PearlHeart Book 1

Journeys of
PearlHeart

Keilani McConnell

First published by Spirit Lion, an imprint of Nine Lions, 2025

Hardcover ISBN: 978-1-963482-00-3
Paperback ISBN: 978-1-963482-01-0
Ebook ISBN: 978-1-963482-02-7

Cover art and interior graphics by Keilani McConnell

Text set in Libre Caslon Text

keilanimcconnellart.com

To my family

The
Fourth World

Draconi

Isla

Haliae

Phoenae

Pantha

Pica Pica

Ursi

Daerce

Unys

Pertes

The North...

The South

Paradi

Pagu Island

Campi

Delphy

Xiphi

Lady Azalea's Island

Panthog

Butej

Cunica

Sudines

Selachuu

Tecla

Grist

Corxae

Ullia

Lotinx

N
W E
S

1

PearlHeart sails beneath a starry sky.

Three flags wave from the top of the mainmast. Lanterns hang aloft and on both decks, casting the wood in a warm glow. The mainsail and foresails as well as the jib and pusher are set to catch the gentle breeze, guiding them steadily along on their journey. The sailors on watch – on since midnight – stand in the nest, along the starboard and port rails, and at the wheel.

Near the end of the hour, the watch begins to change. Sailors who have been resting come up from the crew's quarters to relieve those that have been out. One sailor now off watch goes to a bell hung near the galley door and rings it – four times for four in the morning. The sound echoes over the ship and the empty ocean around them.

Slowly, the sky begins to brighten.

At six, Captain Rath, a man with long dark orange hair, light clothes, and a blue-green waist scarf leaves his cabin and walks out to the main deck. He greets his crew before going below to the cargo hold.

Once inside, he walks up to three crates – two low and

long, one tall – and a barrel which are all secured to the floor.

He goes to the taller one first and checks the contents – a large bottle of ink and a thick packet of paper – writes in his logbook about their condition, then focuses on one of the lower crates.

When he lifts the lid, there is moss inside. He removes the wire rack it is nestled on, revealing two small but vibrant green plants. He smiles at them, then gets to work, carrying the rack with moss over to the barrel containing fresh water and rinsing out any ocean salt the moss may have picked up during their travels. Afterward, he replaces it in the crate, gently pressing the moss down so it can continue to protect the plants from the salty air. He does the same for the second low crate – containing two more of the plants – then writes in his logbook.

Back on the deck, the sun has begun to rise and *PearlHeart* glows orange. Rath goes to the upper deck to join his first mate and navigator, Fenrir, who is on watch at the wheel.

Fenrir smiles. His short brown hair is bound with green and brown beads and his clothes are simple in similar colors. "Good morning. How were your grandmother's plants?"

"Good morning," Rath says. "And they are well. I am very glad to see it."

Fenrir hums, eyes on the ocean ahead. "When I told my father your grandmother had ordered plants from Cunica, he thought it was very interesting. He says she always had gardens, even when she lived on Sudines."

"That is what Grandmother told me as well." Rath's green eyes soften. "She has so many on her island now. I enjoy seeing how much they grow each year."

"As do I."

Around them, the sky continues to color the sails pink and orange and the ocean a brilliant turquoise.

At eight, the bell rings again and Rath and Fenrir join the growing line to the galley to have breakfast. The little cook aboard *PearlHeart*, Phillip, hands them their dishes, saying, "I hope you enjoy!" He is wearing a clean apron and a yellow bandanna over his bald head.

They eat inside at the table, surrounded by crew members talking and laughing or sitting on the benches secured around the room. The door is left open, letting in the cool Summer breeze.

Afterward, Rath returns to his cabin to study, write letters, and mend some of his clothes before going back out to the main deck to watch his crew and update his logbook. He eats lunch outside, then goes below to have his daily tea and talk with the ship doctor and his personal doctor, Carlos, an older, well-dressed man with gray hair, in the infirmary.

As the sun dips below the horizon and the sky grows darker, Rath goes aloft, lighting the lanterns. They shine like little stars as those above begin to come out. Back on the deck, he stands near the port rail, tracing a constellation with his finger. He smiles when he finishes.

Fenrir joins him, having just taken the evening navigation check. "We're making good time," he says, settling next to his captain.

"That is great to hear. Thank you for your work."

"I'm happy to do it. This has been ... " Fenrir looks at the crew, talking amicably with one another and listening to the familiar flap of the sails and the waves carrying them onward. He laughs softly. "Well, it is very different from my home on Sudines. Even from the previous ship I served on."

Rath thinks. "You said that was a hundred years ago?"

"Yes." Fenrir gestures. "Pan ships – made by the God Vocalise – haven't changed much in that time, thankfully, but *PearlHeart* is different." He pauses, then says instead, "The similarities were a relief to me when your grandmother asked if I would consider applying to be your first mate and navigator. It was good for me, too – I had spent a hundred years doing little to nothing on Sudines before she did." Rath frowns, but Fenrir says, "It is true. Although younger than me by centuries, you've already done far more with your twenty-five years than I've done with my four hundred and twenty-five. I rarely see you idle on or off *PearlHeart.*"

A flush spreads over Rath's freckles. "I am glad to help."

Fenrir smiles fondly. "I wonder how you would have fared with one hundred years of idleness."

"I do not believe I would have been very happy."

"I am certain you would not have." Fenrir turns toward the deck again and the crew on the lines. "I enjoy this. Although only four and half years here, they are my most treasured ones."

"Mine as well."

They stand at the rail for a while longer, then part ways, wishing one another good night before they both go to sleep.

For the next few days, they travel to Rath's grandmother's island.

During that time, Rath tends to the plants they are delivering to her, checks the other cargo, eats with his crew, and plays cards with Fenrir in his cabin.

They have just finished a game when there is a knock on the door.

Rath opens it and the sailor on the other side says, "Captain, a Phoenae airship is hailing us."

They all go outside and the sailor points northeast.

There, a golden ship approaches. Balloons filled with hot air keep them aloft, heated by bright phoenix resting on perches beneath them. The flag of a Phoenae Messenger Airship with a phoenix design on it flaps from the mizzenmast.

Rath says to his crew, "Heave to!"

"Yes, Captain!"

Working together, they adjust the sails and turn the wheel so that *PearlHeart* comes to a bobbing stop. By that time, the Phoenae airship's shadow is over them and they all wait, looking up at the golden hull.

The hatch opens and a rope ladder swings down. Its weights *thunk* on *PearlHeart's* deck and Rath winces.

A man in golden clothes climbs down, glances around with displeasure at the ship, then settles on Rath and Fenrir, who stand in front of the crew.

He holds out a tube. "A Phoenae message, from Councilman Georgio Lewis of the Alliance to Lord Rath Lewis and also to Fenrir Mata, son of Councilman Fevrier Mata."

Fenrir inhales quickly, but says nothing. Rath steps forward. "Thank you very much for delivering this." He accepts the message and opens it. As he spreads the shimmering golden scroll between them and they read, Rath's eyes widen and Fenrir's darken.

The messenger speaks. "Fenrir, your father has returned home to Sudines citing health concerns due to his advanced age. As he is no longer able to perform his duties as the

Councilman of Sudines, by tradition, law, and verdict of my god, the Elder God Merp and Ruler of the Fourth World, you are to inherit your father's role in the Council and immediately travel to Phoenae to do so. Do you have any objections?"

"No," Fenrir replies. He turns to Rath, taking his arm. "Rath, we must speak."

"Of course."

They start toward the captain's cabin.

The messenger, startled by their abrupt departure, shouts, "Hey! Wait!"

Rath pauses long enough to turn and bow. "I sincerely apologize. Please excuse us."

As they leave, the messenger stamps his foot.

When they are inside, Rath waits as Fenrir breathes for a few moments, calming himself. Then Fenrir faces Rath and asks, "May I see your father's message again?"

Rath nods and hands it to him.

Fenrir slumps at the table, reading, while Rath quietly sits across from him. When Fenrir finishes, he rubs both temples and inhales deeply. He moves the gold parchment back over to Rath.

Upon seeing Rath's expression, Fenrir says, "It is all right. My father is very old – even by the standards of his and my people and all of those with Hep's Traits." He stands. "I will retrieve my belongings. Will you accompany me below deck?"

Once in the crew's quarters, they whisper near Fenrir's hammock.

Fenrir says, "I am sorry, Rath."

Rath shakes his head. "There is no need to be."

As he pulls his side satchel over his shoulder, Fenrir frowns. He suddenly gasps. "The North. We – you are sailing there after your grandmother's delivery. You need someone to take my place before you do."

"I will. It will be all right."

Fenrir nods, but still looks concerned.

When they return to the deck, Fenrir joins the messenger by the rope ladder. "I am ready."

The man huffs. "Finally." He begins climbing.

"I will not be traveling to Phoenae," Fenrir continues and the man whips around, a shocked look on his face. "I respectfully request that I be taken to Sudines where my father is. I will correspond with the Council via letter during that time and travel to Phoenae afterward. Do you accept my request?"

The messenger hesitates. After a moment, he flicks his hand – an irritated little golden flame shoots out, demonstrating Merp's Traits – and he says, "Very well. We shall board and you shall go to Sudines first. Then Phoenae." He continues up the ladder.

Fenrir turns toward Rath and bows deeply. "I am departing now, Captain."

"Please have safe travels," Rath says.

Fenrir rises, takes a step forward to do something else, then turns around and walks to the ladder instead. Following the messenger, he climbs higher and higher until he reaches the hull and disappears inside. The hatch shuts.

Rath and his crew wait until the airship has continued on – southwest, to Sudines – and the morning sun shines over *PearlHeart* again.

Then they sail due west to the small green island on the horizon – Lady Azalea's Island.

2

For the rest of their journey, Rath takes Fenrir's role, acting as helmsman during the four to eight watch in the morning and evening as well as getting their bearings throughout the day.

During his off hours, he checks on the delivery below and writes letters to the captains he knows in the Pantrog Merchant Ship Guild, inquiring as to whether they know of any navigators or first mates who may be available mid-season.

He asks William and Phobos, the Paradi messengers during the early afternoon to deliver the letters. Phobos, a bird of paradise with magenta and yellow feathers, is William's bird partner and the two have been with one another since birth. William has two of her feathers tucked into the ribbon tying back his braided hair. After William carefully folds and binds the letters with twine, Phobos flies off with them in her talons to the nearest Paradi Message Tower where it will be sorted and delivered.

Two days later, a small green island appears on the horizon. The following morning, on Rath's twenty-sixth birthday, *PearlHeart* arrives.

Up in the nest, Felix calls, "Lady Azalea's Island, ahead!" and his bird partner with yellow and orange feathers, Triphonius, gives a triumphant "Caw!" from his shoulder.

However, as they come closer to the private dock on the northern coast of the island, something in the sky catches Rath's eyes and he looks up.

There, three Pagu fly. They are small, about six inches tall with glittering eyes and gently tipped ears. One wears pink, the other green – a pair of glasses shine on their face, too – and the third wears purple with a brown side satchel over their shoulder. The trio flies over *PearlHeart*, going to Lady Azalea's Island as well, where they disappear into the bright green trees.

After *PearlHeart* docks, Rath gathers members of his crew to help carry the crates of plants and bring them down the gangplank where Azalea, Rath's grandmother, is waiting on the beach.

She is short, with gray hair tied up in a bun with a green ribbon and leans on a carved wooden cane. Her smile is lit with the morning sun and it grows when she sees her grandson approach.

Rath kneels and they hug one another tightly.

"I am so glad you arrived here safely," she says.

"I as well, Grandmother."

As they part, Carlos joins them. He bows. "Lady Azalea."

"Good to see you, Carlos," she says, then to his crew, "And all of you as well!"

They beam. "You too, Lady Azalea!"

Azalea suddenly frowns, looking around. "Where is Fenrir?"

"Sudines," Rath says, "with his father. Fevrier is unwell."

Azalea grips her cane. She sighs. "I see. When I saw Fevrier this past Winter, I had thought he looked ... " She swallows. "Thank you for telling me. I am glad Fenrir can be there with him at this time." She straightens, placing her cane firmly in the sand. "Now, I'll show you where to bring my plants this year."

"Thank you, Grandmother."

She guides all of them up the beach and to a small path through the forest, where many Pagu have homes on her island.

As they walk, Pagu fly above them and in between trees, playing with one another. More return to their homes, under mushrooms or in little huts made out of dried grass. One Pagu is hanging up their laundry on a small clothing line while others are baking cookies in their homes. A few wave to Rath, recognizing him, and he waves back.

When they exit the forest, they come out into the sun on a large bright green lawn, not far from a mosaic of a turtle with two bright green eyes. Ahead, there is a three-story home with a covered patio, nestled within the trees.

However, to Rath's surprise, his grandmother takes them right, down the path to the gate leading to the back gardens. They walk alongside the house, past tall windows to their left and a hedge to their right until they reach the top of a hill which overlooks all of Azalea's gardens.

Down and to the right is Azalea's West Garden which is also her private garden that Rath has never seen. It is enclosed by the hedge and a gate covered in ivy. A turtle pond rests in front of it with two small turtles paddling in the water.

Directly across from it is the East Garden, one that Rath helped begin. It is on a low hill and the flowers there are arranged in a circle, ordered in the colors of a rainbow. Small flagstone paths lead in between the different shades. Near it, there is also a wooden gazebo with hanging plants and a patio leading back into the house.

Azalea takes them due south, down the hill, past the West and East Gardens and down another hill into the southern forest.

Above them, the branches stretch out, providing shade. Azalea says to Rath, "I would like you to plant these in the South Garden."

"Right. The South Garden." He pauses. "I apologize, Grandmother. I do not recall you having a South Garden – only the East and West."

They exit the forest. Azalea grins and her wrinkles disappear. "That's because it's new."

Rath turns forward.

In front of them, there is a large clearing surrounded by trees. Before, Rath remembered it as being covered in grass, but now the ground has been dug up and overturned, ready for plants.

"Grandmother!" Rath says, elated.

Azalea laughs. "I thought your plants could be the first ones. What do you think?"

Rath squeezes her hand in response. "That sounds wonderful. Thank you."

As the crew gathers and those carrying the crates set them down, Rath explains what they will be doing. They all look just as excited as he is. Before, the crew had only ever carried plants to be placed inside the home. While they carefully take out the plants and lay them on the grass, Azalea uses her cane to mark places in the soil for them to dig holes and her house staff brings them shovels and gloves to use.

Once the plants are out, Rath kneels next to them, smiling as he watches their leaves lift up toward the sun.

Suddenly, he sees one of the leaves lift and underneath it is the same Pagu he saw earlier that was dressed in pink. Their brown hair is bound in two short tails.

They do not seem to notice Rath as they nuzzle their cheek against the plant, saying to it, "Yes, it sounds like you had a very long journey! But now you're at your new home and what a beautiful place it is!" They turn around, spreading their arms out. But as they do, their eyes lift up and they see Rath. "Oh!"

He flushes. "I-I apologize. I was staring."

"That's all right." They suddenly pause, as if listening. Their eyes light up. "You brought these Mehrin plants here?" they ask Rath.

"Yes, my crew and I aboard *PearlHeart*."

"I see!" They listen some more and nod, then continue, "The plants say that you took very good care of them, cleaning their moss and smiling at them each morning. They only wish you talked with them more!"

"Talked? I see." Rath turns to the plants. "I apologize for not doing so before. I am glad to hear you felt cared for. And I am very happy to see you at Grandmother's safe."

The leaves seem to tremble in delight.

The Pagu says, "Yes! Just like that." They and Rath share a smile.

Hearing them, Azalea walks over and when she joins them, the Pagu steps out from under the plant and brushes off their overalls. They take off their hat and hold it at chest-level. "Hello!" they say to Azalea. "I'm sorry that I did not introduce myself sooner. I have arrived on your island unannounced."

"You are always welcome, Honored One," Azalea says.

Their eyes shine as they hold out their hand to Rath, then Azalea, who shake it with their fingers. "I'm Flower-Pagu. My friends and I are visiting from Pagu Island. We heard Lady Azalea's Island is a most wonderful place!" They clutch their hat. "I absolutely love your gardens, Lady Azalea. And it looks like you're making another?" They look terribly excited.

"Yes, we are." Azalea gestures. "This is my grandson, Rath. He has helped build my gardens for many years."

Rath dips his head respectfully. "It is wonderful to meet you, Flower-Pagu. Would you like to help us plant? We were just about to."

Flower-Pagu's mouth drops open, then they fly up into the air, putting both arms up as they do. "I would love to! Thank you so, so much for asking." They put back on their hat, beaming up at them.

The shovels and gloves are distributed and they all begin. Some sailors start digging holes while others are with Rath, who shows them how to remove the plants from their pots. As they carry them to the garden, Flower-Pagu flies next to them, encouraging the plants. One by one, each is put into the ground and their roots are covered with soil.

Not long afterward, Rath is on his knees tending to the last one. He reaches over and gently pats the ground twice right at the base of the stalk, saying softly, *"Pat, pat."*

Flower-Pagu, who was sitting opposite of him, sees and for a moment they look surprised. Then they smile happily.

A little before breakfast, the South Garden has begun.

Four Mehrin plants wave their leaves from their new homes while Rath, Flower-Pagu, Lady Azalea, Carlos, and the crew all look out at the small beginning.

Azalea invites all of them to eat at her home and together they walk back to it, entering from the side patio. They have breakfast in a long dining room with windows on both sides. Rath sits near the head of the table with his grandmother, Carlos, and Flower-Pagu.

Flower-Pagu nibbles on their sandwich, telling Rath about their journey from Pagu Island. "And we all went really fast, like ... like ... " They struggle.

Rath gestures with his hand, saying, "Like *swoosh?*"

"That was it exactly!" They giggle. Then they look up at the ceiling and gasp. "Oh my!"

Up above, a painted mural stretches from one end of the room to the other, depicting different animals alongside their human counterparts: a dolphin, a rabbit, a snake, an eel; a chimpanzee, a shark, a hawk, a bird of paradise; an eagle, a deer, a crow; a swordfish, a bear, a magpie; a lion, a seahorse, an elephant; a tiger, a wolf, and a turtle. An octopus and its human counterpart are also there, set away from the rest, and both seem to be looking in the direction of three others – a unicorn, a dragon, and a phoenix – and beyond them to a set of bright clouds with three tiny forms.

Flower-Pagu says, "I had no idea this was here! It's wonderful. May I ask who painted it?"

"Penelope, the Goddess of Campi and my mother's goddess," Rath says. "I think it is very beautiful."

"It is!" Flower-Pagu finishes their sandwich, then says, "I think my friends, Bucket-Pagu and Well-Pagu, would love to see it, too. Actually, I really want to introduce you to them, if that's all right?"

"Definitely. I would like to meet them."

Everyone thanks Azalea after breakfast and she invites Flower-Pagu to lunch as well, which they happily accept. Then they and Rath head down the hallway together. Flower-Pagu tells Rath their friend Bucket-Pagu was especially excited to see Azalea's library.

"They love to read!" they say.

Rath leads them to a gallery with two bowl-shaped chandeliers, then to a set of double doors with turtles carved into them. He opens them.

Azalea's library has two levels, full of shelves and windows and a seating area in the center that is bathed in light from the morning sun.

Lying on their stomach on a green cushion on one of the couches, a Pagu wearing green with round glasses is swinging their feet in the air, enjoying a tiny book just their size.

Flower-Pagu says, "Bucket-Pagu! I've brought someone I'd like for you to meet!"

The Pagu looks up, adjusting their glasses. "Oh! Flower-Pagu!" They mark their place in their book, then fly over to join them.

Flower-Pagu says, "This is Rath! He's Lady Azalea's grandson and he told me he and his crew brought Mehrin plants for Lady Azalea from Cunica and then we all planted them and we started the South Garden!" They finish their explanation with a twirl.

"That's great! I'll have to see it." They hold out their hand. "I'm Bucket-Pagu. I really appreciate Lady Azalea letting us come here. Her library is amazing!"

Rath gives them his pointer finger to shake. "It is great to meet you. And I think so as well. My father and I often read in here when we are together."

"Really? What kinds of books?"

"Non-fiction for study. I greatly enjoy learning. May I ask what book you are reading?"

"Fiction." Bucket-Pagu hugs their book to their chest. "It's a new series I'm starting called *Tales of Flight.* It's about a dragon who doesn't think he can fly anymore because of something that's happened in the past, but he's slowly becoming braver with the help of his friends and family." They blush. "I really relate to it. It was very hard for me to travel here from Pagu Island."

Flower-Pagu says, "But, you did it!"

Bucket-Pagu laughs. "I did!" They think for a moment. "Flower-Pagu mentioned a crew. Are you a sailor, Rath?"

"Yes. I am the captain of *PearlHeart,* a Pan ship. We carry different items and provide passage for people wherever they would like to go."

"Oh, wow! You must go to a lot of places, then."

Flower-Pagu says, "Would you tell us about them? It's been a long time since we've left Pagu Island. It would be good to know how the world has changed since then."

Rath says, "I would love to."

Sitting on the couch together, Rath tells Flower-Pagu and Bucket-Pagu about his journeys on *PearlHeart.*

"This will be my fifth year as captain," he says. He tells them about each of his years, sailing to places like Lotinx and Cunica, Pantrog and Haliae, Pica Pica and Campi. "We always start and end on Delphy, my homeland."

Bucket-Pagu says, "Oh! Then Marchand would be your god."

"How is he?" Flower-Pagu asks.

Rath smiles warmly. "I think he is well. I cannot wait to see him when we return to Delphy." He shares with them the different deliveries they've carried – paintings and food, supplies and plants. "We are currently carrying ink and paper for Elvin, the God of Haliae, to be delivered to his home in the North."

Bucket-Pagu says, "That makes a lot of sense for Elvin," but Flower-Pagu says, frowning, "How is the North? We've heard it has become very dangerous for ships there and that Haliae would sometimes freeze in the Winter."

Rath sobers. "I am afraid both are true. To make the journey safely, we arrive during late Summer and leave the area in the Fall to avoid the first snows. My grandmother tells me that it is the Elder God of Draconi, Ara, who makes the Winters as they are."

Both Pagu pause, then nod.

Bucket-Pagu says, "Did she say how exactly he caused them?"

"I do not believe so."

"It's his emotions." They tuck their hands in their lap. "All of the gods have control of the land they have claimed, which allows them to affect the Seasons that occur there."

Flower-Pagu says, "When the Winters in Draconi are dangerous, it means that Ara is upset and hurting. It has always made us sad."

Rath's eyes lower. "I am very sorry to hear that."

Then they ask to hear more about Rath's journeys and as he continues, their faces brighten.

They are all so engaged that they do not notice a small Pagu in purple with black hair and dark eyes softly push open a window in the front of the room. They wear a brown side satchel over their shoulder. They listen for a few moments and when they realize what Rath is talking about, their eyes widen and a sudden look of longing fills them. While Rath speaks, Well-Pagu sits by the window and absorbs every word of the ocean and *PearlHeart* and the places that Well-Pagu has seen, but centuries ago.

The clock chimes twelve and they all start.

Looking up at it, Rath says, "Lunch."

Flower-Pagu says, "Oh dear! Lady Azalea invited me," and Bucket-Pagu, who did not know this, says, "Really?"

"Yes! I'm sure she would be all right with you coming, too!"

"I can't wait!" However, then Bucket-Pagu turns around and says, "Well-Pagu!"

Flower-Pagu waves to them. "Do you want to have lunch at Lady Azalea's?"

Flustered, Well-Pagu flies over to the group. "Invite?"

Rath thinks. "Do you mean would you be invited?" Well-Pagu nods. "Yes, I believe my grandmother would love to have you there. I would like it, too." He holds out his finger. "I am Rath."

They take it and give a firm shake. "Well ... Pagu."

The four travel quickly to the dining room and Rath introduces Bucket-Pagu and Well-Pagu to his grandmother and Carlos. Lady Azalea is delighted but Carlos looks mildly concerned by the sudden addition of three Pagu at the table. He watches as they and Rath talk about the mural above, pointing out different parts to each other. Azalea pats Carlos' hand and he relaxes somewhat.

Looking at the mural from end to end, Bucket-Pagu says, "It really is amazing. It was also very kind of Penelope to paint it. I love that it has her and her siblings."

"As do I," Rath says.

Well-Pagu carefully laces their fingers. "Together."

"Exactly."

Well-Pagu beams at his understanding. They pause to take a bite before saying, "Sailor."

"Yes. I am the captain of *PearlHeart*, a Pan ship."

Well-Pagu clutches their side satchel tightly. "Wonderful." They continue to eat with a little smile on their face.

After lunch, Azalea invites all three Pagu to dinner and they accept. Then Flower-Pagu tells them that they will be showing their friends the South Garden they began earlier that morning.

Rath says, "I hope you all enjoy."

They beam. Flower-Pagu and Bucket-Pagu say, "Thank you!" and Well-Pagu says, "Thank!"

While the Pagu look at the gardens, Rath, Carlos and Azalea have tea outside in the gazebo, as they do every year for Rath's birthday. Carlos brews Delphy Fruit Tea – Rath's favorite –

and after he serves everyone, they take their first sip together, quiet for a moment.

Azalea sets down her teacup and asks Rath, "Would you tell me of your journey so far? Your fifth year as captain. A very auspicious year."

"Of course, Grandmother." He begins with their start in Delphy and the long journey to Lotinx in the southeast for the ink and paper for Elvin, then their stop at Butej to pick up shells, Cunica for Azalea's plants, and Campi to deliver the shells which would then be made into paints.

"I was able to see Mother while we were there," he says. "She traveled to Perin Village where we made our delivery."

"That is wonderful to hear!" Azalea says. "She has become so much more brave than when I first met her. Most from Campi would prefer not to leave their own village, much less travel away from their country and goddess like Marin has done."

Carlos says, "I recall Lady Marin being terrified the first time Lord Georgio tried to teach her how to sail a Delphaen ship. Now, she is quite capable."

Rath smiles. "I agree. I was very grateful to be able to see her." He continues, "It was when we were sailing to your island, Grandmother, that the Phoenae airship hailed us down. They had a Phoenae message for me and Fenrir from Father. They also informed Fenrir that he was to take his father's place in the Council."

"Your father sent the Phoenae message?" Azalea asks. When Rath nods, she sighs. "Fevrier. However, you said Fenrir went to Sudines instead?"

"Yes. He asked that he go there first, then to Phoenae."

"I am glad he did. He needs to be with his family right now." Azalea pauses for a long moment, then says, "Fevrier is very old, Rath. Older than me or Carlos, for he was nearly five hundred when we were both still quite young. Fenrir's family, too, comes from Hep's First, one of the oldest families present on Sudines, with ancestors who lived for a thousand years or more." She puts both hands around her teacup. "I am glad I got to see Fevrier this past Winter. I will pray to Hep for him and his family. Will you pray to Marchand?"

"I will."

She smiles. "Where will you go next?"

"Haliae. It is our last delivery before we return to Delphy."

Sipping her tea, Azalea says, "I am concerned with you doing so without a first mate or navigator. Do you know who you may hire in Fenrir's stead?"

"Not at the moment. I sent letters out to those in the Pantrog Merchant Ship Guild, inquiring about any who may be able to. I will likely receive a reply by the end of this week."

"Before you set off." Azalea nods. "I know that you will find someone wonderful. And who will feel very lucky to be aboard *PearlHeart* and have you as their captain."

Rath reddens. "Grandmother."

She laughs and they continue their tea.

However, once they finish, Bucket-Pagu and Well-Pagu suddenly fly up to them.

Well-Pagu says, "Help?" and Rath immediately replies, "Of course. What can we do?"

Bucket-Pagu explains, "When we were in the South Garden, Flower-Pagu heard another flower. They think it needs help. They're requesting ... " They tilt their head to the side, listening. "A shovel, please!"

"I can get that."

After Rath retrieves one, he joins Carlos, Azalea, Bucket-Pagu, and Well-Pagu – who leads all of them to the South Garden, then into the surrounding forest. They move carefully in between the trees, going into parts where the leaves are thick above them, blocking the sunlight.

Rath is stepping over a large root when he hears Flower-Pagu's voice.

"No, I know that you're very strong! I'm also very, very happy you asked for help and that I was able to hear it!"

They enter an area of low bushes. A flash of pink can be seen at the base of one, right next to something orange.

Azalea takes one look and gasps. "Oh my." Beside her, Carlos is equally startled.

Next to the bush, a wilted orange flower is struggling to raise itself off of the ground. Flower-Pagu is cradling it, their eyes sparkling. When they hear the others, they rub their face with their forearm, then smile. "Everyone! You're here!"

Rath kneels beside them. "What can we do?"

Flower-Pagu looks appreciative. They gently let go of the

flower and step back. "We need to take this one to somewhere where there's lots of sun as soon as possible." They hesitate, then get down on their knees. They pat the ground, creating glowing pink handprints in the grass. "These are where its roots are. Please dig around them."

"Yes, Flower-Pagu." Rath does so carefully, loosening the soil around the plant. Afterward, he hands the shovel to Carlos and gets down on his knees. He pauses for a moment before he gently takes up the flower, pulling it out of the ground. "It will be all right," he says to it. "We're taking you to a new home."

The flower seems to lift a little bit.

As Rath stands, Azalea says, "I know just where to put it, if that would be all right with you, Flower-Pagu?"

"Yes! I trust you, Lady Azalea!"

Azalea guides them through the shade until shafts of light begin to appear. Each one that catches the flower turns the orange brilliant. When they arrive in the South Garden again, Azalea walks over to the Mehrin plants. She looks them over, then nods.

Pointing to the area next to them, she says, "Here."

Flower-Pagu inhales. "That's perfect! It'll be with so many new friends. And the sun!"

Carlos digs a hole to the left of the Mehrin plants and Rath puts the flower in. Then he, Azalea, and the Pagu put soil over its roots. Rath pats the ground twice like he did before, saying, "*Pat, pat.*" He smiles at the flower, happy to see that it already looks far brighter.

A tiny hand takes his finger. He looks down and sees Flower-Pagu. "Thank you for helping, everyone."

"Of course."

After a moment, Flower-Pagu says, "This is a Pantha Flower." Rath starts. Both Azalea and Carlos look sad. "I didn't think ... This may be the last one left." They beam up at Rath. "That's why I'm so glad that it found its way here! It wasn't sure it wanted to ask for help, but it did and now it has a wonderful new home with new friends and the sun ... " For a moment, they close their eyes and take a deep breath. They squeeze Rath's finger, then fly over to sit with the flower. Bucket-Pagu and Well-Pagu join them and they all take hands.

Later, they return to Azalea's home for dinner.

At the end of the meal, a dessert with raspberries is set in front of them and both Rath and Well-Pagu's eyes widen.

Well-Pagu says, "Favorite."

Rath turns to them. "It is mine as well."

They smile at one another, then start to eat.

When they are finished, the Pagu leave for the night, explaining that they are staying with some of their friends in the forest.

Bucket-Pagu asks Rath, "Will you be here tomorrow?"

"Yes, and through the end of the week. Then we will continue on to the last delivery of our journey."

They promise to see one another again, then the Pagu fly toward the forest to the north while Rath and Carlos go in the same direction to *PearlHeart*.

That evening, the crew celebrates Rath's twenty-sixth birthday. Rath plays card games with them and Phillip brings out a raspberry tart as well as other desserts for all to enjoy. As the sky grows dark, Melody – one of the Paradi messengers aboard *PearlHeart* – who has long hair and amber eyes, plays her harp and sings with Demeter, her bird partner with purple and blue plumage. They all talk for a long time before Rath thanks them for a wonderful evening and goes back to his grandmother's home.

He finds her in the front lawn, looking at the mosaic of the turtle, her hand lifted in a prayer gesture. Although Rath cannot see it, a green Spirit Turtle rests on her shoulder. He waits. When Azalea turns around, she smiles and offers her hand.

They enter the home together. As they climb up the stairs in the foyer, Azalea says, "This will have been your second time starting a garden, won't it?"

Rath blinks. "Yes. Although, I am not sure that I started the East Garden."

"You planted the first flower!" Azalea says, laughing. "A Delphy Flower, for the blue-green part of the rainbow."

"That is true."

"You were so surprised when all the colors came together – you had no idea that was what we were building!"

Flushing, he says, "I-I did not. It was beautiful to see."

They pause at the top of the stairs. "And now, you're beginning another one. With your crew." She looks at a row of potted plants resting on small end tables down the hallway. Plaques near their bases say, *Pantrog – The First Journey.* "You and your crew have helped plant many inside, but I've always thought it would be wonderful to start a new garden outside to honor the new path you've taken as a captain."

"Th-That is not necessary."

Azalea squeezes his hands. "It is. It was very brave of you." They walk down the hallway together, passing more plants. "And look where you are now – on your Fifth Journey!"

"Yes!"

They turn to go up another staircase where many paintings – sunsets and beaches and *PearlHeart* – are hung up. Rath looks at them thoughtfully. "Do you think Mother would like to paint the South Garden?"

Azalea grins. "I think it will be hard for any of us to convince her not to!"

"I cannot wait to see it," Rath says, smiling.

They reach the top, where tall windows overlook the back gardens and chandeliers line the wide hallway where there are suites for Rath, his grandmother, his father, his mother, and Carlos.

Rath kneels and hugs Azalea. "Thank you for a wonderful day, Grandmother."

"Happy Birthday, my dear." She squeezes him, then pulls back and brushes his hair out of his eyes. Then they wish each other good night and go to their separate rooms.

3

Throughout the week, Rath spends time with his crew, the Pagu, and his grandmother.

The Pagu join them at tea and for meals and later for cards in the warm sunroom on the second floor of Azalea's home. Then they fly through the gardens with Rath as he tells them his memories from childhood growing up on his grandmother's island.

One day, Rath and the Pagu are in the South Garden. The Pagu are playing around the Mehrin plants while Rath sits in front of the Pantha Flower. He is carving a small piece of wood in his hands in the likeness of the flower and when Flower-Pagu sees, they gasp.

After Rath finishes, he holds it out to them. "What do you think?"

Flower-Pagu's eyes are wide. Each petal has been delicately carved, reaching out to the sun just like the flower in front of them. "It's ... It's beautiful." They laugh suddenly. "Strong! Just like how Lionel wanted them."

"The God of Pantha?"

"That's right." They pause as if to say more, but do not.

"You may have it, if you would like," Rath says.

"Really?" Rath nods and Flower-Pagu reaches out. They tenderly hug the carved flower to their chest, looking up at Rath in wordless thanks.

For the next two days, Rath talks with Flower-Pagu in the garden and reads in the library with Bucket-Pagu. He is starting the first book in the *Tales of Flight* series and enjoying it greatly. Up in the study, he and Well-Pagu pour over maps, sharing the different places they've been.

After Well-Pagu points to all the countries they have seen, Rath says, "You have been to so many!"

"Too."

"I have." Rath looks down at the map, smiling softly. "I wish to go everywhere."

Well-Pagu's eyes shine, then they look down at the map as well.

The following morning, the Pagu leave for a day trip, promising to be back before *PearlHeart* leaves.

While Rath, Azalea, and Carlos are playing cards in the sunroom, Rath tells them, "Flower-Pagu, Bucket-Pagu, and Well-Pagu said that they are visiting the Pagu in the East Village."

Azalea smiles. "You have many times as well. I wonder how they are."

After they finish a round, Carlos says, "I am certain your gift to Flower-Pagu meant a great deal to them. As they said, the Pantha Flower here may be the last one."

Rath says, "I did not know there were flowers in Pantha."

Azalea sighs. "There were. That's how Carlos and I recognized it. We were ... I was just under seven hundred and Carlos would soon turn five hundred, I believe, when we went there." She shakes her head. "My parents were not sure about us going given the people there have a history of fighting, but it's out of their love for it, not for violence. And when I heard that there were flowers there that Lionel had created ... "

Carlos gives a much longer sigh. "You were not to be deterred."

Flushing, Azalea says, "They were beautiful. They *are* beautiful." She takes the deck from Carlos and begins to shuffle. "Plants and seeds are very strong. They can withstand much that many would think they couldn't."

Rath pauses. "What happened to the flowers in Pantha?"

"I am not sure. All I know is that they are gone – what Flower-Pagu said proves that." She deals the cards out. "Pantha used to be a warm land, with tall mountains surrounding wide fields where Lionel and his people would run. Now, it seems it has steadily grown colder due to Ara's Winters in the North." She frowns. "Even as strong as they are, Lionel's plants would struggle in such a climate."

As they all pick up their hands, she continues, "But, that is exactly why I am so relieved that a Pantha Flower managed to make it all the way here. By Pan ship, that is a journey of two months, isn't it?" Rath nods and she smiles. "It was very strong, indeed. I am certain Lionel would be proud of it, too." And they begin to play.

The Pagu return the next day. Flower-Pagu shows Rath a small piece of paper with an idea for him to carve. He studies it seriously and nods.

The next day, he meets with Flower-Pagu, Bucket-Pagu, and Well-Pagu and holds out his hand, revealing three identical shovels carved out of wood. They are delighted.

"Shovel," Well-Pagu says, hugging theirs.

They all help Azalea, Carlos, and the staff in the kitchen garden that afternoon, and the Pagu get to use their shovels to dig up different roots and gather other ingredients to be used for meals from Azalea's private herb garden. Then Rath and the Pagu fill a basket of raspberries and each have one before they bring it to the head chef.

After lunch, Rath checks on those aboard *PearlHeart*. William hands him two letters that Phobos returned with that morning and Rath thanks them before going to his cabin to read.

The first says: *I'm afraid I don't know any navigators who are experienced with the North. I hope you're able to find one for your delivery!*

And the second: *No navigators that I know of, but I have three first mate candidates for you. They can meet you at my home on Pantrog, near Port Pallas on the north coast. I'll have them here for the whole last week of the month if you're able to arrive by then. Let me know!*

Rath looks relieved. He sets both letters aside and starts composing his replies.

He returns to his grandmother's home that evening for dinner and is happy to see the Pagu have joined them again as well.

Well-Pagu is quietly eating their raspberry dessert when they hear Azalea ask Rath, "Did you receive a reply on your inquiries?"

"I did," he says. "I will be interviewing three people interested in the position of first mate on Pantrog at the end of this month. I have already informed the crew."

"That is wonderful to hear." She looks concerned. "But none for navigator?"

"I am afraid not. None that are knowledgeable about the North," Rath says. "I plan to send more letters tomorrow morning after our departure."

Well-Pagu looks up at Rath. "Navigator?" He turns toward them and they continue, blushing, "Listened."

"That is all right. Yes, I am looking for a navigator. It will not be safe to go to the North without one."

"Dangerous," Well-Pagu agrees. They look pensive for the rest of the meal.

Later that evening, Well-Pagu, Bucket-Pagu, and Flower-Pagu are in Pebble-Pagu's home, where they are staying during their visit to Lady Azalea's Island. The three are packing their things to get ready to leave.

Flower-Pagu tucks their embroidery in their knit bag. "Where should we go next?"

"M-Maybe somewhere not so far," Bucket-Pagu says, carefully packing their books. "What about Campi?"

"That's a great idea! What do you think, Well-Pagu?"

But Well-Pagu is looking out the small window at *PearlHeart*, with its twinkling lanterns and furled sails. They clutch their side satchel. "Excuse," they say to their friends – Flower-Pagu and Bucket-Pagu nod – and they exit the home, flying toward the forest path. When they reach it, they turn in the direction of Azalea's home, then back at *PearlHeart*. Unsure of what to do, they finger the strap of their satchel nervously.

Then they hear boots coming from Azalea's.

Well-Pagu turns and sees Rath walking their way, looking

thoughtful.

"H-Hello!" they say.

Rath stops. He brightens when he sees them. "Well-Pagu. How are you?"

"Good." They seem to struggle. "North." They point to themselves. "Know." They open their side satchel and pull out the tiniest compass Rath has ever seen. "Navigate." Well-Pagu holds out their hand. It trembles. "Apply?"

For a moment, Rath is stunned. Then he puts out his finger and Well-Pagu takes it. "I would be honored to have you as *PearlHeart's* navigator, Well-Pagu."

It takes a few seconds for them to process. "True?"

"Yes! Would you be available to see *PearlHeart* tonight? I realize it is late."

"Would!" Well-Pagu says. They look at the Pan ship. "Love."

They both make their way to *PearlHeart* and go up the gangplank. As Rath shows them around, Well-Pagu looks up at the masts and the rigging and the bright lanterns like stars. They talk more in the captain's cabin and fill out Well-Pagu's paperwork, which they sign with a small pen. They beam at their signature below Rath's.

After agreeing to meet early in the morning to cast off, Well-Pagu departs from *PearlHeart,* waving to Rath, their new captain. They quickly fly back to the forest to tell Flower-Pagu and Bucket-Pagu their news.

Both gasp, then all three spin around in joy.

Flower-Pagu says, "That's so exciting!" and Bucket-Pagu says, "You'll do so good!"

Pebble-Pagu comes home and they tell them, too, then all of the other Pagu in the forest. They decide to celebrate with cookies baked earlier that day. As they nibble on them together, they talk about the days to come for Well-Pagu and the journey that they will be embarking on. As the stars come out above, they tuck in for the night. Well-Pagu smiles, cuddled up between Flower-Pagu and Bucket-Pagu in their little bed, looking forward to the next day.

In the morning, Carlos knocks on the door to the captain's cabin. Rath had slept on *PearlHeart* for their last night at his grandmother's.

After Rath responds, Carlos enters. "Did you sleep well?"

Rath is already dressed. "Very." He suddenly says, "That's right – Well-Pagu came to speak with me last night."

"Oh? That would be rather late."

"Indeed. They asked if they may apply for the position of navigator aboard *PearlHeart.*"

Carlos chokes. "They ... Might I ask what you said?"

As Rath ties back his hair with a red-brown ribbon, he replies, "I said that I would be honored to have them." He sees his doctor's expression. "Carlos? Are you all right?"

After a pause, Carlos says, "Yes. This is good. Very good, Master Rath." He is quiet for another moment, then says, "I am truly very happy for you. It is quite auspicious to begin the last portion of our journey in such a way."

"Thank you. And, I agree."

"Will Well-Pagu be arriving this morning?"

"Yes." Rath turns toward his windows, measuring the light in the sky. "I will go out to the main deck now to watch for them."

When they are outside, Carlos says, "Are they performing both roles as Fenrir did? As first mate and navigator?"

"They will only be acting as navigator. They said that they would be 'uncomfortable' performing both."

"I see. Then, it is good that you will be meeting with three candidates for the position of first mate on Pantrog."

"I agree. I am excited to meet them."

While Carlos goes below to the infirmary to do his final checks for their departure, Rath remains on the deck doing the same.

Near five, he hears a little voice from the dock say, "Permission?"

He looks over the rail and sees Well-Pagu waiting at the bottom of the gangplank, dressed in a white shirt, brown pants, and sturdy boots, with their side satchel across their chest.

Rath smiles warmly. "Yes. Permission granted, Well-Pagu."

They beam, then fly up to the main deck of *PearlHeart* to join him.

The crew gathers and Rath says to them, "Everyone, this is Well-Pagu. They will be acting as navigator aboard *PearlHeart.*"

Well-Pagu faces the crowd. "Hello!"

"That's great!" they say and "Hello, Well-Pagu!" Well-Pagu blushes, but smiles.

While Rath speaks with his sail-master, Isaac, on the sail plan, Well-Pagu flies up into the rigging to get their bearings. They take out their sextant and put it up to their eye.

A little before six, *PearlHeart's* preparations are complete.

Before they cast off, Rath and Well-Pagu go back to the beach where Azalea, Flower-Pagu, and Bucket-Pagu are.

While Well-Pagu spins with Flower-Pagu and Bucket-Pagu, Rath hugs his grandmother, saying, "Thank you for a wonderful week. I love you."

"I love you, too, my dear." She nods toward the Pagu. "I see you have a new addition to your crew. Carlos told me."

"Yes! I am very much looking forward to having Well-Pagu aboard."

"I am sure! I am also certain they are, too." She hums. "Did they tell you how long they have been navigating?"

"Three hundred and eighty-seven years."

Azalea laughs. "Such a short time for a Pagu!" She squeezes his hand. "I think you two will work very well together."

"I do, too." Well-Pagu flies up to them and Rath says, "May I ask if you are ready?"

"Are." They pause. Flower-Pagu and Bucket-Pagu are beside them, both carrying their bags like they were at the start of the week when they were flying to Lady Azalea's Island.

Flower-Pagu says, "Rath, we wanted to ask you a question."

Bucket-Pagu fingers one of their shirt buttons. "We ... We wanted to know if we could go with you!"

"Together?" Well-Pagu asks.

Rath looks surprised, then nods. "Definitely. I would greatly enjoy it if you came with us Flower-Pagu, Bucket-Pagu."

The three Pagu take one another's hands, looking thrilled. Flower-Pagu says, "Thank you so much, Rath! I can't wait!"

Bucket-Pagu says, "This will be my first time on one of Vocalise's ships. I'm nervous, but excited, too."

Well-Pagu beams.

Looking up at the brightening sky, Rath says, "We will need to leave now. Are you prepared to do so?"

They say in unison, "Yes, Captain!"

Azalea's staff arrives to see them off. Flora, Azalea's maid, in a light green dress with eyes that seem far older than she appears, hands Azalea a basket of raspberries that she then gives to Rath. "I will see you in the Winter. Please stay safe."

"I will, Grandmother. Thank you."

As they go up the gangplank to *PearlHeart*, Rath and the Pagu wave to Azalea and her staff. Azalea watches Carlos retrieve the raspberry basket from Rath so he can take his place at the wheel. The Pagu sit on the console in front of him. The sails fill and *PearlHeart* slowly pulls away from the island, on course for Pantrog.

4

During the next week, the Pagu slowly acclimate to life aboard *PearlHeart*.

They and Rath agree that it will be safest for them to stay in his cabin and he offers them the left side of the bed and the bedside table on that side, too. They set up their little bed on the left pillow then begin to fill the bedside table with all of their things, including Well-Pagu's charts, Bucket-Pagu's books, and Flower-Pagu's embroidery.

Out on the deck, Well-Pagu is the most adept with traveling in the high winds and Flower-Pagu enjoys them greatly, but Bucket-Pagu seems more unsure and holds onto the safety lines that Rath showed them on the first day. By the end of the third day, however, Bucket-Pagu begins to go up in the rigging with their friends and Rath smiles as he watches them.

The crew is also happy to have the Pagu aboard.

"Flower-Pagu is always letting me know when I need to tend to one of the plants," Phillip, the cook, tells Rath. His green Spirit Rabbit, who has been bonded with Phillip for his whole life, hops up and down on his shoulder in agreement even though Rath cannot see her.

Carlos tells Rath that he and Bucket-Pagu have talked much, particularly during the first days when Bucket-Pagu was still a little uncomfortable. "They have grown far more brave," Carlos says.

The other helmsmen, Franz and Oren, also grow accustomed to working with Well-Pagu and following their directions.

Each day, Flower-Pagu and Bucket-Pagu sit on the rail, watching Well-Pagu and the crew work. However, by the end of the week, they look thoughtful and ask Rath if there is anything that they can do.

At first, he tells them that it is not necessary for them to work, but when he sees their expressions, he thinks carefully and says he has an idea.

Together, they go to Phillip and Carlos, asking if Flower-Pagu can help in the galley and if Bucket-Pagu can work in the infirmary. Both immediately accept. Afterward, Rath and the two Pagu go back to their cabin to sign the paperwork to make it official.

From then on, all three Pagu exit the captain's cabin at six in the morning, Well-Pagu to get their bearings, Flower-Pagu to the galley, and Bucket-Pagu to the infirmary. Rath, at the wheel since four, waves to them as they leave and they wave happily back.

When all three are finished with their work for the day, they sit on the console in front of the wheel where Rath is, looking at the wide ocean ahead and the lantern light all around them and the stars above.

Four days before *PearlHeart* will arrive on Pantrog, Rath and Well-Pagu are in their cabin, going over the route. The wind has picked up since the previous day and it rattles the windows above Rath's desk.

"The Sudines Turtle Migration will pass Pantrog's northwest coast this week," Rath says, his finger on his map on the table. "I would like to adjust our route further east to not interfere. What do you think?"

Well-Pagu, holding their smaller map, marks it down. "Agree."

Later, Rath climbs the mainmast to take a look at the wind gauge. He frowns when he sees the speed.

They reduce sail until they are only using their staysails and jib, the force of the wind pulling them along quickly even so. The Pagu take to bundling up in Rath's scarf while they are outside so as not to be blown away.

Bucket-Pagu says, "Is it normally like this near Pantrog?"

Rath shakes his head. "No. Pantrog has monsoons, however, it is far too late in the season for them. It is also too early for any Winter winds from the North to be here."

"Will we make it there safely?"

"Definitely. We will be all right, Bucket-Pagu."

"Thank you, Captain!"

That evening, the wind increases more.

No one is aloft and everyone out on the deck is straining to see through their hair and clothes whipping around them as they stay close to the lines.

Rath is at the wheel when Well-Pagu is getting the last navigation check of the night. They fly high up into the rigging and Rath watches them with concern.

Suddenly, a furious gust blows through and Rath holds onto the wheel.

He hears a little voice shout.

When he looks up, he sees Well-Pagu has been blown down, heading toward the sea to the south. His eyes widen and he ties off the wheel quickly before letting the wind drag him down the stairs. He runs across the deck to the port railing and stretches his arm out. He catches Well-Pagu just before they go over and cups them with his other hand, shielding them from the rest of the wind.

When it dies down, Well-Pagu opens their eyes.

"Are you all right?" Rath asks.

Well-Pagu nods.

Straightening, Rath looks around. "Is everyone all right?"

"Yes, Captain!" they all reply.

The wind begins to pick up again and Rath says, "We'll stop for the night."

They strike the sails and drop the sea anchor. Phillip and Flower-Pagu serve a quick dinner and they all retreat to their sleeping quarters to eat.

Rath and the Pagu sit at their table, all bundled up in blankets. Suddenly, Well-Pagu gives a violent shiver and Rath nearly drops his spoon. "Are you cold?" he asks.

Well-Pagu frowns. "Am."

"I will get you another blanket." Rath rises, going to his cupboard. "My mother has made many that are your size." As he reaches inside. he asks, "Flower-Pagu, Bucket-Pagu, would you like another as well?"

"Yes, please!" they both say.

When Rath returns, he lays three neatly folded blankets on the table. When the Pagu open them up, they see that they have been embroidered with colorful patterns.

Flower-Pagu wraps themselves in one with flowers. "These are so beautiful! And warm. Captain, you said your mother made them?"

"Yes. She is an excellent seamstress and loves to embroider. She made many of my clothes when I was young."

The Pagu look delighted. Flower-Pagu turns to the others, who nod. "We have a friend that also likes to sew. He's made clothes for all of our friends and family!"

Rath's eyebrows go up. "That is amazing."

"He is one of our closest friends." Flower-Pagu beams.

They hear the wind again outside, less vicious, but enough that they all turn toward the windows.

Flower-Pagu says quietly, "I don't think he would like weather like this."

"He always loves it when it's sunny. He doesn't like clouds or rain – and especially not snow!" Bucket-Pagu says.

Well-Pagu sighs. "Necessary."

Rath understands what they mean. "I agree. Weather of all kinds is. Different plants are only able to thrive in certain conditions."

Flower-Pagu nods. "Like the Pantha Flower!"

"Exactly."

They all get ready for bed afterward. Bucket-Pagu goes under the covers. "It's been a scary night, but we're all making it through together."

"We are," Rath says. "However, I apologize that it has been. Good night, Well-Pagu, Bucket-Pagu, Flower-Pagu. I hope that ... " He begins to drift off. " ... tomorrow is not a scary night for you." Then he has fallen asleep.

The Pagu look surprised. They fly out of their bed and,

together, pull up Rath's covers. Flower-Pagu says, "We hope so for you, too, Captain."

They return to their own bed, cuddle up, and fall asleep as well.

The next morning, the windstorm has passed. Rath, the Pagu, and the crew are awake and out at six, checking how *PearlHeart* fared overnight. Rath had started to climb the mainmast when he suddenly hissed in pain.

Well-Pagu says, "Hurt?"

Rath raises his shirt and sees a large purple bruise over his ribs. "I will see Carlos about this. It must have happened last night." He asks another sailor to go aloft instead.

One sail tore, however, no major damages were sustained. While two sailors work on repairing it, Rath goes down to the infirmary.

Below, Carlos frowns at the bruise. "Did this happen yesterday?"

Rath flushes. "Yes. I did not notice it."

With a sigh, Carlos places his hand over Rath's torso. His hand glows yellow with Sevran's Traits. "No fractures. Only bruising." Bucket-Pagu writes this information down in a little book. Carlos presses his palm down and Rath tenses, then relaxes as the coloring begins to improve. "No bandages will be needed." He looks at Rath. "However, do be careful with it."

"Yes, Carlos."

Three days before they'll arrive on Pantrog, Velt – one of the sailors on the lines – has climbed overboard using a rope secured near the port railing where Rath watches to make sure she is safe. When Velt reaches the ocean, she stretches her arm out, dipping it in the water. Her Delphaen tattoos – representing Marchand's Traits – begin to glow blue-green and a Delphaen message in the same color runs across the water to her, meeting her hand. She pauses as she 'reads' it.

As she climbs back up, the blue-green glow is just fading from her tattoos. She tells Rath, "The Delphaen messenger on Pantrog says that the turtles made it through just fine, Captain. We're clear to go through Hep's Current and dock at Port Pallas."

"Thank you very much."

"Of course! How are your ribs doing?"

"Much better, thanks to Bucket-Pagu and Carlos."

"That's great!" She shows him her palms, which have been bandaged. "Bucket-Pagu helped put salve on my rope burns from the windstorm the other day. They've been a lot of help."

"I agree."

That evening, Rath has just checked the delivery for the last time that day and is walking back into his cabin when he hears Bucket-Pagu say, "Double Berceuse!"

He looks over. The three Pagu are seated on cushions on their bedside table. They are using a deck of small playing cards and Bucket-Pagu has just laid down their hand.

"Good job, Bucket-Pagu!" Flower-Pagu says.

"Win!" Well-Pagu says.

Bucket-Pagu flushes. "Thank you!"

Flower-Pagu notices Rath. "Oh! Hello, Captain!"

"Hello. I apologize if I am interrupting your game."

"You're not!" they say, flying up to him.

Bucket-Pagu joins them. "Would you like to play with us? We normally play this game in pairs, but there's only three of us."

Well-Pagu arrives. "Four!"

Rath nods. "I see. I would love to play."

They all sit at the table and Flower-Pagu quickly explains the rules.

"The game is called Double Berceuse!" they say.

Then they break off into pairs, Rath with Flower-Pagu and Bucket-Pagu with Well-Pagu.

They play a few rounds, switching partners each time and all of them winning at least once.

In the last round, Rath and Flower-Pagu are a team again. Flower-Pagu draws a card, then they both look excited. As they set down their hand, Rath says, "Double ... "

"Berceuse!" Flower-Pagu finishes and the other Pagu congratulate them.

Afterward, they put away the cards for the night and all go to bed.

The following morning, Rath and the Pagu are on the deck, watching the lush canopy of Pantrog grow closer.

Suddenly, William, who is in the nest, says, "Captain? There's something in the water ahead of us!" Phobos gives a startled "Caw!" from his shoulder.

Rath turns.

To the north of *PearlHeart*, a large form rises out of the ocean. The water cascades down and reveals the green carapace of an enormous turtle. A head lifts and emerald green eyes – intelligent and patient – regard them calmly.

Rath recognizes him. "Hep." He asks his crew to heave to.

After they have stopped, Rath goes to the rail.

The turtle seems to smile at him. "Captain Rath! I am so glad to see you."

Rath bows deeply to the God of Sudines. "I as well, Hep. Is there something that I may do for you?"

Hep looks surprised for a moment, then gives an aged, but gentle laugh. "No, no. Actually, would I have your permission to board, Captain? I promise not to get your deck wet."

"Of course."

"Thank you." Then the turtle begins to glow and the light travels onto *PearlHeart*, growing smaller before fading to reveal an older man with gray hair, wearing clothes similar to Fenrir's in greens and browns. He is far shorter than Rath, close to Azalea's height. Rath kneels and Hep grins. "Captain Rath of *PearlHeart*." He looks up at the sails and rigging. "It is good to see that you and your ship are well." He suddenly pauses. "My young Captain, you are hurt."

"Ah, yes. I bruised my ribs during a windstorm two nights ago."

"I am very sorry to hear that. But, Carlos is here with you" – he nods to Carlos, who had come up from the infirmary – "so I would suspect he has already tended to it?"

"He has. And Bucket-Pagu as well."

Hep's eyebrows raise. Then he looks to the Pagu flying nearby and smiles. "I see. That is wonderful to hear. You are truly in most caring hands, it would seem." He sobers. "May we speak, Captain Rath? The Pagu and Carlos, too. Perhaps somewhere private. You may also continue your travels while we do so – I do not wish to delay you."

"I understand. We may speak in the Pagu and my cabin, if that is all right with you."

"You and the Pagu's ... " Hep chuckles. "Well, I suppose it is to be expected they would choose to stay with you. Yes,

Captain, that would suit me just fine. Thank you."

Rath directs his crew to continue sailing, then he, Hep, Carlos, and the Pagu go to the captain's cabin.

They sit at the table and the Pagu sit on their cushions on top of it. At Hep's request, Carlos has prepared tea for them all.

As Carlos pours for the god, Hep says, "Thank you. Like Azalea, I always think that discussions go far better with tea. What do you think, Captain?"

"I believe so as well. I find it to be very relaxing."

After everyone has been served, they take their first sip together. When Carlos sets down his teacup, he studies Hep with some concern.

Hep notices. "Wondering why I'm here?"

Carlos hesitates for the slightest moment. "Yes."

"I thought it was a good time." Hep grins benignly.

Carlos frowns.

Hep takes another sip, then says, "After that windstorm two days ago, I was worried for my turtles. As you likely know, Captain, they migrate past Pantrog on their way to Sudines at this time of year. They were all fine – and now on their way home."

Rath says, "I am glad to hear that."

"While I was out, I thought I might see if the wind affected anyone else – ships like yours. I do not leave Sudines often, so it seems only right I use that time to help others. Then, I saw your ship." Hep's eyes shine. "*PearlHeart* is very distinctive, Captain Rath, in particular your flags. I would guess not many, if any, of Vocalises's Pan ships bear a Delphaen flag as a designation of the captain's god." He frowns. "Did your ship sustain any damage?"

"Only a sail, which has been repaired."

"Good." Hep reaches into his pocket. "I am glad we could meet like this." He holds out an envelope. "A letter for you, from Fenrir."

Rath takes it carefully. "Thank you."

While Rath tucks the letter away, Hep sips, then exhales. "This is wonderful tea, Carlos."

Carlos purses his lips. "I am pleased to hear as such."

"You seem a touch tense. Is it my presence?"

Clearing his throat politely, Carlos says, "You do not leave

Sudines often, as you said." He glances at the Pagu.

Hep understands. "Ah. Yes, everything will be all right – do not worry. The Pagu are present and all who live here or up above know that when they become involved, many good things are preparing themselves to be known." He smiles at Well-Pagu, Bucket-Pagu, and Flower-Pagu. "Now, the other thing I wished to discuss – the windstorm itself. My Spirit Turtles can confirm it came from the North and that can only mean it came from Draconi and specifically, my brother, the Elder God Ara. All of us can influence the weather of our lands given our moods, however, Ara's will is very strong and often, the cold weather he creates brings about early Winters. Its presence this far south indicates that the season this year may also be very severe." He looks seriously at Rath. "Fenrir tells me that your next delivery will take you to Haliae, in the North, correct?"

"Yes."

Hep grips Rath's hand. "Please be careful."

"I will."

Hep relaxes a little, then removes his hand.

They all finish their tea and Hep stands up, brushing off his green clothes. "Well, I think I have startled your crew more than enough for them to have tales to tell during the rest of your journey."

Rath says, "Thank you for delivering Fenrir's letter."

"Of course. He misses you. I cannot say if he wrote that or not, but I thought you should know."

Rath nods.

Hep turns to Carlos. "Thank you for the tea. It was just the thing to help me make the journey back to Sudines."

"It was my pleasure," Carlos says, bowing.

They exit out onto the main deck. Hep glows and soon reappears in his giant turtle form, paddling in the ocean next to *PearlHeart*. He smiles up at Rath one more time, then raises a front flipper in a wave before he dives underwater and swims west, to Sudines.

Later, Rath sits at his desk, reading Fenrir's letter. When his eyes reach a certain line, they fall. He quietly composes a reply.

During their afternoon tea, Rath shares some of what he read with Carlos.

Afterward, Carlos says, "Then Fenrir's father has passed on."

"Yes." Rath sips his tea quietly.

Carlos sighs. "I had thought something more was troubling Hep."

Rath nods.

PearlHeart continues, growing closer to Pantrog.

5

They travel for the rest of the day. As they come closer to Pantrog, other Pan ships sail alongside them and Rath and the Pagu watch them from the rail. Then they look ahead to Port Pallas, where many ships like *PearlHeart* are already docked.

That afternoon, Rath and his sail-master, Isaac, eat lunch together on the deck. Isaac holds out a piece of rope tied in an elaborate knot. "What do you think, Captain? It's a new knot I've been working on and I was thinking of showing it to Vocalise when we were on Pantrog. I think my god would like it a lot."

Rath puts down his bowl and accepts the rope from Isaac. "This is amazing. Would you teach me how to do it?"

Isaac flushes. "Absolutely!"

After they finish eating, they return their bowls to the galley, then stand at the rail. Isaac teaches Rath and after a few tries, he is tying and undoing it deftly.

Isaac says, "That's it!"

Rath laughs. "It is very fun to do." He undoes it once more, then hands the rope back to Isaac.

Isaac ties it himself. "I can't wait to show Vocalise." He

frowns. "Well, if I can find him."

"I remember you saying that he was difficult to find. My father and Marchand have said the same."

Isaac nods. "Most of the time, he shows up when I'm not looking for him. We ask why he's here and he's like, 'Why *am* I here?' Then he just turns into a chimp and leaps away."

"That sounds very confusing."

Isaac shrugs. "That's what he's like all the time. From what you've told me about your god, Marchand, he's not like that, is he?"

"He is more present in Delphy, if that is what you mean. And he has told me that if there is ever a time we need him" – he hesitates – "to send him a Delphaen message." He glances at his bare wrists. "Or ask someone to send one."

"That's really good of him. And I don't mean to sound like Vocalise doesn't care about us on Pantrog, we just don't see him often."

The next day, a little past six in the morning, *PearlHeart* docks at Port Pallas on Pantrog.

Pan ships surround them on both sides, bobbing with sails furled and lowered or raised and ready to sail. Even at this hour, the docks are full of people from different countries.

Pantrog itself is lush and green. Tall, tiered buildings made from orange wood like *PearlHeart's* stand alongside dense, thick trees with large boughs and long vines people can climb up. Many of Vocalise's people prefer to travel on the rooftops, leaping over colorful lanterns strung across the narrow streets of the port town. Vocalise's Traits of balance help them so that they very rarely fall.

As Rath and the Pagu look at the town, Bucket-Pagu says, "There's so many people!" Their eyes widen. "I see a lot of people from Pantha as well!"

Flower-Pagu nods. "I do, too! And their Spirit Lions!"

"Reason?" Well-Pagu asks Rath.

"I am told that it is due to the Selachuu prisons being nearby. Much of the population that was born on Pantha who are now here are former pirates and bandits that were arrested. They have since been released and may take jobs here while on their probation before they are allowed to return to Pantha or go to other countries. However, it seems that a great number have chosen to stay here." Rath thinks. "Actually, Isaac recently told me that a restaurant had opened up near here that serves food from Pantha. He says it's become very popular."

Flower-Pagu says, "Really? Can we go?"

"Definitely. I notified Captain Larox that I would be able to be at his home later this morning to meet with those applying for the position of first mate, so we could go there for breakfast."

The Pagu look excited. "Yes, please!" Flower-Pagu and Bucket-Pagu say and Well-Pagu says, "Breakfast!"

They ask Phillip and Charles – one of the sailors on the lines – if they want to come and both immediately agree.

They go down the gangplank and enter the crowd, staying close to one another.

A tall muscular woman walks past them, carrying a crate to a Pan ship. She asks her Spirit Lion, "Anything yet?" The Lion shakes her head.

When they leave the docks, Well-Pagu flies up high into the sky to find the restaurant. In the streets, there are more people clustered around Spirit Lions. Although Rath, Charles, and Phillip cannot see them, the Pagu can as well as Phillip's Spirit Rabbit.

One man says to the Lions, "Well? Is it still going?"

The Lions nod, flicking their ears as they pace.

Charles looks over. "I wonder what those people are doing?"

Phillip says, "My Rabbit told me that they're all gathered around their Spirit Lions."

Flower-Pagu says, "Maybe they're waiting for news from Pantha!"

Bucket-Pagu nods. "They would know if anything was going on there."

Rath says, "That is true. I hope that the news is good."

Well-Pagu flies down, having heard part of the conversation. They ask Rath, "Coliseum?"

He winces. "Yes, I have been taught that in the past, Pantha's royals proved themselves in the Coliseum by, ah, defeating all who came as a show of strength and right to rule. Afterward, they would feast on the food that was brought to the castle that month." He shakes his head. "However, I am told that the Coliseum has not been used in thirty years. There has not been a royal for the same amount of time and it has made the country very unstable. Their god, Lionel, has not been seen for just as long." He looks thoughtful.

The Pagu do, too, as they continue on.

At the same time, others are leaving *PearlHeart*.

Three sailors with tattoos demonstrating Marchand's Traits – Velt, Franz, and Perri – set out for a trinket shop Isaac had told Perri about earlier that morning. Right afterward, Isaac, William, and Felix – both with their bird partners, Phobos and Triphonius – leave.

As they reach the docks, Triphonius looks at the people leaping across the rooftops. He gives a low "*Caw.*"

His partner, Felix, sighs. "No, Triphonius, we can't race with them!"

William smiles knowingly beside them and on his shoulder, Phobos gives a cheerful "Caw!"

Isaac turns back toward *PearlHeart*. "Hey, Oren! You sure you don't wanna come with?"

Oren, one of the helmsmen, lounges on the upper deck. "And find Vocalise?" He shrugs. "Naw. He's always impossible to find. He sometimes doesn't even show up for the holiday!"

Isaac frowns. "Well, yeah, but ... " He shakes his head. "We'll let you know if we find him!"

"Thanks, Isaac. Hope you do."

Isaac brightens, then leaves with the others.

Carlos arrives on the main deck from below with his medical bag over his shoulder. Near him, standing in the shade of the upper deck, are Melody, Demeter, and Evermore – a young man from Ullia with long pale blond hair bound over his shoulder and dark clothes. A purple scarf covers his eyes. Like others from his country, he is highly sensitive to sunlight, but he can sense those around him and his environment with Erole's Traits.

Carlos asks them, "Would you let others know that I will be at the apothecary shop on Menna Street?"

Melody says, "Yes, Carlos!" and Demeter gives a polite "Caw." Evermore nods beside them.

"Thank you."

As Carlos goes down the gangplank, Evermore asks Melody,

"Will you go to the town?"

She shakes her head. "No. I'd rather stay on *PearlHeart*. What about you?"

He frowns. "I won't. Too many people."

Melody nods, understanding.

As they talk, Carlos walks toward the town. He pauses when something catches his eye in the ocean, however, the moment he looks over, it disappears. He frowns, but joins the crowd on his way to the apothecary shop.

Ahead, Rath, Well-Pagu, Bucket-Pagu, Flower-Pagu, Phillip, and Charles have just arrived at the restaurant. The building is very different from those surrounding it and built with a type of wood that is much darker.

Rath looks at it with interest. "This is Ursian architecture. The wood, too, is from there."

Phillip says, "Shouldn't it be more like what's in Pantha?"

"I am not sure. However, Ursi and Pantha have always had good relations with one another."

They walk up the stairs to the entrance and Rath and Charles open the heavy wooden doors.

Inside, there is a small entryway with a desk, a kitchen behind it, and a large eating area to the left. Maps of the Fourth World are on the walls. Rath is studying them when someone says, "Ya' eating or looking?"

Rath turns and sees a man with short brown hair sitting at the front desk, his bare feet on the desktop. Grinning, he wiggles one toe in a hello. "Hey, there."

Rath waves back with his hand. "Ah, hello. Yes, we are eating."

The man vaults himself up and over the desk, then walks over to them, slouching. "Sure thing. This way! I think." He scratches his jaw as he leads.

They follow him into the dining area, where thick rugs have been laid out beneath the wide tables and a dormant fireplace rests against the inside wall.

Once they reach an open table, he pauses as if sizing it up. "Yup. It's a table all right." He gestures. "This fine? I'm kinda new to this whole work ... stuff."

Rath says, "Yes, it is. Thank you."

They sit down and the man waves his hand behind his back, producing six menus that weren't there previously. He fans them out on the table. "Here ya' are."

After they decide, he takes their menus back, saying, "Sure and sure and done. I'll be back whenever. I dunno how long this stuff takes to cook. Tastes good, though." He gives a lazy wave, then walks in the general direction of the kitchen.

Not long afterward, he comes back with the dishes, all balanced on a wide wooden platter. He lays each of them down quickly.

"Thank you very much," Rath says.

The man raises an eyebrow. "You already thanked me."

Rath flushes. "I apologize."

Both eyebrows go up, then he grins. "Don't. It's kinda refreshing. Hope to see you around, Captain."

"You as well."

After he leaves, they all start on their meals.

"This is amazing," Rath says. He brings a hand to his mouth, smiling. "It is very different. Filling."

Bucket-Pagu turns to Flower-Pagu. "You helped Lionel make it like that, didn't you?"

"That's right! I remember he said, 'Flower-Pagu, I want something that will make them strong!' So, we put our heads together and this is what we came up with!"

Rath says, "That was very wonderful of you to help him."

However, Phillip and Charles look amazed. They say simultaneously, "You've met the God of Pantha?" and "You advised a god?"

Flower-Pagu beams. "Yup!" They shoot their arms up. "To both!'

Phillip and Charles look at each other, then Phillip says to Flower-Pagu, "It's no wonder you know so much about plants – and different dishes!"

"It just takes time and practice, Phillip! You know a lot, too."

"Thanks, Flower-Pagu."

Outside, Isaac, William, Phobos, Felix, and Triphonius are looking for Vocalise.

"Vocalise! Vocalise!" Isaac calls.

William says, "Will that really work?"

Felix says, "He could be anywhere in the country."

Isaac's shoulders begin to fall, but then he suddenly nods, looking reinvigorated. "That's it, I'm shouting it from the rooftops!" And he clambers up the nearest wall.

"Isaac!" William says. He turns to Felix. "You want to follow him up there?"

Felix shakes his head. "I'm good down here."

His partner, however, gives an enlivened "Caw!"

"Triphonius, I told you – we're not doing any races!"

Triphonius twitches his feathers. Phobos looks around, trying to help Isaac locate his god.

On top of the roof, Isaac shouts, "Vocalise! Vocalise! VO-CA-LISE!"

At the restaurant, Rath, Well-Pagu, Bucket–Pagu, Flower-Pagu, Phillip, and Charles are now leaving.

Rath says to the man, now back at his desk, "Thank you very much for helping us today."

"Huh?" He sits up and a chimp folded out of paper falls off his nose. He catches it and starts juggling, but now he has three. He grins. "Yeah, sure thing, Captain. Good luck with meeting those first mates."

"Thank you."

As they exit the restaurant, Phillip suddenly stops and looks up at Rath. "Wait. How did he know about your meeting?"

Rath pauses. "I do not know."

Charles puts in, "He also called you 'Captain,' but I don't think any of us said you were."

"That is true." Rath thinks for a moment, then shakes his head. He pulls out his pocket watch. "I need to go meet with the first mates now. Thank you for having breakfast together, everyone. I truly enjoyed it."

Flower-Pagu says, "You too, Captain!" and the rest nod in agreement.

While Rath goes to Larox's home, the others decide to return to *PearlHeart*. Well-Pagu, however, goes back into the restaurant. All they say is, "Talk," indicating the man behind the desk.

While they walk, Phillip says to Charles, "Do you think Well-Pagu knew the waiter?"and the other sailor shrugs.

At his home, Captain Larox speaks to two men – a man with dark brown hair and one with light blond hair and a black eye patch covering his left eye. The second man also has a short blade sticking out of his right boot and a blue Spirit Lion sits next to him, licking his chops.

Larox says, "Captain Rath should be here soon. Shame Lin isn't here yet. Hopefully he arrives in time."

The first man, Farrow, says, "Maybe the windstorm delayed him?"

"Maybe." Larox frowns. "Never seen a storm like that this early in the season – especially in Pantrog."

"You think it came from the North?"

"Assuredly." Larox pauses. "Come to think of it, Captain Rath will be sailing there next – Haliae, as I told you all. He was looking for a navigator, too, that had experience in that area, but it sounds like he found one."

Farrow stretches. "Hopefully the storm didn't delay *PearlHeart*, too."

The second man, One-Eye, gives a grunt and stomps off, heading outside. He shifts a beaded curtain out of the way as he leaves.

Farrow says, "Where's he going?"

Larox just sighs.

One-Eye stands in the street while people walk around him. He faces north, arms crossed. "He'd better get here soon," he says.

His Spirit Lion shakes out his mane next to him, saying something that only One-Eye can hear.

One-Eye whips his head toward him. "Of course I mean Captain Rath! I don't care if the other first mate doesn't show up. Just means I'm more likely to get the job."

The Lion stares at him. He suddenly scratches his ear.

"I don't care about any news from Pantha."

With a serious look, the Lion begins to pace.

Sighing, One-Eye kneels and catches the Lion on his return trip. He ruffles his mane. "I'm sorry you're agitated about this." He moves on to scratch the Lion's ear and the Lion purrs. "We'll run after this, I promise. Maybe even in other places, too, if I get this job."

The Lion cracks his eyes open.

"I'm getting it. No matter what."

Nearby, Rath is walking to Captain Larox's home.

As he nears an intersection, he steps off to the side and pulls out Larox's letter to check the address.

At the same time, on the street ahead of him, One-Eye stands, still waiting. Finally, he says to his Lion, "We should go back. If Larox is right about Captain Rath, he'll be here when he said."

They start walking. One-Eye hesitates. "Any news?"

The Lion gives him a pointed look, flicking an ear.

One-Eye looks away. "I'm asking for you, not me. I don't like seeing you this on edge."

The Lion starts to nod, then suddenly goes still.

Every other Spirit Lion in Port Pallas freezes, too.

Then in a single moment, they let out a simultaneous roar and the people surrounding them look surprised, then all let out a victorious shout in response.

Calls of "He did it!" and "King Faerohr!" and "Lionel came?" erupt all over the town.

Rath looks up just as two people run past him, tackling each other in a friendly brawl. He stares as they land not far from him, still laughing. He quickly backs away as three more tumble past.

Amid the chaos, he hears a different shout from behind.

He turns around and sees a man fall from the rooftop and into the alley in between the two buildings, landing on his left leg with a *crack!*

Rath rushes toward him. "Are you all right?"

The man holds onto his leg. "I-I was just startled, okay? Wouldn't have fallen if ... Oww ... "

"Your leg may be broken. I am Captain Rath. My ship doctor is nearby. I can bring him here."

For a moment, the man starts to protest, but then he tries to move his leg again and his face twists in pain. "Yes, please."

Behind them, another voice says, "Hey! Mars – what are you doing?"

Three more people crowd into the alleyway.

Mars, the man who is on the ground, says, "Oh, you know,

just ... ”

Rath says, “Please do not move.” To the others, he says, “He’s badly hurt his leg. It may be broken. I’ve offered to bring my ship doctor here.”

The tallest man, with long dark blond hair and thick arm muscles, pats his shoulder. “Small one like you? You won’t make it past this street with how things are.” He grins. “The first new king in thirty years has been crowned – King Faerohr. It sounds like he just showed up at the castle, struck the gong there, and defeated everyone who came to the Coliseum. Not only that, Lionel himself came and told everyone he supports Faerohr as the new king. That’s more than cause to celebrate.” He gestures to himself, then the two with him. “I’m Fleiche. Beren and Tol will stay with Mars and I’ll bring your doctor here. Make sure he gets through.”

“Thank you so much. He is at the apothecary shop on Menna Street.”

“Got it.” Without another word, Fleiche bounds up to the roof and hops over it, out of sight.

While they wait, the celebration in the street continues. Mars says, “Faerohr really beat everyone?”

Beren and Tol kneel next to them. Beren, a man with thick dark brown hair, nods. His eyes are a bright blue. “Yeah. Spirit Lions say he barely got a scratch on him.”

Tol says, “I want to go back to Pantha and see that.”

Mars says to Rath, “Hey, Captain, what do you think?”

“I am, ah, unsure how to feel about proving one’s strength by fighting.”

Tol lightly shoves him, but grins. “I think it sounds exciting.”

Beren laughs. “My parents say it was always a lot of fun, too.”

Mars shrugs. “None of us got to do it. People thought the tradition was dead by the time we were born. But, maybe if we went back to Pantha, we could now?” They all share a look of anticipation. The Spirit Lions swish their tails.

Beren continues, “It sounds like they had the feast afterward, too – with whatever was in the castle from the last king.”

Tol rolls her eyes. “Right. Him. The one that decided to hole up and take it all for himself? My mom always said his father, King Faron, was the last good king.”

Mars says, "My dad said that, too."

Rath hesitates, then says, "May I ask what happened to the king?"

"No one really knows," Beren says. "Many think he ran off to the Ursian mountains after everyone stopped bringing food to the castle." He snorts. "Why would they if he was just going to hoard it all?"

Tol says, "It's hard enough to find food in Pantha without that. Now, most people just find what they can, mostly in groups."

Mars, still holding his leg, says, "But, now, they – *we* – won't have to. If Faerohr's like what the Spirit Lions say he is, then maybe things can go back to how they were and everyone will work together again."

Rath says, "If I may say, I hope very much that they do."

The others smile and Tol slaps him on the back again in a friendly manner.

"Master Rath?"

They all turn to see Carlos, protected by Fleiche, enter the alley.

After scanning Rath up and down – Carlos breathes a sigh of relief – he turns to Mars. "I am Carlos." He kneels next to him. "Let me see." He places his glowing hands over Mars' leg, moving up and down his shin without touching it as he checks it with Sevran's Traits. "Broken. It is likely due to Lionel's Traits of endurance that you are still conscious. I will need to reset it. Fleiche?"

Fleiche, who had been holding a splint, some medical tape, and crutches comes over and hands the first two to Rath, saying, "Don't know how to use either of these," then crouches by Carlos and Mars.

Carlos places his hands fully on Mars' leg. "This may hurt for a moment."

"Okay – OW!"

A Spirit Lion nuzzles his back, saying that it will be all right.

With Rath's help, Carlos secures the splint and binds it with medical tape.

As Carlos eases the pain with Sevran's Traits, he says, "You will need to be off of the leg for at least a month." He reaches into his bag for a pad of paper and writes out a note. "Here are the exercises you will do to strengthen it afterward. I will also write a referral for the doctor here who can treat it and check on its progress. Please see her. I will not be here by the end of today." He tears out a sheet and hands it to Mars.

"I-I promise, Carlos!" Mars reads it over.

Carlos smiles briefly.

Fleiche says, "Stretches? To make you stronger?"

"The muscle will weaken during his recovery." Carlos turns to Fleiche, Beren, and Tol. "Have you three any injuries?"

They look at one another. Fleiche rolls his arm. "Have issues in my upper arm all the time."

Beren says, "I get some pain in my neck."

Tol says, "Shin splints."

"I may have remedies for all of those," Carlos says. "For more serious issues, I will refer you to the doctor here for extended care." Then he says, "Master Rath, were you able to get to your interviews?"

Rath's eyebrows go up. He stands up quickly. "N-No, I did not. Not with the sudden crowd."

Fleiche says, "I could help you get there."

But another voice says, "Naw, I got it."

They all look up.

A tall man with long limbs, brown hair, and a grin is swinging his feet above them on the roof. He raises a bare foot and waves to Rath with his big toe.

"You were the man from the restaurant!" Rath says.

"Sure am."

Carlos frowns at him.

"I can take him there," the man continues, extending a hand to Rath and pulling him up onto the roof. He nods to the others. "Get your things looked at by Carlos – he's the best doctor I've ever met and I guess I've met like a few, or something. He's pretty good." He grins at Carlos. Carlos' expression doesn't change. The man stretches out his back. "Aaanyways ... "

Rath says to the others, "I am glad that you will have your injuries looked at, everyone. Carlos, thank you for doing so. And, I am glad that Faerohr has been crowned as well."

The man and Carlos seem surprised, but Fleiche, Beren, Tol, and Mars all smile. Fleiche says, "Thanks, Captain."

As Carlos helps them, the man next to Rath says, "Let's get

you to where you were going. Larox's, right?"

"Ah, yes. May I ask how you knew that?" Rath follows him over the rooftops, careful of his footing.

"Spirit Lion told me." The man turns around for a moment. "Sounds like he's *pretty* interested in you. The one he's bonded to is one of the first mate candidates."

"I see."

The man hops over to the next roof – a short gap of only two feet – and Rath does the same.

Rath looks at the tiling. "I've never traveled like this before."

"Isn't it fun?"

"I guess it is," Rath says, laughing a little.

After a few more houses, the man suddenly stops, looks left, then turns back to Rath. "You good from here? I've gotta go." He points. "Larox's is just up ahead – the house with the balcony."

"I understand. Thank you for telling me." Rath makes it to the next roof. "And yes, I am. Thank you very much for your help earlier."

"Sure thing, Captain Rath," he says, ruffling Rath's hair. "Hope to see you again soon."

"Y-You as well!"

But when Rath looks up, the man is gone and when he turns around, he's nowhere in sight on any of the rooftops.

Earlier, when the news from Pantha was first released, One-Eye and his Spirit Lion had been in front of Larox's home. After the shouts and play-fighting began, Larox stepped out, saw One-Eye, and said, "What in the world happened?"

One-Eye ducks into the building, away from two people tackling one another. "New king."

Larox's eyes widen. "Really? From what I understand, there hasn't been one in quite a while, right?"

One-Eye nods. Beside him, his Lion's eyes shine.

Larox looks at the people outside, then checks his watch. "Rath should have been here by now. I hope he didn't get caught up in the, uh, celebrations."

"I'll go look," One-Eye says and he and his Lion go back out, making their way through the crowd.

Nearby, Franz, Velt, and Perri are inside the trinket shop.

They watch the people celebrating outside.

Franz says, "I think we should stay in here."

Velt and Perri agree.

Not far from them, Isaac helps Felix onto a rooftop that William and Phobos are already on.

They sit on the edge and watch people get tossed from one crowd to the other in the street. Triphonius looks at it all and gives a low "*Caw.*"

His partner gapes. Holding his bird back, Felix says, "N-No, Triphonius! You can't join them!"

Triphonius puffs out his chest, repeating his "Caw!"

"You don't even know why they're celebrating!"

William pets his bird partner. "Phobos says there's a new king in Pantha."

Triphonius' eyes gleam.

Suddenly, Isaac notices a familiar figure with long dark orange hair across the street from them, hopping over the rooftops. "Hey, isn't that the Captain?"

Back on the street, One-Eye dodges around a cluster of people trying to both hug and race around the block. His Spirit Lion sees them, then begins hopping up and down on all four paws, getting caught up in the excitement.

One-Eye says, "Not right now. Come on – we'll have a better chance seeing him from the roof." He starts to climb. The Lion pouts, but leaps up after him.

Once there, One-Eye says, "Is there any way you can tell where Captain Rath is? He's from Delphy, does he have a Spirit Dolphin?"

The Lion thinks, then shakes his head. He seems unusually pensive for a moment.

While the Lion scratches his ear, One-Eye looks down at the crowd. He huffs when he sees about a dozen arm wrestling matches going on.

Then he hears something to his left and turns.

A man with long dark orange hair is traveling over the rooftops in the direction of Larox's home. The Lion sees, too, and says something to One-Eye.

One-Eye faces the man and shouts, "Hey!"

The man starts, begins to turn, then loses his footing.

One-Eye bounds across the next two rooftops. Just as Rath falls over backward, One-Eye catches his hand. The two stare at one another.

"Hello," Rath says, wide-eyed.

One-Eye grunts and pulls him the rest of the way up, then lets go. "Sorry. Didn't mean to startle you."

"That is all right. Can I help you?"

"You're Captain Rath?"

"I am. May I ask who you are?"

One-Eye holds out his hand again, flushes when he realizes that they just held hands, but keeps it out. "One-Eye. One of the first mates you're meeting with at Captain Larox's house."

Rath smiles warmly, shaking his hand. "I see. It is wonderful to meet you."

One-Eye's flush deepens and the Lion grins beside him. Coughing to cover it, One-Eye says, "That was a good idea to go to the rooftops." He hops across the next gap. He watches Rath follow him with a more careful leap and land safely.

"It was not me. A man I met at a restaurant earlier today helped me up. I've never done anything like this before. I find it very fun."

One-Eye smiles briefly, then focuses on his own footing. "Larox's isn't far from here. I think he was still waiting on one of the first mates to show up – he was delayed – so you should be fine."

"Thank you for telling me. Did you come out to find me?"

One-Eye hesitates. "I did." His Lion stares at him. "Larox was concerned about the crowd."

Rath nods. "It started very suddenly. I heard that King Faerohr was crowned."

"I know. My Spirit Lion told me." One-Eye sighs. "He's excited." He leaps down onto the second floor balcony of Captain Larox's house, then offers a hand to Rath without thinking.

Rath takes it gratefully, then joins him. "I am glad that your Spirit Lion is excited. I think that if this news means that Pantha would have more stability, that would be good."

One-Eye immediately frowns. He looks away. "Yeah." He doesn't say anything more.

Below, Larox hears them and steps outside. "Rath, One-Eye! What are you doing up there?"

One-Eye gestures to the crowd.

Rath says, "Hello, Captain Larox!"

After they climb down, Larox says, "Well, I'm glad that you both are safe, at least." He looks at the people still cheering. "You'd think it was Pica Pica here." Shaking his head, he walks inside and Rath, One-Eye, and his Spirit Lion follow him.

They pass through the beaded curtain and into the room One-Eye was in earlier.

Larox says, "You've got good timing, Lin just got here."

Rath nods, then looks forward. His eyes widen. "Are you all right?"

Another man is now seated next to Farrow. He waves a crutch. "Hey, Captain Rath. I'm Lin." While Rath and One-Eye sit opposite of them and Larox leaves to give them all privacy, Lin continues, "Doing better now. While I was traveling here, some crates got knocked over during that windstorm and broke my foot."

"I am very sorry to hear that."

"Me too." Lin frowns. "I won't be able to do much for several weeks still, so I don't think I can apply anymore – not if you're needing to leave soon. But, I wanted to at least meet you and let you know in-person."

"Thank you very much for doing so. It is good to meet you, Lin."

Lin smiles. "You, too."

Farrow says, "It's a wonder you made it with all that's going on outside."

"You know – that was kinda the weird part. I thought it'd be impossible, but then some tall guy that looked like he was part of the Selachuu Military showed up and helped me through. Everyone just stepped out of the way wherever we went."

"That's unusual he was here. I thought all of them were up in Pantha."

Lin shrugs.

They begin the interviews. Even though Lin cannot apply, he and Rath talk about his career. "Definitely aiming to become a captain one of these days."

"That is wonderful to hear," Rath says.

He speaks with Farrow next. "I've sailed for seven years, first mate with Larox for three," he tells Rath and One-Eye frowns as he listens.

Rath says, "I worked as first mate for Captain Larox as well, though just for a year. It was a great experience."

"Yeah. I'm learning a lot." Farrow hesitates. "I'm afraid I don't have a lot of experience with the North, though. No ships I've worked on go any further than the countries in the South."

"I see. It can be very dangerous there and I am told that this Winter may be more severe."

"Will you still go?"

"If weather permits, yes."

Rath turns to One-Eye last.

One-Eye says, "I learned to sail Pan ships eight years ago when I was released from the Selachuu prisons. Sailor for three, sail-master for three, first mate for two. I have experience sailing in the North, but only on Pantha ships."

Rath thinks. "They do not have sails, do they?"

"No. They're just other countries' ships with the sails torn off." Rath winces and One-Eye coughs. His Lion presses his nose into the couch. "I'm familiar with the currents in the North. I also sailed here on Pantrog during monsoon season."

"That can be a very tumultuous time. I remember doing so myself. They often come unpredictably."

One-Eye nods, relaxing.

Afterward, Rath turns to the whole group. "May I ask why each of you applied?"

Lin says, "Heard good things about you from Larox and about *PearlHeart.*"

Farrow says, "I'd like to be a captain soon, but need more experience."

One-Eye says, "I want to leave here."

They all stare at him.

While his Lion gnaws at his pant leg, One-Eye says, "That's the truth. I enjoy sailing Pan ships – I like going places. Every ship I've worked on has only taken deliveries on Pantrog." He looks straight at Rath. "I heard you go anywhere. That's what I want."

Rath holds his eye for another moment, then smiles. "Me too," he says softly. He extends his hand. "Would you accept my offer to be first mate aboard *PearlHeart*, One-Eye? I believe we would work well together."

One-Eye smiles as he takes Rath's hand. "Same."

Larox rejoins them and they all talk. He says to Farrow, "There will be more positions." Then to Rath and One-Eye, "Will you be going to get One-Eye's papers signed?"

Rath, who had brought all the necessary paperwork with him – he and One-Eye already signed the initial sheets – says, "Yes. I believe there is a Selachuu outpost nearby."

Larox frowns. "There is, but I'm not sure if a soldier is stationed there."

One-Eye says, "We'll check."

Looking toward the open door, Lin says, "It sounds like they're still celebrating out there – be careful you two."

Rath says, "Thank you, Lin."

Outside, the crowd somehow still has the same amount of energy as before.

One-Eye huffs and starts to climb. "Roofs, again."

"Yes," Rath agrees, following him.

Once they reach the top, One-Eye looks around. He points. "The Selachuu outpost is over there. I've had to check in with them multiple times since living in Pantrog." He glances at his Lion. "But, not recently." He and Rath begin walking over the rooftops toward it.

While they travel, Carlos, Mars, Fleiche, Beren, and Tol are exiting the alleyway. Mars is using the crutches. Carlos says, "If you all do the stretches I showed you, your ailments should recover."

"Yes, Carlos!" they say.

Carlos frowns at the people in the street, but the others grin, eager to join them.

However, suddenly the group to their right grows quiet. They look in that direction and see the people move back. Although Carlos cannot see them, the Spirit Lions step back as well as a tall man in a Selachuu Military uniform walks through them. The man has short gray hair and chews on what appears to be a silver toothpick.

The man pauses, nods to Carlos – Carlos nods back – then faces the crowd, but does not say anything.

A Spirit Lion speaks up.

The man says, "No. You're not in trouble."

The Lion licks his chops.

Then another voice makes all of them turn. "Soooo ... "

Up on the nearest roof, a giant chimpanzee sits with his long arms folded in front of him. He grins down at the crowd. "I've been getting some noise complaints. Not telling you all to stop, but I think I've got a better place you can do this all in. I don't mind y'all living here – never have – but ya' gotta remember other people live here along with you. So – want me to lead you to that place I mentioned?"

The silence is broken as several people shout, "Yeah!"

Vocalise, the God of Pantrog, laughs as he sits up. "Alrighty, follow me!" He bounds off the rooftop in the direction of the southern forests.

The man in the Selachuu Military uniform who had made them all quiet smiles for a moment, then walks over to Carlos. Mars, Fleiche, Beren, and Tol have since departed with the others.

"Thank you," Carlos says. He raises an eyebrow. "I had thought I saw you earlier in the ocean."

He nods. "Just checking on things here." Then he looks up and sees Rath and One-Eye disappear over the side of a roof. He frowns. Waving to Carlos, he starts in that direction.

At the Selachuu outpost, One-Eye looks at the note on the door. "He's not here," he says to Rath.

Rath reads, "*Please see the Phoenae airship dock.* That makes sense."

"How?"

"The Phoenae Force will sometimes fill in for absences in the Selachuu Military."

One-Eye offers a hand to Rath, helping him up onto the roof again. "Why wouldn't they just be here?"

"With the exception of messengers and the Phoenae Force, people from Phoenae are not customarily allowed outside of their country. However, they cannot leave their airship for a long length of time."

One-Eye pauses, then nods.

Ahead of them, an enormous tree grows near the coastline.

A spiral staircase runs up its trunk. At the very top is a golden Phoenae airship, hovering next to a dock that stretches out from the tree and over the ocean below.

"It's not too far," One-Eye says. He suddenly looks down at his Lion. "No, we can't run." But at the Lion's insistence, he says to Rath, "Unless you wouldn't mind? It would be faster."

Rath blinks. "No, I suppose not. I've never done so over roofs, however."

"I'm sure you'll be able to do it. You've handled yourself fine."

"Thank you."

One-Eye smiles, then reddens and frowns again. He and his Lion make the first leap, picking up speed.

Rath hesitates for a moment as he measures out the gap, then starts after them.

One-Eye and his Lion slow to match Rath's pace, but soon they're all moving comfortably together. The Lion bounds in between them, tongue lolling happily.

They reach the large tree quickly and slow down.

One-Eye grins, kneeling as he ruffles his Lion's mane. "Liked that?" The Lion accepts all of the attention. To Rath, One-Eye says, "Thanks. He's been restless all day."

Rath is flushed, but looks happy. "Of course. I found it rather fun as well." He pauses. "Will he be all right on *PearlHeart*? There is not much room to run around."

"He'll find other ways to keep busy." The Lion grins – One-Eye huffs, but is smiling – then One-Eye stands and they go up the stairs together, catching their breath as they do. Rath looks out at the port city, the tall trees, and the people racing over the orange-tiled rooftops.

He suddenly stops. "The people are gone that were celebrating."

One-Eye stops as well, one boot on the next step. "You're right." He talks silently with his Lion for a moment. The Lion looks south and One-Eye points. "My Lion says they're over there now. I think I see them."

"I do as well. And a giant chimpanzee. I believe that may be Vocalise, the God of Pantrog."

"My Lion says it is. You ever met him?"

"No. Have you?"

"A few times. He tried to pretend he wasn't a god. My Lion told me he was. They talk sometimes." One-Eye shakes his head. "Doesn't seem like he's around that much. I don't mind." He continues up the stairs and Rath follows him.

They reach the top and approach the Phoenae airship at the end of the dock.

Rath says, "Excuse me?"

A few people with golden hair and eyes glare down at them from the railing, but none say anything.

Instead, a hatch opens from the side of the hull and a woman dressed in a Phoenae Force uniform walks down it.

She stops in front of them, frowns, and says, "Yes? I am Officer Sverellin."

"Captain Rath of Delphy. This is One-Eye. We were directed here by a note on the door of the Selachuu outpost."

Sverellin's eyes crinkle irritably. "What is your business, Captain? If it is those loud people from Pantha disturbing the peace, we've received enough reports and I'll tell you as I did the others: we may be acting in the Selachuu Military's stead, but it is ultimately Selachuu's god, Belle, and his military who are responsible for their actions here. Not us."

"It is not that." Sverellin raises an eyebrow and Rath hands her their paperwork. "I have just hired One-Eye as my first mate. However, he needs his paperwork signed by a Selachuu soldier – or one acting in their stead – so that he may leave Pantrog with us aboard *PearlHeart.*"

"I know the law, Captain," she snaps. She glares at both of them. "And I will tell you again – not our responsibility."

One-Eye grits his teeth. Rath says, "I see. May I ask if you would know where a member of the Selachuu Military may be?"

"All in Pantha as far as I'm aware." She flaps the papers. "Why would you want to hire this man? You do realize that his own negligence will reflect on you as a captain? Let me do you a favor" – her hand suddenly ignites in a golden flame as she uses Merp's Traits and Rath gasps – "hire someone else" – it starts to consume the paper – "and then you won't need paperwork like – " She suddenly stops.

While she spoke, a tall man in a Selachuu Military uniform walked up and took her hand in his own, smothering the flame.

Sverellin stares up at him, her mouth slightly open.

However, before she can find her voice, Rath says, "Belle."

Belle, the God of Selachuu, nods. He snaps the paperwork a few times, completely putting out the fire before handing it back to Rath. He stares at Sverellin. "You realize that burning any official document without due reason is illegal?"

"I-I ... "

"We'll talk. Go over there for a moment. I need to speak with these two."

For a second, she looks like she's about to protest, but then she says, "Yes, Belle," and walks down the dock to wait.

To Rath, Belle says, "Good to see you again. You've just hired this man?"

"Yes. This is One-Eye. Would you know of any other Selachuu outposts on Pantrog that would be occupied currently to sign his paperwork?"

Belle frowns. "None at the moment, unfortunately. Officer Sverellin was right about that. Merp ordered that all of my people were to be near Pantha due to an increase in piracy this year."

One-Eye says, "What are you doing here?" His Lion looks curious.

The corner of Belle's mouth goes up. "Checking on things." He looks to the forest where the people are still celebrating. "Technically, the South is the jurisdiction of my brother, Fierce, and the Butej Guard, but due to the population of those from Pantha here on Pantrog, he insists it's more for the Selachuu Military. We've talked about it a few times." He thinks. "Although, with the news of King Faerohr being crowned and Lionel supporting him, I should be able to move some of my people back down here to sign that paperwork of yours. I can't guarantee that they'll be here soon, but definitely by the end of the month."

Rath says, "I am afraid we will need to travel north before Winter arrives. And I am not leaving here without One-Eye."

One-Eye looks at him in surprise, then an unreadable expression crosses his face. The Lion looks at them both.

Belle raises his eyebrows. He thinks. "North ... " He strokes his chin, then seems to come to a decision. "Hand me that paperwork for a moment."

"Of course."

Belle waves his hand – a pen appears – and he signs it. He hands it back to Rath and both he and One-Eye stare at it, wide-eyed. Belle says, "That won't count as a real signature – I'm their god, not a soldier." He smiles. "But, it will give you permission to be in the South, at least, One-Eye. You'll have to find another soldier to officially approve it before you go to the North. Check the ports as you do customs – the further east you go, the more likely my people will be at them. I'll start sending them back as soon as I can."

"Thank you," Rath says. One-Eye looks at him with respect.

"Sure." Then Belle turns toward the Spirit Lion, who has begun pawing the dock in impatience. He kneels in front of him. "Yes?"

The Lion says something.

"Have I really beaten Lionel in combat?"

The Lion nods.

Rath's eyebrows go up – he is only able to hear Belle's side of the conversation. One-Eye sighs.

"Isn't that what he's told you?" Belle pauses. "A score?" The Lion speaks again and for the first time, Belle looks mildly irritated. "That's not what I remember." He stands up. "I'll talk to Lionel when I get back to Pantha. I want to meet King Faerohr and it's been too long since I've checked on Lionel himself. But, first ... " He looks at the Phoenae Force officer waiting on the dock and frowns. Then to Rath and One-Eye, he says, "Take care, both of you," and walks off.

As they start down the stairs, One-Eye says, "You know Belle?" His Lion looks curious as well.

"Yes. He helped me before. I am deeply grateful for it."

One-Eye and his Lion pause on a step, nod, then continue on.

They reach the bottom of the staircase, still well above the town. The docks are easily visible, with the masts rising up from all of the Pan ships. One-Eye says, "Can we see *PearlHeart* from here?"

Rath looks out across the rooftops to the ships currently docked at port. His eyes immediately travel to the right and he smiles. "Yes. There. With the Delphaen, Pantrog, and Alliance flags."

One-Eye smiles at his expression, then follows his look. He finds the ship with a blue-green flag with a dolphin on it alongside an orange one with a chimpanzee and a golden one for the Alliance.

On a wordless agreement, they start toward it.

In town, Franz, Velt, and Perri are exiting the trinket shop. They have a few bags of purchases.

Franz says, "Seems like things have calmed down." The others nod, then they all walk back to *PearlHeart.*

Not far from them, William and Felix are helping one another down from the roof they were on with Isaac.

William calls up, "You coming, Isaac?"

"In a bit." He waves to them as they depart for *PearlHeart,* then sighs as he swings the knot he made on his finger.

Someone sits next to him.

Isaac watches as they take up the knot, study it, grin, then say, "You make this, Isaac?"

He blurts, "Vocalise!"

Vocalise, now in his human form, laughs and ruffles Isaac's hair.

"A-And yeah, I did. Taught the Captain how to make it, too."

"Good work." Vocalise hands it back to him. He hums. "Captain Rath, right?"

Isaac nods. "He's the best."

Vocalise smiles for a moment, then frowns. "You doing all right? You looked kinda ... " He gestures, but seems to struggle with a word.

Isaac flushes. "Oh. Yeah, I am now." Vocalise frowns and Isaac continues, "I just thought I might not find you before we had to leave."

"Oh." Vocalise stands, pacing the roof and looking up at the sky. "I mean, I can't always be there, right?"

"I guess not."

Vocalise turns back toward him, then sits down again, hands in his pockets. He suddenly says, "Let's go to *PearlHeart* together." He jumps off the roof.

"R-Really?" Isaac joins him.

"Yeah." Vocalise scratches his chin. "I wanna see everyone. Also, I've been told I should *properly introduce* myself to

Captain Rath and the others."

"What do you mean by that?"

"I don't really know. I'm hoping I'll figure it out before we get there."

Isaac stares at his god.

At the same time, Rath and One-Eye are nearing *PearlHeart*.

As they approach, they see Franz, Velt, Perri, Carlos, Phillip, Charles, William and Phobos, Felix and Triphonius, and the Pagu all gathered.

Perri sees them first and waves. "Hey, Captain!"

"Hello, Perri!"

When they arrive, Rath says, "Everyone, this is One-Eye. He has accepted the position of first mate aboard *PearlHeart*."

One-Eye nods to them. The Lion sits up tall.

The crew welcomes One-Eye, saying, "Glad to be working with you," and the Pagu, who can see the Spirit Lion, greet him as well. Flower-Pagu and Bucket-Pagu say, "It's great to meet you!" and Well-Pagu says, "Meet!"

One-Eye says, "You too." His Lion grins.

Velt holds up a bag. "We were just giving things out to everyone. Look, Captain!" She hands him something.

Rath's eyes widen. "A dolphin! It is very well-made." He turns over the metalwork sculpture in his hands.

"It's for you!"

Rath flushes immediately. "Ah – "

Franz says, "We got one for everyone. We all got dolphins." He includes Velt and Perri.

Phillip and Charles hold up theirs. Phillip says, "We got rabbits, like our goddess, Rella!" Charles nods.

Carlos clears his throat. "I have been given a snake." He doesn't say anything more.

Turning to One-Eye, Perri says, "May I ask who your god is? We can go back and get one for you."

One-Eye says, "It's fine." He stares at the metal sculptures. "I'd rather not have one of Lionel."

At that moment, Isaac and Vocalise walk up to them. Isaac says, "Guys, Vocalise is here!"

From the deck, Oren says, "Really?" He hops down to join them.

While Franz hands both Isaac and Oren little chimps – Isaac is thrilled, Oren starts juggling it and some coins from his pocket, smiling – Vocalise strokes his chin, looking at Well-Pagu. "Does that count as a proper introduction?"

Well-Pagu stares at him. They give a small cough.

Vocalise stretches. "Right."

Rath gasps. "You were the man at the restaurant! And who helped me up to the roof. I did not know you were Vocalise at the time, however."

Vocalise ducks his head, scratching the back of it. "Sorry about that. You get to those interviews all right?"

"Yes. Thank you very much for your help."

"Sure thing." Vocalise suddenly grins at One-Eye. "He hired you, huh?"

One-Eye frowns. "Yeah."

"I'm glad. Your Spirit Lion and I were hoping for you." He kneels next to the Lion. He waves his finger, saying, "Try not to gossip too much."

The Lion's eyes sparkle.

Vocalise laughs and stands up. To Rath, he says, "You got any Spirit Animals aboard, Captain?"

"Yes. Phillip has a Spirit Rabbit."

The Rabbit hops once on the cook's shoulder.

"Good." Vocalise looks at the Lion. "You already have someone to talk to."

The Lion licks a paw.

Vocalise laughs again. "You already knew about her?"

The Lion opens his eyes, then looks at the Rabbit. The Rabbit twitches her nose, curious.

To all of them, Vocalise says, "You off now?"

"Yes," Rath says.

Isaac says, "Will you watch us, Vocalise?"

Vocalise jumps. "Uh." He turns to the Pagu. "Um, yeah. I can do that." He seems a little flustered.

The crew of *PearlHeart* board and Vocalise stands on the docks as the gangplank is pulled up. Isaac waves brightly to him and Oren smiles from the deck. Vocalise waves a little back.

Then he sees Rath talking with One-Eye by the wheel – he will be taking them out of port for the first time – and One-Eye smiles as he listens. Vocalise does, too, then waves with one, long, lazy arm as the sails begin to fill and *PearlHeart* pulls away from Pantrog.

As the Pan ship grows smaller, Belle walks up beside him.

Vocalise grins. "Heeey, Belle."

"You should have done something sooner."

Vocalise's smile disappears and he scuffs his bare foot on the docks. "Ah," he says.

Belle sighs. "Lionel's people being able to live here during their probation is a very good thing. I don't want Merp or the Council to have any reason to discontinue it."

"Yeah, yeah. Me neither," Vocalise says, nodding. "So, where are you going?"

"Back to Pantha. I want to meet Faerohr and check in with Lionel."

Vocalise snorts.

Belle gives him a look, then walks to the edge of the docks. He dives, glowing midway through. He hits the water and when he surfaces, it's in his shark form, but Vocalise only sees the fin quickly making its way north.

With a yawn, Vocalise saunters back down the docks to the port town, disappearing in the crowd.

After One-Eye's first watch – it ends at eight that evening – he goes down to the main deck, where Rath is refilling a lantern. One-Eye looks up at the sails and then where they're going, breathing deeply.

He says to Rath, "Good night. I'll be going below."

Rath smiles. "Good night, One-Eye. I hope you sleep well."

"You too."

They wave to each other, then both leave the deck. *PearlHeart* continues north.

6

One week later, they reach the Delphaen Trade Route, a wide strait crowded with ships of all kinds. Pan ships like *PearlHeart* sail alongside them, Delphaen ships – which can travel both above and beneath the water – can be seen beneath the waves, and a few Butej skyships fly over them.

The country of Delphy is to the north, a large, curved island with a long cove, where tropical trees sprout up in between inland waterways. To the south is another country, full of farms and rolling hills, its green fields tinged with yellow as its yearly harvest approaches.

On the main deck, Phillip is with Flower-Pagu. He points at the country to the south. "There's Cunica, my home."

Flower-Pagu brightens. "Oh! It's even more beautiful than I remember!"

"It's getting into harvest season, too. I'm sure Nan and everyone have already been getting ready." He steps away from the rail. "Speaking of which, we'd better get started on breakfast."

Flower-Pagu shoots their arms up. "Yes, Phillip!"

Later, breakfast has been served and Rath, One-Eye, and

the Pagu all sit in the captain's cabin, eating together. One-Eye says, "I'd never seen Delphy or Cunica before. They're beautiful."

Rath smiles warmly. "I think so as well. We'll have some time at Cunica if you would like to see more of it."

"I would. Thanks." His Lion looks excited beside him.

It takes them fifteen days to reach Port Telma on Cunica. During that time, One-Eye looks at all of the ships – above water, beneath, and in the sky – in the busy trade route. His Spirit Lion is beside him, enjoying the breeze.

A week before they will arrive, Rath and One-Eye are just leaving the upper deck when the Pagu fly up to them.

Flower-Pagu says, "Captain, we were wondering if you wanted to play Double Berceuse again?"

"Okay?" Well-Pagu asks.

Rath nods. "Yes, that sounds wonderful to me."

Bucket-Pagu says, "Would you like to join, too, One-Eye? It's a card game our friend invented! We taught the Captain earlier."

"It was very fun," Rath says.

One-Eye says, "I'll join."

The Pagu beam. "Yay!" they all say.

They meet in the captain's cabin and Bucket-Pagu explains the rules to One-Eye.

"We normally play it in pairs, but because there's five of us, we'll play separately. Do you have any questions?"

"No. Seems simple." One-Eye looks at the small playing cards the Pagu provided. "My Lion says that it's an octopus on these cards. Why?"

"That's a – " Flower-Pagu says.

"Secret!" Well-Pagu finishes.

One-Eye stares at them. His Spirit Lion swishes his tail, saying nothing.

They begin to play and Well-Pagu quickly wins the first round. "Double ... Berceuse!" they say.

"Wonderful job," Rath says.

One-Eye frowns. "Again."

Rath wins the second. "Double Berceuse."

One-Eye looks at his cards. "Close."

They play a third round. One-Eye wins this one. "Double

Berceuse."

Flower-Pagu cheers, "You did it!"

Rath nods. "Congratulations, One-Eye."

One-Eye pauses, then smiles. "Thanks."

They play a few more rounds together.

At the end of the week, they arrive on Cunica.

"Port Telma, ahead!" Felix calls out from the nest and Triphonius gives an exuberant "Caw!" from his shoulder.

The Pagu are with Rath on the main deck. Flower-Pagu does a twirl. "Oh, I just love Cunica! It's so beautiful!"

"I agree," Rath says, looking out at the forests, farms, and wide fields everywhere. One-Eye does too, his Spirit Lion next to him.

They dock at Port Telma, a quiet stretch of land with no town to accompany it. Only a small, vine-covered customs house sits at the edge of the dock. Paths lead over hills to farmsteads and run through long fields into deep forests. A calm breeze tugs at the wild flowers growing everywhere.

One-Eye seems far more relaxed as he takes it in. He tenses, however, when his eye settles on the short building. "Is that the customs house?"

Rath follows his gaze. "Yes. We will go there after we load the provisions that Phillip's Nan, Pelline, is bringing."

Suddenly, Phillip trots up to them. "Oh! Captain, there she is! Look!" He points and they all turn.

To the southeast, an older woman pulling a cart is seen cresting a hill in the early morning light.

Pelline arrives and Rath, One-Eye, Phillip, and the Pagu meet her in the stretch of dirt off the dock. She is wearing light scarves and a woven hat. Her gray hair is pulled into a thick braid down her back.

"Nan!" Phillip says, hugging her tightly.

"Good to see you, Phillip," she says. They pull apart and Pelline looks to the others, tipping her hat. "Glad to see you as well, Captain. Are these new members of your crew?"

"That is right."

The Pagu fly forward. "I'm Flower-Pagu!"

"I'm Bucket-Pagu!"

"Well ... Pagu!"

"One-Eye." His Spirit Lion gives his best grin.

Pelline smiles. "Nice to meet you all. Quite an honor to meet the Pagu, too." She claps her calloused hands together. "Well! Shall we do business, Captain? I've got your provisions here."

"Yes. Thank you very much, Pelline."

"Of course. Can't have you going to the North unprepared. It's bad enough most years, but this year ... well, I'll tell you after." She jerks her chin at the hill. "Vern – my neighbor – is coming with extra provisions for Haliae. Was wondering if you would carry them there since you're already going."

"Definitely."

Rath begins directing *PearlHeart's* crew with One-Eye and Well-Pagu's help, loading the crates Pelline brought and securing them both in the galley and the cargo hold.

Afterward, Rath and One-Eye return to the dock where Phillip is sitting on Pelline's now empty cart and Pelline is standing next to him, frowning at the path she traveled earlier. She clicks her tongue. "Don't know where Vern is – he didn't leave much after I did. Sorry for the wait, Captain."

"There is no need to apologize," Rath says. Beside him, One-Eye frowns.

Pelline sits down next to Phillip. "Might as well share the news I've heard. I'm sure it'll be valuable to you all," she says. "We'll have a good harvest this year – lots of rain – but that isn't always good for other things. A heavy rain season always means an early Winter and that the Elder God of Draconi, Ara, is upset."

Rath's eyes lower. "I heard the same from Hep."

Pelline's eyebrows raise. "Hep? The God of Sudines?" Rath nods. "Captain, did your grandmother say anything to you before you left her island? About the North? She has an uncanny sense for things sometimes."

Rath thinks. "She said to 'please stay safe.'"

Pelline considers this, then says, "Well, the North isn't unfamiliar to you and while Fenrir handled it skillfully, I'm sure your current crew will ensure all of you make it there safely."

"I agree."

She sobers. "We heard about Fenrir's father – the Spirit Rabbits let us know. I said a prayer to Rella for them."

Rath nods quietly.

Pelline checks the path again, huffs, then turns back to the group. "I assume you'll be checking in with customs here, Captain?"

"Yes. For the cargo and to ask if they will approve One-Eye's paperwork to work outside of Pantrog."

Pelline shakes her head. "That may be difficult. I heard all of the Selachuu Military are in the North."

One-Eye says, "We were told by Belle that they would start returning to the South and we were likely to find a soldier the further east we went."

"Belle? My ... I suppose that makes sense now how you're here at all, without the military's approval." One-Eye glares and Pelline raises a hand. "Don't look at me like that – I never had a problem with anyone from Pantha. Hard workers. Nice muscles." She studies One-Eye. "You'd do well on a farm." One-Eye doesn't know how to respond to that. "Thing is, not all people are as open – like the young man that's now acting as customs officer. He's from Unys, one of the Amaran Knights. You heard of them?"

"White clothes?"

"Yeah. And long white hair, too. Don't know if he's one of Amara's One Hundred Knights, but if he isn't, he's definitely aiming to be."

One-Eye crosses his arms. "Saw them on Pantrog once. They were full of themselves."

Rath chokes.

Pelline laughs. "I do like you! You chose well, Captain." She continues, "They can come across like that, but they really do mean well – even if they can take that to extremes at times.

"The knight is here to cover for the absent Selachuu soldier. We normally have a Butej guard fill in instead, but that windstorm from earlier was very hard on their skyships. I hear that they and their God, Fierce, are still recovering from it. The Phoenae Force offered to provide one of their officers, of course – on obligation, you understand – but my Goddess, Rella, forbid it." She wiggles her fingers in the air. "Too much fire with them from Merp's Traits. That's why we don't have any Phoenae airship docks on Cunica at all. Rella won't let them near her crops.

"Anyways, I wanted to let you know who you'll meet for

customs so you weren't surprised by a sword in your face the moment you – or, most likely – One-Eye, walked in."

At that moment, they hear a call. "Pelline!"

They all turn. A tall, older man is cresting the same hill Pelline was on earlier next to a young man on a unicorn, both resplendent in white.

"Finally," Pelline says. "Looks like the knight's with him, too."

The Amaran knight, his unicorn partner, and Vern soon join them. Rath notices that the left wheel of Vern's cart is missing a spoke, but the area has been filled in with the white light of Amara's Traits, allowing it to be used.

Vern has kind brown eyes and is wearing scarves like Pelline. He tells them, "Broke a wheel on the way here. This young lad helped me out."

The knight sits tall. He has pink eyes and his white hair is bound with a single tie down his back. His unicorn partner, who shares his eye color, takes one look at the group and snorts in disapproval. "It is the very least that I can do. After all, helping those in need is one of the greatest tasks that an Amaran knight can hope to accomplish." He dismounts, then bows, his long hair flowing behind him. "But, I am forgetting my manners. It is best to introduce oneself at the earliest opportunity. I am Sir Rif and this is Amethyst Rose. We are knights of the Elder Goddess Amara and dream to one day be part of her illustrious One Hundred Knights!" He straightens and smiles hopefully. "At least, that's the plan."

He turns to each member of the group. "I have heard tell of a Miss Pelline whom we would be joining as well as a Captain Rath of Delphy who – " His eyes land on One-Eye and they widen. Faster than Rath can blink, Rif draws a white sword that has materialized, scabbard and all, at his side and points the tip of the blade at One-Eye.

Rif glares. "A man from Pantha. Good Company, would you but give me the word and I will dismantle him."

"No," Rath says immediately. "Please do not, ah, dismantle ... " He cannot finish.

Rif raises an eyebrow. "Then, he is a friend?"

"Very much so."

Rif hesitates. Focusing on One-Eye, he says, "Yet, I have

been told all under Holy Lionel only fight in most dishonorable ways. Many, too, that are here in the South are those that have been released from the Selachuu prisons after being sent there for such crimes as piracy, after which they complete their probation on Pantrog and thereafter ... " He blinks. "Seek gainful employment in many cases." He turns to Rath. "He has?"

"Yes. One-Eye is my first mate. Would you please lower your sword?"

Rif does, but keeps it visible at his side. "I shall. However, it is only because your status compels me to do so."

One-Eye says, "Status?"

"Goodman Vern informed me of the members of this party I would be meeting. Before I laid eyes on you and was forced to act – perhaps preemptively, however, prudently done – I had been about to say, 'Captain Rath of Delphy, who is also the son of Councilman Georgio.'" He bows to Rath. "The lineage of the Council is of the highest rank as nearly all are from the bloodline of the Gods' First. The councilpeople of Delphy traditionally are. Regardless of my own personal feelings on the matter, I am required to obey your will."

Rath looks uncomfortable. "That is not necessary, Sir Rif."

The knight frowns, then looks thoughtful. "Yet, something has now occurred to me. If I may ask, my Good Captain?"

"Of course. Please speak freely."

"You have my thanks. Then, so I will. Why, pray tell, are you addressed by the title of 'Captain' when it is ... " Rif counts his fingers. "At least seven ranks below your birthright?"

"It is because my current position is Captain of *PearlHeart*."

Rif looks at the ship. "Yet, someone of your lineage – well, I shall not speak out of turn. It does not befit a knight of Amara. If you would prefer to be addressed as 'Captain,' then so I shall do."

"Thank you, Sir Rif."

Rif turns to the Pagu. "If I may – what of the Honored Pagu's presence here? I am not rightly prepared to receive their wisdom." Even Amethyst Rose regards them with utmost respect.

Flower-Pagu says, "We're part of the Captain's crew!"

Rif gapes. "His crew?" He faces Rath again. "You have the Honored Pagu as members of your crew?" He stares with something in between awe and terror. "What manner of man are you?"

"Please calm down, Sir Rif," Rath says. "And – I am unsure how to answer your second question. The first is correct."

Rif shakes his head. "Wonders and miracles."

One-Eye speaks. "Is that the extra delivery?" He points to the cart Vern brought.

The farmer replies, "It is. Sorry it's late, Captain."

"That is all right," Rath says. "May we carry it aboard *PearlHeart* now?"

"Yes, please."

"Thank you very much." Rath bows to Rif. "I need to direct my crew now. Please excuse me."

Rif bows lower. "No, no, it is I who have delayed you, Good Captain."

While Rath, One-Eye, and Well-Pagu go up the gangplank to gather the crew, Phillip suddenly says, "Oh! We'd better get the food started for the picnic." He goes up the gangplank, heading for the galley.

Flower-Pagu flies after him. "I can't wait!"

Bucket-Pagu follows as well. "I'll ask Carlos to bring out the blankets!"

Rif hears. "Picnic? Blankets?"

Pelline answers, "Yup. The Captain and his crew always stop here for extra provisions before they journey to the North and it's our tradition to have a picnic before they cast off."

"I see! Thank you for your explanation."

"You're welcome to join us, too, you know."

Rif looks surprised. "Why ... Well, it would not be at all appropriate form to deny such a gracious invitation, yet my other duties may not permit it."

Pelline swats her hand in the air. "Oh, you can get away for a few minutes."

"Then, I will strongly consider what you have proposed."

Vern says to him, "Will you be performing customs for the Captain?"

"You are correct! Until then, I shall remain here, where I am available and unobtrusive."

After the crew has loaded the crates Vern brought, Rath returns to the dock to speak with Rif. Bucket-Pagu had come back out earlier and has been talking with the knight.

Rif says, "Good Captain, this Honored Pagu, Bucket-Pagu, has been regaling me with tales of your voyage thus far! Do you truly make small implements out of wood for their holy fingers to use?"

Rath blinks. "Ah, yes, I do."

"Tremendous! Then to give them to such honored beings, you truly will be blessed." He continues, "Now, may I ask if you are sufficiently prepared for I, the acting customs officer of this fair Port Telma, to verify the state of your cargo on *PearlHeart*?"

"Yes, we are. I also ask that you sign One-Eye's paperwork so that he may officially be a part of *PearlHeart's* crew and journey to the North with us."

"Paperwork? Yes, I suppose that is one of my duties as well." Then he says, "Goodman Vern. I will now be returning your wheel to its previous, broken state."

Vern smiles. "No worries. Thanks again for your help."

"Most certainly!" Rif twirls his hand and the white light that had held the wheel together disappears. It tilts outward without the extra support.

Afterward, Rath guides Rif to the cargo hold so he can check the delivery.

"All are checked and accounted for!" Rif studies his customs log. "I believe I sign here." He does so, then beams at Rath. "Truly, Good Captain, I greatly approve of your quest. To take food to those on Haliae is very noble and honorable, indeed! And ink and paper to Holy Elvin, who loves both so!" He looks around. "However, there is truly so much food! Why would Haliae need so much? I have not heard of any food shortage there and I believe that Lady Amara would know if such a thing had happened."

"I am told that there may be an early Winter and that the Elder God of Draconi, Ara, may be upset which would make it more severe."

"Truly? Then, we are certainly in troubling times. Pray you be safe, Good Captain."

"We will."

They leave the cargo hold together and pass through the crew's quarters where many sailors are asleep in their hammocks.

When they return to the main deck, Rif says, "I must ask —
as this is my first time on a vessel such as this and it does excite
me so – why do so many sleep now in the daylight hours? They
are not all from Ullia, are they? To my knowledge, Holy Erole's
people's eyes are highly sensitive to the sun and prefer to be
awake at night."

"No. Evermore is the only one from there aboard
PearlHeart. Many are resting now because they were awake
helping us sail between the hours of twelve and four in the
morning."

"So early!"

"Indeed. It is needed so that we may travel through the
night."

Rif shakes his head. "That seems terribly inconvenient. If
Amethyst Rose and I are on the ocean at night, we simply make
camp and rest."

One-Eye, who has joined them, hears this and says, "On
top of the water?"

"Of course. With Lady Amara's Traits, it is possible."

One-Eye looks disturbed.

They rejoin the others on land. Pelline, Vern, and some of
the crew have begun to set down blankets in the grassy field
near the dock.

As they walk past them to go to the customs building, Rif
says, "Ah! The picnic that I have been told of!"

"Yes," Rath says. "Would you like to join?"

Rif hesitates. Amethyst Rose walks alongside him and he
puts his hand on her neck. "Miss Pelline asked the same – you
are truly both kind. However, we are currently unsure."

When they arrive, Amethyst Rose stays outside while Rath,
One-Eye, and Rif enter and sit on either side of the desk inside.
Rath hands the paperwork to Rif.

As Rif reads, he slowly frowns. When he reads the second
sheet, his eyes widen. "Holy Belle's signature! Is mine truly
needed in this case?"

Rath says, "Belle told us his was only valid in the South, not
the North."

"I see." Rif lowers the papers, rubbing his arm uncomfortably.
He pushes them back to Rath. "I deeply apologize, however, I
do not believe that I have the proper authority to accept this.

True, I am here in place of our comrades-in-arms, the Selachuu Military, but" – he shrugs slightly – "I am only a Knight-in-Training. One of Lady Amara's One Hundred Knights would be more suitable – or Sir Ronan, our Champion! I truly do not feel I am appropriate to make a decision on this. I am sorry, Good Captain."

"That is all right. Would you know of a Selachuu soldier near here? Belle said that they would be returning to the South."

"Not on Cunica, no. But ... " Rif suddenly gasps. "That's right. Do you know of Renet Island?" Rath nods and Rif continues, "Amethyst Rose and I recently heard from our dear friends and fellow knights, Sir Evera and Garnet Wisdom – whom were sent to Renet Island to do as I am doing here – that they have since left. Gladly, I must say, for I hear that the weather there is customarily terrible. Sir Evera tells me their departure was due to the Selachuu Military returning. The captain now stationed there is named Berkut. It would seem to me that he would have the authority to make this decision," he says, gesturing to the paperwork.

"I understand. Thank you very much for telling us, Sir Rif."

"Of course. You have been kind to me and I wish to help." He looks pained. "You, too, One-Eye, have not given any cause for my actions earlier. Now knowing that Holy Belle approves of your presence here ... " He shakes his head. "No, such actions were rash and very unbefitting of a knight. I duly apologize."

One-Eye raises an eyebrow, but nods.

After they leave, Rif goes to Amethyst Rose and Rath and One-Eye join the others at the picnic. They sit with Pelline, Phillip, and Carlos. The Pagu mingle in between the groups, talking to everyone.

One-Eye's Spirit Lion rolls on the soft blanket and One-Eye smiles at him.

Pelline says, "How is your grandmother doing, Captain? Phillip told me she requested plants from Cunica for her gardens this year – did she like them?"

Rath eats a cracker. "Yes, very much so. And she is well. Actually, she asked that the Mehrin plants be the first to be planted in her new South Garden. It was wonderful to see everyone working together on it."

"I'm sure she was delighted to see it, too. Another garden,

though? Ha! Soon, that island will be covered in flowers."

Rath pauses. "That would be many."

Pelline grins. Then she looks past their group and to where Rif and Amethyst Rose are outside of the customs building. She raises her voice over the chatter of the crew. "Hey! Rif! Do you want a bite?"

Rif replies, "I greatly appreciate your offer, Miss Pelline, however, I must decline!" He pats Amethyst Rose nervously. "The recent tidings that have been shared with us concerning the North have troubled Amethyst Rose and I greatly so we will be having a walk in the forest to put to rest both our thoughts and our hearts." They walk away under the shade of the branches.

Pelline snorts. "He'll come around."

When they finish eating, Pelline asks if Rath can fix Vern's cart. "You still woodcarve, right?"

"I do. And I believe I could."

Vern appreciatively gives him some extra wood to make a new spoke and Rath begins to work on it while the others relax, play cards, or carry their dishes to the galley. One-Eye plays a few rounds of cards with Isaac, Charles, and Oren. Afterward, he and his Lion run around the nearby hills.

As they pass a forest, a pair of rabbit ears pop out of the bushes and an inquisitive nose twitches in their direction. It hops back into the trees, glows, and walks away in the form of a short young woman with brown hair.

When One-Eye and his Lion return, they find Rath has finished the new spoke and Vern is testing it with the wheel.

They approach just as Vern says, "It works great! I can't thank you enough, Captain."

Rath flushes. "You are welcome. I am glad to see that it does."

"You sure that I can't pay you?"

"No, I was happy to do so."

Vern looks thoughtful. He digs into his pocket. "Then, at least let me gift you the rest of the wood and some extra I found. Maybe you could make something for yourself with it."

Rath accepts it, surprised, but deeply grateful. "Thank you."

Vern smiles. He takes up his cart. "Well, I'd best be on my way back. What about you, Pelline?"

"About that time. Good seeing you, Phillip," she says, hugging him.

"Y-You too, Nan!" Phillip says.

Pelline turns to the group. "Great to see and meet all of you as well."

Flower-Pagu says, "You too, Pelline!" Bucket-Pagu, Well-Pagu, and One-Eye nod.

"Best of luck with your paperwork, One-Eye. If Belle says you'll find someone, I'm sure you will."

"Thanks."

Then, with a wave, Pelline and Vern head back up the hill.

After they're out of sight, One-Eye asks Rath, "What do you think you'll make with that?" He looks down at the wood in Rath's hand.

"I am not sure yet. It is Talron wood and very high quality." Rath turns it over thoughtfully and One-Eye smiles, his Lion looking up at Rath as well.

They start packing up the supplies from the picnic, folding up blankets and taking them and any remaining dishes back up to *PearlHeart.*

They pull away from Port Telma, helped by a strong wind to enter the Delphaen Trade Route. One-Eye watches as they pass Cunica, his Spirit Lion and Rath with him.

When he goes off watch later that evening, Isaac and Felix meet him on the main deck. "What did you think of Cunica, One-Eye? It was your first time there, right?" Isaac asks.

"It was ... relaxing. I liked it."

As he, Isaac, and Felix enter the stairway to go below, Felix says, "If you liked Cunica, I bet you'll really like the Captain's grandmother's island."

Isaac says, "Lady Azalea's Island is the best! This year was my first time seeing it."

"We deliver plants to her every year."

"Right," One-Eye says. His Lion's eyes gleam beside him with interest.

They go to their respective hammocks, silently waving good night to one another. One-Eye lies in his, his blue eye glowing with Lionel's Traits which allow him to see in the dark. He shuts it, and with his Spirit Lion near him, falls asleep.

7

They travel through the Delphaen Trade Route for ten days before they arrive at Renet Island, where Sir Rif had said Captain Berkut was stationed.

A steady rain has been drenching *PearlHeart* since the previous day and One-Eye stands at the wheel that evening, frowning under a rain hat. Well-Pagu sits on the console in a wide brimmed hat as well and Rath stands with them, dressed similarly.

Renet Island is small and seems like it was once part of a far larger island, with a single tall, craggy cliff that looks as if it had been bitten in half, letting the sheer face plummet directly into the tumultuous waves below. At the top of the cliff are docks for Phoenae airships, but none are there now.

On the side of the island facing *PearlHeart* is a large fortress that has been built into the rock itself. Fires sputter in the rain, only partially shielded by the outcroppings above.

One-Eye looks at it nervously.

After they dock, One-Eye stands next to Rath, who is addressing his crew. "Everyone! Please go below or to the galley! Change into dry clothes if you need to!"

"Yes, Captain!"

The crew moves eagerly in both directions. Rath turns to One-Eye. "Are you ready?"

One-Eye nods. "Yeah."

They walk down the gangplank. Water sloshes at the bottom, having overtaken the docks. "Please be careful," Rath says.

One-Eye nods again.

While One-Eye's Lion hops on rocks sticking up out of the water, Rath and One-Eye wade through, knee-deep in it, moving closer to the fortress.

One-Eye glances at the building once, then focuses on his footing. "Looks like Selachuu."

"That would make sense," Rath says.

One-Eye stumbles.

Rath catches him. "Are you all right?"

"What do you mean by that?"

It takes a moment for One-Eye's question to register to Rath.

In the interim, One-Eye says, "I'm fine. Thanks."

Rath lets go. He continues, "Carlos has told me that nearly all of the military's territory was originally part of Selachuu."

"How'd it get here?"

"Belle moved the land, Carlos says."

One-Eye pauses. His Lion almost slides off the rock he was on. They exchange a wide-eyed look with one another, then continue on.

They make it up the stone steps leading out of the water and to the heavy metal doors of the fort. Rath knocks on one. "Excuse me?"

There is some shuffling inside, then a Selachuu soldier opens it. "What?"

Rath bows. "I am Captain Rath. This is my first mate, One-Eye. May I ask if Captain Berkut is at this customs port?"

"He is. Here for your cargo to be checked?"

"Yes. And for One-Eye's paperwork to be signed."

The Selachuu soldier's eyes light in understanding. "Right. Come in."

He allows them into a dark entryway. Other soldiers stand by the walls, surveying them. Only a few torches are lit inside and One-Eye's eye glows dimly as he and Rath follow the man that let them in. "Captain's this way," he says.

They come to a hallway with tall windows. Lightning flashes intermittedly, illuminating doors on the opposite wall leading to different chambers. At the end of the hallway, a dark stairway travels up and they start climbing. One-Eye's Spirit Lion walks alongside them.

They continue for a long time until they see a door up above, lit around the edges with the light outside.

"He's out here. Like usual," the soldier says. Then without warning, he opens the door and a sharp wind buffets them. They cautiously move forward as the soldier stays and shuts the door.

They are on top of the cliff, near the Phoenae airship docks. A dark figure is sitting on the wooden planks stretched out over the cliffside, scaffolded beneath.

Suddenly, the form turns as if whoever it was sensed them. They rise and something golden and bright extinguishes in their hand. A Selachuu captain walks over to Rath and One-Eye.

Rath bows despite the wind. "I apologize if I am interrupting. I am Captain Rath of Delphy. This is my first mate, One-Eye. May I ask if you are Captain Berkut?"

The man studies him with golden eyes from beneath his hood. "I am," he finally says. Another gale tears through and he says, "Inside."

They follow Captain Berkut back to the door. The other soldier has since left, so Berkut holds it open, waits until all three of them are inside, then shuts it, plunging them into darkness. Berkut flicks his hand a few times and a golden flame sprouts from it. He lifts it up, illuminating them all. He has deep bags under his eyes. "This way," he says and goes ahead, leading them down with his golden flame. Rath and One-Eye follow.

One-Eye mutters, "He's from Phoenae also."

Berkut suddenly turns. "Something to say, One-Eye?"

"You're from Selachuu, but you have Merp's Traits, too."

Berkut gazes longingly at the flame. "I do, don't I?" He turns back around, continuing down. "Merp would call it a pale imitation of his glory."

They reach the bottom and Berkut extinguishes the flame in favor of the dim lighting on the first floor. He turns to Rath.

"What is it that you need, Captain?"

Rath says, "My ship, *PearlHeart,* is here for customs. We also have been looking for a Selachuu soldier to sign One-Eye's paperwork."

Berkut starts to nod, then pauses. "*PearlHeart?*" He smiles faintly. "What a wonderful name. Would you lead me?"

"Yes."

They go to the front of the fort and exit out into the rain again, then down into the water. Berkut seems undisturbed as if this happens every day.

Soon, they are in the cargo hold. Berkut surveys the contents, writing in a small book. After he finishes, he says to Rath, "I couldn't help but notice that your crew is belowdecks. Did you tell them to go there in this weather?" Rath nods and Berkut continues, "You are very kind to your crew." He turns away, covering his mouth. "I find it ... refreshing."

One-Eye, who is by the door, arms crossed, says, "Done?"

Berkut replies, "Yes, One-Eye. I suppose I will look over your paperwork now."

"Do we have to go back to the fort?"

"My office is there. Unless ... " He glances at Rath. "Would you permit my signing it here on your ship, Captain?"

"Of course. We may use my cabin if that would be all right?"

"That would be ... very kind. Please."

They leave the cargo hold, exit out onto the main deck, then enter the companionway leading to the captain's cabin.

"It's warm," Berkut notes.

Rath replies, "It is. The galley is to our left and it provides heat through the wall."

"I see."

Behind them, One-Eye frowns.

They all sit at Rath's table. Berkut looks over the paperwork. "Everything seems to be in order. I suppose I do not have a problem signing it either."

"Thank you," Rath says.

Berkut pulls out his pen. He begins signing, saying, "Even though it would irreparably mar my reputation where Merp is concerned. He has never approved of anyone from Pantha, much less a former pirate."

Beside Rath, One-Eye tenses.

Berkut hands the completed paperwork to Rath, continuing to him, "Although, Merp never accepts anyone that isn't fully from Phoenae either, so perhaps his dislike of me will be the same." He looks directly at Rath. "From the moment I met you, I knew through Belle's Traits that despite your admission to being Delphaen, you bear none of Marchand's Traits or any others that may be in your heritage. Is that correct?"

"Ah, yes."

One-Eye turns to Rath in surprise. His Lion looks pensive.

"I've never heard of such a thing," Berkut says. "But, I am sure that it has cost you opportunities just as being mixed did for me. We are the same, you and I." He rises. "I will go now. I want to look for more of Merp's airships. But, for what it is worth, I do hope we'll meet again, Captain Rath. Perhaps we can speak more of our similarities." He leaves.

One-Eye speaks first. "You're not doing that."

Rath, who had been rubbing his wrist, starts. "I-I'm sorry?"

"Speaking to him about ... I don't like him."

"One-Eye, that is not very kind to say."

One-Eye pauses, then his expression eases. "He shouldn't have been so forward about that. Whatever happened to you is none of his business."

Rath looks startled for a moment, then nods but seems deeply uncomfortable. "I would agree. I am very sorry to hear about his relationship with Merp. My father had told me that such was the case in Phoenae for those of mixed race."

One-Eye exhales. "At least he signed the paperwork."

"Yes. We will now be able to continue to the North." Rath goes to file away the papers.

When he comes back, One-Eye says, "Thanks. For doing all of this."

Rath smiles. "Of course."

One-Eye smiles back, then they leave together.

8

Three days later, the clouds have broken up and behind them, Renet Island is slowly disappearing in a rainy fog. Immediately around them is open ocean and One-Eye and his Lion stand on the deck, leaning on the rail for most of the morning to see it.

A week later, they come into a bright mist. One-Eye looks at it curiously while he eats his breakfast with Perri, Felix, and Triphonius on the deck. His Lion sniffs it.

One-Eye says, "Haven't seen anything like this before. My Lion says it's from Paradi?"

Felix says, "Yeah. It helps Oracle create her ... Well, it's better if you just see them." Triphonius gives a proud "Caw!" on his shoulder.

Perri nods in agreement.

One-Eye raises an eyebrow and looks at his Lion, but the Lion pouts, not knowing to what they are meaning. He leaps toward the galley, disappearing through the wall.

While they are returning their bowls, One-Eye finds the Spirit Lion lying with his chin on the floor, staring straight ahead. One-Eye pets him. "Phillip's Spirit Rabbit wouldn't tell you?" The Lion shakes his head. "She said it was a surprise?"

The Lion looks up at One-Eye, but One-Eye shakes his head. "I won't ask the Captain. We'll just have to wait and see."

The Lion buries his face in his paws.

Later that day, One-Eye goes to the captain's cabin to play cards. However, when Rath opens the door, he says, "Would you allow a few minutes? The Pagu and I are just finishing up."

"Yeah."

One-Eye pulls out a deck of cards and sets it on the table while Rath walks over to his bed, where the Pagu are seated around a large bound book.

Bucket-Pagu says, "Captain, we think we've decided what we want!"

"That is wonderful to hear!" Rath says as he sits down with them. He watches while the Pagu each point to a spot on the page.

Flower-Pagu says, "I'm getting the pink one with the flowers!"

Bucket-Pagu says, "I'm getting the green one. It has ships on it."

"Purple," Well-Pagu says. "Stars."

"They all look beautiful," Rath says.

The Pagu beam, then Flower-Pagu turns to the table. "One-Eye, do you want to see?"

One-Eye stands up and walks over. "Sure. What is it?" He hesitates for a moment, then sits down next to Rath.

"We're ordering stationery from Paradi! The Captain says we'll pass by it very soon."

Bucket-Pagu nods. "We're going to use them to write to our friends on Pagu Island! We can all talk to each other any time we want, but we all agreed that there's something different about writing a letter!"

Rath smiles warmly. "I think so as well."

One-Eye says to him, "Are you ordering anything?"

"No, I do not believe I need anything. Do you?"

"I don't."

Bucket-Pagu says, "Then, we're ready to order!"

While they fly over to their bedside table to fill out their forms, Rath and One-Eye play cards. After the Pagu are finished, they leave the cabin and send off their order with Demeter, Melody's bird partner. They all wave to the purple and blue bird as she flies off.

Two days later, One-Eye is at the wheel next to Rath. His Lion is studying something to the north that they can't see yet through the mist. As the morning goes on, William, Phobos, and Melody come out and stand by the upper deck. Demeter is still on her delivery. Felix and Triphonius watch eagerly from the nest.

The sun begins to rise and the misty morning is burned away. Slowly, a golden beach is revealed. One-Eye's eye widens as he sees lush foliage appear, then a sparkling river. Homes are visible on either side, going up a tall mountain, bordering a large waterfall that falls all the way down from the top. One-Eye's Lion's ears prick forward as they both see something sitting there – a giant bird with feathers in every color of the rainbow. It seems to regard *PearlHeart* with its large eyes, then raises its head and gives a sonorous "Caw!" It is followed by thousands of bird calls on the island of Paradi and by Triphonius and Phobos on *PearlHeart.*

Suddenly, the rainbows appear, swirling around the island and reaching all the way out to *PearlHeart.* One-Eye sees blue and purple bands pass through the wheel and Rath raises his hand in bands of blue and green. The Spirit Lion starts to trot around excitedly, then leaps over a rainbow and One-Eye laughs. Rath, who can only see One-Eye's reaction, turns toward him, then smiles.

During breakfast, they all eat on the deck. Even Phillip brings out his bowl and joins Carlos, Charles, and Perri by the door to the galley.

One-Eye sits with Rath, Isaac, Oren, and the Pagu. Evermore sits with Melody. He removes just a bit of his scarf while they sit in the shade of the upper deck to see one of the rainbows drift by.

Later, when they are all still on the deck, they suddenly hear a triumphant "Caw!"

"Demeter!" Melody says, looking up at the sky.

However, then they hear a far louder "Caw!" and all turn toward the sound.

There, a great flock of birds is flying toward *PearlHeart.* In the center, flanked by Demeter on the right, the same giant rainbow bird of paradise they saw on Paradi flies.

Soon they are over *PearlHeart.* The large bird turns a rainbow-colored eye on Rath. "Permission to board, Captain Rath?"

He is stunned. "Ah, yes." He stands up and bows. "Permission granted."

The bird seems to smile. She descends, begins to glow, then steps down onto the deck as a young woman with long hair braided with colorful beads and feathers. She is wearing a swirling dress in the colors of a sunrise at the top and a sunset at the bottom. In her arms, she holds a small package and two letters.

She walks up to Rath and bows. "Greetings. Thank you for allowing me to board your ship. I am Oracle, the Goddess of Paradi. I do not believe we had a chance to meet while you were training to be a councilman. However, I have worked with your father and grandfather as well as my brother, Marchand, many times."

"I remember them telling me. Is there something I may do for you?"

Oracle blinks, then laughs. "No, no, I thought I might do something for you." She nods to the package and letters. "I believe the Pagu aboard your ship – Well-Pagu, Bucket-Pagu, and Flower-Pagu – ordered these. And these letters I asked for before I left. They are for you and Carlos."

"I see. Thank you very much. That was very kind of you."

She smiles. "It was my pleasure!"

The Pagu fly up and Oracle hands them their package.

They all open it and Flower-Pagu cheers, "Yay! Our stationery!"

"Thank you very much, Oracle," Bucket-Pagu says.

"Appreciate," Well-Pagu says.

"Of course, my dears." Oracle scans the crowd. "Is Carlos here, by chance?"

Carlos walks up to them and bows deeply. "Oracle."

"Ah! Wonderful. One letter for each of you, from Lady Azalea."

"Thank you again, Oracle," Rath replies and Carlos nods respectfully.

"You are welcome!" Oracle clasps her hands together. "It is a pleasure to see you once again, Carlos."

"As is mine."

"Why, I believe the last time we spoke was on Lady Azalea's Island seventeen years ago. You served the most delicious tea."

"I am pleased to hear as such."

Oracle's eyes turn to Rath. "However, I did not have a chance to meet young Rath then either. The little boy who was always playing with the Pagu in the forest."

Rath blinks. "I see. I apologize if this is rude to say, however, I do not recall seeing you on my grandmother's island."

"Really? Almost all of my brothers and sisters have been to Lady Azalea's to seek guidance from her and – " As she speaks, her eyes settle on Carlos. She frowns. "I am disappointed in you, Carlos. Surely he is old enough to know of such a thing."

Rath's eyebrows go up.

Carlos delicately coughs. "Lady Azalea and I agreed that godly influence was inadvisable for someone so young."

Oracle considers, then says, "Well, I cannot argue with that."

"As to the present ... " Carlos turns to Rath and bows. "I do apologize, Master Rath. It is becoming more apparent that it is needed for you to know of such things."

Rath waves his hand. "That is all right, Carlos."

Oracle nods to the Pagu, who are admiring their stationary by the rail. "It seems that you are still as close as you ever were to the Pagu. It is lovely to see." She thinks for a moment, then says, "Well, I would trust you would like to begin reading your grandmother's letter. Might I ask if you would allow me to stay aboard your ship and see how my dears are doing while you do so?"

"That would be all right with me."

"Thank you." She walks over to join the people from Paradi, who are waiting for her by the port rail. She spreads out her arms. "Hello, my dears!"

"ORACLE!" Felix and Melody say, and their bird partners "Caw!" They all hug one another.

Beside Rath, Carlos clears his throat. "Master Rath, I would like to explain Oracle's words in further detail after you have read your letter, if you would allow?"

"Of course."

They leave to read their letters. Rath does so at his desk,

a soft smile on his face. Carlos does the same in the infirmary, looking thoughtful.

Later, they meet on the upper deck. Carlos says, "Do you remember when your grandmother and I would tell you that we were having special guests?"

"I do," Rath says. "You both dressed in your most formal attire as well. I thought it was very exciting."

"Indeed. I recall you telling us how wonderful we both looked." Carlos pauses. "The special guest was, at times, Oracle, and at others, her siblings."

"The other gods?"

"Yes. Your grandmother and I would offer counsel to them on occasion."

"That was very kind of you both."

Carlos smiles at his comment, then coughs lightly. "What we told them was not always appreciated. However, I do believe – and Lady Azalea agreed – that at the very least, they left far calmer than they arrived." He frowns. "We never wished for you to see a god when they were truly upset. That is why we decided to not have you meet them when they visited. However, I apologize for the confusion Oracle's comments may have caused."

"It truly is all right, Carlos."

Carlos studies him. "You do not appear to be very surprised by this."

"You and Grandmother give very good advice. I have always believed as such."

Carlos straightens his collar. "Thank you, Master Rath."

Just as lunch is starting and the watch has changed, Oracle greets William and Phobos and speaks to them for a time, then walks up to Rath. "I will be returning to Paradi now, Captain Rath."

"I understand. Thank you again for delivering Well-Pagu, Bucket-Pagu, and Flower-Pagu's stationery as well as Grandmother's letters to Carlos and me."

"I was happy to. Thank you for allowing me to see my dears. They tell me you will be off to the North now? To Haliae and my brother, Elvin?"

"Yes, to deliver Elvin's ink and paper as well as extra provisions."

"From Cunica, correct?" Rath nods and Oracle grows serious. "That is very good of you to do so. My brother, Ara, can cause the Winters to be very unpredictable." She steps back. "Safe travels, Captain Rath!"

Rath bows. "Thank you. You as well, Oracle."

She beams. Then she glows bright and the next moment is in her form as a giant rainbow bird. She flies off, trailing sparkles behind her as she soars back to Paradi.

9

PearlHeart sails through the rainbows. On the last day before they go back into the mist, the Pagu are in their cabin working on their letters to their friends and family on Pagu Island.

Flower-Pagu says, "Captain! We've finished!"

Rath looks up from *Tales of Flight: Volume Two.* He walks over. "Would you like to send them now?"

"Yes, please!"

They go out to the main deck together and the Pagu carry their large stack of letters, tied up neatly with ribbons embroidered by Flower-Pagu, all ready to be sent off.

Triphonius takes them proudly, flying to the nearest Paradi Message Tower to do so.

Four days later, they enter sunny skies. That morning, Flower-Pagu flies up to Rath with a little drawing for an idea they had for him to carve. Rath looks at it carefully.

Later that day, One-Eye is returning his dish to the galley when he sees Rath and Flower-Pagu near the stove.

Rath has just installed a wooden panel with hooks that Flower-Pagu can hang their tools on for easy access. They now have so many that the little cup Phillip had given them cannot hold all of them.

Flower-Pagu has just hung up the last tool – their spoon.

"There!" they say. "Oh! Captain, it works so wonderfully! Thank you so much!" They hug him and Rath laughs.

"You are very welcome, Flower-Pagu!"

One-Eye smiles and his Spirit Lion grins.

Over the next days, Rath talks with Flower-Pagu about the different flowers they have seen on the countries they pass – Butej, Xiphi, Tecla – and discusses the second *Tales of Flight* book with Bucket-Pagu. Every evening, he stands by the rail with Well-Pagu while the stars shine down on them both.

Two weeks after leaving Paradi, they enter a dense fog. All of the lanterns are lit and they keep them on day and night as they travel.

Three days later, Rath and One-Eye are by the starboard rail. They have scarves on to stave off the chill of the fog. Rath nods to the white expanse to the south. "Unys is there," he says.

As his Lion squints, One-Eye shakes his head. "I can't see anything. That's where the Amaran Knights are from?"

"Yes. At times, we have seen them and their unicorn partners traveling across the ocean."

One-Eye's eyebrows go up. He frowns. "Right. They can do that."

They exit the fog by the end of the week. The day is overcast, but bright. The crew seems more relaxed now that they can see the ocean more clearly around them.

One morning, Rath, One-Eye, and Well-Pagu are on the upper deck when Felix calls out, "Captain! An Amaran knight is approaching!" and Triphonius gives a bold "Caw!"

PearlHeart heaves to, pausing so that the knight can ride up. His outfit has far more ornaments than Sir Rif's did. "Hail! And salutations!" he calls out.

"Hello, Sir Knight," Rath replies from the rail.

"Might I have permission to board your vessel? I find it far more appropriate than to shout more words across such an expanse and instead directly to those ears which need hear them!"

One-Eye stares – his Lion flicks his tail – but Rath says, "I understand. Yes, permission granted."

"You have my thanks, Good Captain." Then, with a wave

of his hand, a white glowing ramp appears from the side of his unicorn up to the starboard rail of *PearlHeart.* He dismounts, walks up, and steps onto the rail before hopping down onto the deck. He looks about. "What a quaint and homely ship." He turns to Rath. "And it would be yours, my Good Captain?"

"Yes, that is right." Rath bows. "I am Captain Rath of Delphy. It is wonderful to meet you."

The knight bows, but not quite as low. "It is a pleasure to meet you, Good Captain Rath. I am Sir Ronan, Lady Amara's current Champion of her illustrious One Hundred Knights. I am not oft in these parts as I am ever by her Lady's side. However, a quest was required of her – nay, destined for her to take – and as such I was given a most honorable one as well in her absence and that is to – " He hesitates for a moment, studying Rath. "Delphy is your place of origin, you said?"

"Yes."

"Hm. If we may talk later, my Good Captain. I believe – no, I am sure – it would be to your benefit."

"Of course."

One-Eye frowns beside them.

Ronan continues, "Now – as I was saying – my quest. My Lady Amara has tasked me with the most honorable duty of warning such ships as yours of the dangers of the North. You see, two months prior to this moment, an out-of-season storm struck this area. Are you well-versed in this characteristic of the North? By which I mean it's unpredictable nature?"

"I am. We have sailed this route for the past four years."

"Good. I am glad to hear you have the necessary experience for such an area. However ... " Ronan lowers his voice. "If we may speak of something else? Before you progress onward?"

Rath nods and they step aside from the others, closer to the rail.

Ronan studies him. "My Good Captain, how have you remained hidden?"

"I-I'm sorry?"

"Surely, you are aware that there is not a god who has their divine protection over you."

Rath winces. "That is true."

Ronan takes his hand. "Then, why have you not sought out Lady Amara? Why, it is well known that she aids in the deciding of Godly Guardianship. Now, Lady Amara may be off on her quest, however, I am certain she will return soon. All you must do is come with me to Unys and she will have your god decided."

"Ah, Sir Ronan, I apologize. However, my god has been decided."

"When?"

"At my birth."

"As is customary. Yet, my Good Captain, as I have said, you do not have the sign of any such protection. As her Champion, Lady Amara's Traits allow me to see such things."

"I understand. Even so, I very much consider my god to be Marchand, as he was before."

Ronan tugs Rath's hand. "Yes, I recall you saying you hailed from Delphy, yet no sign of Marchand's is to be seen about you. I insist that you accompany me to Unys to have this matter resolved. Surely this venture is not more important. Why must you go to the North when your lack of god puts you in far more danger?"

"We are traveling to Haliae to deliver ink and paper to Elvin and extra provisions to the people there. They may have a more severe Winter this year and I wish to help them if I can."

Ronan blinks. "That is quite a noble quest, indeed." He shakes his head. "Yet – it would not take long to travel to Unys – my loyal partner, Opal Starlight will carry us!" There is a snort from the water below. "*I* will carry you!"

He pulls on Rath's hand again and this time, notices Rath wince. He looks down at their hands, then lets go. "You have my deepest apologies. I did not mean to injure." Swirling his finger, he uses Amara's Traits to create a small strip of white light and points at Rath's wrist. It wraps around it, but does little good as a bandage. Ronan lets it disappear. "I cannot do anything, I am afraid."

"It is all right. And, I sincerely apologize, I cannot go with you."

Ronan looks concerned, but takes a step back. "Very well. Your quest is truly noble, indeed. To journey forth to the people of Haliae, bearing sustenance and ink and paper for the god who loves them." He falters, blushing. "Quite noble, indeed." He coughs. "I suppose it would be – ah – ignoble of me to delay such a quest that truly is deserving of the utmost haste and – " He pauses then, quite flushed, looks Rath right in the eyes and says, "Fair travels, my Fair Captain." He hops over the railing and onto his unicorn. "Away, Opal Starlight!"

They gallop off. Rath watches them.

"Give me your hand."

He turns and sees One-Eye has walked up to him. "Of course." When he does, One-Eye holds it in his left hand and raises his right. He hesitates for only a moment, then puts that hand over Rath's wrist. It glows yellow and Rath's eyes widen. A warmth fills his wrist and the strain eases.

One-Eye takes his hands away. "Sevran's Traits. My Spirit Lion says it came from my mom's side," he says. "You should get it looked at by Carlos, too."

After Rath tells the crew they may continue on, he and One-Eye go below. While Carlos checks Rath's wrist, One-Eye stands by the door with his Spirit Lion.

Carlos pulls his hands away. "It will heal fully within two days. There is no need to wrap it – only be mindful of it." Rath nods. "You said One-Eye healed it just now?"

"Yes."

Carlos looks over at One-Eye. "Fine job."

One-Eye frowns, unsure how to take it.

As he walks over to them, Carlos continues, "Have you ever healed anyone but yourself?"

"No" – One-Eye glances at Rath – "never wanted to before."

Rath's eyes widen and he flushes slightly.

Carlos looks between them. "I see."

One week later, they pass the small island of Pica Pica to the east. Its tall, brightly colored buildings rise up in contrast to the overcast gray skies. A continual sound of cheers, laughter, and talking can be heard from it. As *PearlHeart* passes, confetti flits through the air and puffs of colored smoke erupt, inciting even more cheers.

Isaac stares at it. "They really do party all the time."

Perri giggles. "That's Pica Pica for you."

From the rail, One-Eye stares at it and Well-Pagu frowns, both not liking the noise.

To the west, there is a dark area known as the Phoenae Sea. It lays directly beneath the country of Phoenae high up in the sky. The area has continuous storms and all ships stay well away due to the weather that sometimes spins out of it.

It starts to rain the next day and continues into the third when they arrive at the Southern Selachuu Military Base, positioned at the border between Daerce and Pantha.

The base is built into a long cliffside, stretching far to the north where it disappears in the rain. Selachuu ships come and go from dark sea caves, worn down by the continual waves.

After they dock, Rath leaves *PearlHeart*, walking toward one of the caves. He passes low stone buildings where soldiers spar with axes and swords while others sharpen their blades on whetstones.

Inside the sea cave, lanterns provide little light and water drips down from the ceiling. Rath reaches a building built into the back of the cave wall and knocks on the door. "Excuse me?"

The door opens and a tall Selachuu captain with short brown hair appears. He has a tin mug looped around his belt. "Customs?" he asks.

"Yes, I – " Rath suddenly sees another man is inside, leaning against the desk. "I apologize if I am interrupting."

Belle, the God of Selachuu, smiles a little. "You're not, Captain." He walks over. "Heard One-Eye got his paperwork signed by Berkut?"

"That is right."

Belle nods. He turns to the Selachuu captain. "I'm going north."

"Yes, sir." As Belle leaves, the captain pats his pocket as if looking for something, then says, "Book. One moment." He returns, now holding his customs log and extends his free hand to Rath. "Captain Farbourne."

"Captain Rath."

They leave together. As they exit the sea cave, Farbourne looks up at the dripping entrance. "Miserable place." He turns ahead and his eyebrows raise when he sees *PearlHeart*. "Fine enough ship."

After they board, they check the cargo and when they return to the main deck, Farbourne is saying, "Ghastly place, the North. Almost worse than here." He suddenly grins. "You see those Amaran Knights? Sir Ronan and Opal Starlight? They've been trotting around south of here."

"Yes, Sir Ronan asked to speak with us."

"Warned you about the North, did he? We had that storm two months ago and I heard it became a windstorm further south, but otherwise things are normal – unpredictable, as they always are. Storms like that could mean Winter's coming early, but you can never be sure." He shrugs. "Anyway, the people in Pantha have been different recently. That king of theirs ... Hey, do you have anyone from Pantha aboard? They might want to hear this."

"My first mate is," Rath says. He asks One-Eye if he would like to and he walks over to them. Beside him, his Spirit Lion's eyes gleam with interest.

Farbourne continues, "No one knows how he's done it, but King Faerohr's rallied most of Pantha behind him – though, Pantha's God, Lionel, backing him likely helps. Food has been scarce there for a while, but they've definitely been working hard to find and carry all they can to Pantha Castle. Almost none have been by the Daerce border for the past few months and piracy has been down on the ocean, too. Some people are starting to compare Faerohr to the last good king Pantha had – King Faron. Seems just about as strong as him, too, given what we've heard about him in the Coliseum." He frowns. "The weather's just getting worse up there, though. Even with all of them working together, seems like it would be hard to find enough food for everyone. What do you think, One-Eye?" One-Eye just glares at him. Farbourne seems unfazed as he turns back to Rath. "Anyway, you're clear to go to the North. You should make it to Haliae just fine by leaving now. Safe sailing, Captain."

"Thank you very much, Farbourne. I hope you are well here."

"Thanks. Not much to look forward to," he says, gesturing behind him. "It's a fair ugly chunk of rock – but, I thank you all the same, Captain."

They sail north, the Southern Selachuu Military Base on their starboard side.

As they travel for the next two weeks, the temperature rapidly drops. All bundle up in more layers, puffing out clouds with their breath while on watch.

Three weeks after that, One-Eye is standing by the rail with his Lion and Rath, looking toward Pantha. Mountains extend over the entire coastline with small paths through them leading to the country's wide plains. His Lion's eyes are bright, but One-Eye looks away, turning his eye forward instead.

Two islands are there. A small, low island closer to Pantha and a larger one with a mountain in the center more near the Phoenae Sea. He asks Rath, "Mella is the one to the east? Haliae to the west?"

"That is right. Well-Pagu says we are set to arrive one week from now."

Three days later, they pass Mella Island and four days after that, Felix calls out from the nest, "Haliae, ahead!" while Triphonius gives a triumphant "Caw!"

Ahead, Haliae looks like it has been recently dusted with snow, from the trees at the base of the mountain all the way to the marble buildings on the top. *PearlHeart* approaches from the southern coastline with One-Eye at the wheel, Rath beside him, and Well-Pagu sitting on the console.

Suddenly, a terrible cry pierces the overcast sky and everyone jumps. They have enough time to look in its direction – north – before a sharp wind screams toward them, carrying with it a blizzard. In a moment, Haliae disappears and in the next, the storm hits *PearlHeart* and the crew.

On the upper deck, Rath opens his mouth to speak, but gasps instead as his boots begin to slide backward, then lift up off the deck.

One-Eye sees. "Hey!" He lets go of the wheel to go after Rath, shouting, "Isaac – the wheel!"

Isaac clambers up, his feet glowing orange as Vocalise's Traits help him maintain his balance over the growing ice on the deck. "G-Got it, One-Eye!" He holds onto it with all of his strength while Well-Pagu clings to the console and other members of the crew grab onto what they can.

One-Eye grips Rath's hand just as he flies over the rail. They hold there for a moment, then One-Eye stretches out his other hand.

Rath lifts his with an effort, nearly making it to One-Eye's.

At that moment, another cry fills the air and with it, another gust. Rath's hand slips out of its glove and One-Eye watches as he flies off with the wind, disappearing in the snow. One-Eye doesn't hear the mizzenmast behind him creak or Well-Pagu, hands pressed together and glowing purple, say, "Help!"

Unseen by One-Eye, Rath disappears, leaving purple sparkles.

The mizzenmast comes down behind One-Eye and his Spirit Lion tackles him, sending him out of its path. One-Eye hits his head on the deck and is knocked unconscious.

Below, in the captain's cabin, Flower-Pagu and Bucket-Pagu hold hands, glowing pink and green. Simultaneously, they say, "Help!" and *PearlHeart* disappears from the storm, leaving pink and green sparkles.

10

One-Eye wakes up on the deck.

The sky is overcast and the snow has stopped. Carlos hovers over him against the dim light. "Don't sit up yet."

One-Eye frowns up at him.

Carlos puts his hand behind One-Eye's head. It glows yellow. "Having Sevran and Lionel's Traits prevented a concussion, however, you will still have a painful bruise for a few days."

"I'm fine." Carlos removes his hand as One-Eye sits up. He looks around the upper deck. The mizzenmast has fallen, taking out a chunk of the stern railing and crew members are hauling away sawed off pieces so that the weight doesn't capsize *PearlHeart*.

One-Eye stares at the place for a long time. Suddenly, he looks at Carlos.

Carlos raises his hand. "Talk to the Pagu. They requested to see you when you awoke."

In less than a minute, One-Eye is pacing in the captain's cabin. On the bedside table, the three Pagu are bundled up in both their blankets and those from Rath's mother.

One-Eye is saying, "He flew overboard. He's – "

"No," Well-Pagu says very softly.

One-Eye stops and his Spirit Lion butts his head against his legs until he runs a hand through the Lion's mane. He relaxes a little. "Where?"

"South."

One-Eye pauses. He nods. "Right."

"Okay," Well-Pagu assures him.

One-Eye doesn't say anything to that. "We have repairs to make. Then, we'll sail ... south." He looks at the Pagu. "Are you all right?"

Flower-Pagu answers, "We're a little cold."

Bucket-Pagu says, "But, we'll be better soon."

"Rest," Well-Pagu says.

"Yeah." One-Eye hesitates. Then the Pagu watch him leave.

To the south of where *PearlHeart* is, there are sunny skies.

A set of nine isles – eight small ones surrounding one larger one – bask in the warmth. In the ocean to the north of the main isle, Rath lies over a piece of driftwood, unconscious.

Suddenly, a wave moves toward him. A small Pagu flies above it. As they near Rath, a voice below the water says, "Ah! There he is. Just as you said he would be, my dear one." The creature swims beneath Rath, then carefully lifts him up and off of the driftwood. Rath groans and the two look alert. The creature says, "Oh dear, I believe he is hurt. We shall get him to River-Pagu immediately!"

"Yes, Berceuse!" the Pagu says.

They travel back toward the main isle.

Hours later, Rath wakes. He finds himself inside a small hut with many beautiful fabrics covering the walls and floor. A warm candle glows beside him. His right shoulder is immobilized by a sling. He tries to sit up but a sharp, tearing pain bursts in that shoulder when he moves.

A voice gasps and a hand reaches out to him. "Oh! Peace, my dear. Do not move just yet." The hand gently pushes him down and Rath complies, breathing heavily. As the throbbing slows, he looks up into the face of a man with long brown hair. He has purple eyes and a matching set of earrings that glint in the candlelight. "There. Just rest now." Rath tries to nod, but even that strains his shoulder. The man above him frowns, concerned. He looks to something or someone else in the hut for a moment, then turns back to Rath. "My dear ones tell me you have had a long journey and I am afraid not a very pleasant one."

Rath struggles to remember. It must show on his face, because a Pagu in a turquoise doctor's coat and gloves flies into his field of vision and says to the man, "Berceuse, he needs more sleep."

"I agree." His eyes focus on Rath again just as Rath's eyes begin to close. "Rest easy, my dear. You will be all right." Berceuse's eyebrows suddenly go up. "Oh. He is already asleep."

"It is for the best with the state that he is in," the Pagu replies.

Berceuse toys with his hair nervously. "He will be all right, won't he, River-Pagu?"

"Absolutely. Well-Pagu sent him here with great care."

"Bless them." Then Berceuse reaches forward and brushes Rath's hair from his eyes. "I cannot imagine the place he came from. I do believe he had snow on him when we found him." He shivers. "Well, I am sure he will be both hungry and thirsty when he awakens. I shall retrieve both."

River-Pagu nods. They settle at Rath's side, sitting on their knees with their gloved hands resting atop them. "And I will stay with my patient. Thank you, Berceuse."

Berceuse smiles on his way out. "Of course, my dear one." His earrings glint and he is gone, out into the sunshine.

River-Pagu watches Rath. After a moment, they reach out and pat his hand gently. "You will be all right," they say firmly.

On *PearlHeart*, Velt is repairing a staysail that tore during the storm while One-Eye speaks to everyone.

"Well-Pagu says the Captain's south. That's where we'll go after the repairs are finished."

"Yes, One-Eye!" the crew reply.

Evermore, who had been in the shadow of the upper deck, asks, "Then ... he is alive?" Melody is next to him, holding his hand.

One-Eye glances at him. "Yeah. He is."

Later that night, they are nearly finished. The railing on the upper deck has been restored and the mizzenmast has been carried off. The first section of the new mast has been installed and awaits the next two pieces. The staysail Velt repaired is also finished and has already been hauled back up into place.

One-Eye speaks to them in the light of the lanterns. "We'll finish the rest in the morning and sail right after. Thank you for your work."

"Of course, One-Eye!"

As the crew go to their watch or below to sleep, Isaac hops over to One-Eye. "Hey. Anything else I can do for you? How's your head?"

"Fine. Sevran's Traits let me heal fast."

"That's good."

One-Eye pauses. "You?"

Isaac rolls his shoulders. "A few bruises. Carlos says nothing major." Then he nods to One-Eye. "Good night."

"Night."

Isaac leaves and One-Eye soon follows him.

Rath wakes up again.

Before he can try to rise, Berceuse says, "Allow me to help you up. Easy ... There."

"Thank you." In the time that Rath was sleeping, a dozen or so cushions have been placed behind his back. They all have different fabrics similar to those in the hut. Rath tries to focus on Berceuse. "I apologize. I do not know your name."

"Berceuse. The God of Oct."

Rath blinks slowly. "The ... octopus."

Berceuse looks surprised, then he smiles. He gestures to two Pagu that fly up to him, one wearing an orange skirt and sleeveless top and the other in turquoise. "This is Feather-Pagu, who guided us to you and River-Pagu, a very talented doctor of ours." Then he picks up something on the floor next to him. He holds up a cup and an odd fruit that Rath has never seen. "I've brought you food and water."

"Thank you," Rath says again. Berceuse hands him the cup first and he drinks from it slowly. After he has finished, the god hands him the fruit. Rath takes it with his left hand, looking at it thoughtfully.

"It's called Together Fruit," Berceuse supplies. "I invented it myself – with my dear one's help, of course."

A spark of awareness lights Rath's eyes. "I see." He takes a bite and they widen, looking more at ease. "This is wonderful!"

Berceuse beams.

As Rath continues to eat, Berceuse and the Pagu do as well.

After they finish, Berceuse reaches for a stack of clothes next to him. "I did these while you were sleeping. The poor things had many tears." He holds out the overshirt, jacket, and hat Rath had been wearing on *PearlHeart* when he fell overboard. A single glove lays on top of them all. "I could never find the other glove, however. Would you like me to make you another?"

"I ... " Rath struggles.

River-Pagu intervenes. "He is not up to deciding right now, Berceuse," they say. They hold out a small pill to Rath. "Here. It will help with the pain."

Rath takes it.

Not long afterward, Berceuse helps him lie down again and he falls asleep immediately. He looks more relaxed now, but his breath hitches every so often as his shoulder pulses in pain.

River-Pagu frowns at the sling they, the other Pagu, and Berceuse wrapped over Rath's injury. "His shoulder must be reset, Berceuse. We need Carlos, his doctor."

"I agree. You tell me he is quite talented." Berceuse turns to Feather-Pagu. "My dear, might I ask if you have heard anything?"

Feather-Pagu replies, "I just spoke with Well-Pagu. They say the acting captain of *PearlHeart*, One-Eye, has informed everyone that repairs will be finished tomorrow and they will sail south afterward."

"Repairs? Oh dear ... " He looks to Rath. "I do hope they arrive soon."

The following morning, everything on *PearlHeart* has been repaired or replaced and the sails have been set. Isaac reports, "We're ready, One-Eye!"

"Thanks." One-Eye is at the wheel.

Slowly, *PearlHeart* picks up speed, heading south. As they travel, Well-Pagu joins One-Eye. He asks, "Are you better?"

"Much!" Well-Pagu replies. They sit on the console and

look ahead.

As they travel, the skies remain overcast. One-Eye watches the coastline of Pantha change, knowing where they are based on it.

When it is nearly noon, he huffs and asks, "How far?"

"Here," Well-Pagu replies.

One-Eye's eye widens and simultaneously he hears the gasps of the crew.

Up above, the clouds suddenly recede, replaced by a brilliant blue that they haven't seen for months. The sun shines brightly. The Pantha coastline fades away, becoming sparkling ocean. Then, further ahead, two isles materialize, both full of brilliant colors. The crew watches them fully form as they pass. One-Eye finds his words long enough to say, "These aren't supposed to be here."

Well-Pagu agrees. "Hidden."

At the same time, Feather-Pagu flies up to Berceuse, who is sitting outside the hut with a large group of Pagu. "Berceuse, *PearlHeart* is nearly here!"

"I understand, my dear one." He looks at the other Pagu clustered around him. "Well, shall we meet with them?"

"Yes!" they all say.

River-Pagu, from the hut says, "I will stay with my patient while Carlos is brought."

"Thank you, my dear one."

They go to the north beach.

On *PearlHeart*, One-Eye watches as a far larger isle begins to appear. Flowers of all colors grow in the shade of tall trees. He sees a man with long brown hair, surrounded by a group of Pagu, walk down the beach. The man gives a tentative wave. One-Eye frowns.

Carlos joins him on the upper deck and says, "I'd best go with you."

One-Eye nods.

They lower the sea anchor a little out from the main isle. One-Eye and Carlos descend on one of the small boats and One-Eye rows them toward the largest isle. It is warmer here and the sun shines down on them both.

When they reach the shore, the man calls, "Um, greetings!"

"Hello!" the Pagu all say.

After they get out of the boat, One-Eye drags it to the shore. They walk up the beach to join the man and the Pagu.

"I am Berceuse, the God of Oct," the man says. "The young man you are looking for is this way. I will lead you to him."

Carlos says, "Thank you."

They walk through large-leafed plants under a thick shade that makes the sunlight appear even brighter.

One-Eye follows, suspicious, but when he glances at Carlos, he looks focused and calm. They enter a clearing with an unlit fire pit and cushions set about it – one big and many small – a fresh water pool, and a hut.

Berceuse walks them to it, drawing aside the fabric covering the door. "He is here."

One-Eye takes one look inside, then enters quickly, forgetting about Berceuse. Carlos' face tightens in concern, but he says nothing as he walks in.

The Pagu dressed in turquoise meets them. They bow. "I am River-Pagu. I have tended to Captain Rath since his arrival on the Isles of Oct."

Carlos dips his head. "Thank you for your help, Honored One."

"Of course. It is my assessment that his right shoulder has been dislocated. It must be reset before it can heal properly."

One-Eye, who had sat down next to Rath, says, "Why hasn't it yet?"

River-Pagu responds calmly, "I nor my friends can complete this procedure with satisfactory results. Berceuse was scared he may not do it correctly."

One-Eye relaxes somewhat. "Fair." He pauses. "Sorry."

River-Pagu nods.

Sitting down as well, Carlos says, "One-Eye, you will need to help. I can reset it, however, it will be very painful. You must hold him and heal him with Sevran's Traits while I do so."

"Right."

Carlos moves Rath's hair back. "Master Rath? You must wake."

Rath stirs. "Carlos?"

"You will be all right. One-Eye and I are here."

Rath listens, but seems unfocused. Carlos helps him sit up, then One-Eye holds him around the waist. Carlos begins removing the sling and bandages that Berceuse and the Pagu put on.

Carlos lifts Rath's arm slowly. Rath groans into One-Eye's shoulder.

Then with one swift, strong movement, Carlos resets it and Rath shouts. He goes limp except for his deep breaths. Carlos immediately begins easing the pain with his traits and One-Eye does the same with his own. Rath's breathing slows until he falls asleep.

Carlos removes his hand. "It will now heal properly. Thank you, One-Eye."

"Yeah."

With One-Eye holding him, Carlos immobilizes Rath's right arm and shoulder again. One-Eye stares at the fabrics on the floor, layered at least three deep. Afterward, Carlos says, "You can set him down now."

After he does so, Carlos settles the pillows around Rath and pulls up the blanket. He sits back and looks at Feather-Pagu and River-Pagu. "Thank you for your aid. There was no additional damage."

River-Pagu says, "I am glad to hear this," and Feather-Pagu says, "You are most welcome, Carlos!"

Carlos looks at One-Eye, who does not seem to have any intent of moving. "He will need to rest now. And you must inform the crew that we will not be leaving for several days at least."

One-Eye gets up abruptly and leaves.

Outside, Berceuse approaches him. "How is he?"

One-Eye glares at him. "Carlos says we won't be leaving for several days." He inhales, then says more calmly, "His shoulder's been reset. He should get better now."

"Oh, thank goodness. You all are welcome to stay on my Isles of Oct as long as you need."

One-Eye frowns, but nods. He walks off toward *PearlHeart.*

On the beach, he moves the small boat out into the ocean. His Spirit Lion seems to say something and he grunts. "I know he helped." The Lion hops in and One-Eye joins him. He begins to row. "He's still a god."

Later that afternoon, Rath opens his eyes.

"He is awake!" Berceuse says, sitting next to Rath's bed.

Carlos, near him, says, "Would you bring the food and water?"

"Most certainly." Berceuse leaves.

Carlos helps Rath into a seated position. "How do you feel?"

"Very tired." He frowns. "I believe I injured my shoulder."

"It was dislocated. One-Eye and I reset it three hours ago."

Rath looks startled. There is a clarity to his eyes that wasn't there before, but a strain remains as he adjusts his position. "I remember One-Eye. And ... "

Berceuse walks in. "I have brought food and drink for all." He hands a cup to Rath. "For you, my dear."

"Ah, thank you." Rath takes a sip. Then he looks at Berceuse, who has already started eating. "I apologize, may I ask if you are Berceuse, the God of Oct?"

"That is right. You remember!"

"I am afraid there is not much I do of the previous day. However, I remember you and two Pagu, I believe. River-Pagu and Feather-Pagu?"

The two fly up to him, each holding little cups of water. "That is us!" Feather-Pagu says.

"It is good to see you recovering," River-Pagu says.

Rath replies, "I see. And thank you."

Berceuse gestures to them. "River-Pagu tended to your health – they are a very talented doctor – and Feather-Pagu communicated with Well-Pagu so that your crew could find my Isles."

"I understand." Rath dips his head slightly to both Pagu, careful of his shoulder. "Thank you very much for doing so. I greatly appreciate it."

River-Pagu smiles and Feather-Pagu says, "We're always happy to help!"

Suddenly, Rath's eyes widen as something they said registers. "My crew."

Carlos holds up his hand. "Many have bruises and One-Eye was saved from a concussion due to Sevran and Lionel's Traits, but all are well."

Rath relaxes. "I am glad to hear that. Thank you very much

for telling me." He takes another sip, then looks at Berceuse. He suddenly flushes. "Ah, I apologize. I asked for your name – before, that is – however, I do not believe I introduced myself."

Berceuse hands him some fruit. "Peace, my dear. You may introduce yourself now."

"Thank you. I am Captain Rath of Delphy."

Berceuse raises his hand to his mouth. "Oh! Delphy. Then, you must be one of my brother Marchand's."

"I am." He pauses, thinking. "It occurs to me now that I have not heard of a land called Oct."

"I am not surprised, my dear ... no, my Captain." Berceuse smiles at the title. He spreads his hands. "Oct – or, my Isles of Oct – are the isles that we are currently on. As for why it is likely you would not have heard of them, well, I hid them and myself over one thousand years ago."

Rath listens, however, he begins to look tired.

Carlos says, "Perhaps you should rest again, Master Rath?"

"I believe so. I apologize."

Berceuse shakes his head. "There is no need. We may talk more when you awaken – well, if you would like?"

"I would like that greatly."

Berceuse beams.

Carlos helps Rath lie down again while Berceuse, Feather-Pagu, and River-Pagu clean up from lunch.

Berceuse is just leaving when he sees One-Eye approach. "Ah – One-Eye, correct?"

"Yeah." He looks at the hut. "Is he awake?"

"Not anymore. We ate and drank and now he's resting again."

One-Eye's expression changes into a mixture of disappointment and relief. He sits on one of the cushions. Several more larger ones have appeared since his last visit and he uses one of the those. Berceuse sits across from him. They are silent for a long moment.

Berceuse shifts uncomfortably. "I feel as though I have upset you."

"It's not you," One-Eye says. "It's all of you."

"I'm not sure I understand."

"Gods. That's what I mean."

"Oh." Berceuse rubs his knees. "Well, I cannot say we are

all perfect. My sister, Amara, certainly has much to say on that subject in regards to me."

One-Eye's eye lights with surprise. Then he studies the unlit fire pit. His Spirit Lion peers at Berceuse with interest.

They don't say anything more until Carlos comes out. Carlos' eyebrows go up when he sees them together. "One-Eye," he says.

"I informed the crew. They understand," One-Eye says. "How is he?"

Carlos sits with them on another larger cushion. "Very tired. And still in pain, I am sure. Feather-Pagu and River-Pagu are staying with him now."

Berceuse beams. "My wonderful dear ones!"

Carlos says to One-Eye, "I will be staying here until he is well enough to return to *PearlHeart.* What will you do?"

"Go back and forth." One-Eye exhales. "Talk with him."

"You may be able to later tonight when he eats his dinner."

One-Eye looks up quickly. He trains his eye on Berceuse. "Do you mind if my Spirit Lion and I run around here?"

"Well, no. I suppose not."

"Thanks." One-Eye stands. He leaves with his Lion before Berceuse can respond.

As soon as he and his Lion reach the trees, they start running. They travel easily along the paths that wind their way through the foliage and Pagu watch them as they go by. The shade grows thicker, then thins out. The sun bursts through as they arrive on the beach. One-Eye slows and his Spirit Lion matches his pace. They look out at the turquoise waters and the sunny skies more indicative of the South.

His Spirit Lion says something.

One-Eye whips his head in his direction. "Berceuse is causing the weather here?"

The Lion nods.

One-Eye looks up at the sky. "Of course." He seems to have more to say, but doesn't. "Let's keep going."

The Spirit Lion grins. They set off again.

They do not return until much later, when the sun is setting. One-Eye finds Berceuse and Carlos outside, sitting on the cushions. Berceuse waves his hand and a fire appears. "There," the god says.

One-Eye frowns.

Carlos notices him first. "Welcome back, One-Eye."

"Thanks." One-Eye sits. He does not say anything, staring at the ground and not into the fire that suddenly appeared. "When?"

Berceuse seems puzzled by his abruptness, but Carlos responds with a look at his watch. "Now."

One-Eye is already up and walking to the hut.

Once inside, he sits next to Rath's bed. He nods to River-Pagu and Feather-Pagu. Then he looks at Rath, still sleeping. His chest rises steadily, but every so often the action causes him to wince.

Carlos enters and Berceuse follows.

After they sit down, Carlos says, "Master Rath. It is time for dinner."

Rath stirs and One-Eye's eye softens.

As Carlos starts to help Rath up, One-Eye moves over to help as well. Rath blinks away the sleep from his eyes as they do and when he fully registers the other person helping him, they widen. "One-Eye."

One-Eye flushes at the proximity. He nods, then settles next to Rath against the wall of the hut. Carlos raises an eyebrow, but says nothing. If Berceuse notices, he does not either, but he does smile as he raises two large Together Fruits. "Shall we eat?"

"Yes, please," Rath responds.

With everyone's help, they divide up the fruit.

"All you must do is touch the stem swiftly! Like this!" Berceuse says, demonstrating with his pointer finger.

Rath says, "Like *tap?*" and when he does so, he watches in amazement as the fruit divides into four even sections.

"Yes! Just like that."

They begin eating. After Rath swallows a bite, he asks One-Eye, "How are you?"

One-Eye chokes a little. "Fine." He turns more toward him. "How are you?"

"Better. Thanks to Carlos, River-Pagu, Feather-Pagu, Berceuse, and ... " Rath hesitates, then meets One-Eye's eye. "You." He flushes deeply, looking away as One-Eye reddens further. "That is, I believe you were, ah, here when Carlos reset my shoulder. You held me."

One-Eye swallows hard on his next bite. He nods with an effort.

"Thank you for doing so."

One-Eye finds his words. "I wouldn't have just – " He huffs, then changes the subject. "The crew's fine. *PearlHeart's* fine. You're ... all right. I'm glad." He takes another bite of his fruit, ending the conversation.

"I am as well." Rath continues his own fruit slowly, looking thoughtful.

Berceuse suddenly speaks. "That's right. My Captain, you were asking about my land earlier, the Isles of Oct, correct?"

"Yes. You said you had, ah, 'hid' them and yourself over one thousand years ago."

One-Eye looks over at him as he speaks, surprised, then turns to Berceuse as the god says, "That is correct."

One-Eye thinks. "That would make sense why I didn't think they were supposed to be here." He says to Rath, "We're not far from Haliae. We're by the Ferint mountain range of Pantha. They were the mountains that we passed a week ago."

Rath's eyes widen, startled.

Berceuse says, "I cannot say I know them, but the world was very different when my Isles were created." He sighs. "All I recall is being near Drynad."

Carlos stops eating.

One-Eye says, "Haven't heard of it."

Rath suddenly gasps. "I believe I have seen a land named that on one of Grandmother's maps. One that was drawn of the Third World, the one before this."

Berceuse leans forward. "Truly? That was a very long time ago, my Captain."

Carlos gives a polite cough. "Master Rath's grandmother is over nine hundred years old."

"Oh!"

One-Eye starts coughing. When he recovers, he turns to Rath. "Your grandmother?"

Rath nods. "Yes. She is from Sudines and has Hep's Traits. Carlos does as well."

One-Eye stares at Carlos.

Carlos evenly replies, "Over seven hundred. That is all I

will say."

One-Eye looks back to Rath. "How old are you?"

"Twenty-six."

"Me too. How long will you live?"

"To around one hundred, Carlos says. An average Delphaen lifespan."

One-Eye frowns, then he realizes why. He nods. "Same as me." He goes back to eating his fruit.

Rath looks surprised. "That is true."

When they are all finished, Rath says, "Thank you for having dinner with me, everyone. I truly enjoyed it."

Carlos, One-Eye, and the Pagu smile. Berceuse says, "Of course, my Captain!"

While the God of Oct gathers up the leftovers then leaves, Carlos talks with River-Pagu and Feather-Pagu, and One-Eye speaks with Rath, who is lying down now. "I'll be coming back and forth from here and *PearlHeart* until Carlos says you're ready to leave."

"I understand. Is there anything I can do for you?"

One-Eye lifts his hand, then firmly puts it back down. He shakes his head. "No. Just rest. I'll handle everything on *PearlHeart* for now."

"Thank you, One-Eye." Rath falls asleep. One-Eye stays with him for a moment, then stands up and walks toward the doorway.

Carlos hears him pass and says, "Good night, One-Eye. Thank you for your help today."

"Yeah. Thanks to all of you," he says, including the Pagu. They smile. "Night."

He walks outside into the evening air. Berceuse is sitting by the fire, sewing. Other Pagu fly around him. One-Eye lifts his hand in a short wave. The Pagu see and wave eagerly. Berceuse notices and gives a hesitant one back. Then One-Eye walks through the forest, reaches the small boat, and rows back to *PearlHeart* to go to sleep.

11

The next morning, three Pagu leave *PearlHeart*. Pink, green, and purple fly toward the largest isle of the Isles of Oct. They enter the forest and find Berceuse, who is gathering Together Fruit for breakfast with the other Pagu. He sees them and gasps.

"Ah! My dear ones!" They fly up to him and he looks at each of them. "Why, I believe it has been a very long time since we have last seen each other, Flower-Pagu, Bucket-Pagu, Well-Pagu."

Flower-Pagu twirls. "Hello, Berceuse!"

Bucket-Pagu says, "I agree. I think it was over seven hundred years ago."

"Long," Well-Pagu says. Then they say, "Captain?"

Berceuse nods seriously. "Yes. Carlos should be waking him now for breakfast. Will you join us?"

They all say, "Yes!"

Rath is sitting in the hut with Carlos when the Pagu Trio of *PearlHeart* enter.

"Captain!" they say.

Rath's eyes widen. "You three ... " They fly over and hug him. He brings his left hand up to hug them back gently. "I am so happy to see you." As they pull away, Rath's eyes look a little wet. "How are you?"

"We're better now that we're here!" Flower-Pagu says.

"It wasn't a long time, but it was a really scary time," Bucket-Pagu says.

Well-Pagu points at Rath's immobilized shoulder. "Healing?"

"Yes. Thanks to Carlos, One-Eye, River-Pagu, Feather-Pagu, and Berceuse."

Well-Pagu looks relieved. "Glad!"

Berceuse walks in. "I've brought food for everyone!"

Rath replies, "Thank you very much, Berceuse."

As Berceuse settles and begins distributing the fruit, Flower-Pagu says to Rath, "We thought we would stay and have breakfast with everyone!"

"That is wonderful to hear. I am very happy that you are."

They beam up at him.

During the morning, the Pagu Trio of *PearlHeart* stay on the Isles of Oct. They share breakfast with Rath, Carlos, Berceuse, Feather-Pagu, and River-Pagu – whom they also reunite with – then talk for a long time with their captain until he grows tired. He rests and they nap with him, in a little makeshift bed beside his.

Later that day, One-Eye arrives. Rath, now awake and looking far brighter with the Pagu with him, smiles up at him. "Good afternoon, One-Eye."

"Good afternoon." He sits with them. "Thought you would want to know what happened on *PearlHeart* while you were here."

"I would."

Flower-Pagu and Bucket-Pagu rise. "We're going to go talk with Berceuse!" Flower-Pagu says.

"He asked us during breakfast if we needed any more clothes for him to make. We had some ideas for him."

"I see. That is very kind of him to do so."

They wave and Rath waves back with his left hand. Well-Pagu stays as part of the leadership on *PearlHeart* and One-Eye sits next to them.

One-Eye begins, "We were dismasted. It broke a third of the stern railing. Staysail was torn. All are repaired now –

mizzenmast, railing, staysail. No other damage."

Rath's hand is lifted to his mouth. As he fully registers One-Eye's words, he nods. "I understand. Thank you for telling me, One-Eye." He looks at him and Well-Pagu. "And thank you for all that you two have done. As well as the crew."

"They're glad to hear that you're all right. We ... " He frowns, then says instead, "What do you want to do about the Haliae delivery?"

"I cannot say. I do not wish to progress if the weather is still dangerous in the North."

"I don't know about there, but it was overcast where *PearlHeart* ended up. Even stranger is the weather here."

"The Isles of Oct, you mean?"

"Yeah. It's blue skies." One-Eye glances at his Spirit Lion, who is sitting beside him. "My Spirit Lion says it's because of Berceuse."

Well-Pagu speaks. "True."

They both look toward them, then Rath says, "I see. I have been told by Bucket-Pagu and Flower-Pagu that the Gods' emotions can often affect the weather."

One-Eye crosses his arms. "There was a cry before the storm hit us. My Lion says it was Ara, the Elder God of Draconi, which means he must have caused it." He shakes his head. "I don't like having to depend on the weather if it's being caused by a god. What do you think?"

Rath considers for a long time. "I heard the cry as well at the start of the storm. It would seem that Ara is very upset right now." He leans back carefully. "I am not sure it would be safe to continue with that in mind." He winces. "However, I am concerned about Haliae. I have been told about some Winters where they are trapped indoors until the following Spring. If this Winter surprised them, they may not have the supplies to survive during that time. We would need to carry those to them."

Afterward, One-Eye goes back to *PearlHeart* and Rath takes another nap.

When he wakes up, Flower-Pagu, Bucket-Pagu, and Well-Pagu show him the new garments that Berceuse made for them. Flower-Pagu has a new belt, Bucket-Pagu has a new vest, and Well-Pagu has a new hat. Rath looks delighted when he sees them. "Those all are amazing!"

"Berceuse is a wonderful designer!" Flower-Pagu says, spreading their arms out.

Bucket-Pagu says, "Do you remember how we said that our friend made all of our clothes?"

Rath replies, "I do."

"Berceuse is that friend!"

"Really?"

"Yes! It's been a very long time since we have seen him, though."

The other two Pagu nod.

All three stay for dinner, then spend the night there as well, sleeping peacefully next to Rath.

In the morning, Carlos and Berceuse help Rath out of the hut. Flower-Pagu, Bucket-Pagu, Well-Pagu, Feather-Pagu, and River-Pagu are there as well.

"There," Carlos says. "Some walking will aid your recovery, however, do be mindful of keeping to even ground."

Rath says, "Yes, Carlos."

Berceuse claps his hands together. "Why don't we go somewhere? We could go to the beach – "

Carlos coughs lightly. "Even ground, Berceuse."

"Then we will merely stroll through the forest on the paths. What do you think, my Captain?"

"I would love that."

Berceuse takes his good arm, tucking it into his elbow. "It is settled." He winks. "And worry not, my Captain, I will ensure that the ground is very even for you."

"Thank you very much for doing so, Berceuse."

While Carlos stays in the clearing, Rath, Berceuse, and the Pagu travel together on a path in between the trees.

As they do, Rath looks around. "There are so many beautiful flowers here. I have never seen many of these varieties."

"I created them with my dear ones' guidance. Do you like flowers?"

"Very much so. My grandmother has many on her island. She now has three major gardens – the West Garden, the East Garden, and the South Garden. The South Garden began four months ago. Everyone on *PearlHeart* helped to start it with the Mehrin plants we brought from Cunica."

"That sounds absolutely wonderful! I am sure that the Pagu would approve as well." Berceuse taps his chin. "May I ask for your grandmother's name?"

"Yes. Her name is Azalea Lewis."

"Ah! Lady Azalea! I knew it!" They pause and Berceuse looks around at the Pagu with them. "We all know Lady Azalea, however, I must admit I have never met her. Many of my dear ones – the Pagu – live on her island and the island near it, Pagu Island. They tell my dear ones here about it. Do you spend much time on your grandmother's island, my Captain?"

"Yes. I spent much of my childhood there."

"Oh! Then, you must have met many of my dear ones."

"I did. They always brought much peace to me when I was around them."

Berceuse seems surprised for a moment. Then he smiles, looking fond. "I see."

At the same time, One-Eye arrives at the clearing.

Carlos is there, sipping tea. He sees One-Eye look at the cushions, then the hut, then Carlos himself. Carlos says, "Master Rath is taking a walk with Berceuse and the Honored Ones."

One-Eye drops down onto a cushion. "Why do you call the Pagu that? 'Honored Ones.'"

"Because they are."

One-Eye frowns. His Spirit Lion says something and One-Eye turns toward him. "You're not going to ask either?"

The Spirit Lion seems almost nervous. One-Eye sighs and starts petting him as he waits.

It is not long before Rath, Berceuse, and the Pagu return.

Rath's eyes light up. "One-Eye. Good morning."

One-Eye smiles briefly. "Morning."

With Berceuse's help, Rath sits on the cushion next to One-Eye.

Berceuse looks at them together, then announces, "I will go retrieve lunch for us all. Will you be staying, One-Eye?"

One-Eye stares at him. It takes him a moment to respond with politeness. "Yes."

"Wonderful. I will be sure to bring enough back for all." He walks back into the forest with many of his dear ones following.

Well-Pagu, Bucket-Pagu, Flower-Pagu, Feather-Pagu, and River-Pagu join Rath and One-Eye on their own small cushions.

One-Eye asks Rath, "Why does he go get food? Can't he just make it appear?"

"I'm sorry?"

One-Eye points to the fire pit. "Two days ago, he just waved his hand and a fire started."

"I see. Like ... " Rath waves his good hand. "*Whoosh?*"

"Yeah. *Whoosh.*"

Across from them, Carlos chokes on his tea. The Pagu look delighted by the term.

Rath says, "Carlos, are you all right?"

Carlos lowers his teacup. "I am, Master Rath, thank you." He says to One-Eye, "Gods cannot simply make anything appear when they wish it to and some may not wish to make appear the things they can."

"They can definitely mess up the weather," One-Eye says.

Berceuse and the Pagu return and they eat together. While they do, the other Pagu on the Isles of Oct introduce themselves to everyone. A Pagu with a ruffly skirt and a pretty flower in their hair introduces themselves to Rath – "I'm Petal-Pagu!" – while One-Eye and his Spirit Lion speak with two Pagu dressed in dark green and red – "I'm Moss-Pagu!" and "I'm Cave-Pagu!"

After they finish eating, Rath rests, One-Eye returns to *PearlHeart*, and the Pagu Trio of *PearlHeart* go with him. They promise to come back to the Isles of Oct after dinner.

At that time, Rath is sitting outside near the fire with Carlos, Berceuse, Feather-Pagu, and River-Pagu. He is looking up at the stars, tracing a constellation. Berceuse sees and says, "Do you like the stars, my Captain?"

"I love them." Rath flushes. "Ah, that is ... That is true. They have always been very important to me."

Berceuse nods. "Their constellations tell the stories of my siblings and I."

"They do."

One-Eye and the Pagu enter the clearing. Flower-Pagu says, "We're back, everyone!" They fly up to Rath, Bucket-Pagu and Well-Pagu close behind.

Rath laughs. "I see. Welcome back, Flower-Pagu. You too,

Bucket-Pagu, Well-Pagu." Then he sees One-Eye and smiles warmly. "Good evening, One-Eye."

"Evening." He sits down with him, then looks up at the stars. "Heard they had stories." He glances at Berceuse. "Also heard they were about the Gods."

Berceuse tugs on his hair nervously. "Well, yes."

Rath looks thoughtful. "I do not believe Grandmother told me a story about you, Berceuse. May I ask where your constellation is?"

"Most certainly, my Captain." He points up. "It is near Merp's and Feint's."

"All right."

"Now, look for nine bright stars – one brightest and eight surrounding it – just like my Isles of Oct."

Rath searches. His eyes light up. "I believe I see it."

One-Eye stares at it, too, frowning.

Berceuse continues, "That is *Berceuse's Isles*. It tells of the time when I hid myself and this place. It is ... well, it is not the happiest story, but perhaps I will tell you one day, my Captain, if you would wish?"

"I would." Rath dips his head respectfully. "Thank you very much for being willing to do so."

"Do you know many of the stories?"

"Yes. Ah, that is, those that my grandmother has told me."

Carlos coughs politely. "Master Rath has heard all but two, including yours, Berceuse."

Berceuse replies, "My!" He looks at Rath inquisitively. "Would you tell me one, my Captain? I know them, of course, but it has been a very long time since I've heard them told. If you are well enough, that is, and all do not mind."

"I believe I am. And I would love to, Berceuse. The constellation stories have always brought me much peace. May I ask if there is a specific one you would wish to hear?"

"Hmm ... what about Elvin's?" Berceuse gestures north. "I am told he is likely the closest sibling I have to where my Isles are, yet like all of my siblings I have not seen him in a very long time."

Rath looks sad at the thought. "I see. I will tell Elvin's story, then." He starts to gather his thoughts, then looks to the others. "Would that be all right with everyone? I apologize for not asking sooner."

Carlos says, "Certainly, Master Rath."

Flower-Pagu shoots their arms up. "It's all right with us, too! We would love to hear Elvin's story again!" Bucket-Pagu and Well-Pagu nod beside them.

One-Eye hesitates, then settles back, leaning a little closer to Rath. "I'll stay." He seems to have more to say, but doesn't.

"Thank you very much, everyone. I will begin."

"Elvin's constellation is near the center of the sky and thus is often used by navigators to find due north. It appears as a band of seven stars with one brighter star in the center. They are known as Elvin's People.

When my grandmother told me this story, she prefaced it with this disclosure: from the moment of his birth, Elvin loved order. When the Third World ended, everything was in chaos and it affected Elvin greatly. His love of order made the destruction around him very painful to bear. Like the other gods during this time, he wished for something that he could do to help, but he and his eagles could do nothing against the winds that buffeted them from the storm that tore the world apart.

A group of humans came to him during this time. They told him that if they were to all go to a large mountain seen in the distance, that they would be safe. In the state Elvin was in at that time, he did not believe them. He would rather try to think that if they stayed where they were, they would be safe and the storm would end. So the humans, disheartened but accepting, moved on.

As Elvin remained with his dear eagles, he looked beyond, wondering why the humans would rather leave and why they would endanger themselves to travel to the mountain. He worried for them and with his great eyesight, he peered forward to see how they were. The humans were struggling greatly. The winds buffeted them like it did him and his eagles and he saw many lose their footing as they walked toward the mountain they were sure would protect them from the storm. Another gust blew the entire group over and that is what made Elvin's decision.

Gathering up his eagles, Elvin flew toward the humans and

right when he was above them, he pulsed his wings – strong – against the wind, expressing his intent to protect the humans below him. The storm receded, but was still very dangerous. Elvin then partnered each human with an eagle who blew back the winds, clutched onto their humans' shoulders for support. They forged a path through the storm by working together and finding order within it.

They arrived at the mountain and Elvin claimed it as his own for him, his eagles, and his people and called it Haliae. The people with him were the first that he gave his protection to – humans and eagles both. Their traits became their communication between one another no matter what distance and their brilliant eyesight. On Haliae, Elvin shielded those he cared for into the next world, where their descendants still live today."

Rath takes a breath.

The group is quiet while the fire burns and the Pagu look into it, reminiscing. Carlos thinks and One-Eye seems conflicted as his Spirit Lion peers up at him.

Berceuse breaks the silence. "I had forgotten how my brother was in times such as these." He tugs at his earring and looks across the fire. "My dear ones tell me that a storm is in the North – that it struck you and your crew, my Captain, and that it is the reason why there was snow on you when you first came here." He rubs his hands together. "They also tell me that in this world, my brother, Ara, affects the weather in this area and often causes severe Winters. Is that true?"

Rath says, "Yes. That is what I am told."

Looking pained, Berceuse says, "Ara is very strong. Like all of us, the strength of his effect on the world around him is driven by his emotions. He must be very upset. And Haliae ... " Suddenly, he gasps. "How is Haliae? My brother Elvin's island?"

"I cannot say for its current state. However, when we approached it four days ago, it was covered in snow."

"So early in the season!" The god combs his fingers through his hair. "I do hope that Elvin and his people are all right."

One-Eye speaks. "What about your people?" They all turn to him. "I don't know all of the Gods' stories, but I know enough that they all chose someone. We've been here for over three days and I've seen no one but the Pagu."

Berceuse puts his hands down. "You are correct." He looks uncomfortable. "Well, I never chose any. I hid only myself, my dear ones – who were with me at the time – and my Isles." He frowns. "My sister, Amara, tells me that I was a coward – to hide myself when I could have helped other humans like the rest of my siblings. I doubt that even after a thousand years she has forgotten my decision." He exhales, blowing some hair out of his face. "But, enough of that. Thank you for telling me my brother Elvin's story once again, my Captain. It has ... Well, it has made me think of many things I have not for some time." Then he looks into the fire alongside the Pagu, his mind on centuries past.

The next morning, Berceuse swims in the ocean in his octopus form. Feather-Pagu is with him.

"I will just take a small look outside to see how Haliae is doing," Berceuse says. His tentacles twitch nervously. "Oh dear, I do not even know if it is close enough to see from here!"

Feather-Pagu pats his big head. "You will need to swim a little further out, but you can do it."

"Yes, my dear one. Ohh, what if it is still snow-covered, like my Captain said? Or worse?"

"It will be all right, Berceuse."

"Thank you, my dear one."

He swims on. The ocean seems to grow colder the further out he travels from his Isles. Finally, he stops.

"This is the edge," he says. Then he glows purple and a veil is lifted, revealing a very different ocean and sky. Heavy clouds hang overhead, muting the color of the waters Berceuse tentatively swims out into. "Well, it is not terribly bad – except for all of these clouds!" As they continue on, he turns to his left. "Where is Drynad? And what is that horrible shadow in its place?"

Feather-Pagu replies, "That is the Phoenae Sea. The majority of Drynad was raised up into the sky by Merp and became his country of Phoenae."

"Merp? Yes, my new brother, though we have never met." He turns to the right. "Is that Lionel's country, Pantha? It's so large!" He sees something else. "Oh! And what is that?"

"A Selachuu military base. They watch for any pirates from Pantha in the ocean here."

"Pirates? Oh, dear. But, Selachuu ... My brother Belle." Berceuse swims forward. "Ohh, he would know what to do in a situation like this."

Berceuse and Feather-Pagu travel throughout the day.

On the morning of the next, a few white flakes begin to fall from the sky. One lands on Berceuse's head. "Oh!" He looks up. "Snow! I do not like snow."

"We must go further, Berceuse."

"Yes, my dear one." Feeling more nervous, Berceuse does.

As they travel that afternoon, the snow continues to fall in clumps until it is thick around them.

"Oh dear ... Feather-Pagu, I will begin a barrier."

"Yes, Berceuse!"

Berceuse begins to glow purple again. However, this time it forms a sphere around him and Feather-Pagu. Warmth spreads out from him to the walls of the bubble, melting the snow. "There. Much better. How are you, my dear one?"

"All warm!"

"I am so glad!" He swims, a soft purple glow among the white.

Within an hour, they reach the edge of the storm.

"Oh goodness, I do not believe we can go any further safely," Berceuse says.

Feather-Pagu looks very sad. "Haliae and Mella Island are within it, Berceuse," they say.

"But – " He raises his voice. "Elvin? Elvin, are you and your people all right?" There is no response. "Elvin?" He shivers. "Surely this storm has not continued since it struck my dear Captain and his crew, has it?"

"It has. It is growing. Well-Pagu, Bucket-Pagu, and Flower-Pagu sent Captain Rath and *PearlHeart* out of the storm just before they were to arrive on Haliae. Now it is far past."

"Oh my ... My brother Ara must truly be very upset." He turns around. "Come, my dear one, we must get out of this cold!"

"Yes, Berceuse!"

Berceuse returns two days later to the clearing looking

exhausted. The Pagu have retrieved breakfast this morning and the others are already eating. A cluster of Pagu bring food to Berceuse and Feather-Pagu as they sit down.

"Here you go, Berceuse and Feather-Pagu!" they say.

Berceuse takes his wearily. "Thank you, my dear ones."

Feather-Pagu says, "Thank you!"

As Feather-Pagu begins to eat, Berceuse looks at his food. He takes a bite, chews, then lowers the fruit.

Carlos clears his throat. "Berceuse, I was just telling Master Rath that he is fit to leave for *PearlHeart.*"

Berceuse's eyes widen. "Truly?" He turns to Rath and smiles. "That is wonderful, my Captain. Then you are well?"

"Yes," Rath says.

Berceuse pauses. "Where will you go after this?"

"I cannot say. Our next delivery would take us to Haliae" – Berceuse starts – "however, I do not know if the storm we encountered earlier this week has continued or if it is safe to proceed."

"The storm has continued." They all look at Berceuse. He finishes his fruit, leaving the rind, and sets it down neatly. "I saw it two days ago. I believe I still have snow on me despite my barrier!" He shakes his head. "My dear one, Feather-Pagu, says that it is growing as well. It was well past Haliae and Mella Island when we saw it."

Rath's eyes fall. One-Eye glares at the ground. The Pagu are quiet and Carlos frowns, saying, "That is very concerning."

"It must mean my brother Ara is very upset, indeed." Berceuse sighs. "We could not see anything past his storm."

Rath raises his head too quickly and winces. He lifts his left hand to his right shoulder. "Really?"

"Yes! Only white."

"That is terrible."

Berceuse tugs on his hair. "Will they be all right on Haliae? I cannot imagine this is the first time that they have had a storm like this."

"I do not know. However, yes, they have had similar storms before. I am told that at least one in this generation has trapped them inside until the end of Spring."

"Oh dear! And what you are bringing – your delivery – is it food?"

"Yes. And ink and paper."

Berceuse smiles for a moment. "For Elvin, I am sure. He must be ... " He suddenly looks down, rubbing his hands together. When he raises his eyes, he says, "Do you believe you will continue on, my Captain? To Haliae?"

Rath looks pained. He shakes his head. "No. Not if the storm has continued. We cannot do so safely."

"But if I came, would you?"

Rath's eyes widen.

One-Eye's eye narrows. "What would you do?"

"Protect everyone. Protect *PearlHeart* so that it may make the journey safely. As a god, I do have a similar talent as Elvin – if I use my will, I can create a barrier to drive back Ara's Storm just as in his constellation story. Of course, Ara is many times stronger than me ... I am the weakest of my siblings, but – "

Feather-Pagu pats his hand. "You can do it, Berceuse."

"Thank you, my dear one." He continues to Rath, "It would be far easier to maintain such a barrier if I'm not in the cold ocean. I would dearly love to see my brother Elvin and help him and his own if I can. However, it is your decision, my Captain."

"I ... " Then Rath dips his head in profound respect. "I would greatly appreciate you coming with, Berceuse, so that we may journey to Haliae safely."

Berceuse nods, but looks nervous. "Then it is decided. Is there anything I need? I've never been on a ship before."

"No. You may bring anything you may wish for."

"I see." He eats some more of his fruit and looks up at the blue sky.

Afterward, with One-Eye's help, Rath walks to the beach where the small boat waits to take them back to *PearlHeart*. Flower-Pagu, Bucket-Pagu, Well-Pagu, and Carlos go with them. Berceuse, Feather-Pagu, River-Pagu, and the large cluster of Pagu that inhabit the Isles see them off.

Rath is settled in the small boat, then speaks to Berceuse. "We will leave tomorrow morning at six, if that is all right with you?"

"Most certainly!" Berceuse toys with his hair. "Well, it is rather early – no, I shall be ready, my Captain."

"Thank you."

One-Eye stares at Berceuse. "I'll be here at five-thirty to

row you there." There is an unspoken *Be ready.*

"Yes, One-Eye."

Then Berceuse and his dear ones watch Rath and the others row toward *PearlHeart.*

Once they reach it, they are pulled up to the deck. As One-Eye hops off and offers a hand to Rath to help him, the crew all gather around, shouting, "Captain!"

"Ah, hello," Rath says. He steps onto the main deck and looks around, his shoulders relaxing. "It is so good to see everyone."

"You too, Captain!"

Rath gathers his thoughts, then says, "Berceuse, the God of Oct, has asked to accompany us on our delivery. He tells me that Ara's Storm is past Haliae and Mella Island now, however, he will be able to protect *PearlHeart* and everyone on it with his barrier so that we may travel there."

The crew look surprised, then determined. They nod.

"One-Eye, Well-Pagu, Bucket-Pagu, Flower-Pagu, and Carlos have told me that everyone helped with the repairs on *PearlHeart.* Thank you very much for your help. I greatly appreciate it." The crew beam. "I ask that we leave tomorrow morning at six. Thank you for all that you do!"

"Thank you, Captain!"

As the crew talk among themselves, One-Eye turns to Rath. "I'll show you the repairs."

"Thank you."

They go to the upper deck first.

Throughout the day, One-Eye and Well-Pagu update Rath on the state of *PearlHeart.* He listens carefully. At the end, One-Eye says, "I can handle the logbook until you can use your arm again."

Rath looks surprised, then smiles. "Thank you. I would greatly appreciate that."

"Sure."

On the Isles of Oct, Berceuse spends his last day.

He lies in his clearing, looking up at the blue skies. He eats with his dear ones. Then, as the stars come out above, they sit beneath them.

" ... I cannot create both a barrier over *PearlHeart* and

maintain my Isles. It would use far too much energy."

The Pagu nod. "We know, Berceuse," Petal-Pagu says.

He looks concerned. "Then where will you go?"

The Pagu look at each other. Then they nod and smile up at their dear friend. "We will go on a journey as well! To the Pagu of Pagu Island. It has been a very long time since we've seen them."

"Oh! That sounds absolutely wonderful."

"It is!" They gather around him. "We hope that you find Elvin well, Berceuse."

"I hope so as well, my dear ones."

He looks up at the stars.

12

Early the next morning, One-Eye rows to the largest isle.

As he does, Berceuse walks out of the forest and onto the beach. He turns to the Pagu who came with him. "Please have a safe journey, my dear ones. I love all of you."

"We love you, too, Berceuse!"

They give each other one last wave before the group of Pagu that have lived on the Isles of Oct for so long fly off south on their way to the Pagu of Pagu Island.

After they have left, Berceuse steps through the sand to where One-Eye waits. He climbs into the boat.

One-Eye asks, "You're not bringing anything?"

"No, I can just – " Berceuse starts to wave his hand.

"Never mind."

They row to *PearlHeart* in silence. Berceuse looks at the tall ship as they approach. Once they have been hauled up, One-Eye steps down onto the deck and Berceuse follows him. Rath is already there to meet them. "Good morning, Berceuse."

"Good morning, my Captain."

He stands by the upper deck with Bucket-Pagu and Flower-Pagu. As the sails begin to fill and *PearlHeart* starts to move, he raises a hand to his mouth. "My ... " The Pagu smile next to him.

PearlHeart sails under blue skies – north – away from Berceuse's Isles of Oct. They pick up speed under the fair weather. After fifteen minutes, Berceuse steps forward, facing the upper deck where Rath is standing with One-Eye and Well-Pagu. "My Captain, I will now allow *PearlHeart* to exit this area."

"I understand. Thank you, Berceuse!" Rath says.

Berceuse takes a deep breath. With Flower-Pagu and Bucket-Pagu next to him, he walks toward the prow and stands before the blue skies and turquoise waters. Then he clasps his hands together and begins to glow purple. The blue up above recedes, replaced by a deep gray that turns the ocean a dark blue and behind them, the Isles of Oct melt away.

PearlHeart now sails under overcast skies. Pantha is to their right and the Phoenae Sea and its storms are to their left. A chill comes over the ship as the warmth of the sun disappears. Berceuse shivers.

Afterward, Rath guides him to the guest cabin. "Would you be all right with staying here?" He opens the door with his good hand and Berceuse looks in.

The room has two portholes, a table with two chairs, and a cozy bed tucked into the right wall with an embroidered blanket placed over it. Berceuse sees it first. "Oh!" He strides over, then sits and examines the stitching. "This is beautiful." As Rath joins him, he asks. "Did you sew this, my Captain?"

"No. My mother did."

"Ah! Is she from Campi, perchance? These stitches look very much like my sister Penelope's. I use them all the time in my work."

"She is. And I see."

"Your mother is very talented," Berceuse says, smiling. He looks around at the room. "Yes, this would be wonderful, my Captain. Thank you."

"Of course."

Berceuse thinks. "That's right. Before your crew arrived on my Isles, I had asked if you would like me to make you a second glove. Do you remember?"

"I believe I do."

"I am more than happy to. Or, what about a new pair? In

case you find the other."

Flushing, Rath waves his hand. "I cannot ask for you to do that."

"I am offering, my Captain. It would bring me great joy."

"Then, I would greatly appreciate it, Berceuse. Thank you."

"Most certainly!"

Rath leaves to allow Berceuse time to settle in. "I will start working on your new gloves today!" the god calls after him.

"Thank you again."

Rath turns and almost walks into One-Eye, who says, "Gloves?"

"Yes. Berceuse has offered to make me a new pair."

One-Eye nods to his right. "Left your other one in your cabin. The one that came off."

"I see. Berceuse tells me he fixed the one that was with me. Thank you for telling me. I will let Berceuse know as well."

One-Eye nods.

That morning, Berceuse eats breakfast on *PearlHeart* for the first time. He takes his dish back, saying to Phillip and Flower-Pagu, "It was absolutely divine!"

Phillip is flustered. "Th-Thanks!"

Flower-Pagu shoots their arms up. "You're welcome, Berceuse!"

Berceuse notices the hooks in the wall near the stove and the little tools hanging from them. "What is this? My, are these yours, Flower-Pagu? They are beautifully made!"

"The Captain made them!"

"Truly? He is quite talented."

"He also made shovels for Bucket-Pagu, Well-Pagu, and I so that we could garden together!"

Berceuse gasps, placing his hands over his heart. "That is absolutely precious!"

That afternoon, Franz and Velt are out on the deck, eating. Franz stares at the storm ahead nervously. "We've got a god with us. It'll be fine."

"It definitely will!" Velt says.

One-Eye, who was eating with Oren, looks up when he hears this. He glances at Berceuse, who has finished his meal and is looking at the storm as well.

Afterward, One-Eye, Rath, the Pagu, and Berceuse meet on

the deck. Flower-Pagu says, "We thought we'd all play Double Berceuse if that was all right with everyone!"

"That sounds wonderful," Rath says. "I would like to."

One-Eye starts to say, "Sure – " but stops. He looks at Berceuse. "You invented it."

Berceuse toys with his hair. "Well, yes."

One-Eye scowls.

"Really?" Rath says. "That is incredible."

Berceuse blushes, laying a hand on his cheek. "Why, thank you, my Captain!"

They all sit at the table in the captain's cabin. One-Eye glares at Berceuse, who looks uncomfortable.

Rath says, "We have six players here. We could play Double Berceuse in pairs."

Flower-Pagu looks excited. "You're right, Captain!"

One-Eye doesn't hesitate. "We're pairing, Captain."

Rath starts. "Y-Yes, One-Eye."

Well-Pagu flies up to Berceuse. "Team!"

"It would be my pleasure, my dear one!"

Flower-Pagu and Bucket-Pagu link arms. "Then we'll be together!" Flower-Pagu says and Bucket-Pagu nods.

They play through the afternoon. One-Eye holds the cards for them while Rath manages the drawing and discarding with his good hand.

Four turns later, One-Eye sets their hand down. "Double..." he says.

"Berceuse," Rath finishes.

Berceuse beams. "Wonderful job, you two!"

One-Eye frowns at him. He picks up the cards and starts to shuffle. "Again."

They play several more rounds, choosing different partners each time. Well-Pagu and Flower-Pagu win next, then One-Eye and Bucket-Pagu, and finally Rath and Berceuse win the last.

"Double," Berceuse says and Rath finishes, "Berceuse!"

They smile at each other.

One-Eye looks across the table at them, still frowning. He stands up. "I need to go to my watch."

Rath says, "I will go outside as well. It is nearly time for dinner." The Pagu nod next to him.

They gather up the cards and Berceuse says, "Thank you all for playing. It is one of my most favorite games I've created."

"I believe it is wonderful," Rath says.

One-Eye just nods.

Rath eats dinner with the Pagu and Berceuse, then joins One-Eye at the wheel. One-Eye stares at the storm ahead.

Finally, he says, "I thought he'd be better at it." Rath looks confused and One-Eye explains, "I thought Berceuse would be better at ... Double Berceuse. He invented it."

"That is true."

They pause.

One-Eye says, "It's good. The game."

Rath brightens. "I believe so as well."

One-Eye looks uncomfortable. His Spirit Lion watches him curiously.

During the next day, *PearlHeart* grows closer to the edge of Ara's Storm. The temperature drops and most of the crew eat in the galley where it is warm, looking nervous but determined, trusting in their captain and everyone else aboard *PearlHeart*.

That morning, Berceuse sits in his cabin, knitting. He holds out a finished light green glove. "There."

Bucket-Pagu and Flower-Pagu, who are with him, cheer. "It looks wonderful, Berceuse!" Flower-Pagu says.

Bucket-Pagu says, "You did a really great job."

"Thank you, my dear ones." Then he takes it and the glove he had already finished and stands. Like everyone else on *PearlHeart*, he, too, is wearing warmer clothes, with a large purple scarf around his neck. "Shall we go give these to our Captain?"

"Yes!" the Pagu say.

Outside, the storm is far closer now and snow has begun to fall over them. Berceuse looks up at it, concerned. "This is further south than when it started before. The storm must have grown."

Near them, Rath is speaking with One-Eye and Well-Pagu. One-Eye is saying, "When is he going to do something?"

"I cannot say," Rath says.

Well-Pagu sees Berceuse and the others approach. "Here," they say.

Rath and One-Eye turn.

Berceuse joins them. "I am ready to begin my barrier, Captain," he says. "However, before that ... " He smiles and holds out the gloves. "I just finished these. I hope that they keep your hands warm."

Rath takes them carefully, amazed by the stitching. "Thank you so much, Berceuse. They are beautiful."

"I am glad that you like them." Berceuse hesitates. "I cannot guarantee that my barrier will make it be as warm as on my Isles – we will be in my brother Ara's Storm, after all and as I said, my power is not nearly as great as his – " The Pagu give him an encouraging look. "But, I will do my best. I will keep you, your crew, and *PearlHeart* safe, my Captain. That I promise you."

Rath does a careful bow. "Thank you, Berceuse. I greatly appreciate it." He rises. "Please let me know if there is anything I can do to help."

"I will, my Captain." He looks toward the prow. "May I sit there?"

"Of course."

Rath, One-Eye, and the Pagu watch as Berceuse steps forward, walking past both masts. He sits cross-legged and closes his eyes. He starts to glow purple. The snow continues, growing thicker and Berceuse concentrates. Soon, his glow begins to grow, spreading out from him like octopus limbs until it hugs all of *PearlHeart* in its warmth. Then it spreads beyond, reaching past the flags up above and down to the water's surface surrounding the ship, creating a dome over them. Any snow that comes near it melts. To the crew of *PearlHeart,* the snow appears to have stopped entirely and they look up at it in wonder.

The god continues to focus, his purple barrier glowing brightly over the ship.

PearlHeart sails as if it never left the overcast skies, toward Haliae.

13

Later that day, Phillip comes out to ring the bell. "Lunchtime – whoa." He looks up at the purple barrier, amazed. "I mean, lunchtime everyone!"

"Come and get it!" Flower-Pagu says next to him.

Rath and the others eat in the galley. As they are leaving, Rath pauses when he sees that Berceuse has not left his spot near *PearlHeart's* prow.

Flower-Pagu asks, "What is it, Captain?"

"I am concerned about Berceuse. I do not believe he has left to eat lunch. However, I do not wish to disturb him to ask."

Carlos, who ate with them, responds, "As a god, Berceuse does not truly need to eat. It does replenish his strength, however, during this time it is not something he can afford to do. I am certain he understands that and did so from the time that he said he would protect *PearlHeart.*"

Rath nods. He is wearing the green gloves that Berceuse made for him.

For the next three days, *PearlHeart* travels under Berceuse's barrier.

One afternoon, William and Phobos are talking in the galley

with Isaac. William is sipping a warm drink. "It was really good of Berceuse to help."

"Right?" Isaac says.

Out on the deck, Rath is standing with the Pagu and One-Eye, looking north. Ara's Storm is directly ahead.

That night, they enter it.

Rath, One-Eye, and Well-Pagu stay awake and remain on the deck when they do. They watch Berceuse and the purple glow around *PearlHeart*, and the sky steadily darkening above them.

Suddenly, *PearlHeart* tosses back as if hit by an enormous wave. They hear a wind shriek past.

However, the barrier holds and while the wind has picked up within it, it is manageable for the crew working the lines.

Rath and the others stay outside for another hour, then go inside to sleep.

When Rath comes out the following morning, the sky is still dark. He looks up into the thick, heavy clouds above them, tinted purple by the barrier, and the snow that melts when it comes too close.

He turns toward Berceuse, still seated by the prow.

The god suddenly tips to the left.

Rath starts forward, but he feels a little hand on his arm.

When he turns, he sees that it is Well-Pagu. They shake their head and Rath immediately understands. Ahead, Berceuse rights himself, but is clearly struggling under the weight of the storm.

The Pagu go to talk to Berceuse later and check on him frequently during the day. That night, they ask if Rath can tell them more of the Gods' constellation stories. He agrees and they sit on the rail, all bundled up in the cold. Even One-Eye stands with them, listening to stories about Fierce, the God of Butej, and Hep, the God of Sudines.

As Rath speaks, Berceuse hears him and straightens. When Rath and the others are going to bed, the barrier glows more steadily.

Berceuse holds it for the next two days.

On the night before they are to arrive at Haliae, another wind shrieks past, rocking *PearlHeart* backward and forcing the crew to tighten their grip on the lines. But this time, Berceuse strengthens his barrier and it brightens all around them. They hear the wind go past, but it sounds distant. Ahead, Berceuse sits tall, hands clasped together.

In the morning, Berceuse opens his eyes. He can see the rising mountain in the center of Haliae appear in front of him and he smiles very briefly, then continues to concentrate.

That evening, they arrive at Port Efrin on Haliae.

They sail to the docks – they are empty from what they can see – with Franz at the wheel. Rath, One-Eye, and Well-Pagu are on the upper deck with him, watching their progress the best they can through the snow falling outside of the barrier.

When they come to a bobbing stop, Franz exhales. "We did it."

Rath takes his shoulder with his good hand. "Excellent job, Franz."

"Thanks, Captain."

As they go down to the main deck, One-Eye says, "What now? Where do you normally take the delivery?"

"The southeast side of Elvin's Peak. There, the crates are hauled up with a pulley system to the city above."

One-Eye peers at the top of the center mountain of the island. The white city is almost invisible in the snow. "Is anyone even up there?"

"I do not know." Rath runs a hand through his hair. "They could also be inside the mountain itself, if the city was deemed unsafe."

"It's hollow?"

"Yes. However, I cannot say that is where they are now." Rath looks out at the snow, too. "We will need to find someone. There was always someone near the pulley system on our previous deliveries."

One-Eye shakes his head. "I'll go." Rath frowns. "This isn't too different from the winters in Pantha. It's not as bad on land and I'll have my Spirit Lion with me."

"I understand. Thank you, One-Eye."

Evermore steps forward. "I will accompany One-Eye, with your permission, Captain. Once I am on the island, I will be able to tell if any others are nearby with Erole's Traits."

"That is a good idea. Would that be all right with you, One-Eye?"

One-Eye turns to Evermore. His scarf is gone and his pale yellow eyes are somehow bright in the dark blizzard. "Fine," he says.

Evermore gives a slight nod.

Rath looks to both of them. "Please be very careful."

One-Eye says, "We'll be back soon."

Rath watches as One-Eye and Evermore go down the gangplank. The barrier only extends halfway down it and when One-Eye steps through, he is immediately surrounded by the blizzard. Evermore gasps behind him as he exits. One-Eye holds up his arm and trudges on, saying, "Come on!"

"Behind you, One-Eye," Evermore says.

They walk forward through snow that comes up to their knees. One-Eye's Spirit Lion, head low, moves next to him. Following the docks, they reach the mainland.

One-Eye asks, "Do you sense anyone?"

Evermore shakes his head. "No. None nearby." The trees ahead are tall with dark green needles, each branch covered in snow. Evermore stops. "There. Someone is near."

One-Eye looks ahead. In between gusts, he can make out the base of the mountain. "Captain said there was usually someone close to Elvin's Peak."

"They are not outside. But, yes, they are in that direction."

As they walk, One-Eye glances at Evermore. He has recovered from his initial step and continues forward with a distant look in his eyes as he senses his surroundings.

"You don't seem fazed by this," One-Eye says.

Evermore's eyes flick toward him, becoming present for a moment. "My training has taught me not to be." They pass through branches that are stiff with ice. "But ... being under the barrier of a god ... did unsettle me."

One-Eye glances over again. He looks forward. "Same."

He does not see Evermore's startled, then quiet look.

They exit the forest and approach the side of the mountain. One-Eye scans the area, but does not see anyone. Before he can ask Evermore, a voice calls out in a strange, muffled way, "Here! Over here!"

They look right at the mountain. As they move in the direction of the voice, a grinding sound – rock against rock – starts and soon, they see why. A dark, rectangular entrance has appeared in the mountain. The voice, now clearer, calls, "This way!"

One-Eye and Evermore pick up their pace and duck inside. As soon as they do, they hear the same grinding sound and One-Eye sees two people with ropes managing a pulley system. It is rigged over a slab of rock that, in the snow, looked like it was flush with the mountainside and now has been lowered to close the entrance. Above, a man – the one who called out to them before – with an eagle partner on his shoulder stands on a scaffolding. His clothing is lit by a strip of light that One-Eye sees is from a slit cleaved into the wall, allowing the man to see out, but too small for One-Eye and Evermore to have seen from the outside. The man hops down to greet them.

"Hey! Glad to see you made it in safe. Sven said to keep an eye out for someone, but I didn't really believe anyone would make it."

Before One-Eye can respond, another voice calls out, "Rath! Is that – " A young man near Rath's age with black hair parted on one side and an eagle partner perched on his left shoulder join them. His look of relief fades to one of confusion as he looks at them. "Evermore and ... "

"One-Eye. First mate aboard *PearlHeart.*"

Immediately, understanding lights the man's eyes. He straightens his robes – long sleeves and pants ending at the knee where they are tucked into boots. "My father told me that Fenrir had to leave suddenly. I am glad that Rath found someone else. I would assume he found a navigator, too, if you are all here."

"Well-Pagu."

"A Pagu?" He puts a finger to his chin. "That does make sense for Rath." He steps forward and extends his hand. One-Eye shakes it. "I am Lord Sven, son of Councilman Hailcorn of Haliae." He gestures to the eagle on his shoulder. "This is Pema." She peers at them with intelligent eyes. "My father is currently still in Phoenae serving in the Council, so I am the acting representative of Elvin on Haliae. Rath and I know each other from when we were training to be councilmen. His father and mine have been friends for a long time." He falters. "Is Rath all right? I would have thought he would be here."

One-Eye thinks on how to answer that. "He's on the ship."

"Oh, thank goodness."

"We brought the delivery. Wondered where to bring it. We brought extra provisions, too."

Sven rubs his face. "Bless you." He looks behind him, where the small entry area opens up into a much larger space full of people sitting around fires, bundled up in blankets. "In here, please. I will make room. Elvin will bring his up to his office." He says, "Do you think it will be possible to bring them through the snow?"

"That's up to the Captain."

Sven nods. The wind howls outside and he glances toward the entrance. "It's been like this since last week. I'm glad that we got everyone inside." He frowns. "I hate to send you out again, but we could really use those provisions and Elvin, his ink and paper. We'll be watching for you. Unless you can't make it." He pauses. "How did you get through Ara's Storm? That's what the Spirit Eagles tell me this is. I don't know a lot of about ships, but this seems like it would be dangerous."

One-Eye hesitates. "A god helped us. Berceuse."

Sven blinks a few times. "Berceuse? I haven't heard of a Berceuse." He shakes his head. "I'll tell Elvin – he'll likely want to know. Maybe – " He stops and says instead, "Good luck out there. We'll hopefully see you back soon."

"Yeah."

The stone slab is lifted again, then One-Eye and Evermore exit.

On *PearlHeart*, Rath waits on the deck with Carlos and the Pagu, all tucked into their winter gear.

Suddenly, the barrier around them wavers. When Rath looks up at it, Carlos turns to Berceuse and the Pagu look in the same direction.

They hear boots on the gangplank.

Rath exhales in relief. "One-Eye, Evermore. How are you?"

One-Eye shakes the snow off of his hair. "Fine. Met Sven. You know each other?"

"Yes, since we were children. How is he?"

"He really wants those provisions."

"Do you believe it is possible to carry them there?"

One-Eye thinks. "It would be doable with two people

carrying and one person watching."

"Then that is what we will do. Thank you, One-Eye. You as well, Evermore."

Evermore bows.

Rath gathers his crew and soon, the crates are being carried off. One-Eye stands near the edge of the barrier on the gangplank, saying, "Stay steady while you step through!"

"Yes, One-Eye!"

Evermore is beyond, near the forest. "The entrance to the inside of the mountain is this way," he says.

The delivery to Haliae makes a steady line toward the mountain. Rath watches the best he can from the ship, Carlos and the Pagu with him.

When they arrive, the stone slab is lifted and the group enters the mountain with much relief.

Under Sven's guidance, they take the crates to the central room, a large circular space with a ceiling that reaches all the way to the mountaintop. A staircase winds around, leading to different levels with tunnels that go to various rooms. Many of the tunnels are dark, as most of the people are on the ground floor, but a single one near the top glows brightly.

As One-Eye looks at it, Sven calls up, "Elvin! Your ink and paper are here!"

The light dims for a moment as if a something has blocked it, then One-Eye hears a rushing sound. Suddenly, a large eagle flies out, descending to the floor in a spiral. He flaps a few times before he lands, then puts one enormous talon on the crate of ink and paper. "Finally! You have no idea how long I've waited for this. Why – " He stops and looks around. "Where is Captain Rath? I wished to give him my thanks in-person – so to speak."

One-Eye grits his teeth. "On his ship."

Elvin peers at him. "And who would you be?"

"One-Eye. His first mate."

"And one of Lionel's, too! Perfect, that is just perfect!"

"Why, I have been attempting to improve relations with Pantha for some time! It is very good to see you as part of Captain Rath's crew and very good of him to hire you! Now, this ink and paper is quite instrumental, for I am currently – "

"Elvin," Sven says. "One-Eye says that *PearlHeart* was able to sail here because they were helped by a god. Berceuse?"

Elvin stops. "Berceuse?" He glows briefly, stepping forward as a tall man with gray hair pulled back in a short tail and wearing robes similar to Sven. "Truly? My brother Berceuse is with you?" he asks One-Eye.

"Yeah."

Sven asks, "Who is Berceuse? I've never heard Father or you speak of him."

Elvin looks sad. "Because he left a very long time ago. None of us ... Well, I did not think I would ever see him again. Yet, he is here." He bows to One-Eye. "Please. I would very much like to see my brother again, if you would guide me to him."

One-Eye looks very uncomfortable. "Sure."

Sven says, "I would like to see Rath, too, if that is all right."

The three of them leave, following the sailors that brought the crates and are now returning to *PearlHeart*. As they move through the storm, Elvin thrusts up his arm, his long sleeve flapping. "My! This is dreadful! This isn't the same storm from last week, is it?"

Sven responds, holding his arm in a similar way, "Yes. I told you, Elvin. And about how restless the Spirit Eagles were?"

Elvin rubs his nose. "I do not remember."

Sven sighs.

One-Eye says, "Can't you do something. As a god?"

Elvin turns to him suddenly. "Oh! Quite right." He lowers his arm and in that single gesture, a light blue barrier surrounds them like a pair of wings, melting any snow that comes near and reducing the wind around them. He strides forward. "Now, come on, *PearlHeart* awaits."

Sven brushes the snow off of his robes as he and One-Eye follow. They meet members of the crew on their way back and – seeing the barrier – they all cluster inside for the return trip. By the time they reach the gangplank, the whole group is within.

As they approach the purple barrier, Elvin strokes his chin. "Yes! This is most certainly my brother Berceuse's work." He quickly steps up the gangplank. "My brother! Are you there?" The crew follows close behind.

When they enter Berceuse's barrier, Elvin releases his own. He sees Rath, Carlos, and the Pagu. "Ah! Captain Rath."

He strides forward and bows. "Thank you very much for your efforts in bringing my ink and paper."

Rath seems startled by his sudden entrance. "Of course, Elvin. I am happy to do so."

Sven comes up beside them. "And the provisions. Thank you, Rath, it's – " He suddenly Rath's sling. "What happened?"

"Ah – "

Elvin has moved on at this point, having spotted Berceuse. "There you are! Berceuse!"

While Rath explains to Sven – "*You fell off your ship?*" – Elvin sits cross-legged in front of his brother. The God of Oct is still concentrating and has his eyes closed. Elvin notices the barrier tremble. Then he pats his knees and adds his own energy to stabilize it. All look up at the mix of light blue and purple now around them.

Berceuse opens his eyes. He blinks a few times, then sees Elvin's grinning face. "Brother! You are all right!"

They lean forward and embrace. "Well, of course! Haliae has weathered storms such as this before."

As they part, Berceuse frowns. "Brother, I do not think that this is one of Ara's storms that will go away so easily."

"Yes, there was that storm – twelve years ago? But, that, too, dissipated."

"My dear ones do not believe this one will." Berceuse gestures. "They believe that it will ... grow."

Elvin's glasses slide down a little. "Oh."

Near him, Rath has just finished explaining to Sven what had happened to his shoulder.

Sven rubs his face. "Let me get this straight – you were hit by the same storm we were hit by a week ago, fell off your ship, and somehow ended up on the Isles of Oct, the home of Berceuse, the God of Oct, who even I didn't know about, and who also tended to you until your crew arrived, then offered to help you finish your delivery to Haliae by making a barrier around *PearlHeart* so you could all sail here?"

"Yes," Rath says.

Sven shakes his head. "You need a year off."

"I would prefer not to."

Sven takes his hand fondly. "You probably wouldn't know what to do with yourself." He frowns. "And ... I can't imagine anything will be quite as dangerous as what happened ten years ago, but I still do worry. I'm sure Marchand does, too. He thought you were dead before."

Rath nods quietly.

Sven shakes his head. "I'm sorry. I have a feeling you've gotten over it more than the people around you." He looks around *PearlHeart.* "But, I'm glad to see you and your ship are here safe. And all of your crew – new members, included. Where'd you meet One-Eye?"

Rath brightens. "On Pantrog."

One-Eye, not far from them, sees his expression while talking about their meeting – warm and relaxed – and relaxes as well.

A few minutes later, they gather together with Elvin.

Elvin clears his throat. "My brother, Berceuse, has told me that this storm is perhaps not like others from Ara and that it may grow, not diminish over time."

Sven asks, "What should we do?" Pema looks at her god.

"We will watch it for now. However, you have my promise, Sven and Pema, that if you deem it to be too dangerous, I will listen to you and we shall make plans for what to do afterward." Looking embarrassed, Elvin continues, "I've been rather wrapped up in my proposal for Pantha. I apologize for not listening to you like I should. We will be working together closely in the future just like your father, Fritz, and I are doing now, thus communications must be open on both sides. Still, you have my apologies." He bows.

Sven and Pema are stunned. "That's all right, Elvin." He straightens. "I will speak to you if and when the storm becomes unsafe for Haliae." Pema nods in agreement.

Elvin grins. "Perfect." He turns to Rath. "I would advise that when you are able to, Captain, that you sail back to the South. Berceuse tells me that the storm has grown quickly and it would be best if all of you left as soon as possible."

"I understand."

Elvin asks Sven and Pema, "Shall we go?"

Sven pets his eagle partner. "Yes – actually, just a moment? We'd like to say goodbye to Rath."

"Of course. Thank you again for delivering my ink and paper and provisions for Haliae, Captain Rath," he says, bowing.

"You are welcome, Elvin."

While Elvin goes to say goodbye to Berceuse and speak with the Pagu, Sven takes Rath's hand in place of a hug. "Be careful."

"I will. You too, Sven, Pema."

"We definitely will." Sven blinks. "It surprises me that Elvin's entrusted me with such a decision. I'm also surprised he's changed his mind so readily about the storm. Just this morning he was convinced that it would dissipate by the holiday." He looks over at the two gods and the Pagu. "I wonder what Berceuse told him." He moves on, "Anyway, I hope you are able to get home safely. We'll do our best here. Thank you again for bringing the provisions and Elvin's ink and paper."

"Definitely."

They squeeze each other's hands one more time, Pema gives a respectful nod, then Sven and Pema depart with Elvin. As they go down the gangplank, the light blue fades from *PearlHeart's* barrier and Rath sees an orb of it surrounding Sven, Pema, and Elvin as they make their way back to the mountain. The barrier around *PearlHeart* returns to a pure purple, but it seems a little brighter this time.

Soon, *PearlHeart* is sailing south.

At the wheel, One-Eye looks ahead, thinking.

Later that evening, he is in the captain's cabin. The Pagu are with them and all are eating raspberries at the table.

"Thought he'd be ... " One-Eye starts.

Rath looks up.

One-Eye shakes his head. He eats another raspberry. "Elvin. He listened. I didn't expect that."

"To Sven, you mean?"

"Yeah." One-Eye sits back. The Pagu nibble on raspberries in between them. "Got the feeling from Sven that he wasn't listening before. When we were in the mountain." He pauses. "Didn't know a place like that existed. I liked seeing it."

Two days later, they sail out of the storm. Outside Berceuse's barrier, the blizzard turns to light snow and, finally, overcast skies.

The afternoon of the sixth day, Berceuse releases his barrier and stumbles to his feet. Rath sees and walks over to him, holding out his hand.

"May I help you, Berceuse?"

Berceuse takes it heavily. "Yes. Thank you, my Captain. I think I may take a very long nap. Then perhaps something to eat. Dinner will be soon, yes?"

"It is."

Smiling, Berceuse says, "Then, if you would have it with me, I would be greatly delighted."

Rath's eyebrows go up. "Of course." With Rath helping him, they walk to the guest cabin.

After Berceuse is in his bed, Rath says, "I hope that you rest well, Berceuse."

"Thank you, my Captain."

They continue to sail without Berceuse's barrier. The Pantha coastline is more visible now, and with it, the Selachuu military bases. Selachuu ships come and go from the sea caves.

After Berceuse finishes his nap, he, Rath, and the Pagu eat dinner, then they play Double Berceuse. Later that evening, Berceuse speaks with Carlos on the deck and watches the crew aboard *PearlHeart.* Then he looks ahead to where his Isles of Oct would be, although they are hidden now.

Berceuse approaches Rath, One-Eye, and the Pagu the next morning. "My Captain?" he says.

Rath smiles. "Hello, Berceuse. What can I do for you?"

Berceuse looks at him fondly, then says, "I wished to announce my departure." He gestures. "This is near the area where my Isles of Oct are. However, I do not believe that I will return to them. Or, that they will remain here." He taps his cheek. "I haven't decided yet on that." He continues, "I did greatly enjoy seeing my brother Elvin again. It was not as frightening as I thought it would be. I would like to see my other siblings as well – and my dear ones, too, that are likely already on Pagu Island." He gives a gusty sigh. "I miss them terribly." He looks up at the sky. "I can already tell that it is warmer here. I do not believe that you will be in danger of Ara's Storm this far south." He takes Rath's arm. "However, do be careful, my Captain."

"I will."

Berceuse looks around. "I have truly enjoyed being here on *PearlHeart.* Thank you for allowing me to sail with you. I am certain we will meet again." He winks. "I still need to tell you my constellation story, after all."

"I would love that." Rath bows. "Thank you for your help, Berceuse, in protecting us from Ara's Storm. I have truly enjoyed your company."

"And I!"

One-Eye says to Berceuse, "Thanks." He doesn't say anything else. Berceuse smiles tentatively.

The God of Oct gives them a wave, then leaps into the air. He glows, becoming an octopus halfway through his descent. Rath and the others watch as he swims away from *PearlHeart* – south – to warmer waters, his siblings, and his dear ones.

14

As *PearlHeart* travels, the skies continue to be overcast. Three days later, it begins to rain and the next, they arrive at the Southern Selachuu Military Base for customs.

When Rath knocks on the door of the building inside the sea cave, Farbourne answers. "Well, I'll be." He takes a swig from his mug. "Captain Rath. Come back from the North?"

"Yes."

As they begin walking to *PearlHeart*, Farbourne continues, "Heard it suddenly got a lot worse there. The Spirit Sharks are saying it's Ara's Storm. What happened to your shoulder by the way?"

"I fell off my ship."

Farbourne stops. He looks at Rath and gives a low whistle.

They board *PearlHeart* and Farbourne checks their empty cargo hold. When they return to the deck, Farbourne waves to One-Eye and he joins them.

"From everything I've heard," Farbourne says, "Ara's Storm is still going on. Also heard the King of Pantha, Faerohr, is still alive and well. Borders have been nearly empty of Lionel's own – seems all of them are too busy finding food to make it through this Winter. Only a handful of pirates, too." He turns to One-Eye. "You think you'll ever go back to Pantha?"

One-Eye responds immediately, "Never."

"Fair." Farbourne says to Rath, "You're good to leave. Glad you made it back now – sounds like they'll be closing off the North soon due to the storm. Belle's deemed it dangerous enough."

Rath looks surprised, then nods. "I understand. Thank you for letting me know."

They sail away and Farbourne waves to them from the shore.

PearlHeart passes Pica Pica the next day. Despite the cloudy skies, the inhabitants of the small island continue to cheer and laugh just as they did before. A pink cloud explodes over the tall buildings followed by a yellow one and a green one. More cheers and whistles erupt from below immediately after. One-Eye stares at the island while he is at the rail. Well-Pagu does, too. Both frown.

A week after that, One-Eye is leaning on the port rail next to Rath and the Pagu when he sees something ahead of them. His Lion peers forward, too. "Great," One-Eye says.

Rath turns to look just as William calls out, "Captain! An Amaran knight is approaching us!"

Not long afterward, Sir Ronan has boarded *PearlHeart*. His purple eyes brighten when he sees Rath waiting on the deck. "Fair Captain Rath! I had thought that I recognized this vessel as yours. Not many Pan ships bear a Delphaen flag." He sees Rath's arm bound in a sling and gasps. Taking Rath's free hand, he says, "Fair Captain, what has happened to your shoulder?"

"I dislocated it."

Ronan releases his hand and begins to dig into a white pouch at his hip. "Fear not, for I have come readily equipped for such a situation." He brandishes a white roll. "From the good, if not eloquent people of the Southern Selachuu Military Base, I have made the fine and most prudent purchase of bandages! I am currently working on the expertise to wield them."

"Th-That is all right, Sir Ronan. It has already been wrapped."

Ronan lowers his bandages. "So it has." He returns them to his pouch. "Which is a fine thing – for such things must be cared for in the most expedient fashion to prevent them from worsening. However, for next time – ” He flushes suddenly. “Er – not that I expect there to be a next time, Fair Captain, but should the situation arise once more – and I do pray that it does not – ” He puts his hands on his hips. “I shall be prepared!”

“I see. That is very prudent of you.”

“Is it not?”

One-Eye approaches them just as Sir Ronan continues, “Now, how was your journey? I have heard concerning tales of a great storm of Lady Amara’s brother and Elder God of Draconi, Most Holy Ara. I pray that you did not encounter it.”

“Ah – ”

One-Eye speaks. “Captain. We need to keep sailing.”

Ronan frowns at One-Eye over Rath’s shoulder.

Rath says, “One-Eye is right. We need to continue on.”

Ronan releases his hand with care and steps back. “I understand. Now, on any other such occasion, I would urge – no, insist that you accompany me to Unys, Fair Captain, as the matter of determining your god I can tell has still not yet been resolved.” He sighs. “Yet, Opal Starlight and I spoke for a very long evening and have decided that as my Lady has yet to return from her quest to the North and her last words given to us were to warn the good people of the South of the weather there, we must remain here. Though it pains me to see you unprotected, Fair Captain. Thus, when Lady Amara returns, I shall explain the situation to her and surely, with her guidance, it will be resolved.”

“Sir Ronan, I apologize. However, I do consider Marchand to still be my god.”

Ronan looks conflicted. “Yet ... No, I shall not delay you further. Such would not be befitting my position as a knight and least of all as my Lady’s Champion of her One Hundred.” He pauses. “Although, I would still like to hear of your journey – how your noble quest to Haliae fared. Perhaps we could correspond by letter?”

Rath blinks. “I would love that.”

Ronan beams. “Then it shall be done! I shall send you a proper inquiry as to the details of your most noble quest to deliver provisions and ink and paper to the fine, orderly people of Haliae and most eagerly await your response. It shall be delivered by the holiday, I promise you!"

"Thank you very much, Sir Ronan."

Ronan hops up onto the railing, makes an illustrious bow, then descends on his white ramp. "Fair travels, Fair Captain!" He disappears and from below, they hear, "Opal Starlight! We must procure ink and paper at once to forge a fine letter for details on *PearlHeart's* most noble quest!"

Opal Starlight snorts.

In the coming days – now a month since leaving Haliae – *PearlHeart* enters the fog around Unys. One-Eye glares at where the island must be when they pass it.

After a week, they exit it. Few signs of the storm are this far south and while cloudy, the skies above them are blue. The crew looks up at it happily. On the same day, Rath exits the door leading to below with Carlos. He is no longer wearing his sling. When he joins One-Eye and Well-Pagu on the upper deck, they are both glad to see his shoulder is healed.

They enter the mist surrounding Paradi again and later, its rainbows. While they are there, Melody and Demeter bring down two letters for Rath and Carlos – they are both from Lady Azalea.

In the last month of Fall, they arrive at Renet Island, where Captain Berkut is still the acting customs officer.

On that day, One-Eye leans against the rail and watches Rath and Berkut return from the cargo hold.

Berkut is saying, "It is truly a pleasure to see you again, Captain Rath. You are on your way home, then?"

"Yes. *PearlHeart* will undergo maintenance and repairs during the Winter before we set sail for our route in the Spring."

Berkut nods. "Then, that is the season I will look forward to."

They depart not long after and Berkut watches them go. *PearlHeart* leaves the darker skies surrounding Renet Island and joins other ships of all kinds in the Delphaen Trade Route. Several Phoenae airships are in the sky as well. They travel toward the large port in the capitol of Delphy – Priage Port. The waters become clearer the closer they are to it and the sun shines.

One-Eye is at the wheel when they arrive and the crew of *PearlHeart* ends their fifth year.

15

The crew bustles around, taking down sails and hauling them below. Rath does a final check with One-Eye and Well-Pagu. Phillip and Flower-Pagu prepare the galley plants for their journey back to Cunica, then Phillip packs his dishware and tools and Flower-Pagu tucks theirs into their little knapsack. Bucket-Pagu helps Carlos store herbs and medicine that will keep in a locked chest and pack the rest to be taken by both of them. Bucket-Pagu now has a little suitcase perfect for them and their study books.

After everyone is done, Rath and his crew gather on the deck one last time. Rath thanks them for their work that year and the crew thanks him in turn. Then sailors are going down the gangplank, hugging each other before going off to their homes on Delphy or across the ocean, for which they will board various ships to reach.

Evermore, Melody, and Demeter say goodbye on the docks. They squeeze each other's hands, then Melody and Demeter watch as Evermore joins others from his country and god to take a Ullian ship back to Ullia in the far south.

Not far from them, One-Eye talks with Oren as he waits for

his ship to Pantrog.

"Bet Vocalise would like to see you again," Oren is saying.

One-Eye grunts.

"Captain'll be in Pantrog for a bit of the Winter, too."

One-Eye's eyebrows raise in surprise. He looks over at Rath, who is currently hugging Isaac.

As they pull away, Isaac says, "So, I'll see you in a few months, Captain! My family can't wait to see you again."

"Yes. I will be there. And me neither," Rath says. "Take care, Isaac."

"You too, Captain!"

They wave to each other. One-Eye walks over to Rath just as Carlos – who was near him in the crowd with the Pagu Trio of *PearlHeart* – says, "Master Rath?"

Carlos nods ahead and Rath looks to where three people are. One-Eye sees them, too. One is an older man with short, gray hair. He is wearing a sleeveless shirt that fully shows his Delphaen tattoos from his wrists to his shoulders and up his neck. Next to him is a younger man with slightly longer brown hair and a woman with hair in a shade similar to Rath's. They all see Rath and both relief and joy spread across their faces. One-Eye watches as Rath moves through the crowd to them and the four embrace.

Carlos smiles, then notices One-Eye. He looks at him curiously for a moment, then he and the Pagu slowly make their way over to Rath and the others. With a nudge from his Spirit Lion, One-Eye follows.

Georgio, Rath's father, hugs his son tightly. "It is so good to see you and your crew safe – you're all safe, correct?"

"Ah – "

Carlos joins them. "Lord Georgio, Master Rath did sustain an injury in his right shoulder during the journey."

Georgio holds his son at arm's length. Marin, his mother, raises a hand to her mouth in concern. Georgio says, "Is it all right?"

"It is currently healing," Rath says.

The older man, Rath's grandfather, Garreth, speaks. "What happened, Carlos?"

Carlos clears his throat. "Perhaps it would be best to speak when all are seated."

Georgio says, "I would agree. You've had a long journey and perhaps an even longer one with – " He stops, looking pained. "Carlos is right – we'd best all discuss this when we've returned to your grandfather's home."

Rath replies, "Yes, Father." He sees the Pagu and One-Eye – more awkwardly to the back, but there. He smiles. "Father, Mother, Grandfather, may I introduce you to the new crew members aboard *PearlHeart?*"

Georgio says, "Absolutely."

"Thank you. This is One-Eye, our new first mate, Well-Pagu, our new navigator, Bucket-Pagu, our infirmary helper, and Flower-Pagu, our galley helper." Then to them, he says, "Everyone, this is my father, Georgio, my mother, Marin, and my grandfather, Garreth."

One-Eye, Bucket-Pagu, and Well-Pagu nod. Flower-Pagu says, "It's a pleasure to meet you!"

Garreth says, "You as well. We're all about to head to my home to eat. You're welcome without question there – just don't mind the Butej guards looking over your shoulder every other moment."

One-Eye says, "Why's that?" His Lion's ears perk up.

Garreth waves a hand dismissively. "A directive from their god, Fierce." He sizes up One-Eye. "One of Lionel's. Good for you, Rath."

Rath flushes. "Thank you, Grandfather."

Flower-Pagu says, "We would love to see your home!"

Bucket-Pagu nods. "Then, afterward, we'll fly to Pagu Island to see our friends and family."

Well-Pagu smiles. "Home."

One-Eye says, "I'll come. Then I'll search for work around the docks here on Delphy."

Garreth laughs. "That's what I like to hear." He looks at Rath and One-Eye in turn. "You're a good match. I can tell." He strides through the crowd, waving behind him. "Well, come along, then!"

Georgio calls, "Yes, Father!" As they follow, he frowns and says to Marin, "He's doing that thing again."

Marin blinks. "What, dear?"

"That he means something more than what he's saying, but I don't know what."

She pats his arm. "I'm sure he'll tell you if you ask."

"That's true."

One-Eye walks beside Rath and the Pagu fly with Carlos, who is walking beside Georgio and Marin.

They go north until they reach the city of Priage. One-Eye looks at the walkways and waterways that run through the city, people with Marchand's Traits both walking and swimming through. Arches are everywhere – as bridges and on the roofs of homes and bordering the walkways. Plants grow around them and blue-green crystals glint near the base of most buildings.

When they reach an incline, Garreth falls back beside Rath and One-Eye. "Are you going to speak with Marchand after this?" he asks Rath.

"Yes. I cannot wait to."

"I'm sure he's looking forward to your customary visit as well." He directs his next question to One-Eye. "You're staying in Delphy, then?"

"Planned on it."

"It would be the most efficient. I'd assume you came to know my grandson from Pantrog?"

One-Eye looks momentarily surprised. "Yeah."

They walk under the shade of the wide leaves above. Garreth's eyes are a deep blue-green, sharp and intelligent. "Most people from Pantha that find themselves on Pantrog were ones that had been sent to the Selachuu prisons. Piracy?"

Rath chokes a little.

One-Eye answers, narrowing his eye, "Yeah."

"Thought so." He turns to Rath. "You didn't know?"

"I do. One-Eye told me during his interview."

"Good. If you're going to be associating with this man, you should know something like that for your own safety, Rath."

"Yes, Grandfather."

Moving on, he says to One-Eye, "You'd have a yearning for better ships after that, wouldn't you?" He turns to Rath and explains, "Pantha ships don't have sails. Lionel's own rip them off the second they get their hands on one. Shame to the beautiful things."

"One-Eye has told me," Rath says, wincing.

Garreth focuses on One-Eye again. "Consider yourself lucky to have been on *PearlHeart* and with a captain like Rath."

He nods ahead. "Home is this way." He moves forward.

One-Eye looks unsettled after he does. He glances at Rath, but he seems thoughtful.

When they reach the top of the hill, Georgio, Marin, Carlos, and the Pagu are there. Georgio calls, "Father, pause for just a moment!"

"You've been sitting up in Phoenae for too long! Come on, son," Garreth says, already halfway down.

"Yes, Father."

As they follow him, One-Eye turns to Rath, who still looks like he is thinking. "What is it?"

Rath starts. "May I ask why they do so? Ah, 'rip' the sails off?"

One-Eye crosses his arms. "Because it's a show of strength. They don't like sails moving the ship for them. They prefer oars."

"I see."

"Vocalise's ships are better. *PearlHeart* is. Your grandfather was right. I wanted to sail a ship like yours even back in Pantha."

"I am glad that you are able to do so."

One-Eye nods. He hesitates. "The piracy doesn't bother you? Me, that is."

Rath looks surprised. He thinks, then says, "No. It does not. I cannot say that I understand why you did so, however, I am not you."

"Money. Didn't enjoy it. Also – " His expression tightens. His Lion looks up at him, but he says nothing more.

They reach the bottom of the hill. A wide path leads up to a tall mansion where Butej guards stand on every terrace, landing, and corner.

"That's where you live?" One-Eye asks.

"For a time when I was younger, yes. Not anymore."

"Because you became a captain?"

Rath pauses. He shakes his head. "No. It was before that." He looks at the mansion. "Before I lost my traits ten years ago, I was to succeed my father as Councilman of Delphy. It is what I trained for most of my life."

"Sven told me that's how you two met."

Rath smiles. "Yes. He is a very good friend of mine." He continues, "The Elder God of Phoenae, Merp, told me I was not fit to be a councilman due to my mixed blood and my traits from Marchand being weak. He did not believe it was appropriate for me to live in a house given to the one who would become a councilman."

One-Eye's Lion looks up at both of them. "Then where did you go?"

"My grandmother's island. She and Carlos raised me. Grandfather chose to stay here and my father is in Phoenae three-quarters of the year. My mother – "

Garreth calls out, "Rath, One-Eye, up here!"

"Yes, Grandfather!" Rath says.

They go up the stairs, passing each Butej guard as they do.

When they arrive, Garreth takes the handles on the front doors. "It's big," he says, "but I don't use a lot of it. It's just me here most of the time, after all. Minus the guards, but they don't talk much."

He opens the doors.

Inside, there is a large foyer with many waterways running through it, supplied by waterfalls that cascade down either side of the two staircases in front of them. The sound of water is everywhere. Blue-green crystals – Delphaen crystals – are set where sconces would be, dimly glowing.

Garreth looks unimpressed as he walks in. "Merp said he had it designed with traditional Delphaen architecture from hundreds of years ago in mind. Marchand tells me that his architecture has improved since then. I agree." He walks up to a bowl of water spilling over its edge and sends a Delphaen message. Almost immediately, he receives a reply. "Food is ready to be served. We'll eat and talk in the small dining room."

"Thank you, Father," Georgio says.

They follow Garreth through the right hallway into a room with tall, arched windows that look out onto the sea. Rath and One-Eye turn toward them, but One-Eye frowns when his gaze meets with the silent Butej guards.

Garreth holds the door open to the next room for them all. One-Eye goes in last and Garreth says to him, with a nod to the guards, "Just don't say anything around them you don't want them to know. They'll remember anything. It's why I prefer to communicate with Marchand's Traits if possible. Yet" – he turns to where Rath is talking happily with his family and a sad look crosses his face – "we'll have to speak normally. Not just for you, but for my grandson."

"I know."

Garreth looks surprised for once. Then he nods as if this confirmed something. "Good." He enters and One-Eye follows.

Inside, the table is already set. Butej guards stand by every window.

They sit down and begin to eat. Garreth says to One-Eye, "Traditional Delphaen food – not much variety, I'm afraid. Merp won't allow much else." He takes a bite. "You ever been on a Phoenae airship?"

"No."

"They're situated the same – same traditional menu, segregated seating, segregated rooms ... "

Georgio looks pained. "Father."

Garreth jerks his head toward the guards. "They can say whatever I do back to Merp. He knows well how I feel. It isn't going to change what he does about it."

One-Eye asks, "Why is it segregated?"

"Because he doesn't like mixing cultures, that's why."

Beside him, Rath lowers his eyes. His mother, too, is quiet.

After they all finish, Rath says, "Thank you very much for the food, Grandfather. It was wonderful."

Garreth smiles a little. "With you saying it, I believe it." He stands up. "We'll go to the sitting room. The one room we can be in peace."

Inside, no Butej guards line the walls and One-Eye relaxes. Garreth sits in a chair and sighs. "All right. Now, we can talk. Mostly. I learned long ago they listen at the walls."

After they all sit, Garreth fixes One-Eye and the Pagu with a level look. "I hope you know that despite all this, you are welcome here. It's still my home, no matter what others insist must reside in it."

One-Eye nods.

Flower-Pagu says, "That's all right! We've really enjoyed it here so far."

Garreth's expression softens. "Really? I'm glad." He sits back. "Now, Rath. Your journey? Then Georgio has some news to share with you as well that you may or may not know about already."

Rath says, "Of course, Grandfather. We began this year sailing to Lotinx for Elvin's ink and paper."

As his grandson speaks happily about his journey on *PearlHeart,* a change comes over Rath's grandfather's face. The harsh lines around his forehead and eyes ease into something more like what came from smiling and laughing and he settles back into his chair as if it is comfortable, not as rigid as when he first sat down.

"Then, we arrived on Cunica to pick up the plants that Grandmother ordered."

Garreth's eyes flicker with sadness. "Curious how she chose Cunica this year." He laughs a little to cover a brush at his eye with his knuckle. "I'm sure it has some deep meaning she hasn't told anyone yet." He moves on, "How was Cunica? I recall it being very beautiful at that time of year."

"It was. The fields were all an amazing color that I had not seen before."

Garreth relaxes even more. "I'm sure you enjoyed it," he says softly.

Rath goes on, speaking about traveling west through the Delphaen Trade Route and entering the open ocean beyond it. "It was when we were traveling to grandmother's island that Fenrir and I received your Phoenae message, Father, and Fenrir needed to leave."

Georgio nods. Marin holds his hand.

Garreth exhales. "My Spirit Dolphin informed me about Fevrier." Then he asks, "Did Azalea like the plants?"

"Yes." He suddenly looks at his parents. "Do you ... "

Georgio pats his wife's hand. "We know about the South Garden. Azalea sent us both a letter. And Marin ... "

Rath's mother's eyes are sparkling. "I saw it. It was absolutely beautiful. The plants that you brought there with your crew, are wonderful, Rath." She leans back, reaching for something by her chair. "I had to paint it. Garreth, would you like to see?"

Garreth leans over, reaching out. "Please."

She holds it out to him and he takes the frame delicately. He says nothing as he smiles at the painting of four Mehrin plants and one Pantha Flower. He hands it back to Marin, mouthing, *"Thank you."*

She smiles. After showing Rath, One-Eye, and the Pagu –

they are all amazed – she carefully sets it down.

Garreth takes a deep breath. "South Garden ... Hmm. Has she or Carlos ever gotten around to teaching you Sudines philosophy, Rath? It is part of your heritage as well."

Rath shakes his head. "No, they have not." He thinks. "Grandmother says she believes that she and Carlos are not the ones to teach me."

Garreth frowns. He looks at Carlos. "I'm not getting anything out of you, am I?"

Carlos lifts his hands. "I have no answer to give."

"Well, if Azalea says it'll happen – it will. Keep your ears open for it," he tells his grandson.

"I will, Grandfather."

Rath continues on, talking about their time on Lady Azalea's Island and the Pagu. Garreth does not say anything while he speaks of them, but at the end, he says. "Navigator. Perfect." He does not elaborate.

They are all quiet as Rath tells them about the windstorm and Hep meeting them. Georgio in particular looks distant.

Then Rath explains how he met One-Eye on Pantrog. His parents' eyes widen at his encounter with the people from Pantha, but Garreth says, "Of course they're excited! It's been too long since Pantha had a royal. Did Mars and the others have their ailments cured?"

Rath turns to Carlos, who nods. "Yes, they were primarily minor, barring Mars with the broken leg."

Marin says, "The poor dear. I hope he fully recovered."

"Then you hired this young man," he says, looking at One-Eye. He smiles and says nothing more.

Rath tells them about how he met Vocalise and saw Belle again, then their journey to Cunica. Garreth asks, "And how is Phillip's nan. Pelline, doing?"

"She is well. She and her neighbor, Vern, brought provisions for *PearlHeart* and Haliae. Like Hep, they believed that the earlier windstorm would herald an early Winter."

Garreth's smile fades. "Right. That." He exchanges a look with Georgio. "We'll get to that later on. Now, did you have that picnic again?"

"Yes. It was wonderful."

Garreth settles back as Rath talks about getting One-Eye's

paperwork approved on Renet Island with Captain Berkut. Marin looks surprised when he tells them Oracle brought their delivery from Paradi. Rath continues with them meeting Sir Ronan and Opal Starlight on the ocean and later Captain Farbourne at the Southern Selachuu Military Base.

Garreth asks, "Were the people of Pica Pica still partying?"

Rath blinks. "I believe so."

He nods as if it was a philosophical question.

"We sailed north afterward, then – " Rath stops suddenly and turns to One-Eye, who had been busy listening. Rath flushes. "I apologize. It occurs to me that we crossed the Isles of Oct at that time, but we did not see them."

One-Eye thinks back. "Sounds right to me."

Garreth glances up at the mention of Oct, but Rath's parents look bewildered. Georgio says, "The Isles of Oct? I'm not sure if I've heard of a place."

Before Rath can, Garreth answers, "Because it doesn't exist. In a way." He looks to Rath to continue.

"We sailed north and just before we arrived on Haliae, *PearlHeart* was struck with Ara's Storm."

His parents lean forward. Marin asks, "Was everyone all right?"

Georgio says, "Was that where your shoulder was injured?"

"Yes – and, ah, Carlos tells me that many in the crew had bruises. He says that One-Eye was saved from a concussion due to Sevran and Lionel's Traits."

Garreth gives a nod as if he suspected this.

Georgio asks, "What happened? Did you stay where you were?"

"I cannot say. I flew over the stern railing. One-Eye caught me. I believe that is when I dislocated my shoulder."

Garreth gives a huffed sort of laugh, but his eyes are fragile. "Better that than falling off entirely."

"I did. My hand slipped out of my glove."

Garreth's eyes flame. He turns them on One-Eye.

"I apologize. I do not remember much of what happened until I awoke on the Isles of Oct with Berceuse, River-Pagu, and Feather-Pagu."

Georgio breathes a sigh of relief. "The Pagu were with you. Good." He asks his father, "Do you know someone called

Berceuse?"

"Marchand's brother." Georgio looks startled. Garreth continues speaking, returning his eyes to One-Eye. "Fill in the blanks. What happened?"

One-Eye frowns back at him. "We were dismasted. My Spirit Lion threw me out of the way before the mizzenmast broke a third of the stern railing. I was unconscious. I woke up and we were somewhere different – out of the storm, south of it. Well-Pagu told us the Captain was further south, so that's where we went once repairs were done. We found him on the Isles of Oct with Berceuse, the God of Oct, and the Pagu that live there." He hesitates, then says to Rath, "You weren't coherent until Carlos reset your shoulder. I don't know what happened before that."

Rath thinks. "Berceuse mended my clothes. My arm was bound." He blinks. "I believe we all ate Together Fruit. It was very good. Then, River-Pagu gave me medicine and I rested until you and Carlos arrived." He winces. "I do not remember a great deal of my shoulder being reset except pain and you holding me."

Carlos carefully watches the expressions in the room. Rath's parents' eyebrows go up and Garreth's eyes narrow. He says to One-Eye, "You were there for him."

One-Eye, now a deep red, says, "Yeah."

Garreth's expression loosens and he falls silent, thinking.

Rath says, "I remained on the Isles of Oct for the rest of the week in order to recover. Carlos stayed with Berceuse, the Pagu, and I while One-Eye visited us from *PearlHeart*. Well-Pagu, Bucket-Pagu, and Flower-Pagu also came on the second day."

The Pagu smile up at him. They are seated on little cushions on the table in the middle of everyone. "We did!" Flower-Pagu says.

"We wanted to make sure you were okay," Bucket-Pagu says.

"Concerned," Well-Pagu says.

Rath frowns. "I apologize. I appreciate you doing so."

Georgio speaks. "Then – I hate to ask – did you make it to Haliae?"

His son surprises him by saying, "Yes."

Garreth grins and a youthful liveliness comes to his face. "Berceuse," he says. "You got that old god to leave his Isles?"

Rath flushes, raising his hands. "Ah – Berceuse offered to protect us with his barrier as we traveled north to Haliae. He dearly wished to see his brother Elvin, he told me, and make sure he and his people were all right."

"I see." Garreth barks out a laugh. "Could convince a dragon out of his home. 'Course, more proof of that is right beside him."

Rath seems confused. "I-I'm sorry?"

One-Eye glares at Garreth.

Garreth spreads his hands. "Although, Pantha or Pantrog aren't places that would take much convincing to leave for someone like you, would they, One-Eye?" One-Eye doesn't answer that and Garreth turns back to Rath. "Sorry, Grandson. Continue. Don't mind me."

"It is all right, Grandfather." Rath continues, "With Berceuse's help, we arrived on Haliae. One-Eye and Evermore found Sven, Pema, and everyone else inside of Elvin's Peak and everyone in the crew helped to deliver the ink and paper and extra provisions under their direction. I am very grateful for everyone's help. Elvin spoke with Berceuse on *PearlHeart* and I spoke with Sven and Pema, who arrived as well. Elvin then told me that it would be best if we sailed south as soon as possible. We did." He goes over their return journey with Berceuse's departure, Captain Farbourne, Sir Ronan, and Opal Starlight.

"Sir Ronan said that he would be sending me a letter," he says and One-Eye frowns next to him.

Then he tells them about Unys, Paradi, Captain Berkut, and finally – home.

Afterward, they all are quiet for a long moment. Then Marin says, "How is your shoulder, Rath? Carlos said that it is healing?"

"Yes. It is much better now."

Garreth studies his grandson. "I'm glad you had your crew with you. The gods and the Pagu, too. You handled yourself well in that situation."

"I am glad as well. And, thank you, Grandfather."

Garreth smiles for a moment. Then he grows serious again

and sighs as he turns to his son. "Georgio, you should inform him of what you heard in Phoenae during the Council."

"Yes, Father." Georgio pauses to gather his thoughts. "Rath, Councilman Hailcorn of Haliae informed me before the Council ended that, due to Ara's Storm on Haliae, he and Fritz are unable to return there by Phoenae airship."

Rath's eyes fall. "I see."

"There isn't any way to get messages to Haliae right now – the Paradi Message System has been unable to access many regions in the North due to the storm and the Selachuu Military is having to rely on either Selachuu ships or Spirit Sharks for theirs." He relaxes. "Thanks to you and your crew, I can tell Hailcorn that the people on Haliae will be all right. He's on Pica Pica right now, ready to go to Haliae the moment the Selachuu Military clears the area for travel. I can send a Delphaen message informing him about the state of Haliae from what you've told me."

"Thank you, Father."

They go outside to the beach behind Garreth's home. Georgio walks up to the ocean and rolls up his sleeve. His Delphaen tattoos extend all the way to his shoulder. They watch as he concentrates, closing his eyes, and his tattoos begin to glow a warm blue-green. The light travels down his arm and into the ocean, where it shoots away toward the east. He shakes out his hand as he stands. "It'll need to go through Paradi, where the Delphaen Relay will carry it forward to Pica Pica."

Rath says, "Thank you again, Father."

Garreth clears his throat. "Will you be off to Azalea's now?"

Georgio says, "We'd best."

Marin says, "It was wonderful to see you again, Garreth."

"And you, too, Marin. You as well, Carlos." Then to the Pagu and One-Eye, "Good meeting you all."

One-Eye nods. Flower-Pagu says, "You, too, Garreth!"

Bucket-Pagu says, "Thank you for the food."

Well-Pagu says, "Good."

Garreth's eyebrows raise, then he laughs. "Really? Well, I'm glad." He turns to Rath last and gives him a strong hug. "Take care – of your shoulder and the rest of you."

"I will, Grandfather." As they pull away, Rath says, "I truly enjoyed seeing you. I hope you have a wonderful Winter."

"Thank you, Rath."

As Garreth walks back to the house, where Butej guards stand on watch, the others move further down the beach to where two Delphaen ships are – a medium-sized one and a smaller one.

The Pagu see them. Well-Pagu frowns, looking up at Rath. "Delphaen?"

"Yes," Rath says. "I cannot use them underwater, however, Marchand made modifications to them two hundred years ago to allow everyone to be able to use them – above water or below."

"Appropriate."

"Mother and Father will use the medium-sized one to sail to Grandmother's and I will use the smaller of the two to sail to Marchand's Bay, then to Grandmother's as well."

Flower-Pagu says, "We'll be flying to Pagu Island now! To see our friends!"

"That sounds wonderful. I hope you have a safe journey."

"You, too, Captain!" Flower-Pagu and Bucket-Pagu say and Well-Pagu says, "Too!"

They wave to everyone, then start flying west.

Georgio asks, "Where will you go, One-Eye?"

"Anywhere I can find work."

Georgio thinks. "Leighran Port – try there. They're always looking for customs officers over the Winter. It's on the western coast."

"Thanks. I will."

Marin says, "You could go to Priage Port and rent a small ship if you would like. It would be faster than walking."

One-Eye shakes his head. "No, I'd prefer going on land." He ruffles his Spirit Lion's mane. "Want to see Delphy more."

Marin smiles. "I understand."

Georgio, Marin, and Carlos set out, heading west to Lady Azalea's Island.

After they wave to them, Rath says to One-Eye, "I hope you are able to find work at Leighran Port and that your journey there goes well."

"Thanks. You too. Where will you be most of the Winter?"

"My grandmother's island – ah, Lady Azalea's Island. It is

further to the west."

One-Eye hesitates. "I'll … send you a letter."

Rath's eyes widen. "That would … ah, that is, I would … " He flushes deeply. "I apologize. I would greatly appreciate that, One-Eye."

Seeing his reaction, One-Eye turns red as well. "Sure."

"May I – that is, would you like to sail with me until Marchand's Bay?" Rath stops. "Although, it now occurs to me that you said you would prefer to go by land. I sincerely apologize."

"It's fine. I'd like to go with you." One-Eye glances back at the Butej guards. "I'd rather get off your grandfather's land, then travel on my own. Thanks."

"Of course."

Rath unties the mooring lines of his ship, then offers One-Eye a hand. One-Eye takes it and the ship tips as they both balance themselves on it. While One-Eye sits by the tiller, Rath lowers the triangular sail.

"Do you want me to handle this?" One-Eye asks, gesturing to the tiller.

Rath turns, looking surprised for a moment. He smiles. "Yes, please. Thank you." He sets the sail. "I normally have it set in the direction I am going. We will sail far easier with you here." The Spirit Lion grins at One-Eye as he reddens again. Rath does not see as he grips the line secured to the sail and they both watch it begin to fill. They move away from the shore, going east.

As One-Eye watches the coast go at a faster pace, he asks, "What were you saying earlier? When we got to Garreth's house." Rath glances back. "About your mother."

Rath winces. "My mother was not allowed to be at my grandfather's home either. Merp disapproved of Father's marriage to her."

"That's ridiculous."

"For a long time, it was illegal for members of the Council to marry outside of the country they represented. My grandfather changed this so that he could marry my grandmother, who is from Sudines. He changed it again so that Father could marry Mother." He angles the sail and One-Eye follows the direction, matching it with the tiller. "Grandfather tells me that when

Merp approves proposals, he often asks for an addendum." One-Eye frowns and his Lion sneezes. "His addendum to the first change was that both people had to be full-blooded. My mother is not, so Grandfather worked to change the law again so that people in the Council could marry whoever they wished to regardless of their heritage." He exhales. "I am very grateful for it."

One-Eye nods. "You had mentioned before that Merp thought your traits from Marchand were too weak?" Rath winces again and One-Eye immediately regrets saying it. "Why would that matter?"

"Councilpeople and their respective god guide others in the use of their traits. Those in the Council often carry far stronger ones than others. Marchand tells me this is due to many families – including my own – being descended from their god's First – the first human he gave his traits to in the previous world. Grandfather believed if he could train me – his traits are very strong – that Merp would see that I was capable of being a councilman. However, I could not send Delphaen messages very far, so Father asked if I might send letters instead. Merp said I could not. I have knowledge of the capabilities of people with Marchand's Traits, but not the ability to do so." He is quiet for a time, thinking. One-Eye is, too.

Suddenly, Rath says, "I apologize. May I ask if that answered your original question?"

"Yeah. It did." One-Eye looks at the ocean around them. "So, you'll never join the Council?"

"No. It is unlikely."

"Did you want to?"

"Yes, I did. My father explained to me from an early age what I would be doing – helping people and collaborating with other countries. I thought it sounded very exciting." He shakes his head. "I accept that it is now not what I am doing and that I have found something very dear to me – sailing with everyone on *PearlHeart* and helping people by carrying deliveries or offering passage to them. And ... " He glances back at One-Eye. "When you said that you wanted to go everywhere – when we were on Pantrog – I wish for that, too."

In response, One-Eye smiles and Rath returns it happily. The Lion grins at them both, his mane blowing in the wind.

They travel further until they sail beneath the long leaves of Delphaen trees. When One-Eye looks up, he sees that Rath's eyes aren't blue-green like his grandfather's, but a bright green, like the leaves up above.

Rath says, "Here is Marchand's Bay." He adjusts the sail and they slow as they come to a gap in the coast. One-Eye guides them using the tiller into a large waterway which leads to a private beach. A man sits there, appearing to be contemplating something. He has long gray hair that is blue-green at the tips.

One-Eye says, "Could you stop at that shore?" He points to the beach in front of them.

"Of course."

While Rath ties the boat to a small wooden stump, One-Eye says, "Thanks."

"You are very welcome. I hope that you have a wonderful Winter and that you are able to get a job at Leighran Port. I, ah, look forward to seeing you in the Spring."

"You too."

He waves and Rath waves back. With one last look in the god's direction, One-Eye goes up the beach, then onto a path leading back to Priage Port, his Spirit Lion beside him. Rath watches him disappear, then turns and walks alongside the waterway to Marchand, the God of Delphy.

16

Within ten minutes, Rath has reached Marchand.

His god sits cross-legged, thinking. Rath waits politely until he turns and his blue-green eyes brighten at the sight of his own. "Rath!" He wastes no time in getting up, his long hair dragging but somehow never catching on anything. He gives Rath a warm hug. "It is so good to see you safe."

"You as well, Marchand."

They sit together in the sand, Marchand sitting cross-legged again and Rath on his knees.

Marchand says, "I was concerned when I heard about Ara's Storm in the North, but then I saw *PearlHeart* sail into Priage Port and knew that everything was all right. How are you? How was your journey? I want to hear all about it."

Rath laughs, greatly at ease around his god. "I am well. And it was good. I would love to tell you about it, Marchand."

His god beams and settles back, relaxed, as he begins to listen.

When Rath finishes, Marchand is sitting upright, eyes wide and his mouth slightly open. He stands up and paces. "You – " He sits down abruptly. "But, you're all right?"

"Yes, Marchand."

He stands up and paces again. "Berceuse, my brother ... Ara ... Haliae." He turns back to Rath. "But, you have three Pagu aboard *PearlHeart* now?"

"We do."

"That is good." Marchand pauses as if assessing whether or not it is. He throws his hair back behind him and sits. "I'm glad you and your crew are safe. I'm not ... " He sighs. "Ara should have been more aware of what he was doing." He shakes his head. "I've been thinking about Haliae since you arrived. It sounds like whatever Berceuse told Elvin means that this is one of Ara's more dangerous storms. Georgio also came here when he returned from the Council to tell me that Hailcorn and Fritz are currently on Pica Pica. They can't even spend a proper holiday on their own island, much less see Sven and Pema or the rest of their people."

"Unfortunately, there isn't anything we can do except wait it out and hope that it ends soon." He frowns. "Did the Pagu say anything about the storm while you were on Haliae?"

"I do not believe so."

Marchand nods, considering. Then he remembers something. "You said that Berceuse told you he was going to visit his siblings and then the Pagu?" Rath nods. Marchand looks a little put-out. "He didn't visit me." He rubs his chin. "He probably went to Pagu Island first. I'd like to visit him, but the Pagu have rules about their island. Has your grandmother told you?"

"Yes. It is considered a Holy Site of theirs. Others are only allowed with permission."

"Exactly. With his connection to the Pagu, I'm sure Berceuse will be welcome even without letting them know ahead of time. The Pagu that left his Isles may have even gained it for him, knowing he'd likely go there. But, me ... " He pats his knee, looking determined. "Well, maybe I can catch him before he gets there. There's still time before the Delphaen Celebration and I'd really like to see him. What do you think, Rath?"

"I think it would be very good if you did."

"Then I'll do it." Marchand reaches over and takes Rath's shoulder. He looks at it for a moment, then focuses on Rath. "I always enjoy you coming here to tell me about your journeys. I hope you'll continue to do so every year."

"Of course." Rath blinks rapidly. "That is – I would truly enjoy that."

Marchand holds his shoulder for a moment longer, then stands. He offers Rath a hand. "Where are you off to now, Captain?"

"Grandmother's."

"Then, I'll set off with you. Pagu Island is in the same direction, after all. Would you mind if I swam next to you for a time?"

Rath beams. "Not at all."

They walk down the path together toward Rath's ship. Rath unties it and sets the sail. Next to him, Marchand leaps into the water. He glows midway through, enters the water with a splash, and rises as a dolphin. "Are you ready?"

"Yes, Marchand!"

They swim and sail together – west – toward Pagu Island and Lady Azalea's Island.

While they do, other members of *PearlHeart* are making their own way home. Franz, Velt, and Perri travel on a Delphaen ship together in the waterways of Delphy. They are able to breathe underwater due to of Marchand's Traits. Their Delphaen tattoos glow as they talk excitedly.

Days later, Isaac and Oren arrive on Pantrog. They wave to each other, then Oren disappears into the crowd and Isaac goes to his house. When he reaches it, his little sister Sophia tackles him and he grins.

By the end of the week, Charles and Phillip are in Cunica. They walk together for a few days, then go separate ways to their homes.

The following week, William, Phobos, Melody, Demeter, Felix, and Triphonius arrive on Paradi. Oracle comes to greet them and they all collide in a group hug.

Nearing the end of the month, Evermore steps off of his ship onto the desolate land of Ullia, a set of six islets arranged in a ring. He and others walk toward to a small, raised hill in the ground with a door in it that leads to the real country underground. A man in a hood and long pale blond hair like Evermore's stands there. He tells them, "Erole is away. In Phoenae. You'll wait until he returns."

They all nod. Evermore frowns.

Further northwest, Well-Pagu, Bucket-Pagu, and Flower-Pagu fly to Pagu Island. They smile, looking forward to seeing their friends and family again.

North of Delphy, as the sun starts to dip, Rath stops for the night. Marchand is still with him in his dolphin form. As Rath lies down in his ship, Marchand speaks to him from the water. "I hope you sleep well, Rath."

"Thank you. You as well, Marchand." Under the starry night sky, Rath falls asleep.

Marchand smiles, then very seriously looks at his own. He closes his eyes, sleeping near Rath.

Under the same night sky, Berceuse lies on Pagu Island with his dear ones.

Berceuse is saying, " ... and I told my Captain that I would tell him my story and show him my constellation."

"That's wonderful, Berceuse!" Leaf-Pagu says, kicking their feet in the air beside him.

"Isn't it?" Berceuse looks up at the stars. "I hope he will be with his family soon – and resting!"

"Us too!"

The following morning, a giant hawk – Fierce, the God of Butej – flies over the Southern Seas. He keeps a keen eye on the different countries below him as he flies. He travels west over Cunica, scanning the farms and fields. The first snowfall has begun to cover the land. He looks north across the Delphaen Trade Route. There, it still appears to be Summer, but a cool breeze flows over Delphy's waterways and walkways. Satisfied, the hawk moves on.

It is when he is soaring over Pantrog that he suddenly hears, "Hey! Fierce!"

The hawk banks immediately and descends. He steps down onto a roof as a young man with brown hair tied up with a brown-red ribbon and a short cloak, the uniform of the Butej Guard. "What is it? Have you seen Feint's own in the area?"

Vocalise, who had called out to him, scrubs the air with his hand. "No, no – nothing like that. Wanted to hear if you heard the news." Fierce looks alert and Vocalise quickly continues, "Berceuse is back. He's here in the South."

Fierce's shoulders loosen. "I know. I saw him swimming here weeks ago."

"You did? So, you've already talked with him?"

Fierce stiffens. "No. I saw no reason to."

Vocalise frowns. They walk along the rooftops. "I'm gonna try to see him. I bet he's going to Pagu Island."

"That did seem to be his trajectory." Fierce glances at his brother. "However, I would hope that I do not need to tell you that we cannot visit there without the Pagu's permission."

"I know, I know. That's why I'm going to try to catch him before he reaches there." He rests a foot on the steeple. "Aren't you wondering how he is?"

"If he was swimming and currently with the Pagu, he is fine."

"Naw, I mean – do you want to see him?"

Fierce considers. "No. I am very busy right now."

"Yeah, with the people from Corxae." Vocalise looks south, toward the Selachuu cliffs. Beyond them is the small island of Corxae, where Feint – the God of Corxae – and his own live. "They haven't done anything for years. I don't think they ever did anything."

"Then you would be incorrect, Vocalise." Fierce adjusts his cloak. "I have to return to my survey. Was there anything more you needed?"

"Just wanted to see how you were doing."

Fierce blinks, caught off-guard. "I am fine. You are right, I have not seen any of Feint's outside of Corxae for years." He frowns. "However, that does not ensure it will not happen again." Then he is off in his hawk form, flying away. Vocalise watches him and shakes his head.

On Paradi, Oracle is listening to Melody and Demeter tell her about what happened while they were on *PearlHeart.* The goddess' eyes widen. "Berceuse? Really?"

Melody says, "Yes. He seemed very kind." As Oracle ponders this, Melody sighs. "I hope Evermore made it back to Ullia safely."

Oracle squeezes her hands. "I am sure he did, my dear." She hesitates, then says instead, "Berceuse is likely going to Pagu Island. Maybe I can find him before he does. It has been far too long since we've seen each other. Perhaps I can encourage my other siblings to come with me to find him. Ohh, it would be wonderful to have everyone together again."

Melody smiles and Demeter gives a "Caw!" in agreement.

At the same time, near Delphy, Rath and Marchand part ways. Marchand, in his human form, hugs Rath on his small Delphaen ship. "You have a safe journey the rest of the way."

"I will. Thank you very much for traveling with me. I greatly enjoyed it."

"I did, too." Marchand nods to the island of Campi, which is to the northwest of Delphy. "I thought I would stop by Campi to see if my sister Penelope, your mother's goddess, would like to see Berceuse, too."

"That is a great idea!"

Marchand smiles at his reaction. "I'm hoping she'll come. She can be reluctant to leave her island, as you might know." He nods once more to Rath. "Take care."

"You as well, Marchand."

They wave to each other and Marchand leaps off the ship. While he swims north in his dolphin form, Rath continues east to his grandmother's island.

A week later, Marchand is swimming when he suddenly hears a shout. "Hey! Marchand!" He turns back and sees Vocalise, in his giant chimpanzee form, lands on a rock sticking out of the ocean.

"Vocalise! What are you doing here?"

"Trying to find Berceuse before he reaches Pagu Island."

Marchand laughs. "I'm doing the same. Actually, I was going to see if Penelope wanted to join. Want to come with?"

"Sure."

Marchand swims and Vocalise makes great leaps from rock to rock, both on their way to Campi.

While they do, Oracle flies west. She passes Renet Island and is continuing over Cunica when she sees two white rabbit ears stick up out of the snow. She lands. "Rella! This is a surprise."

The two ears move up to reveal a white rabbit. It glows and turns into a short young woman with brown hair. "I wasn't sure if you would light down," Rella, the Goddess of Cunica, says.

Oracle ruffles her feathers. "It is rather cold. What are you doing out here?"

"I wish to see Berceuse. I've heard he's traveling to Pagu Island. Would you take me to him?"

Oracle's eyes shimmer hundreds of colors. "Well!" She dips her head. "You need only ask, my dear."

"Thank you, Sister." Rella climbs on.

Oracle pumps her wings and lifts off, her rainbow sparkles intermingling with the shimmering snow. "How was your Harvest?"

"Pleasant. It yielded much." Rella chews on a nail, looking north. "Ara is causing a severe Winter."

"That is what I hear as well. Have you heard of Haliae?"

"Of course. It will pass. The Seasons change. They always do."

"Do you think it will interrupt your holiday on Cunica?"

"No. We will adapt. I am sure Elvin is doing the same."

Oracle rises higher. "My Councilwoman, Isis and her bird partner Mica, tell me that Councilman Hailcorn and his eagle partner Fritz were unable to travel home to Haliae this Winter."

"That is unfortunate."

"I am hoping that he can make it back to Haliae for the holiday at least."

Rella nods, thinking.

"He's on Pica Pica now," Oracle continues.

"What? They are noisy."

"I think they are bright and festive!"

"Vocalise gives them his extra decorations every year. Even so, they use all of them and more every month for their celebrations. It is wasteful." She frowns. "And noisy."

"We all spend our holidays in our own way, dear sister."

"Very true."

They continue on.

North of them, Marchand and Vocalise have reached Campi. It is a small, low island with a large lagoon that opens up to the ocean. The water in the lagoon is fresh water, made so by Penelope's Holy Site, which is beneath it. While Marchand swims in the inland waterway, Vocalise hops onto the beach, turns into his human form, and walks alongside. They travel past small huts, laundry lines with brightly embroidered fabrics, and people quietly painting.

When they reach the lagoon, they find a group of people in the water with a tiny seahorse speaking to them. "Now, kick your legs! There, that's right! It's hard, but we can all do it together if we try!"

"Yes, Penelope!" the new swimmers call back.

Penelope, the Goddess of Campi, now in her seahorse form, notices Vocalise and Marchand. "Oh dear, oh dear – my brothers are here! Did I forget a date? I am always forgetting one."

Marchand lifts himself out of the water in his human form. "No, no." He grins as his brother sits down next to him. "Vocalise and I thought we'd ask if you'd like to see Berceuse. He's likely traveling to Pagu Island right now."

"Berceuse! Oh my!" The seahorse turns to the swimmers. "Everyone, we will take a break! Please relax and come out of the water if you need. The safety lines are there for everyone!"

"Yes, Penelope!"

As they do, Penelope swims closer to her brothers. "Berceuse," she repeats. "He's really here?"

"That's what Rath says," Marchand says.

Vocalise adds, "Isaac and Oren told me."

Penelope does a nervous turn. "Oh dear! But ... what if we don't find him? Or what if he's already on Pagu Island? It would be so disrespectful to go there without permission ... "

"That's why we're planning to see if we can find him before he gets there. Vocalise and I can help you travel so you don't have to swim," Marchand says encouragingly.

Penelope does another turn. "I don't know ... What if he came here?"

Vocalise stretches his feet out. "He could. But it might be nice for you to get out, Sis."

"I know, I know, but ... well ... " She droops. "I just don't know."

Marchand holds up his hand. "That's all right. We just wanted to let you know. We can tell him that you'd like to see him."

Penelope perks up. "Oh! That would be ... Well, that would be wonderful. Thank you so much, Marchand." She swims around. "I wonder if he's done any more sewing. Of course he has. I'm sure the Pagu clothes he's made are beautiful." To her brothers, she says, "Do you think he'll stay this time?"

"I can't say."

Penelope looks worried for a moment, then determined. "I ... I will think about it! Leaving Campi to find him, I mean. He'll have to leave Pagu Island eventually, right? I could watch for him from here."

"I would think so. It's still the Pagu's Holy Site, even though he has a strong bond with them. I think it would be great if you saw him."

"M-Me too!"

As they get ready to leave, Vocalise says, "Take care, Lil' Sis!"

"You too, Vocalise, Marchand!" Penelope watches them go. She sighs.

Marchand and Vocalise travel for three days. As they grow closer to Pagu Island, they hear a bright bird call in the sky above. Marchand looks up. "Oracle! Is that Rella with you?"

Oracle glides lower. "Yes! Are you trying to find Berceuse as well?"

Vocalise leaps off another rock. "Thought we might!"

Rella says from Oracle's back, "We are not unique."

"I don't think that's a bad thing," she replies, eyes sparkling. They continue on together.

At the same time, Well-Pagu, Bucket-Pagu, and Flower-Pagu have arrived on Pagu Island. Flower-Pagu says, "We're here, everyone!"

They reunite with their friends and family, all of them saying, "How was your journey?" and "You went so far!" and "There was such a terrible storm."

Berceuse, who had arrived earlier, says, "It is so good to see you again, my dear ones!"

Flower-Pagu says, "You, too, Berceuse!"

Bucket-Pagu says, "It was a long journey. But, a really good journey, too!'

Well-Pagu is glowing with happiness. "Loved."

The Pagu ask, "Can we hear about it?"

And the Pagu Trio of *PearlHeart* say, "Yes!"

When they finish their story – all clap happily, having thoroughly enjoyed it – Well-Pagu asks Berceuse, "Family?"

Berceuse jumps. "Ah, have I seen my family yet?"

Well-Pagu nods. "Visit."

Berceuse toys with his hair uncomfortably. "Well, I thought I would come here first, then ... " He sighs. "You're right. I've completely avoided them. I even swam past several of their countries." He grows thoughtful. "This world is so different from the previous. And beautiful. It only now occurs to me I am seeing it for the first time." He suddenly stands up. "A-All right. I deeply appreciate you allowing me to stay here. However, I think now it may be best that I ... " He looks at all of the Pagu. " ... leave."

The Pagu say, "We loved having you here!" and "You can do it, Berceuse!" and "They'll be so happy to see you!"

"I-I certainly hope so."

Berceuse makes his way to the beach and the Pagu go with him to see him off. He takes a very deep breath, steps toward the ocean, and wades in. Then he turns into his octopus form and swims a little way out. He looks back, raises a tentacle in a wave – the Pagu all wave back, cheering him on – then, feeling more confident, he swims away from Pagu Island.

"Would Delphy be the closest?" he says. "No, Campi, I believe. Oh, I would love to see Penelope again." He continues to swim.

At the same time, not far from him, Oracle suddenly gives a chirp of joy. "I-I see him! There, everyone!"

They all go a bit faster.

Berceuse, still studying Campi and deciding if he wants to go there, is passing by an outcropping of rock when suddenly a giant chimpanzee lands on it and a cheerful voice says, "Hey, Berceuse!"

Berceuse shouts.

However, then he looks up, blinks a few times and says in amazement, "Vocalise?"

Vocalise waves a giant hand. "Heeey."

Marchand swims up and Oracle flies toward them with Rella on her back.

Berceuse looks around. "And everyone! What are you all doing out here?"

Marchand says, "Coming to see you. We thought you might be going to Pagu Island and hoped to catch you before you did."

"Oh! I just left. But – " Berceuse gasps. "You came to see

me? Well ... " He shifts, nervous.

Oracle lands on the rock next to Vocalise. "Yes! We all wanted to the moment we heard you had left your Isles." Rella peers over Oracle's back and Berceuse can see her eyes are wet.

Berceuse looks down. "I-I suppose it has been a long time."

Rella takes a deep breath, then says, sounding perfectly calm, "Let's go to Campi. Penelope will want to see you, too, and I don't want to hug you while you're in the ocean."

They all laugh at that. Berceuse says, "Yes, please! I would like that greatly."

As they travel, Berceuse says thoughtfully, "Penelope ... I hope that we do not overwhelm her."

Vocalise, mid-leap, says, "Nawww."

Penelope is highly overwhelmed when they arrive.

She is now in her human form, a short young woman with freckles and wavy orange hair, like Rath and his mother's. "O-Oh dear. I ... " She takes a deep breath. "I am so happy to see you again, Berceuse."

"As am I." When they had arrived on Campi, he, Marchand, Vocalise, and Oracle changed in their human forms. Rella had immediately locked Berceuse in a hug around his waist. She has not since let go.

"B-But ... I'm not ... I don't have anything prepared for so many people or a visit. Or ... " She looks around at the tiny village around them – Perillee Village, the small capitol of Campi – and sighs, her shoulders falling. "Oh, dear."

Marchand takes her shoulder. "We don't want to inconvenience you. I'm sure most of us can simply camp out on the beach, with your permission."

"Oh! Camping ... " Penelope considers this.

Vocalise suddenly points at the beach. He says nothing.

"Yes, Vocalise?" Marchand says.

Vocalise shrugs. "Just claiming that sand pile before you do."

Marchand stares at him for a moment, snorts, then lightly shoves his brother. Vocalise laughs.

Penelope claps her hands together. "That's ... That's a perfect idea! Ohh, a camping trip with everyone together. This will be so much fun!"

Vocalise says, "I mean, we're not really going far or anything."

Oracle touches his arm. "But, I think that's lovely. We'll be by your lagoon, too, Penelope!"

"You're right! I could still do my morning swim and afternoon swim classes." Looking far more confident, she says, "All right! Follow me!"

"Yes, Penelope!" they all say.

They follow the goddess down the twenty feet to the beach. Penelope studies the area carefully, then nods. "Here!"

All of them smile but Vocalise, who says, "But, this is nowhere near my sand pile."

Penelope is undeterred. "Vocalise, lying in a sand pile is no way to camp. Why, we need tents" – she waves her hand and supplies appear – "and a fire pit" – she waves her hand again – "and some food ... " She waves her hand some more.

As the rest of them watch her assemble all of the items needed for a camping trip on the beach, Berceuse says, "I had forgotten how detailed our sister was."

Marchand says, "And very organized."

Rella finally lets go of Berceuse. "Come on. Let's help." She walks forward to start putting up a tent.

Together, they help Penelope. While they do, the people of Campi look at them curiously, but smile.

Once they have finished, the local baker and cook of the village, who provides meals for everyone, comes by with a basket of cookies. She hands it to Penelope, saying, "I hope you enjoy them!"

"Thank you so much!" Penelope hugs her own. While the woman walks back to her hut, Penelope sits down and hands the basket around, each of them taking out a cookie.

They all look expectantly at Berceuse.

Berceuse notices and swallows. "Um ... yes?"

Oracle says, "Well, we would love to hear what you've been up to – "

Rella says, "Talk."

Berceuse jumps. "Y-Yes, dear sister." He pauses, thinking. "I hardly know where to begin!"

Marchand says, "You don't have to tell us everything. A thousand years is quite a lot of time to recount."

"Assuredly."

"So, just start with what you thought was important."

Penelope says, "Then, if there's anything more we want to know, we can just ask. Does that sound good?"

"Yes!" He thinks for a moment, then begins.

He mostly tells them about his Isles of Oct – none of them have seen them – and his dear ones and the different games that they played and the clothes that he made for them and the hikes that they would take. "I truly love being on my Isles," he says.

Marchand says, "They sound beautiful." The others nod in agreement.

"Your lands are as well! Or, at least, what I can only imagine are them. The Pagu told me much about the Fourth World, but this is my first time seeing it. It is so different from the previous and so much larger."

They all quietly nod.

Vocalise says, "Yeah. It's pretty good," and many of them relax.

Berceuse frowns. "Although, now that I speak of what I have done, it does not sound like a great deal. Surely not as much as you all have done within that time."

Vocalise flops down on his back and looks up at the sky. "I dunno about that."

Marchand says, "We've all done things for our own – it sounds like you've made the Pagu happy in a similar way."

"Thank you, Marchand," Berceuse says, brightening. He leans forward. "Now, tell me – what of you? What have you done during these years?"

Taking turns, they all do.

At the end, Berceuse pauses. He stands up and paces a little. They all watch him.

Then he turns around, throws his hands out, and says, "I truly have done nothing!"

Marchand raises his hand. "Calm down."

Berceuse sits down again. "You have helped create cultures and ships and taught your own different talents and given them traits ... You have protected them all these years and grown truly beautiful lands."

The others exchange a look.

Oracle says, "It's all right, Berceuse. We chose to aid the

humans – doing so brought many responsibilities, many of which are not always easy."

Vocalise makes a small noise, but says nothing.

Berceuse sighs. "Yes, while I've taken little to no responsibility, just like Amara told me."

Marchand's eyebrows raise. "You remember that?"

"Of course. Our sister can be terribly frightening when she is angry." Berceuse tugs his earring. "And she was not entirely incorrect. I just wanted a safe place away for myself and my dear ones far away from everything. I did not intend for it to last over a thousand years. Then my Captain came and it was a very stark reminder of the world that existed outside. The one that, as a god as well, I should be helping with."

Rella nudges him. "Don't forget you protected *PearlHeart* so they could get to Haliae and help Elvin and his own."

"It was very difficult, but I am immensely glad that I did." Berceuse smiles a little. "I was so happy to see Elvin. Just as I am to see all of you." He straightens, waving his hands. "So – I am through with comparing. Tell me more about your lands and your own. I wish to hear it because I want to know more of what you have done during these years."

Vocalise sits up. "An' you'll tell us more about what you've done."

Penelope says, "I want to hear more about the clothes you've made."

Marchand says, "The hikes sounded fun."

Oracle says, "And the different features of your Isles!"

Berceuse says, "I would happily tell you all!"

They talk through the morning, working through the cookie basket that Penelope's own brought. When it is lunchtime, Oracle waves her hand and a meal appears. "This food is what Flower-Pagu, my own, and I came up with for Paradi."

Berceuse clasps his hands together. "I cannot wait to try it!"

Afterward, they take a walk on the beach, then swim together in Penelope's lagoon. Marchand helps Penelope with her afternoon swim class while the others watch from the side.

As the sky grows dark, Marchand starts to wave his hand to make a fire, but Penelope shakes her head. "No, no. We should all learn how to make a fire on our own." She kneels by the fire pit, waves her hand to bring herself a rock and a stick and diligently begins spinning it against the other. It starts to smoke.

Berceuse says, "I do not believe One-Eye was very appreciative when I made a fire appear."

Marchand blinks. "One-Eye." He nods. "That's right. You've met Rath's new first mate. Rath seems quite happy with him."

Berceuse laughs. "They seem to work very well together." His eyes shine, but he says nothing more.

The flame grows and Penelope blows at it. It becomes larger until they are all able to wave their hands, making sticks appear that they then add to it.

Penelope says, "I suppose it's all right to use our abilities to keep it going." The others agree.

No one speaks for a while after that, all enjoying the warmth from the fire. Finally, Marchand says to Berceuse, "Thank you. For taking care of Rath."

Berceuse's eyes widen. "Of course! Although, I cannot say that I was the most useful in that situation. That was most certainly River-Pagu and Feather-Pagu."

Marchand smiles for a moment. Then, sobering, he says, "What do you all think of this storm of Ara's?"

"It will pass. It always does," Rella says.

Berceuse hesitates. "My dear ones do not believe it will."

She stares at him. She thinks, then shakes her head. "That is not right. Spring will come. It will ... " Frowning at the fire, she says, "Ara is not allowed to change the Seasons for everyone."

Vocalise says, "Sounds like he's trying to." He flicks another stick into the fire with his foot.

Oracle says, "I wonder what has upset him so greatly."

Berceuse says, "I've thought the same thing."

Marchand suddenly says, "That's right. Amara is supposed to be visiting Ara. She always does every five years. With her strength, she surely made it through his storm. She may know what has caused Ara to be upset."

The others look doubtful. Berceuse speaks. "I had thought that their relationship was not the best."

"No, it's not, but I do think that Amara has made efforts of reconciliation."

Oracle says, "Perhaps I'll fly to Unys after this and see if she was able to find out anything. It worries me to hear that this storm may not end as they always have."

Vocalise leans back. "I don't think she made it there."

Rella says, "Neither do I."

Oracle asks, "Why not?"

"I dunno," Vocalise says. "A few things."

Rella nods.

They talk for a while longer, sharing more about their lands, then go into their tents – Penelope, Oracle, and Rella share one while Berceuse, Marchand, and Vocalise share the other. In their little campsite on Campi, they fall asleep.

To the far east, a lone unicorn gallops. She travels south past the long Pantha coastline, then Daerce, and finally arrives in the sea to the northeast of Unys. Sir Ronan and Opal Starlight are there and see her.

"My Lady Amara," Sir Ronan breathes. He dismounts and stands on a disc of pure white beneath him and Opal Starlight. He bows deeply and Opal Starlight lowers her head.

The unicorn before them slows, glows, then walks forward as a woman with long white hair and a tight expression on her face. Her long sleeves drag in white puddles on the ocean surface. She lifts her hand. "Rise, Sir Ronan and Opal Starlight."

Once they do, Amara opens her mouth to continue, but stops. She gestures. "What are these extra accessories, Sir Knight?" She is referring to the small pouch at his hip.

"This?" Ronan pulls it forward. "Why, my Lady, I have made the most prudent and dutiful purchases of bandages, ink, and paper! I keep them at my side at all times and have most seriously practiced the art of bandages on my own being as Opal Starlight has not yet deemed me proficient enough for her. My penmanship, while already at a great standard, I practice as well as I aspire to present in an even more noble fashion so that I may deliver a reply letter of great quality to my Fair Captain."

Amara's white eyebrows raise. "Your – " She frowns. "Your meaning eludes me, Sir Knight, and I advise for reasons of haste and the most troubling news that I have received in the North that I must impart onto you that you speak with the common tongue."

"I am smitten with Captain Rath. I wrote him a letter."

Her pink eyes flare. "Such blunt infatuation is unbefitting

of a knight of any station, but far more so that of my current Champion, Sir Ronan."

"My Lady, you commanded – " Opal Starlight casts him a look and he falls silent.

Amara continues, "I will not hear of this again. Such implements – especially for such a task – are unneeded at this time. Do I speak clearly for your ears, Sir Ronan?"

"Yes, my Lady."

She calms herself. "I was unable to dutifully complete my quest in the North."

"My Lady! I scarcely believe that someone of your effortless grace and most noble of intentions would even approach such an outcome."

"It is true, Sir Ronan. My brother Ara's Three Dragon Guardians would not allow me to pass into Ara's land of Draconi."

Ronan sighs. "I see. Then, as they are mightier than even the Gods, it was duty-bound that you turn back."

"Indeed. They seek a most noble – if misguided notion – that they protect my brother in doing so." She pauses. "The storm – Ara's Storm – continues in the North. It has grown well past Haliae and Mella Island."

"That is truly troubling to hear. You wish for me to stay to warn the good people who seek to journey to the North?"

"Certainly. Such is a most noble and dutiful task. I trust you will remove the pouch and its contents."

Ronan hesitates a moment. "Yes, my Lady."

She fixes him with a look, then says, "I encountered my brother, Belle, in the North. I had truly set out to warn my other brother, Lionel, in his country of Pantha of the dangers he and his people may face in such a storm. Belle insisted that Lionel would not heed such warnings. Most truly, I cannot deny this, yet it is still the most valiant of efforts to do so in the face of such certainty."

"Truly."

"Belle has been warned and his military will disallow those attempting to go to the North. However, I wish for you to remain here to continue to do so as my Champion of my One Hundred Knights."

Ronan bows low. "It has and will continue to be done." He

shifts. "My Lady, if I may – "

"Do speak freely now. My tidings have concluded and while I wish to think on them, my ears are open to the concerns of the world that yours may have heard."

"With utter grace, you speak, my Lady, and I am most grateful for such." He clears his throat. "This Captain Rath – "

"I said no more talk of such things, Sir Ronan."

"Pray, my Lady, it has nothing to do with such feelings that I may hold for this man, but for the dire circumstances that I fear he may be in."

"What circumstances?"

"He has no god that has claimed him."

Her eyes widen. She thinks. "Rath. Of course. The young captain." She raises her chin. "I have been told, Sir Ronan, and I shall repeat to you, that Captain Rath's situation is not to be affected by I nor you and you shall abide by this."

"Yes, my Lady. Yet" – he clears his throat – "my Lady – if I may, once more – might I ask who has told you such and denied what is truly your most sacred and ancient of duties?"

"Lady Azalea. She is Captain Rath's grandmother."

"Then, he truly comes from ancient and most noble blood!" He flushes.

"Yes. His father is Councilman Georgio of Delphy." Ronan chokes. "Yet his situation is to remain untouched. So Lady Azalea has said."

Ronan bows again. "Then, so it shall be, though it pains me so to see the Fair – ah, Captain Rath in such danger given his lineage and no god to protect him." He rises. "Although I do not know Lady Azalea directly, I know from my position at your side, my Lady, that her words you will heed as nobly as I heed yours."

"True." Amara looks toward the distant, foggy area of Unys. "I shall go now. I must think about my brother Ara's state and the storm he has created."

Ronan and Opal Starlight bow once more. "Yes, my Lady. I shall be here as you have commanded as your ever faithful knight."

Amara nods once, then runs across the ocean. It lights up in small white discs under her bare feet. She glows then turns into her unicorn form, galloping on silver hooves toward Unys.

17

On Delphy, One-Eye runs with his Spirit Lion along the coastline. They join a path leading up a hill and under shade, slowing as they pass other people. One-Eye looks exhilarated and his Spirit Lion grins widely. As they go down the hill, Leighran Port comes into view. One-Eye looks at the masts rising up from all kinds of ships coming and going. Then he walks over to the harbormaster's house to seek work.

It is not long until he has spoken with the harbormaster, Seyline, and she says, "Yeah. Always could do with more customs officers." She looks over One-Eye's papers. "Captain Rath, too? He's highly responsible. If you've been working under him, I've got no worries about having you here."

"Thanks."

They leave the house and walk up a lane next to the ocean. Seyline says, "We've got housing here for those who are just working over the Winter, like you. Of course, if you've got something else already, you can commute from there."

"Don't." He hesitates, realizing that *PearlHeart* was going to be his answer.

They stop in front of a small home with a stone path

leading up to the front door and trees on either side and in the back. Seyline smiles. "Then, this is all yours. No roommate or anything. You'll start tomorrow."

"Right."

Seyline leaves and One-Eye walks toward his house for the Winter. He moves aside the cloth over the door and sees a simple, single room with a bed, a well in the center customarily used for sending Delphaen messages, a small desk, and a kitchen area. He sits down next to the bed and looks at the clear water in the well, thinking as he pets his Spirit Lion, who is now lazing on his lap. Outside, the ocean shimmers under the bright sun, easily viewable from his doorway.

There, far to west, Rath sails. He is nearing his grandmother's island and feels more at ease as he grows closer.

A giant hawk flies above him, then descends. The God of Butej, Fierce, lands on his ship in his human form. Rath says, "Fierce."

"Rath. Are you well? Have you had any encounters with the people from Corxae?"

"Yes, I am. Thank you for asking. And, ah, no. Evermore tells me that none boarded *PearlHeart* during our journey."

Fierce relaxes. "That is very good to hear." He thinks of something. "If you see an octopus swimming near here, do not be concerned. He is my brother, Berceuse." Recognition lights in Rath's eyes and Fierce asks, "You have seen him. Or, know him?"

"The latter. I met Berceuse on the Isles of Oct four months ago. He protected *PearlHeart* with his barrier so that we could reach Haliae through Ara's Storm."

Fierce looks shocked. "That is very different from the Berceuse I knew." He looks ahead, where a small green island is on the horizon. "I am sure your grandmother will be pleased to see you well."

"I cannot wait to see her."

Fierce smiles a little. He turns toward Pagu Island, a tiny isle to the northeast of Lady Azalea's Island. "I am glad that Berceuse will not trouble you. And that he helped." He still seems to have trouble comprehending it. "My guards tell me that you are now accompanied by three Pagu and a man from

Pantha on *PearlHeart.*"

"That is correct. Well-Pagu, Bucket-Pagu, Flower-Pagu, and One-Eye."

"Lionel's own concerns me." Fierce takes a breath. "However, Pantha is not my jurisdiction – it is Belle's. You feel safe around him?"

"Very. He is a wonderful friend of mine."

Fierce's eyebrows go up. He scans the horizon again. "The people of Pantha are unpredictable, but if One-Eye makes you feel safe ... " He sighs. "My guards noticed nothing alarming about him while you were at your grandfather's home. I will trust their judgment and yours."

"Thank you, Fierce."

Fierce looks sad. He and Rath have similar brown-red ribbons tying back their hair. He places a hand on Rath's back. "I will be leaving now. Take care."

"You as well."

Fierce nods seriously. Then he turns into his hawk form and flies away.

Rath arrives at his grandmother's the next morning. The other Delphaen ship that his father, mother, and Carlos took is already there at the private dock. As Rath sails close to the shore he sees them and his grandmother waiting for him. When he reaches the dock, he quickly ties off his ship and runs to meet them. After greeting his parents and Carlos, he kneels and hugs his grandmother. She hugs him warmly back.

They eat breakfast together, then Rath and Azalea go to the South Garden, where he tells her about the rest of his journey on *PearlHeart.* While he does, the Mehrin plants wave their leaves happily and the Pantha Flower raises its head toward the sun – it has grown a new bud.

"My!" Azalea says. "You have had an excitable time – and all in only half a year!"

"Indeed."

She muses, "Berceuse, though ... Ha! Marin's just begun touching up our octopus in the dining room's mural."

"I see."

Grinning, she continues, "I am looking forward to meeting One-Eye. He sounds like he's made of stern stuff, like all of Lionel's own." She suddenly gasps. "I wonder how they are doing in Pantha – with Ara's Storm."

"I do not know. I hope that they are all right."

"As do I."

They walk through the East Garden afterward, then Rath goes up to his rooms. In his sitting room, he sits at his desk and begins writing letters to send out for the holiday. He works late into the morning, finishing just before lunch.

On his way to the dining room, he carries his letters – a large stack with three smaller ones on top – to the Paradi Messengers on Azalea's island, who he finds on one of the balconies. "Excuse me, may I ask if you would be willing to deliver these, Mehr, Felidan?" he asks.

Mehr brightens. "Of course, Master Rath!" and his partner bird, Felidan, gives a happy "Caw!"

Soon, the bird is off with a small package of letters in her talons to the nearest Paradi Message Tower.

Rath's letters go out to his crew, friends, and family.

Franz and Velt, who are neighbors on Delphy, read theirs by the beach. Perri looks at hers at her table. She also received one from Isaac.

Isaac receives his on Pantrog. His mother calls from the kitchen, "Is your captain definitely coming to stay the night next month?"

"Yeah! He says so right here!" Isaac says.

Oren reads his on Pantrog as well.

William, Phobos, Melody, Demeter, Felix, and Triphonius all look at their letters on Paradi.

Charles receives his on Cunica, as does Phillip, who shows a particular line to the rabbit family that lives with him and Pelline.

The line says: *"... and I hope that the rabbit family is well and warm for the holiday."*

They bounce happily.

On Ullia, Evermore looks at his and breathes a sigh of relief before tucking it carefully into his pocket.

Fenrir finishes his quietly on Sudines. He looks a little sad, but smiles as he refolds it.

One-Eye reads his while in his house on Delphy, sitting against the wall. His Spirit Lion is resting on his lap, but one ear is pricked back for any comments One-Eye might say. One-Eye does not say anything, but he does look flushed. The last line of his letter says, *"I hope you have a wonderful Winter. I am truly glad to have met you."*

Rath's grandfather, Garreth, also on Delphy, looks at his on the beach behind his home, his feet stretched out toward the ocean. His Spirit Dolphin flips in the waves next to him.

On Campi, Berceuse, Marchand, and Penelope – who are still camping with Vocalise, Rella, and Oracle – have theirs, smiling softly at the contents.

On Pagu Island, Well-Pagu, Bucket-Pagu, and Flower-Pagu read their letters with absolute joy.

Less than a month later, Felidan returns to Lady Azalea's Island with letters from many crew members for Rath.

Mehr hands Rath a neat stack of letters and one rolled up note with a white ribbon. "These are for you, Master Rath."

"Thank you very much."

He goes to his rooms to read them. He starts with the roll – it is from Sir Ronan and has quite a substantial length. He spends ten minutes reading it. Then he looks at those from his crew – from Franz, Velt, Perri, Isaac, Oren, William and Phobos, Melody and Demeter, Felix and Triphonius, Charles, and Phillip and Pelline. None are from Evermore because mail is not allowed out of Ullia. He reads Fenrir's and below it, One-Eye's.

He looks flushed as he reads it.

After he sets them aside, he reads one from Marchand – his grandfather often does not send a reply, preferring to speak in person – Berceuse, Penelope, and finally, three little letters on the bottom – one pink, one green, and one purple. However, beneath them, there are two more – one turquoise and one orange. He very carefully opens them and reads his letters from the Pagu. The turquoise is from River-Pagu and the orange is from Feather-Pagu.

When he leaves his rooms to go to dinner, his eyes are red. Carlos walks with him. "Are you all right, Master Rath?"

"Ah, yes," he says. "The Pagu – Flower-Pagu, Bucket-Pagu, Well-Pagu, River-Pagu, and Feather-Pagu – sent me letters for the holiday. They were all very kind."

Carlos nods, understanding. Then he casts a curious look

at the bulky envelope in Rath's hands. "Might I ask whom that is for?"

"Sir Ronan." Rath looks at it. "I believe I answered all of his questions."

Carlos does not say anything.

Winter goes on for everyone.

Rath and his mother bake cookies together, smiling and laughing as they cut them out in different shapes. They sandwich them together with raspberry jam spread in between. Georgio and his mother, Azalea, play cards in the sun room. She wins many times. Carlos sips tea peacefully beside them.

On Delphy, Franz helps his family clean the house for more relatives to show up. Velt spends time with her sister, Vann, at their family's ship shop. Perri talks with the Spirit Dolphins that appear in her family's pool and shows them the metalwork dolphin she got in Pantrog. Around them, Delphy is looking more and more like the holiday is approaching, with lanterns and blue-green flags going up. Marchand, now returned from Campi, walks with Garreth through Priage, looking at them.

On the west side of the island, One-Eye watches strings of Delphaen crystals go up as he checks ships. When he walks back to the harbormaster's house, people are putting up some over it, too.

Similar preparations are underway in Pantrog. More lanterns are hung and children run over the rooftops, holding sticks with streamers on them. Others are racing, practicing for the big holiday race. At his home, Isaac helps his little sister, Sophia, set the table while his brothers run around and his mother shoos them out of the kitchen. Oren, who lives in a smaller home out in the country, sits on his roof. Vocalise joins him and Oren casually copies his god's pose. Together, they watch the excitement happening in the larger cities.

Phillip and Pelline are drying and storing what they can to prepare for Winter on Cunica. The rabbit family that lives with them brings them twine to tie up each jar. Charles talks with the rabbits near his home as the snow continues to fall and food cooks inside. Later, Pelline surprises Sir Rif and Amethyst Rose – who are still stationed on Cunica – with a pie.

On Paradi, the sun is going down. William, Phobos, Felix, and Triphonius cheer as Melody, Demeter, and other musicians perform on a stage for the holiday. Oracle watches them, beaming with pride.

Erole, the God of Ullia, has returned to his country. They have no celebration as he listens to every report from his people about news they have heard from all over the Fourth World.

Sitting in his office on Renet Island, Captain Berkut looks up in the direction of Phoenae.

Near the Southern Selachuu Military Base, Sir Ronan watches for ships atop Opal Starlight late into the night. Suddenly, a wave appears beside him and a Selachuu ship surfaces. Captain Farbourne comes out of a hatch in the roof. Ronan meets him and Farbourne unclips a second tin mug from his belt loop. He fills it and Ronan looks at it, then takes a dubious sip. They sit together on the roof of the ship while Opal Starlight stands primly beside them. They look north toward Pica Pica, which is still partying, but to a much higher degree due to the holiday.

For Sudines, celebrations are calmer. Fenrir, his mother, his sister, her wife, and Hep sit quietly together and have tea. The stars are bright outside. They take their first sip together.

Inside Elvin's Peak on Haliae, Sven and Pema eat with Elvin and the others. They are huddled close, torches bright as they talk with one another and Ara's Storm blows outside.

On Butej, Fierce returns to his mountain and sits, watching the lights and colors from the surrounding countries, each celebrating their holiday. On his country, solemn kites are flown in a quieter show of the season. Fierce watches them, then turns his eyes to a blue-green glow in the sea to the west of Delphy.

From the east beach of Lady Azalea's Island, Rath and his family are looking at the same area and on Delphy, One-Eye is also as he stands in the crowd on Leighran Port.

On Lady Azalea's Island, Georgio steps forward and, tattoos glowing, dips his hand in the water. On Delphy, One-Eye watches as others with Marchand's Traits do the same. Garreth sends one out from his private beach near his home.

All of the Delphaen messages travel toward that blue-green glow in the sea, swirling and brightening the area. Something swims around them – a dolphin – gathering up all of the messages – well wishes for the coming year. Marchand swims around them faster and faster until they are all gathered up into a great glowing ball. Then he swims low and shoots up toward it, pushing it with his nose until he and it are out of the water in a great leap. At the same time, the ball bursts, sending blue-green sparkles all over the area.

Rath watches them on his grandmother's island.

One-Eye looks at them on Delphy. His Spirit Lion tries to eat one.

On Pagu Island, the Pagu watch, too, dancing and giggling in the sparkles.

Berceuse, who is spending his holiday on Campi, looks entranced. He takes in the sight next to Penelope, hands clasped together.

In Pantha, a very different holiday is occurring.

Inside the Coliseum, King Faerohr, a young man with long brown hair and wearing a thick cloak, throws a much larger man over his shoulder. As he hits the ground, Faerohr turns to two others that are running at him, slides in between them, and grabs their hands as he does so to pull them together, then down. As he hops back onto his feet, a cheer goes up around him from the crowd entirely made up of those he has already defeated.

A lion stands on one of the crumbling sections of the walls and roars. "That's another! Come on, who's going to take him down!"

Faerohr looks up quickly. "Lionel, not helping!"

Lionel, the God of Pantha, bounces in excitement. "Three more for you, Faerohr!"

Faerohr turns toward them.

He surprises the trio by running right up to them, then making a leap onto the shoulders of the first, landing behind him and throwing him over his head and into the other two, finishing off the last of the fighters. As the three pull themselves up, they grin at their king, then join in the cheers from the rest of the crowd.

Breathing out visible clouds in the cold air, Faerohr waves his hand, officially ending the matches in the Coliseum. As a group, they start heading up the mountain to Pantha Castle, where they will feast on the food that was found that month.

Lionel pads beside Faerohr in his lion form, then glows and turns into his human form – a tall, muscular man with brown hair, a beard, and dark blue eyes. "What a fight! Not a one to beat you!"

Faerohr does not look as enthused. "I thought holidays were supposed to be different."

"Huh? What do you mean?"

"Like, decorations and lights. Music." Lionel squints like these are unfamiliar terms. Faerohr smiles and says, "I've heard the Delphaen Celebration in particular is beautiful."

Lionel looks defensive. "Where'd you hear that?"

"I read about them in books."

"Right. Those." Lionel rolls his eyes. They continue walking. "Now, I'm thinking with all this cold, we have Coliseum fights twice a month instead of once – keeps the blood flowing, you know?"

"I do. But, the weather has been concerning." Faerohr looks up into the snow. "This is one of the heavier Winters, isn't it?"

"Yeah. What about it? Just means Ara's angry about something. It'll pass. In the meantime – what better way to bulk up?" He turns back into his lion form and strikes a pose in front of Faerohr. "Us against the elements! I love it!" He sits down. "And I hate it."

Faerohr stares. He rolls his hand. "Go on."

Lionel shakes out his mane and continues up the path. "I like getting stronger – I like you all getting stronger. Just ... do we need more wood for the fireplaces?"

They reach Pantha Castle, a large structure built on a mesa, four stories tall with battlements surrounding the large keep, its towers frozen in the snow. As Faerohr pushes open the heavy doors, he says, "We always have some. I've asked it's brought along with the food."

"Good. That's where I'm going." Lionel trots in.

Soon, they are all sitting by the fires, eating and laughing. Faerohr sits on a couch and Lionel rolls on the floor in front of the flames. Faerohr watches, sipping a hot drink, then says, "You know. I could arrange for a rug."

Lionel stops. "Don't need one." He rolls over so abruptly, Faerohr cannot tell if it was intentional or he lost his balance.

The lion says to the fire, "Rugs are for the weak."

Faerohr nods, taking another sip. He continues, "So, when you say us against the elements – isn't it really against your brother Ara? Since he's causing this storm."

Lionel rolls back over. "No. He's just upset. The weather's different."

"But you just said – "

Lionel bares his teeth.

Faerohr sighs, dropping it.

The wind howls outside, rattling the ironbound windows. A few people look up at it, then return to their meals. Faerohr says, "It would seem that Haliae would be facing the same that we are here. Are they prepared for it?"

Lionel snorts. "Doubt it. They're not really strong." He shifts uncomfortably. "Though, I guess they can just go inside their mountain. Elvin might like the extra time – he can write more of those things for the Alliance. Proposals or ... whatever." He bats a paw. "He keeps wanting Pantha to join the Alliance."

Faerohr looks interested. "You've received letters from him?"

"Duh. All of the royals have. None were interested."

"What would that mean for Pantha? The Alliance, I mean."

"How should I know? Every time Elvin and I talk, he keeps going on about peace and cooperation – benefits ... "

Faerohr hones in on that. "Like what?"

"Food. Emergency supplies. Support." Lionel flicks his tail. "Ha! Like we need that."

The wind howls again. Faerohr finishes his drink. "Maybe we should consider it." He tilts his head. "Given the weather?"

Lionel studies Faerohr. "You're not afraid, are you? I didn't back a king who turned coward at some snow." He adds, "It'll go away by Spring. Always does." Then he closes his eyes and immediately begins to snore.

Faerohr takes his lead and lies down on the couch. He looks at the rattling windows, then closes his eyes, falling asleep next to the warm fire.

18

On Lady Azalea's Island, Rath says goodbye to his grandmother. He hugs her tightly. "I love you."

"I love you, too, my dear." She grins as they pull away. "I cannot wait to see you in the Summer."

He laughs. "Neither can I."

Azalea says goodbye to Georgio, Marin, and Carlos. Then, with Rath on his small ship and Georgio, Marin, and Carlos on the medium-sized one, they set out. Azalea and the staff watch them go from the beach.

Twelve days later, One-Eye is working at Leighran Port. He has just checked a ship and is speaking to the captain. "You're clear to go."

"Yes, sir!" the man says and goes up the gangplank to tell his crew.

One-Eye returns to the harbormaster's house and places his book in a small basket on the desk in the front. Seyline sees him and says, "Good work, One-Eye. Have a good rest of your day."

"Thanks."

He waves to his co-workers, who are playing cards during their break, then steps out into the late afternoon sun. His Spirit Lion swishes his tail happily. One-Eye pets him as they begin to walk home. However, just as they are turning the corner, the Spirit Lion stops and suddenly points his nose west.

"What?" One-Eye asks.

However, when he looks over, he sees Rath is tying off his small ship at the docks. Afterward, Rath begins to walk toward the town. One-Eye moves in his direction and his Spirit Lion follows.

"Captain!" he says when they are close enough to be heard.

Rath starts. When he turns, his eyes brighten and he opens his mouth, shuts it in a surprised smile, then says, "One-Eye. How are you?"

"Good. Are you on your way to Pantrog?"

"Yes. My ship leaves tomorrow. I was just about to go to the inn here."

"Stay with me." One-Eye coughs, reddening. "I have a house up there. You could ... If you want."

"I would love to." Rath flushes. "Ah, that is, if that is all right."

"I'm asking. Do you want to?"

Rath pauses. "Yes. Thank you, One-Eye."

They walk up the path together. Rath asks how his work is and One-Eye asks about his family. The Lion trots alongside them happily.

As they walk up to the front of One-Eye's house, Rath says, "Grandmother would like to meet you."

One-Eye stops. "Why?"

"She said you seemed to be built of 'stern stuff.'"

One-Eye frowns, but nods. He holds back the cloth covering the front door, letting Rath enter.

Rath looks around. "It is wonderful."

One-Eye hesitates. "Do you want to eat? There's also tea in the cupboard. I don't know how to brew it, though."

"Yes, please. Do you have a tea kettle?" One-Eye nods. "I would be able to brew it. Carlos has taught me."

"Sure." One-Eye reaches in the cupboard and pulls both out while Rath gets to work starting a fire beneath the stove. "Never had tea before. I don't know what kind this is." He looks at the tin. "Delphaen Fruit Tea?"

Rath stands up abruptly, surprising them both. "That is my favorite."

"Good." One-Eye smiles a little as he sets it down on the counter and reaches for the cups. Beside him, Rath gently blows on the growing fire, the smoke rising up and through a hole in the ceiling.

Soon, they are both seated at the low table, taking their first sip together.

Rath looks relaxed and happy. One-Eye looks curious. He nods. "It's good. Makes sense why it's your favorite. You like sweet things, right?"

"I do." Rath suddenly reaches into his pack, pulling out a small embroidered bag. "That's right – my mother and I baked cookies at my grandmother's. I thought I would have them now. Would you like some as well?"

"Yeah. Thanks."

One-Eye finds a plate and Rath gently pours the cookies out of the bag onto it. They talk, eating them and drinking tea while One-Eye's Spirit Lion rolls on the floor next to the warm stove.

They spend the afternoon together, then get dinner at a local restaurant. They sit at a table on the roof beneath tall Delphaen trees and near blossoms that run up the sides of the building and over the roof's railing. They return to One-Eye's house afterward and play a few rounds of cards before getting ready for bed.

One-Eye reaches into a cupboard. "Found some extra bedding in here you can use."

"Thank you very much," Rath says, accepting the blankets from him. "I had expected to stay in the inn down the street, so I did not bring any."

"You don't spend money this way."

"That is true. Thank you very much for allowing me to stay here, One-Eye."

They sleep across from one another, with the well in between them. Rath falls asleep quickly. One-Eye looks over at him, turns away, and falls asleep.

The next morning, One-Eye gets ready to leave for work. He says to Rath, "You can stay here until you need to leave for Pantrog. When is that?"

"Around noon," Rath says.

"I'll be on lunch. I want to see you off."

"Of course." Rath smiles. "I hope you have a wonderful morning at work, One-Eye."

"Thanks."

When he reaches the harbormaster's house, One-Eye retrieves his customs log, then begins checking ships. Around noon, he quickly walks back to his house.

He finds Rath inside tucking a book into his bag. The only part of the title One-Eye can see is *Tales of.* Rath looks up and smiles when he sees One-Eye, then they leave together, heading toward the docks.

They reach a long line of people waiting to board a Pan ship bound for Pantrog. While the passengers ahead walk up the gangplank, Rath says, "Thank you, One-Eye. I truly enjoyed your company."

"Me too," One-Eye says. "Spring? See you then?"

"Yes. I cannot wait."

They wave to each other then Rath joins the line to board the ship. One-Eye watches it sail off before walking back to his house.

It takes Rath a week to sail to Pantrog. He spends much of his time reading or looking out at the other ships in the Delphaen Trade Route. Tikari Port, where Isaac lives, slowly comes into view.

When he arrives, he finds Isaac's house, a larger home in a more wealthy district. Isaac comes out and hugs him, saying, "Captain! How are you?"

"I am well. How are you? How was your holiday?"

Isaac grins. "Great. We've got food ready. Come on inside."

They sit around a large table with the rest of Isaac's family. He has two older brothers, two younger brothers, one younger sister, and one baby sister that his mother and father take turns holding during the meal, bouncing her on their laps.

Isaac says, "We had a lot of games during the holiday – I saw Vocalise a few times, too!" He takes a few more bites. "Then, we had the big race. I came in third this year!"

"That is amazing!"

One of his older brothers, Nari, says, "Oren got second. He

works on your ship, too, right, Rath?"

"He does, as a helmsman."

Nari turns to Isaac. "You ever gonna do that?"

"Maybe at some point. I probably will if I'm ever a first mate."

His mother, Verletta, speaks. "Are you heading to the North again this coming year, Captain?"

Rath nods. "Yes. To deliver ink and paper to Elvin on Haliae."

"I didn't know if it was passable again yet," she says, frowning. "Last I heard, the Selachuu Military still had it closed."

Rath stops eating. "I had not heard. I apologize. Thank you for telling me." He looks thoughtful as they continue their meal.

Later that evening, as the sun is going down, Isaac and Rath climb up onto the roof. Rath says, "One-Eye and I ran across the rooftops when we were on Pantrog before. It was very fun."

"I knew I saw you before!"

They sit down. Ahead of them, hundreds of lanterns are strung in between the houses. The large Pantrog trees tower over them, their long leaves trailing down.

Isaac suddenly digs into his pocket. "Oh, right. I wanted to give you these. Ma made a batch just for you."

Rath flushes. "I do not know how to feel about that." He takes the bag Isaac offers him and opens it. His eyes widen.

Isaac continues, "Ma enjoyed it a lot! She really likes you. Says she's really glad we met."

"I am as well." Rath reaches into the bag and pulls out a small candy with an elaborate design, thin, and sparkling with sugar. "I love these! I haven't had them since last year."

"Now, you've got a whole bunch to last you until the next!"

"I am not sure they will last for another two months." Rath seems completely serious and Isaac's eyebrows raise. "Would you like one?"

"They're for you!"

"I would like to share."

Isaac grins. "Sure." He takes the one Rath offers him.

They eat together as they look at the sunset over Pantrog.

Later, Rath and Isaac are inside again, slowly following Isaac's little sister Sophia who is hauling a large bundle of bedding to the room they will be sharing for the night. Isaac slides the door open and she waddles in, then dumps the bedding down. She points, saying to Rath, "You'll sleep here. Next to Isaac."

Rath nods. "Thank you very much for carrying it, Sophia. You did a wonderful job."

She beams with pride. Then she squirms. "Can I have one of the Pan treats Ma made?"

Isaac gapes. "Sophia! Those are for Rath!"

However, Rath reaches for the bag in his pocket. "Of course. Here you are."

"Thank you, Captain!" She takes one and runs off.

"She is so energetic," Rath says.

Isaac says, "Just wait until she's a bit older. I bet you she'll be winning the big holiday race when she can enter."

Rath looks amazed. "I see." He gestures. "I remember when she was ... this small."

Isaac lies on his stomach on his bedding while Rath starts to arrange his own. "Yeah. We've known each other for a bit, huh?"

"Indeed. I am very happy for every year," Rath says as he continues to smooth out the blankets.

They sleep peacefully that night.

The next morning, Vocalise is walking over the rooftops when he hears a familiar voice in the street below.

"Thank you very much for allowing me to visit. I truly enjoyed it."

He looks down to see Rath – with Sophia determinedly clasping onto his hand – bowing to Isaac and his family

Verletta says, "We always like having you." Her husband, Heiran, who is holding their youngest, agrees.

Sophia says, "Can I go with you, Captain? I want to sail a ship like you and Isaac."

Rath kindly shakes his head. "I am afraid not. However, Isaac tells me that you will begin sailing lessons soon?" She nods. "I think that is very exciting."

"Yup! I can't wait!"

Isaac reaches down to pick up Sophia and she immediately crawls up onto his shoulders. "How about this," he says. "After you've started your lessons, we go and see Rath on Delphy instead of him coming here. What do you think?"

"Really?"

"Yeah! It'd be a perfect first trip."

As Sophia cheers and Isaac's two younger brothers – twins, named Cherin and Meira – ask if they can also come, Mevrin, his oldest brother, says, "She's gonna be a captain before any of us," and Nari just sighs beside him.

Up on the roof, Vocalise smiles.

While Rath makes his way back to the docks, Vocalise hops down and walks next to him. "Hey, Captain."

"Vocalise!"

"You heading off now?"

"I am. To Delphy to prepare *PearlHeart* for our next journey."

"You going to Haliae again this year?"

Rath stops. "I cannot say." As they continue, he says, "Isaac's family tells me that the Selachuu Military has yet to lift the travel restrictions in the area."

"That's true. I'm glad you know. I was going to tell you if you didn't." They reach the docks and pause. "Well, wherever you're going, be safe, all right? I like you."

"I like you as well, Vocalise."

Vocalise just grins.

Then they wave to each other and Rath goes up the gangplank of the ship he is taking back to Delphy.

It takes him another week to arrive and when he steps off onto Priage Port, he sees his mother, father, grandfather, and Carlos waiting for him.

"There he is!" Garreth says.

While they travel east, toward a Phoenae airship dock near Priage, Marin asks, "How was Pantrog, my dear?"

"It was wonderful. I also saw One-Eye at Leighran Port. He allowed me to stay at his home while I waited for my ship."

Carlos' eyebrows go up, Georgio looks curious, and Marin smiles. Garreth says grudgingly, "Kind of him."

"I thought so as well. It was truly good to see him."

When they reach the dock, a golden Phoenae airship is approaching.

Georgio sighs. "There it is."

When it arrives, it lowers next to the dock. A hatch opens from the side and a Phoenae Force officer exits. He gestures to the opening impatiently.

Georgio hugs his family. "Take care, everyone. Rath, have a safe journey."

"I will, Father."

As Georgio walks toward the ship, the officer gives a slight nod to Garreth, nothing to Marin, Carlos, or Rath, then the hatch shuts as soon as Georgio enters. The ship begins to rise again.

Garreth huffs as he watches it. He escorts them to another part of the beach, saying to Marin, "I've arranged for a ship all your own, my dear, to take you back to Campi."

"Thank you, Garreth."

There, they find a small Pan ship with a four-person crew, ready to depart.

Rath hugs his mother tightly. "I love you."

"I love you, too, my dearest one." She pulls away, holds his cheek for a moment, then kisses his forehead. Rath blinks a few times, his eyes wet. Then one of the sailors puts down the gangplank and Marin walks up. She waves from the deck as they sail off.

Afterward, Garreth asks Rath, "Now to *PearlHeart* for you?"

"Yes."

When they reach Priage Port, they can see *PearlHeart* bobbing in the distance. They start to join the crowd, but Garreth takes Rath's arm before they can move further. "I'll say goodbye now."

"Of course, Grandfather."

Carlos politely excuses himself to give them privacy and walks ahead.

While he does, Rath and Garreth hug one another, then Garreth holds his grandson at arm's length. "Take care of yourself, your crew. Let them take care of you, too."

"I will."

Garreth looks over Rath's shoulder and sees that Carlos is now with One-Eye, Evermore, and the Pagu, who had already arrived, and all are waiting next to *PearlHeart* for their captain. "Good group. Safe travels, Captain."

"I agree. Thank you."

Rath waves happily to him as enters the crowd and Garreth waves back, then watches as Rath reunites with his crew and they all go up the gangplank together.

Rath, One-Eye, and Well-Pagu meet with the maintenance workers for their report and welcome other members of the crew throughout the day. Rath hugs Phillip when he arrives. The sails are checked and belongings are placed. The crew works together until they are ready to cast off.

With One-Eye at the wheel, Well-Pagu on the console, and Rath next to them, *PearlHeart* sails away from Priage Port, beginning their sixth year.

19

Two weeks into their journey, Rath and One-Eye are playing cards in the captain's cabin.

One-Eye says, "Have you ever been to Tecla?"

"Yes. A few times with my father." Rath draws, then lays down his cards. "Double Berceuse."

One-Eye smiles. "Good job." Then, "Again."

"Yes, please."

As they play, One-Eye asks, "So, where did your father and you go? In Tecla, I mean."

"Maro's Library. It is underground, but very vast."

One-Eye glances at his Lion. "Maro's their god?" Rath nods and One-Eye hesitates. His Lion swishes his tail beside him. "Do you think you'll have time to visit it while we're there?"

"I am afraid not. The library is in the center of the island, on a small piece of land surrounded by a lake."

"The plant shop we're going to is closer?"

Rath brightens. "Yes. I cannot wait to see the plants there. Teclan plants can be very wild. There are several in my grandmother's East Garden. I always enjoy seeing them."

"I'm looking forward to it. We'll go there after Tecla, right?"

"Yes. And Lotinx before that."

One-Eye frowns. "For the ink and paper. Does Elvin even need it? Every captain I talked to while doing customs at Leighran Port said that Ara's Storm had continued and was growing."

Rath's eyes fall. "That is what I heard on Pantrog as well. The order still came from Lotinx, however. It seems they believe it will be less severe when we travel to the North."

"It better be."

After they finish their last round, Rath says, "Would you ... May I ask if you have played Marchand's Twist before?"

One-Eye's eyebrows go up. He smiles a little. "Learned it on Delphy. I liked it better than Double Berceuse."

"I love both. Would you like to play it sometime?"

"Definitely."

They go out onto the main deck, Rath sees that the skies ahead are darker and a steady rain falls over the island there.

William calls out, "Renet Island, ahead!" and Phobos gives a "Caw!"

They arrive and Captain Berkut boards to check the cargo hold. When he is finished, he stands on the flooded docks with Rath and One-Eye.

"Will you be going to the North again, Captain Rath?" Berkut asks.

"I believe so. We will be picking up a delivery for Haliae after this."

Berkut looks pained. "Pray you will be safe. The Selachuu Military has yet to allow travel." He sighs. "However, perhaps in the Summer it will be open again."

"Indeed."

Berkut lingers. His eyes look more alert than the previous year. "It was good to see you again, Captain Rath." He shifts. "I am not for writing letters, but I hope your holiday was well?"

"It was. Thank you. May I ask how yours was?"

"Pleasurable. Many airships to watch." Berkut pauses. "But, I must admit to finding joy in seeing your ship arrive."

"I am happy to hear that. And, I see."

They say goodbye and Rath turns to go up the gangplank. One-Eye moves to join him but Berkut says, "A moment, One-Eye?"

One-Eye glares at him. "We're leaving."

"Is Captain Rath unattached?"

One-Eye nearly trips.

"I had assumed not." At One-Eye's expression, he adds, "Come now – you should not be worried about any interest I might have. I see how the Captain is near you. I accept that." He glances up at Rath, who is already on the deck, then nods to One-Eye. "Good afternoon."

"Yeah." One-Eye goes up the gangplank.

PearlHeart sails east, into the mists surrounding Paradi. At the end of the week, the crew celebrates Isaac's birthday. He is now twenty-six. Phillip brings out an orange cake and they all help light the candles. After Isaac blows them out, they all cheer.

As slices are handed around on plates to everyone, Rath pulls out a small gift, wrapped up in cloth. "I made this for you, Isaac."

"Really?" Isaac hurriedly opens it. He pulls out some pieces of wood in irregular shapes. "It's a block puzzle! What does it make?"

Rath laughs. "You will need to put it together."

Isaac hugs him. "Thank you so much, Captain!"

They pass Butej ten days later. While they do, a giant hawk watches their progress from the top of his mountain. One-Eye, at the wheel, sees him.

"Who is that?" he asks.

Rath, who is beside him, replies, "Fierce, the God of Butej."

"You've met him?"

"Yes. He was there when I lost my traits. He often checks on me during the Winter."

One-Eye's eye widens, then narrows as he looks up at Fierce. The hawk regards him calmly back.

A week later, they pass the three thin isles of Xiphi, the low round island of Tecla, and the heavily forested island of Grist. Beyond that is Lotinx, a country far larger than the other three. They dock on the north side, where all of the buildings are made out of sturdy stones harvested from the rock quarries to the south. The streets are narrow, with canals running through them and bridges over them for people to cross. Open windows reveal laundry lines hanging between buildings and people talk and laugh on either side of them.

PearlHeart bobs peacefully at port. The gangplank has been lowered and Rath, Isaac, William and Phobos go down it.

The docks are busy this early in the season, but not overflowing as they were on Pantrog. Ahead, a man with a friendly face approaches them. He raises a muscled arm. "Hey! Rath, Isaac, William, and Phobos!"

Rath says, "It is very good to see you, Estival."

Estival, the son of the Councilman of Lotinx, grins. The Spirit Elephant next to him regards all of them with twinkling eyes. "Yeah! You guys, too. Here for the ink and paper?" Rath nods and Estival pauses. "Is there even any place for it to go to? My dad said Sven's dad and Fritz are still on Pica Pica."

"I did not know that. We will not go to Haliae until this Summer, however."

Estival understands. "Ara's Storm might clear up by then. Got it."

They follow Estival through the crowd. As they walk, he says, "Everyone is talking about the storm. Sounds like it's messed up some Pertan trade routes, but, what can we do? Doesn't seem like anyone can sail through it."

They cross a bridge over a canal to a line of shops. Estival goes to one with a painted sign with an illustration of a pen and holds the door open for everyone. "Here we are!"

The shop is small with narrow aisles. Stacks of different weights and types of paper are in racks. They walk past ink bottles and various types of quills until they reach a desk where a man waits. He sees them and brightens. "Captain Rath for Elvin's delivery?"

"Yes, that is right."

The man reaches for a crate. "Was told to expect you." He places it on the desk. "Can't really believe you're going to Haliae, but good luck anyway."

"Thank you very much."

Isaac and William carry the crate out of the shop with Rath and Estival following them.

Estival says to Rath, "I'm worried about Sven and Pema. I know he told us all about that time when they were iced in until the following Spring and they were all right, but ... that sounds awful! How was he when you saw him, Rath?"

"I believe he was concerned. However, Elvin told him that if he and Pema deemed the storm too dangerous, that they would take further action."

"He did?" Estival whistles. "I honestly can't believe his dad hasn't made him councilman yet – he's always been the best out of all of us with that stuff and it's obvious that Elvin trusts him." He makes a face. "Actually, my dad has been talking about the same – stepping down and having me take over as Councilman of Lotinx. I'm only twenty-four! I'm really hoping he was joking."

They reach *PearlHeart* and Estival sees One-Eye on board. "Oh! I don't remember seeing him."

"That is One-Eye. He became my first mate after Fenrir left."

"I see!" Estival suddenly turns to his Spirit Elephant. "My Elephant says he has a Spirit Lion with him, so that'd make him from Pantha. Have you heard about their king, Faerohr?" Rath nods. "It sounds like he's done a lot of good for the country. My god, Helios, says that it's about time Pantha started working together again." Then he asks, "Where are you off to next?"

"Tecla, for my grandmother's plants."

Estival thinks. "Lotinx, Tecla, Delphy – you'd think you were still training to be a councilman with all the travel you've done in the past five years. This is your sixth, right? As captain?"

"That is right."

"That's really amazing. I mean, what led to it wasn't – that sounds terrifying – but the rest? It's neat. Take care, Rath, all right? Nice seeing you again, too, Isaac, William, and Phobos!"

"You, too!" Isaac says.

"Take care," William says and Phobos gives a happy "Caw!"

"It was wonderful seeing you again, Estival," Rath says. "We will see you next year."

Estival nods. "Oh, definitely. Just as long as my dad wasn't serious about making me councilman by then. I'm not ready for that sort of thing. Bye, Rath!"

As Rath goes up the gangplank with his crew, Estival looks up at *PearlHeart* thoughtfully. One-Eye sees him staring and Estival waves to him. One-Eye awkwardly waves back. Estival smiles.

PearlHeart pulls away, sailing north toward Tecla.

They travel for another eight days. During that time, Isaac finishes the wooden puzzle that Rath gave him for his birthday. He shows it to Rath excitedly, who is happy to hear that he likes it. It is in the shape of a Pantrog tree.

The next evening, *PearlHeart* arrives at Port Paka on Tecla. It is quiet but the arid breeze brings talk from further in town, where lanterns are filled with glowing Teclan herbs.

Rath has gathered One-Eye and Oren. "My grandmother tells me that the shop she would like plants from is in the town just to the east of here. She has requested three of the same."

Oren raises an eyebrow. "What kind? You usually say."

Rath runs his hand through his hair. "She says ... she would like me to choose. I am very nervous about it."

As they start down the gangplank, One-Eye asks, "Why?"

"It is a very important decision. They will go in Grandmother's South Garden. I would like to pick ones that would be suitable."

"If she asked you to choose, then I think she wants ones that you'd like."

Rath looks uncomfortable. "But – " He pauses. "That does make sense."

They reach the end of the docks and start down a road with stone walls on either side. As it dips, they come to a bridge that arches overhead, a single lantern illuminating the entrance. They go beneath it and on the other side, the road begins to ascend. Many lanterns are now set into the walls on either side of them. The sounds of talking grow louder, funneling into the enclosed road.

A worker is there shaping a staircase with glowing orange hands as he uses Maro's Traits. Two children suddenly run down the street, laughing as they chase one another. They pat the wall next to the worker, leaving handprints in the stone and the worker shakes his head mildly, then smoothes them out.

Rath, One-Eye, and Oren reach the top of the hill. A small plaza is there, with a mosaic spiraling around the center. People dance beneath lanterns and paper decorations while others watch and eat, sitting at tables and standing by the surrounding shops and restaurants.

"This must be Paka Plaza," Rath says. He scans the streets connected to it. He brightens. "I believe that is Pern Street, where Grandmother said the shop was located."

They go around the perimeter of the plaza. Rath looks at the dancing in the center as they do, having never seen it before. One woman tosses her hand up in a flourish and Rath mimics the gesture at waist level while he walks.

Shops line both sides of Pern Street and a warm breeze kicks up the dust on the ground. People quietly talk in groups, relaxing away from the festivities or on their way home. Rath and the others continue until he sees a shop sign with a lizard on it.

The shop is small and simple, with cactus plants sitting outside and on the two long window sills on either side of the entrance. The door is propped open by a stone.

They enter and once inside, Rath inhales quickly.

The room is filled to the brim with plants – hanging and in beds and in clay pots. A small path done in a similar mosaic as the plaza outside runs between them.

As Rath takes it all in, a swinging lantern appears ahead of them, illuminating a scuttling lizard and a short man with kind eyes. "Why hello." He joins them. "Don't often get visitors on Saturdays – everyone's out in the plaza. What can I do for you?"

"Your shop is beautiful," Rath says. The man's eyebrows go up and Rath flushes deeply. He bows. "I sincerely apologize. I am Captain Rath of Delphy. This is One-Eye and Oren, who are members of my crew. My grandmother, Lady Azalea, has asked that I find plants for her South Garden here. She has asked for three of the same kind."

The man brightens. "Azalea! And her grandson ... I see." He extends his hand to shake Rath's. "Azalea is a great friend of mine – and one of my longest. It's a pleasure to meet you, Captain. My name is Maro."

"It is wonderful to meet you," Rath says. However, beside him, One-Eye frowns, recognizing the name.

"Now, as for the plants ... Well, your grandmother said for you to find them, so why don't you look around? I should have enough of all of them for you to take back three to her South Garden." He pauses. "South Garden, you said?" Rath nods and Maro chuckles. "So, she's started her third." He muses on this as he walks off to fill more lanterns with Teclan herbs that glow for Rath and the others to see by. He says over his shoulder, "I'll be wandering around – just find me when you decide which ones you like."

"I will, Maro. Thank you very much."

After Rath leaves, Oren asks One-Eye, "You want to look around, too?"

"I don't know about plants," One-Eye says. He looks over at Rath, kneeling, very carefully studying a small, perky plant in the soil. The lantern light makes his hair a bright orange. One-Eye flushes, then walks in the opposite direction. "Let's go this way."

Oren looks at Rath, then One-Eye, then shrugs and follows.

For the next hour, Rath, One-Eye, and Oren explore the shop. Rath looks at a hanging plant near a lantern. Oren points out a particularly spikey one to One-Eye. One-Eye's Spirit Lion studies a bulky cactus. While Rath is looking at another low-growing plant, the lizard from before joins him and peers up at him with beady eyes. Rath extends his hand and the lizard looks at it then places his scaly palm on one of Rath's fingers. Rath smiles. Afterward, the lizard goes back to Maro, who leans on his desk at the back of the shop. A conversation seems to occur between them and Maro looks happy.

Later, One-Eye and Oren find Rath near the center of the shop, studying the same small, perky plant he had started with. Rath hears their footsteps and stands. "I believe I have found the plant I want." He hesitates.

One-Eye frowns. "What's wrong?"

"I am very uncomfortable with buying something that I have chosen."

"Haven't you bought anything for yourself?"

"Supplies."

One-Eye nods down to the plant. "That one?"

"Yes. It reminds me of Flower-Pagu."

"That's not the reason you're getting it?"

"Ah, no. It does remind me of Flower-Pagu, however, it makes me happy to look at. I believe that is a good sign."

One-Eye does not say anything for a moment. "Yeah. It is. So, get it. Or, them. You're getting three, right?"

"I am." Rath smiles at the plant. "I believe I will. Thank you, One-Eye. Please excuse me." He walks away. "Maro? I have chosen which plants I would like."

"Wonderful!"

Back by the plant, One-Eye stares at Rath's back, deeply flushed. Oren looks at the two of them again, then sagely nods.

Soon, Maro and Rath return. Rath gestures. "This is the one."

"Ahh, I see." Maro nods. "Meka plants are small, but very hardy." One-Eye's Spirit Lion hears this and looks at the plant with newfound interest. "Pick the three you would like and I'll have them dug up for you and put in travel pots."

"Thank you very much." Rath sits on his knees and studies them. When Maro returns with a shovel, he shows him which ones he would like and Maro digs them out.

Soon, they are all by the counter at the back and the plants have been stored safely in a crate.

"Glad you found what you wanted, Captain," Maro says.

Rath smiles. "I did. Thank you very much, Maro."

"Of course." Maro scratches the back of his head. "Though, if you want ... I'd like your opinion on something. Seeing as you're Azalea's grandson, you've seen a lot of gardens."

"I have seen my grandmother's."

"And her's are one of the highest standards. Do you have a moment?"

"I do."

Maro says to One-Eye and Oren, "You're welcome to come, too. Even if you don't know much about plants, it's always good to get outside opinions."

One-Eye says, "Sure," and Oren nods.

Maro leads them behind the counter, through a short hallway, then out a back door. The evening breeze blows inside as he opens it.

Outside, a rock garden with different cacti sprouting up alongside rock formations and mosaics cover the entire area. In the center, the mosaic forms a lizard with two orange eyes glinting in the lantern light.

"This is amazing," Rath breathes.

Maro flushes. "Thanks. Glad you feel that way."

"It's different," One-Eye says.

"That's all right. I know Lionel's own aren't much for gardens."

One-Eye frowns, but before either of them can continue, Oren says, "Huh. That lizard mosaic kind of looks like the turtle one at Lady Azalea's."

Maro says, "Probably because the same person did it. I did, actually."

Rath says, "Really? You are very talented."

"Thank you. It was the least I could do for Azalea after all she's done for me." He pauses. "I'd love to see her gardens again some day. The last time I visited, she had just started her West Garden, but I don't think she's ever let anyone see that one, has she?"

Rath shakes his head solemnly. "No. Grandmother says that it is her private garden."

"She needs that. I would like to see the others, though. You mentioned a South, so she must have done an East."

"That is right."

"They would be remarkable to see." He sighs. "Someday. Maybe ... " He looks at his garden for a moment, then turns back to Rath and the others. "Thank you for looking. It's something I've been working on for a long time now – although most of that time was getting up the confidence to do it. But, I'm happy with how it's been turning out so far."

"It is beautiful," Rath agrees.

They leave afterward and Maro waves to them from his open front door. The lizard perched on his shoulder makes a quick flapping gesture at them with his arm. Rath, holding the crate with plants, nods back while One-Eye and Oren wave.

As they walk down Pern Street, Rath smiles at the crate and One-Eye glances at him, then flushes as he looks ahead instead. Oren puts his arms behind his head, whistling.

When they reach Paka Plaza, Oren says, "So, we're staying the night here, right, Captain?"

Rath starts. "Ah, yes."

Oren jerks his thumb to the surrounding restaurants. "Why not get something to eat here? Bet the others would want to, too."

"That is a wonderful idea. I would like that very much." Rath looks down at the crate again. "I just need to bring Grandmother's plants to *PearlHeart* and then I can ask the others."

One-Eye coughs. "I'll go with you."

Oren says, "I'll check out what looks good here." He stretches casually and saunters off.

One-Eye walks beside Rath, who is looking at the dancing again. They reach the hill, pass under the bridge, then arrive at the docks to board *PearlHeart*.

Rath carefully secures the crate in the cargo hold, then pulls out his logbook. He writes in it happily.

Then he, One-Eye, Charles, Isaac, Melody, Demeter, and Evermore return to the plaza. They sit together at one of the outside tables, trying the Teclan food from the restaurant that Oren recommended.

Rath and One-Eye sit next to each other as they eat and talk. All around them, the lanterns glow warmly over Paka Plaza.

20

During the beginning of *PearlHeart's* sixth journey, Oracle, the Goddess of Paradi, had begun flying east in her bird form, toward her sister Amara's island, Unys.

She now flies through the fog surrounding it, a spot of color in the white. Ahead, the shadow of an island begins to appear. As she grows closer, she can see a beach, then a path running its way through tall needled trees all the way up to the top of a hill, where the fog pulls away to reveal a glowing white castle.

Oracle lands on the beach and shakes her feathers. "Oh, I always forget how damp it is here!" In her human form, she makes her way up the path.

It takes her several hours to reach the castle, however when she does, the Amaran knight and unicorn partner stationed at the gate recognize her immediately.

"Holy Oracle!" The knight bows and her unicorn partner dips her head. "It is truly a pleasure to see and welcome you to Castle Unys. I am Sir Lunra and this is my partner, Awakening Turquoise."

"Thank you." Oracle cocks her head to the side. "I came here seeking my sister, Amara. Would you know if she is here?"

The knight looks pained. "I am afraid she is not. A most pressing duty – nay, destiny – has compelled her to ascend to the high land of Phoenae to confer with her brother and Ruler of the Fourth World, Most Holy Merp."

"I see. That is concerning." Oracle looks around. "It does not appear that there are as many knights here as I am accustomed to seeing. Are they out as well?"

"Yes. With both good intentions, yet unfortunate times. Many of the Amaran knights are in the Southern Seas, attending to the customs ports that were left by our fellow protectors, the Selachuu soldiers, though some have since returned and gone on to other most noble tasks. Still more are on the waters – such as our leader and Lady Amara's chosen Champions, Sir Ronan and Opal Starlight – who are further to the east, warning good travelers of the dangers of the weather to the North."

"Would you know if the storm there has continued? Or grown?"

"I do not, Holy Oracle. I have been tasked with remaining here by Lady Amara's most elegant order so that I may receive travelers and notify them of the state of Unys and its protector, Amara."

"I thank you for doing so, Sir Lunra and Awakening Turquoise." Oracle thinks. "Then, I believe I will head north next. I am concerned for my brother Elvin and the storm that has overtaken Haliae. I wish to see if there is anything I can do to help."

Lunra's eyes shine and Awakening Turquoise looks on with admiration. "A most noble and valiant task!" Both bow again. "I wish you the greatest success – if I may be so forward to do so – in both endeavors and add my strength if not by presence but by word and spirit. I shall pray, Holy Oracle."

"Thank you."

Oracle leaves Unys and travels through the fog again in her bird form. A few days later, she exits under overcast skies. It is not long until she sees Sir Ronan and Opal Starlight standing on the ocean, the waters glowing white under Opal Starlight's hooves. "Oh, poor dears," Oracle says as she descends. "Greetings, Sir Ronan and Opal Starlight, Champions of my sister, Amara!"

Ronan, who had been looking at a small pouch in his

hands, raises his head abruptly. He dismounts and bows. Opal Starlight lowers her neck. "Holy Oracle! Truly a miracle it is to behold you in such a place and time. I am currently on orders from my Lady Amara, however, it is only fitting for a knight and far more for my Lady's Champion to endeavor to do what I can for one such as my Lady's sister."

"Thank you, Sir Ronan." Oracle flicks her head to the Southern Selachuu Military Base, which is not far from them. "Might I ask why you are on the ocean? Despite the weather, I would believe that one of Belle's bases would be more comfortable."

"With the most high and due respect, Holy Oracle, comfort does not always equate to the tasks that my Lady sets forth for me." He glances guiltily at the pouch. "But, it is with honor that I stand where my Lady has tasked me to so that I may warn the fair ships and" – he falters – "That is, to warn the fair ships of the dangers that are currently present in the North so as to protect the fair – good people on them."

Oracle studies him. "If I may, you seem troubled, Sir Ronan."

"I am, Holy Oracle. My Lady ... " He shakes his head. "Well, it is not something that she would wish me to speak of."

Oracle pauses. "Did Amara say that you had to remain in this spot exactly?"

"Well, no, but her words were clearly that I stay."

"So that you may warn ships." She comes upon an idea. "But, it is the job of the Selachuu soldiers to check every ship going to the North. Why not go to their base and do your task set by my sister while they do theirs? I'm sure they wouldn't mind either."

Ronan hesitates. "Well, we have traveled to land and specifically that of Holy Belle's bases for provisions and" – he glances at the pouch one more time – "other accessories that are not suitable for a knight of my station."

"Let's go there right now. At the very least, it will give us time to talk!"

Ronan and Opal Starlight look at each other. His partner snorts. "Very well. Opal Starlight reminds me that we have not trained for the many days that we have been camped atop the ocean and that in doing so, we are abandoning a great tenant of being a Knight of Amara."

"Ohh! The Selachuu soldiers are always up for sparring!"

"They are indeed!"

As they move in the direction of the base, Oracle says, "Now, tell me about that pouch."

"Well, I wished to write a letter of reply ... "

While they travel, Ronan tells Oracle of meeting Captain Rath of *PearlHeart* and the letters they exchanged over the Winter. As they are arriving at the Southern Selachuu Military Base, Ronan says, holding a stack of papers in his hands, "And he replied! Receiving it brought me great joy and yet deep regret that Lady Amara disapproves of such a thing."

"I am very sorry to hear that, Sir Ronan."

He sighs and tucks the letter back in his pouch. "It is truly the life of a knight to be faced with one's own duty and not for such things as a forbidden love. But, it did make me happy for a time."

Oracle flies lower. "Has Amara forbidden a friendship with Captain Rath?"

"Well, no. No, she hasn't. Yet, she wishes to speak of him not."

"I do not believe a friendship – a comradery with such a person that brings you joy – is anything unchivalrous."

"Very truly spoken. I shall think." He raises his eyes. "Ah! And here we arrive at the base." Ronan waves his hand and a white ramp made from Amara's Traits appears for Opal Starlight to walk off of the ocean and up to the land.

Captain Farbourne, who had been honing his sword on a whetstone, sees them and smiles. "Hey, Sir Ronan, Opal Starlight." He looks up at the giant rainbow bird. "Hey, Oracle."

"Hello!"

Ronan says, "Holy Oracle, this man, the good Captain Farbourne, is the one that procured for me ink and paper with which to write my letter – and bandages so that I may practice the art of healing!"

"Oh my!"

Farbourne takes one last look at his sword, tests the edge, then stands up, resting it on his shoulder. "Wasn't using the ink and paper much. Bandages, sometimes, but had extra."

Ronan beams. "Such prudence!"

Farbourne grins.

Oracle lands. "Captain Farbourne, may I ask as to the state of the North?"

"Bad. Worse than here." He unhooks his mug from his belt, opens it, and takes a swig from it. "By a lot. No travel three hundred miles north of Pica Pica."

"Oh dear."

Ronan nods. "Which is precisely why my duty is so important."

Oracle says quickly, "Captain Farbourne, would you mind if Sir Ronan and Opal Starlight stayed here to perform their duty set by my sister Amara? To ask ships where they will be headed and warn them about the dangers of the North."

"Sure. It's pretty much what we're doing, too."

Surprised, Ronan says, "Why, then we truly are upholding a most common and righteous cause!"

Farbourne shrugs. "Guess so." He hooks his mug back to his belt. "Well, if you and your partner are staying for longer, do either of you want to spar?"

Ronan unsheathes his sword, which materializes at his side. "With great pleasure!"

Opal Starlight whinnies in approval.

Oracle smiles. "Before you do that – would you know how my brothers Belle and Elvin are doing?"

Farbourne says, "Yeah. Think Sven and Pema – the acting representatives on Haliae – deemed the island too dangerous, so from what I hear, Elvin sent one of his Spirit Eagles to Belle. Turns out they and the other Spirit Animals can move through the storm just fine, though they're a little disturbed by it. Right now, Belle's working on evacuating the people on Haliae south to Pica Pica. Most of our ships are up north right now to take them."

"Oh!" Oracle lifts off. "Then, I'd best go help them. And, if I may, Sir Ronan, I would keep the pouch."

He frowns. "Holy Oracle ... "

"I believe it is the most honorable thing to do. After all, Captain Farbourne very kindly procured you the bandages, ink, and paper that are being carried within it. And, I am certain Captain Rath took a great deal of care in writing his letter to you." She tilts her head to the side.

Ronan understands slowly. "It would be highly dishonorable

to dismiss both kindnesses." He lays the pouch on a stone bench. "Very well, I will keep it then – just, not on my personage."

Farbourne taps his sword on his shoulder. "I've got a place to keep it, if you want."

Ronan beams. "Many thanks, Captain Farbourne!"

As Oracle flies away, the two begin sparring – a glowing white sword against a dark steel blade. Next to them, Opal Starlight paws the ground and snorts. Two Selachuu soldiers immediately get up to train with her.

Oracle flies north. Within days, she passes by Pica Pica. The festivities have continued despite the growing darkness beyond.

A week later, she arrives at the edge of Ara's Storm. She concentrates until a magenta glow surrounds her. Bracing herself, she plunges into the storm.

Outside of her barrier, large snowflakes rush past and a bitter wind shrieks. Oracle pumps her wings, flying on.

Further north, Belle stands at a watch tower, looking at the distant shape of Pantha Castle. He chews on his silver toothpick.

A Selachuu general approaches. "All of the ships are ready, Belle."

"Thanks. Keep an eye on things here."

"Yes, sir." They trade places and Belle walks over to the opposite rail of the watchtower. He dives over and midway through, glows and turns into his shark form. He splashes into the icy water then surfaces, glowing blue-gray. Over a hundred Selachuu ships wait next to him. "Three of you – with me."

Their captains, sitting on top of the hatches, reply back, "Yes, sir!" They enter their ships and alert their crews.

They go underwater and begin to move. Belle concentrates and his glow surrounds them, too. The uncertain rocking of their ships in the tumultuous currents level out. Then, swimming in the middle of them, Belle and his Selachuu ships move toward Haliae.

They arrive eight days later. Belle gives a signal to his captains below water to remain where they are, then swims up. He turns into his human form and steps onto the snow-covered beaches of Haliae.

"Elvin!" he shouts.

A dim, light blue glow appears. "Belle?" Then Elvin, surrounded by the glow, runs forward. He takes his brother's hands. "Thank you so much."

"It's fine. Are your people ready?"

"They are. Sven is fretting that he waited too long to make his decision. Is it still possible to leave?"

"Should be."

They suddenly hear a call from above. Oracle lands beside them, adding her glow to their own in a swirl of magenta, light blue, and blue-gray. "Brothers! I've heard what is to be done and I've arrived to help."

Elvin chokes a little. "Thank you, Oracle."

"It's appreciated," Belle says. He thinks. "You'll have to fly low to get your barrier in range of my Selachuu ships. Guide these three to Pica Pica and I'll return with three more from my base."

"Yes, Brother!" Oracle flies off to get into position.

As she does, Elvin says, "And I will help my people board."

They part, Belle back into the ocean and Elvin to the mountain.

When he enters through the stone slab, Sven and Pema are there standing by the door. Sven says, "Did they – is Belle ... He's here, right?"

"Yes, yes." Elvin's eyes sparkle. "And Oracle, too! She flew all the way from Paradi to help. We'll be able to get everyone to Pica Pica far faster."

"Bless her!" Sven says and Pema looks relieved.

"Would you have the first three groups gathered? I will help them board Belle's ships."

"Yes, Elvin." Sven and Pema leave.

When they return, Elvin uses his barrier to help the first group through the storm and to the beach. There, they enter Oracle's barrier and are helped inside the ships by the Selachuu soldiers. Once all three are full, they take off – south – toward Pica Pica with Oracle flying above them.

Elvin watches them go, then returns to the mountain to be with his people until the rest of the ships arrive.

From inside Pantha Castle, Faerohr watches the storm.

They had just had the bout in the Coliseum and finished

their meal. Many are sleeping around the castle, most near the different fireplaces.

He suddenly hears Lionel say, "What?"

Faerohr turns and sees his god in his human form, talking with a Spirit Lion. As the Spirit Lion scratches his ear, Lionel says, "Bunch of weaklings ... "

Faerohr walks over. "Who?"

"Haliae." Lionel looks at the Spirit Lion. "Says they're being evacuated."

"Isn't that a good thing? I mean, for them. For us ... " Another gale rattles the windows.

Lying down on his back, Lionel says, "Just because it hasn't ended yet doesn't mean it won't. And if it doesn't, tough it out!"

Faerohr frowns. "It's nearly Summer. Have any of Ara's Storms lasted this long?"

"One nearly thirteen years ago, I think." He sits up and shakes out his hair. "But, that was just Ara getting upset about something. It didn't last forever."

Faerohr ruffles the Spirit Lion's mane, considering. "How are they leaving Haliae?"

"Sounds like Belle's ships." The Spirit Lion says something and Lionel's eyebrows go up. "Oracle's here, too? Good for her."

Faerohr listens. "Barriers?" He says to Lionel, "Can you do that?"

"Well, duh. Mine are the strongest, too." He pauses. "Almost. They're stronger than Elvin and Oracle's definitely. Belle and I are probably equal." He glows and turns into his lion form, where he busily begins cleaning a paw.

"Then ... why haven't you done anything?"

"'Cause I don't need to. You all are strong. We'll survive. Ha! I bet tales will be told of how we all braved the storm! Us – against nature!"

"And Ara."

"Him, too. And we won!" He bares his teeth in a grin.

The Spirit Lion, invigorated by his god's words, leaps at him and they begin to tussle. Faerohr sighs and sits on the couch, watching. Finally, he says, "If we joined the Alliance, would we be granted the same aid that Haliae is receiving?"

Lionel stops. He has won the tussle and bumps noses with the Spirit Lion before getting off of him. The Spirit Lion stands up, shaking out his mane. "This again. Yeah, I guess so."

"Seems like it would be a good idea."

Lionel growls. "No, Faerohr."

"Just a suggestion."

The god walks in a circle, then flops down. The Spirit Lion disappears. "I'm telling you, you don't need the Alliance with me here. I'll keep all of you you safe. I promise."

Faerohr pauses, then rises to lay another log on the fire. Afterward, he sits next to Lionel – snoring already – and runs his hand through his god's mane.

21

Two months later, *PearlHeart* has arrived at Renet Island. Captain Berkut has just helped them with customs and is returning to the main deck with Rath. He says, "The plants that you selected are ... interesting, Captain."

Rath smiles. "I find them to be wonderful."

Berkut returns it, fond, but nothing more. "I hope they find the rest of the journey safe."

"As do I."

Berkut's expression grows more serious. "I was notified of something you may need to be aware of. Haliae has been evacuated. I am told that the last of Belle's ships arrived this past week."

Rath looks startled. "I see."

"I cannot say what that will mean for your delivery there, however, I would think that you will receive further instructions."

"I agree. Thank you for notifying me, Captain Berkut."

"Of course. Safe travels, Captain."

As *PearlHeart* sails away, Berkut and Rath wave to one another, then Berkut returns to the fort.

For the next fifteen days, they sail through the Delphaen Trade Route. As they are exiting from the western side, a giant rainbow bird flies over them. Oracle gives a call, then asks, "Captain Rath! If I may board your ship?"

"Yes, Oracle!"

She lands and turns into her human form. She looks tired, but relieved. "I trust that you have heard of Haliae being evacuated."

"I have. Captain Berkut on Renet Island told me."

Oracle nods. "Thankfully, they are now all on Pica Pica. I am so glad that Sven and Pema can see Hailcorn and Fritz again." She holds out a note. "This is from Elvin. He is now on Pica Pica, too. It's instructions for what to do with his ink and paper."

"I understand." Rath takes it, then bows. "Thank you very much for bringing this to me."

The goddess beams. "It is my pleasure. Are you off to your grandmother's now?"

"That is right."

"I wonder ... " She does not finish. Instead, she says, "I will go inform the rest of my siblings of what has happened. Safe travels, Captain Rath!"

"You as well!"

After Oracle leaves, Rath goes to his cabin to read his note from Elvin. Once he is finished, he asks One-Eye and Well-Pagu to join him and they sit at the table together. Rath says, "Elvin has requested the ink and paper be delivered to Pica Pica instead. He does not know when he or his people will be able to return to Haliae again."

One-Eye frowns. Well-Pagu looks sad.

Rath shifts uncomfortably. "I thought I would see if any further help was needed – on Pica Pica. Without our journey to Haliae, we would have at least a month left of travel before returning to Priage. I've written a letter in reply to Elvin to ask if there was anything that we may be able to do while we are there."

Well-Pagu smiles and One-Eye says, "Fine with me."

That evening, Rath is in the cargo hold with the deliveries. He has already checked the ink and paper and is now looking at the Meka plants from Tecla. He fingers a leaf very carefully and wishes it a wonderful night, then smiles and writes in his logbook.

Two weeks later, they arrive on Lady Azalea's Island.

Azalea is waiting on the shore for them when they do. Rath meets her and they hug one another warmly. One-Eye comes down to the beach and Rath stands up to introduce him. "Grandmother, I would like you to meet One-Eye. He is now the acting first mate on *PearlHeart* and a dear friend of mine."

One-Eye flushes at the last comment. He says to Rath's grandmother, "Azalea?"

She grins. "You've got it." She studies him. "Hmm ... Pertan descent as well?"

He nods.

She holds out her hand. "Good to meet you, One-Eye. I've heard about what you've done for my grandson and for his ship and crew. Thank you."

One-Eye's eyebrows raise. He takes her hand. "Yeah." Then his Spirit Lion says something to him and he asks her, "You have a Spirit Turtle?"

She smiles and the Turtle waves with one little foot from her place on Azalea's shoulder. "That's right. We have been bonded from our birth. She tells me that you share a similar bond with your Spirit Lion?" One-Eye nods again and Azalea laughs. "I am sure they will have much to talk about!"

They walk on the forest path together. One-Eye's Spirit Lion carries Azalea's Spirit Turtle on his head and they talk amicably with one another. Well-Pagu, Bucket-Pagu, and Flower-Pagu have joined the group as well and many from the crew walk behind them. Rath retrieved the crate of plants from Tecla and now carries it.

"I cannot wait to see which ones you chose," Azalea says.

"It was difficult to do so." He looks down at the crate. "However, I am very happy with them." He flushes deeply. "That is – I hope that is not inappropriate to say given that they are for you, Grandmother."

Azalea laughs. "Not at all! You and your crew started my South Garden; I thought it was only right that we continue to work on it together."

"That would be wonderful. Thank you very much."

When they reach the South Garden, all help with the

planting. Rath pats the ground twice at the base of the last Meka plant, saying, *"Pat, pat,"* and Flower-Pagu beams up at him.

Afterward, everyone relaxes there or in other parts of the gardens. One-Eye's Spirit Lion sniffs a plant in the South Garden with two bright orange flowers. Looking at it also, One-Eye asks, "That's the Pantha Flower?"

Azalea replies, "Yes. It's a hardy one! I am very glad Flower-Pagu found it so they and my grandson could transplant it here."

"Never seen anything like it in Pantha."

Azalea sighs. "Pantha looked like a very different country centuries ago. The Winters have gotten far worse in recent decades, too."

"They've always been bad."

"Not before. Winter came and left, warmed by Spring. Does your Spirit Lion remember this?"

One-Eye turns to his Lion, then his eye widens. "He does."

Azalea smiles, but it is sad. "Draconi, too, has grown colder over the years. The Seasons are very important there, however now it is a frozen land all year. Ara, too, has grown steadily more upset. This storm may be the culmination of that. In some ways, I am not surprised – but certainly not pleased – that this is now happening. Ara's grief is something that has lasted for a very long time." She pauses, thinking, then says to Rath, "It seems you will not be going to Haliae this year, correct?"

"That is right. Captain Berkut and Oracle tell me that Haliae has been evacuated to Pica Pica."

"Good. I do wonder how Pantha is ... " One-Eye tenses and she continues, "I will not argue that your god is the most responsible, One-Eye, but he does care about his own."

One-Eye snorts. "I don't believe that."

Rath looks surprised and Azalea says, "Then, I will defer to you. It has been a very long time since I've spoken with Lionel. However, I had hoped he had improved."

One-Eye begins to retort, but his Spirit Lion gnaws his hand and he pauses. "You've met Lionel?"

"Yes. A long time ago. When the royals still worked together with their people. However, from what I have heard, King Faerohr has now been doing the same."

"Captain Farbourne said that, too."

Azalea nods. Then she gently touches One-Eye's arm. "You are free to go wherever you like on my island, my dear. We have meals here that you are also welcome to join, but not required."

"Thanks." He steps away. "I'll go running now."

"Of course."

Rath says, "I hope you enjoy."

One-Eye's look softens for a moment, then he trots off. He breaks into a run when he reaches the trees. Afterward, Azalea sits down in the chair brought out for her by her staff and Rath sits in the grass next to her.

"Now, tell me how you found these ones," she says, referring to the Meka plants.

Rath smiles gently at them and does.

Throughout the morning, One-Eye runs with his Spirit Lion and Rath tells his grandmother about his journey so far. Later, Rath and Azalea have tea with Carlos in the gazebo to celebrate Rath's twenty-seventh birthday.

When One-Eye returns to the South Garden, Rath is there again, working on something in his hands. One-Eye steps closer and sees that it is the same wood that Vern gave him last year for fixing the wheel on his cart while *PearlHeart* was at Port Telma on Cunica. Rath does another careful nick, then sets the carving down in the grass to compare it with the Meka plants. One-Eye hears him say, "I am so glad that you made the journey safely."

One-Eye frowns. "Did you just talk to that plant?"

Rath turns quickly. "Flower-Pagu says that they – ah, the plants, that is – can listen and like to be spoken to."

One-Eye sits with him, looking at the plant, too. His eye turns to the Pantha Flowers. "My Spirit Lion says that Pantha was different before – like your grandmother said. But, she's at least nine hundred years old, right?"

"That is correct."

One-Eye pets his Spirit Lion. "He says it had more definite seasons before – it wasn't always cold and the Winters weren't always terrible."

"I see." Rath looks at the flower thoughtfully.

One-Eye stands. He offers his hand. "It's almost breakfast. Do you want to eat together?"

Rath takes it. "Yes, please." He gathers his wood carving

and the shavings with his other hand, then stands. They walk to Lady Azalea's home together.

Once inside, Rath guides him to the dining room. One-Eye sees the mural on the ceiling. "Why is it only the Gods?"

"I cannot say. However" – Rath gestures toward the white clouds with three small forms within them – "I never felt that the three there were gods."

One-Eye studies them as well.

Rath says, "That's right. Mother recently restored the octopus – Berceuse – near them."

They begin walking. One-Eye says, "Did she paint it?"

"No. Mother's goddess, Penelope, originally painted it when grandmother's home was finished twenty-two years ago."

"Makes sense it would be gods, then."

They sit down at the head of the table with Azalea, Carlos, and the Pagu. Azalea smiles. "Good to see you, One-Eye. Did you enjoy your run?"

"I did. Thanks. Your island's ... nice."

"Thank you."

"How is it yours? Did you buy it?"

Rath and Carlos' eyebrows go up.

Azalea takes it in stride. "No. It was gifted to me."

"By who?"

"Marchand. However, Belle helped."

The first course is brought to them. One-Eye says, "Why? And helped with what?"

Azalea laughs. "You would have to ask my grandson that." She sobers. "However, part of it was to help our family."

One-Eye hesitates, then understands. "Right."

Near the end of the meal, glass goblets with frozen treats come out and Rath looks at his with wide eyes. It has raspberries in it. Azalea grins as he begins to eat and One-Eye smiles at him.

The Pagu sit across the table, nibbling on theirs, each with a single, perfect raspberry on top.

After they finish, they go out to the hallway and Azalea says to One-Eye, "I was glad to see you came."

"Yeah." He asks, "Did you ever go to Pantha again?"

"No. I only went there once, when I was far younger. For a long time, Hep's people did not travel far from Sudines. In some ways, it is still that way." Then she says, "One-Eye, my grandson tells me that you play cards with one another?" One-Eye nods and she grins. "Would you like to play together while you're here? Perhaps this afternoon, after lunch?"

One-Eye looks interested. "Sure."

They part ways then. Carlos and Azalea go to walk in the gardens, One-Eye goes back to *PearlHeart* for a nap, and Rath returns to the South Garden to check on the Meka plants with Flower-Pagu.

Once they are there, Flower-Pagu says, "They're all doing so well! I'm so happy to see it!"

"I am, too. It is wonderful to see how much they grow each year."

Flower-Pagu beams, nodding.

Later that morning, Rath is in the library with Bucket-Pagu. They are finding the next *Tales of Flight* books to borrow for the rest of their journey. Bucket-Pagu says, "And here are books five, six, and seven!" While they take out the Pagu-sized copies on the smaller shelf beneath, Rath pulls out the same, human-sized books from the one above.

Both holding their books, they smile at each other. Bucket-Pagu wiggles their feet in the air. "I can't wait to see where it goes from here! Book four ended on such a cliffhanger!"

"I agree. It was very surprising."

They go to the first floor of the library to read. Rath sits in his chair and Bucket-Pagu lies next to him on their green cushion.

After that, Rath is outside with Well-Pagu talking about the differences between Pan ships and Pagu ships, which Well-Pagu navigated on previously. They say, "Below."

"So, the galley is below on Pagu ships?"

Well-Pagu nods.

"I see. The reason we have the galley above is so that Phillip can get the direct sunlight for his plants. Otherwise, it sounds as though Pagu Ships are very similar to Vocalise's."

"True!" They pause. "Choose?"

"Why did I choose to sail a Pan ship?"

Well-Pagu nods again.

"Because it was what I was able to sail. After I lost my traits, I told my grandmother that I wished to help people and that I would also prefer to stay near the ocean. I had read that Vocalise's ships were able to be sailed by people of all traits. The thought made me very happy."

Well-Pagu's eyes sparkle, understanding what Rath means.

They go to the forest path to meet Flower-Pagu and Bucket-Pagu, who had asked that they come there right before lunch. "This way, Captain!" Flower-Pagu says, leading them.

When they reach a certain point, the Pagu fly off of the path and Rath follows them, careful to not step too close to the small Pagu homes. Before they have gone too far, the trio stops and Flower-Pagu says, "Ta-da! What do you think?"

Rath looks and his eyes light up. A small picnic has been set out on many small blankets with baskets of flowers for decorations and Pagu everywhere.

All of the Pagu say, "Happy Birthday!"

A little overwhelmed, but smiling, Rath says, "Thank you very much, everyone. This is a wonderful surprise." He sits down on his knees next to the Pagu.

"Of course!" the Pagu say in unison and Well-Pagu says, "Course!"

They all begin to pass around baskets of food. Pebble-Pagu flies over to Rath with one full of small cookies.

"Here you go, Rath!" they say.

"Thank you very much, Pebble-Pagu."

While they fly off to serve others do, Rath eats his small cookie.

He returns to Azalea's for lunch and afterward, he, One-Eye, Azalea, Carlos, and the Pagu meet in the sun room to play cards.

Azalea says to One-Eye, "My grandson has told me that you have played Double Berceuse and Marchand's Twist together, but today I want to play a different game. Do you know Sudines Piece?"

Carlos coughs, but says nothing.

One-Eye says, "No."

"All right. Then I'll teach you."

After she does, One-Eye frowns. "Then who wins?"

Azalea smiles benignly. "No one does, dear. It's all about your personal experience in the game."

"Then it's not a game." One-Eye turns to Rath. "Do you play

it?"

"Yes. I would often play it with Fenrir, my previous first mate. I find it to be very reflective."

One-Eye turns to Azalea. "Fine. I'll play a round."

"Wonderful!"

Carlos deals and they begin to play. Each only have three cards in their hands. They draw and discard in a circle. Finally, the last card is drawn and discarded. They are quiet for a moment.

Then Azalea sighs. She looks around the table. "Well? How did the round go for everyone? I had all three of the correct cards for the whole game."

Carlos nods. "I had the third, but not the first two."

Rath says, "I had the first, however, not the second or third."

One-Eye says, "I didn't have any of them."

Azalea smiles kindly. "Sometimes it happens that way." She gathers up the cards. "Now, shall we play Marchand's Twist?"

"Yes, please, Grandmother," Rath says, Carlos nods beside him, and One-Eye looks relieved.

They play several rounds before parting ways. Rath and One-Eye have dinner on *PearlHeart* and afterward, One-Eye walks with Rath toward the South Garden. "Found something when I was running with my Lion earlier. Thought you'd want to see," One-Eye says. They come out to the north beach. "What do you think?"

Rath smiles. "It is beautiful."

One-Eye suddenly realizes something, flushes, and covers his face. "Right. You grew up here. You've probably already seen this."

"I-I have, however, I do not mind seeing it again." Rath hesitates. "This is the beach where my mother would arrive from Campi. I would sit below in the sand waiting for her ship."

"She didn't live here, did she?"

"No. She thought it was best she live on Campi so as not to upset Merp. He did not approve of me learning about that side of my heritage."

One-Eye glares at the ocean and his Lion looks troubled. "How often would she come?"

"Only once a year. During the Winter." Rath exhales. "Even so, Grandmother said that it was important that I understand all aspects of my heritage. She and Carlos taught me much about Sudines and my grandfather and father taught me Delphaen culture. My mother did not wish to disobey Merp, however, she did begin to show me more of her culture from Campi when I was older. And she always made my clothes for me." He brightens. "She makes wonderful blankets. Many of them are on *PearlHeart.*"

One-Eye nods. "She also paints – and restores, like the mural. I remember seeing her painting of the South Garden while we were at your grandfather's house. It was amazing."

"Yes! Many paintings of hers are hanging in my grandmother's home. Would you like to see them?"

One-Eye agrees and they go together. Inside, Rath guides them to the third floor staircase, where Marin's paintings are hung on the right-hand wall. One-Eye and his Lion listen as Rath tells them where each is from. When they reach the top of the stairs, One-Eye says, "They're beautiful," and Rath smiles appreciatively. Then they both look out the tall third floor windows to the gardens below. The sun is beginning to set, making the flowers glow orange.

Azalea walks up the stairs with Carlos and sees them. She says, "There are guest rooms on the third floor if you are interested, One-Eye."

One-Eye shakes his head. "Thanks. But, I'll sleep on *PearlHeart.*" He asks Rath, "Will you sleep here?"

"Yes." He wishes his grandmother and Carlos good night, then says to One-Eye, "May I ask what you think of grandmother's island?"

"It's nice. It's peaceful."

"I agree. I have always felt that here"

"It's home," One-Eye says.

Rath looks surprised, then his look softens. "It is. I consider *PearlHeart* my home as well."

One-Eye smiles briefly, then says, "Sleep well."

"You as well, One-Eye. Good night."

"Night."

Rath goes to his rooms – One-Eye sees him carefully touch the petal of a blue-green flower sitting on a small table outside of his door – then One-Eye returns to *PearlHeart* to sleep.

22

At the end of the week, the crew of *PearlHeart* prepares to cast off from Lady Azalea's Island. Once they are ready, Rath goes down to the beach to hug his grandmother.

As they pull away, Azalea says, "Be careful."

"I will, Grandmother."

She smiles. "And say hello to Hailcorn and Fritz for me. I'm sure he's much relieved now that Sven, Pema, Elvin, and the rest of their people from Haliae are on Pica Pica with him."

"I agree. And, I will do so."

Then Rath walks up the gangplank. He waves to his grandmother and her staff from the upper deck as *PearlHeart* sails away.

In Pantha, Ara's Storm is far worse. The Coliseum is empty. Pantha Castle is full of people, clustering around the different fireplaces and shivering as they eat. Faerohr walks around, handing out blankets. Lionel follows him, looking conflicted.

Faerohr holds out two different colored blankets to a shivering woman. "Blue or green?"

"Blue, please!" She takes it and sneezes.

Frowning, Faerohr walks over to the nearest fireplace and throws more wood in, then returns to Lionel, who mutters, "I can't believe we're doing this. It's Coliseum Day! We're supposed to have our bout, *then* eat!"

"In this case, I think it's necessary we skip the first, Lionel." Faerohr looks out at the storm that has frozen the windows shut. "It's gotten harder to find enough food for everyone, too. Have you given any more thought to us joining the Alliance? Or maybe a barrier?"

"I don't know. And the second ... can't. Not over all of the Pantha." Lionel struggles. "Ara – when he's like this, mind you – Ara's Storm is stronger than what I can handle."

Faerohr nods, looking almost relieved. "Thank you for being honest."

"Yeah. Still don't think we need the Alliance, though. Doubt they'd do anything for us."

Suddenly, they hear two resounding knocks from the front doors. Faerohr goes to open them, saying, "Oh, good. More people are finally coming in. Lionel, would you get some blankets from ... wherever you get them?"

Lionel waves his hand and a new stack appears.

When Faerohr opens the doors, Belle is standing there. "King Faerohr?" the God of Selachuu asks.

"Yes." Faerohr steps aside, letting him inside.

Belle looks around at all of the people around the fireplaces. He turns to Lionel, who is holding a stack of blankets. "You've changed."

"I'm cold," Lionel says.

Belle nods.

Faerohr glances at both of them. "I have a feeling you know each other."

Lionel says, "That's Belle. My brother."

Faerohr looks surprised. "God of Selachuu." To Belle, he says, "I don't think any of ours have come near the borders. I wouldn't imagine many pirates on the ocean, either, with the weather."

"No, there haven't been." Belle's lips quirk up for a moment. "That's been the weird thing lately." He crosses his arms and regards Faerohr. "By next month, you'll have been king for a year."

"That's right."

"Any thought of what you'll do about all of this? What about you, Lionel?" He gestures to the group of people.

Lionel looks at Faerohr. "Don't."

But Faerohr says, "I'm thinking of joining the Alliance."

Belle's eyebrows go high. He gives a short, low laugh. "All right. I like him, Lionel."

Faerohr says to his god, "We need this. We can't survive if this storm continues like it is."

Before Lionel can respond, Belle says, "It will continue." He takes out his toothpick. "From what I've heard, the Pagu say that it isn't going to end. It's going to continue to grow."

Lionel clamps his mouth shut.

Faerohr thinks. "The Pagu ... Right, I've read of them."

"Where?" Belle says to Lionel, "I didn't think your castle had a library."

"It doesn't. Faerohr, where did you read about them? Or the Alliance?"

"In books, like I told you."

Belle says, "Stolen?"

"No. I did some traveling in Ursi. I offered to help a man named Berne with a building project and in exchange, I got a room and access to books belonging to him."

"I see." Belle continues, "You'll need to write a letter to join the Alliance. After you do, I'll get it to the Council as fast as I can. Have you thought of what you might need? I can get some arrangements for evacuation done ahead of the Council's decision."

Lionel crosses his arms. "You really think they're going to accept Pantha?"

However, Faerohr says, "We're not evacuating."

They both turn to him in surprise.

"I thought a lot about it." Faerohr looks up at Lionel. "I think – for now – if we only get the necessities – food, clothes, medical supplies – that we should be fine in Pantha Castle. We'll last through this storm. Besides, the only options for us to go to would be Haliae, which has already been evacuated, Ursi, which can be friendly with Pantha, but they're also territorial over their own resources, and Daerce, which, given Pantha's recent history with bandits crossing their border, seems very unlikely they'll accept us at this time. They're technically not part of the Alliance and have no obligation to allow us in, either."

"You're right." Belle glances at Lionel as if to say *Where did you find him?*

Rubbing his chin, Faerohr continues, "Actually, where are the people of Haliae? Is their councilperson still with them?"

"Pica Pica. Elvin, Councilman Hailcorn and his eagle partner, Fritz, and his son who will succeed him, Sven, and his eagle partner, Pema, are there now."

"Didn't Elvin of Haliae begin the Alliance?" Belle nods. "Then, why not give the letter to them? It would be a good idea to establish connections and could help our chances of joining the Alliance."

Belle grins. "Good idea. Hailcorn can easily send a Phoenae message to the Council and we wouldn't run the risk of the Phoenae messengers interfering or changing your letter."

"Would they do that?"

"Merp doesn't like the idea of other cultures working together. He might not do anything directly, but his messengers might."

"Then, please do. Thank you, Belle."

Faerohr quickly goes to the room he has claimed as his study and writes the letter. When he returns, he hands it to Belle, who gives them a short wave and leaves, going back out into Ara's Storm.

As they return to the main room, Faerohr says to Lionel, "If Merp doesn't want other cultures working together, why in the world would he accept something like the Alliance existing? Although, given he's ruler of this world, that would technically make him ruler of the Alliance as well."

Lionel huffs. "How should I know? The Alliance was always more of Elvin's thing – he came up with it. Don't know why you'd want to be a part of a bunch of weaklings who just discuss things all the time."

"They are offering us aid."

"Not yet, they're not."

Around them, people are saying, "I'm hungry!" or "Yup. Still cold ... " and "Hey! Toss another log on the fire!" and "Nice blue blanket!"

Faerohr says, "I'll check on the fire."

Lionel nods. "I'll look for more food."

To the west, *PearlHeart* has just arrived at Port Telma in Cunica.

Both Phillip's nan, Pelline, and Pelline's neighbor, Vern, have met them, each with their carts. Pelline says, "We brought food for both you and the people from Haliae now on Pica Pica. Since you aren't going on as long of a journey, I trust you'll do what's right with the provisions you don't use."

"Yes, Pelline," Rath says.

They load the crates onto *PearlHeart* and the rest of the crew begins to prepare the picnic, but the mood seems subdued.

Isaac says as he shakes out a blanket, "Do you think they'll ever be able to get back to Haliae?"

William responds, "I hope so."

Franz smoothes out another blanket with Velt. "It still sounds so scary – isn't the storm growing, too?"

"Yeah. That's what I heard," she says.

Nearby, Rath returns from the customs building with Sir Rif and Amethyst Rose to check the cargo. Both look a little more relaxed than they did the previous year. "Miss Pelline has truly been so kind to me," Rif says. He blushes. "She brings me pies." Turning to his unicorn partner, he continues, "And the most wonderful hoof rub for Amethyst Rose! It has truly charmed us to the country life."

Rath says, "I am glad to hear that."

They go up the gangplank, then below to the cargo hold. Rif checks the delivery and does not hesitate in signing off. "I most certainly approve!" He beams at Rath. "Once again, I find you on a most noble quest to bring provisions and ink and paper to the people of Haliae who" – he frowns suddenly – "who are now on Pica Pica. Oh, Lady Amara, for such things to happen ... I do pray that Most Holy Ara's Storm dissipates so these good people may return home."

Rath nods soberly. "I do as well."

They return to the deck, then to the dock where the picnic is ready on the grass up ahead and others have already begun eating. Pelline calls out, "Rif! You're joining this year!"

"Y-Yes, Miss Pelline!" Rif looks around. "Oh! I see pie!" He turns to Rath. "Shall we eat together, Good Captain?"

"Yes, please."

They sit on the same blanket as One-Eye, the Pagu, Carlos, Phillip, Pelline, and Vern. Even Amethyst Rose kneels in the grass near them. Rif offers her an apple and she takes a delicate nibble, then the whole fruit. One-Eye does not look sure about them joining them on the blanket, but the Pagu are delighted.

Not long afterward, Pelline and Vern head back to their farms. Before Rath boards *PearlHeart*, Rif asks to speak with him. The knight is currently pulling something out of his pocket, saying, "My Good Captain, We made this for you." He holds out a small woven grass charm. "Amethyst Rose and I sought out the most wonderful grasses of Cunica to make this. In Amaran culture, this symbol is said to aid one against troubling thoughts."

Rath bows low. "Thank you very much, Sir Rif, Amethyst Rose." He accepts it. "It is very beautiful."

"It is made from Amara's Herb. Amethyst Rose and I prayed over it. It will not die. We were surprised to find such a thing here. However, Cunica is known for its great, fertile soil. I hope that it finds you and your crew safe during your quest, Good Captain Rath."

"Thank you again, Sir Rif."

Rath boards, waving to Sir Rif and Amethyst Rose and *PearlHeart* sails off, heading east.

While they do, Belle travels south. He climbs out of the water at the Southern Selachuu Military Base in his human form. Captain Farbourne and Sir Ronan are seated on a bench, tending to their swords when he arrives. Opal Starlight is flicking her tail next to them, eating some apples.

Captain Farbourne sees Belle first and stands. "Sir." He sheathes his sword with a *shick*.

Belle nods to him. He looks at Ronan and Opal Starlight. "Good to see you here. Both of you."

The unicorn dips her head.

Ronan stands, sheathing his sword as well – it disappears at his side without a sound. He bows. "Thank you for your words, Holy Belle."

Belle frowns at the title, but does not say anything. Instead, he turns back to Farbourne. "Gather up all the ships again. They're going to Pantha."

Farbourne's eyebrows raise, then he grins. "Yes, sir."

"To bring emergency supplies."

Farbourne looks surprised. He nods. "Yes, sir."

Ronan says, "Supplies? Truly?"

Belle replies, "Yeah. Their king requested it due to Ara's Storm." To Farbourne, he says, "Tell them to have all of the ships loaded immediately so they're ready to leave when I join them."

While Farbourne leaves to carry out the order, Ronan exchanges a look with Opal Starlight. "If there is anything we could do to help such a noble cause – "

"No. Stay here. Oracle told me that your goddess wants you here, warning others about the North. You'd best stay to do that. Thanks for your work."

Ronan bows again, as does Opal Starlight. "It is my most cherished duty!"

Belle smiles a little.

Farbourne returns. "They're ready."

"Good. I have to go to Pica Pica first, but I'll meet them before they enter Ara's Storm."

"Yes, sir."

Belle leaves, diving into the ocean and surfacing in his shark form.

Ronan, Opal Starlight, and Farbourne watch. Ronan muses, "Miracles abound. To think that Pantha would accept such supplies – I do not believe I have heard of them ever doing so before."

Farbourne shrugs and takes a swig from his mug. "Seems like they're changing."

"Most truly."

Opal Starlight tosses her head.

Belle swims north. As he goes past the long military base, ships that have heard the order peel off and begin traveling alongside him. Five days later, Belle moves away from them and turns west to go to Pica Pica. Confetti starts to drifts over him the closer he gets and the cheers bounce off the waves. He arrives at the South Port, where he turns into his human form. There are people everywhere. Some with eagle partners on their shoulders see Belle and bow respectfully to him. He nods in turn and asks, "Councilman Hailcorn, Sven, and Elvin. Where are they?"

They point him in the direction of the large clock tower in the center of the city. Belle walks through the streets. Colored smoke explodes above him. He passes a large fountain, then walks up the steps to the front doors of the tower.

Up above, Sven, Pema, Hailcorn, and Fritz are on the seventh floor balcony, sitting at a table together. Elvin is there, too, reading a letter by the railing.

After he finishes, Sven says, "What did Rath say?"

Elvin looks up. "Well, he understands that they will deliver the ink and paper to Pica Pica instead of Haliae and wishes to thank me for notifying him. He also asks if there may be anything that he and his crew may do while here in Pica Pica. Not delivering to Haliae will mean that they have at least one open month of travel."

Hailcorn smiles. "That's very kind of him. Any ideas?"

Elvin nods. "Distribution of the supplies around Pica Pica always needs help. Going by sea would likely be faster than across the land."

"Good idea."

One of Hailcorn's aides appears at the door. "Councilman Hailcorn, Lord Sven, Elvin. Belle is here with a message."

As they all turn to the door with wide eyes, Belle steps through. "Can't be here long. Meeting others." He holds up a letter. "This is for all of you. From the King of Pantha, Faerohr."

Their eyes grow larger. While Belle waits, Sven, Pema, and Elvin crowd around Hailcorn, who reads the letter out loud. *"Our intent to join the Alliance ... "* They all gasp. Hailcorn reads, more quickly, *" ... we have deemed Ara's Storm to be too dangerous and therefore request immediate aid as due any country part of the Alliance."* He turns to his god. "Elvin, what do you make of this?"

Elvin is stunned. He steps away, pacing the balcony. "Well, it's ... incredible! I fully accept."

"As do I." Hailcorn frowns, bringing his hand up to Fritz. "But, the Council will be another issue."

Elvin strokes his nose, thinking. "Now, normally we wouldn't be able to offer any aid before a country is admitted into the Alliance, but, given the storm..." He looks at his councilman.

Hailcorn understands. "We could invoke immediate aid given the circumstances." He rubs his chin. "We can get everything organized while the Council discusses the proposal officially. By the time we're done, they should have reached a decision."

"I already have my ships sailing there," Belle says. "They'll need my help once they get into the storm. I'll go rejoin them now."

Elvin says, "Thank you, Belle."

Belle nods and leaves.

The others look at each other.

Sven asks, "Do you think that the Council will agree to accept them?"

"I am sure of it," Elvin says, beaming.

Hailcorn says, "Given they're not asking for much besides basic necessities – they're not even asking to be evacuated – I'd say the chances are good. The unique situation in Pantrog has also done well to grow relations between those from Pantha and elsewhere, further improving the chances."

Sven thinks. "Rath does now have a first mate from Pantha. I wonder what he would think of this ... "

Hailcorn says, "I'll forward the letter to the Council myself and include my support of Pantha joining the Alliance. Then, we'll only have to wait for their answer."

23

Far to the west, on Campi, Berceuse lies on the beach while Penelope embroiders a blanket. He stretches out. "It is truly beautiful weather! I almost feel like I'm still on my Isles of Oct." He frowns, however.

Penelope sees and says, "What is it, Berceuse?"

He sits up. The sand falls off his hair. "Well, I cannot help but feel guilty that we have such a beautiful sky here and Elvin and his people ... From what I hear, they cannot even go home."

Penelope shifts uncomfortably. "That's true."

"Isn't there something that can be done? My dear ones said that Ara's Storm would not end – that it would only grow larger. Isn't there a way to stop it?"

"I mean ... " Penelope accidentally pokes her finger with her needle and sucks on it. "Well, that is, if it's *Ara* causing it, wouldn't that mean that ... " She clears her throat. "That *he* would be the only one able to, um ... "

Berceuse leans forward. "End it. Ohh, you are completely correct. That, um, *does* make it rather difficult, doesn't it?"

Penelope just nods.

"What about Merp? I have never met our new brother, but

wouldn't this be his decision, as the ruler of this world?"

"I ... " Penelope fumbles with her needle again, then finally lays her embroidery in her lap. "I'm not sure. Merp doesn't really leave Phoenae. Ever."

"And Phoenae is far above the clouds, isn't it?"

Penelope nods. "You would need a Phoenae airship to get there. Or one of our siblings that can fly."

Berceuse gives a gusty sigh. He flops back down. "Before, anything like this would be the responsibility of the current ruler. Yet, Merp has done nothing?"

"I mean, we don't know that for sure, but ... " She sighs. "I don't like the situation either."

They are both quiet, thinking.

Finally, Penelope says, "Y-You know what we do when we're not sure? I mean, us gods."

"Ask the Pagu?"

"That's right! However, we've found someone else in this world that's been a great deal of help. Two people actually, though one of them might be unavailable right now ... "

Berceuse sits up again. "Who would the other be, then?"

"Lady Azalea."

Recognizing the name, Berceuse beams. "You mean, my Captain's grandmother?"

"Yes! She's always been very kind to us. Um, and the other person is Carlos. He makes wonderful tea. But, he's on *PearlHeart* right now."

"His tea is absolutely divine! I remember it from when we were on my Isles!"

Penelope smiles. "Whenever any of us have been unsure on what to do, we've gone to seek their advice. She and Carlos traveled for a while before, but for the past twenty-three years, she's been on her island. I think even Amara has sought out her advice."

"Truly! Then, we shall go there!"

Penelope suddenly pales. "Um ... " She fidgets with her blanket. "I-I don't know. That's a really far place and ... Maybe I should just stay here ... "

"That was my exact thinking before I left my Isles. And look at all the good that it has led to!" He blushes. "Well, *I* think it has led to much good."

Penelope takes his hand. "It has. It's been *so* wonderful to see you. I'm just not sure if ... " She coughs. "I don't know if I'm ready for that right now."

Berceuse stands up. "I understand. I do. Then, I will go. Thank you so much for having me on Campi for so long."

"Of course! You're ... you're really sure?"

"Yes! I have already made the journey here all the way from my Isles of Oct."

"That was a really long way and ... you're okay." Penelope bites her lip. Then, she sets down her needle and blanket and looks up at Berceuse very seriously. "Berceuse, take my hand."

Berceuse looks surprised. "Of course."

"Now, walk us both to the beach so that – " Her toe touches the water. "Eep!" Berceuse looks at her and she shakes her head, saying, "No. Keep going." But she makes distressed sounds the further out they go. When they are up to their calves in the water, Penelope freezes. She looks at the ocean, stretching out for miles until Lady Azalea's Island, which is a tiny dot on the horizon. She starts to turn around, hesitates, then says, "Berceuse, tell me we're going to Lady Azalea's Island!"

"We're ... " Berceuse says confidently, "We're going to Lady Azalea's Island!"

"Yes, we are!" With a terrified shriek, Penelope jumps into the water. Berceuse joins her.

They both resurface, Berceuse in his octopus form and Penelope in her tiny seahorse form. "I-I'm ready!" she says.

"Then we shall go!" Berceuse says and sets the pace. Penelope pauses for only one more moment before swimming forward and soon, alongside her brother.

It takes them ten days to reach the island. They rest each night and look up at the stars. Berceuse tells Penelope about how he promised to tell Rath his constellation story.

"Really?" Penelope says, surprised. "I haven't even heard it."

Berceuse colors. "Parts of it I am not very proud of. However, I feel that my Captain will accept that and who I am."

"We will, too, you know. Your family."

Berceuse pauses, then nods happily. "I know." He sighs. "It's just more difficult to discuss the previous world with everyone. With everything that happened right at the end."

"I understand that. It's only when you're ready."

"Thank you, Penelope."

When they arrive, they step out onto the beach in their human forms. Berceuse takes in the bright, warm sand and the flagstone path leading into the forest. "Oh! What a beautiful place!"

Penelope wrings out her hair. She still looks nervous, but is smiling. "Isn't it? I really, really like it here."

"I can see why!" They join the forest path. Berceuse looks around. "My dear ones!"

The Pagu wave at both of them.

As they continue on, Berceuse says, "So, you said that our siblings have all been here?"

"I think so. I know almost everyone has talked to Lady Azalea and Carlos, whether or not it was here."

"She only began living here twenty-three years ago?"

"That's right. Rath's twenty-seven right now and he started living here when he was four years old."

"Ah, I see! I remember him telling me he spent much of his childhood here."

Penelope stops and Berceuse looks back at her. "Yes. Merp didn't approve of him living anywhere else – on Delphy with his father, grandfather, and grandmother or on Campi with his mother."

Berceuse looks stunned. "Why in the world would that be?"

"Because of his traits. Being from multiple heritages made Marchand's Traits very weak with him." She flushes, determined. "I never thought it was a problem. Neither did Marchand or anyone else. But, Merp ... " She shakes her head. "Marchand gifted Azalea this island – it used to be a part of Delphy – and Belle moved it here. They didn't think Merp would be able to disallow Rath or his family from being together here."

Berceuse is quiet for a long moment. "I see."

Penelope takes his hand and they keep walking. "Of course, I knew Rath when he was younger – he's been to Campi – but most of us never met him while we were here. Azalea and Carlos asked that we not bring our problems to him. Oftentimes, I think he would be out with the Pagu, camping or having picnics, or hikes ... "

Berceuse smiles a little. "That sounds lovely." But they are both quiet as they cross the lawn, past the turtle mosaic that Maro created and to the front door.

Once they reach it, Berceuse hesitates. "Do we knock?"

Suddenly, the door opens, revealing a harried-looking Flora, who is Azalea's maid. She takes them both in. "Good afternoon, Penelope. Is this ... "

Berceuse stands up tall. "I am Berceuse, the God of Oct. We have come to seek Lady Azalea's counsel. Have we been, ah, expected?"

Flora glances to her left quickly. "Not exactly. Right this way, please."

She guides them to the back gardens. Berceuse looks admiringly at the flowers. "So many colors!"

"Aren't they beautiful?" Penelope asks and Berceuse nods in agreement.

They are still looking around when Flora suddenly stops and curtsies. "Lady Azalea, the Goddess of Campi, Penelope, and the God of Oct, Berceuse, to see you!"

"Thank you, my dear," Azalea says.

Berceuse and Penelope turn. Their eyes widen.

Several of their siblings are crowded underneath the gazebo roof. At the tea table, starting from Azalea's right, are Marchand, Oracle, Vocalise, and Rella. Standing by one of the pillars, is Fierce, who seems restless. He glances once at Berceuse, then turns away, looking even more irritable.

As they walk up the steps, Azalea smiles at them. "It is good to finally meet you, Berceuse. And to see you, Penelope. It has been some time."

Penelope says, "M-Me too. It has."

Berceuse says, "You as well. I hadn't known so many of our siblings would be here, however."

Marchand sighs, setting down his teacup. "We're all at a loss of what to do about Ara's Storm. It's nearly Summer and it's still continued." He waves his hand and two more chairs appear for his siblings.

Once seated, Berceuse says, "It is concerning us as well. That is why we arrived – Penelope advised that we seek Lady Azalea's counsel on the matter." He turns. "Brother, would you like to sit as well?"

Fierce stares back at him. "I had hoped for a private

meeting."

Azalea says, "My dear, this affects you as well."

Fierce steps away from the pillar and bows to her. "With all due respect, Lady Azalea, I do not believe it does. My matter concerns your grandson and his safety, not Ara's Storm in the North." He exhales. "I need to return to my duties. I pray you will excuse me."

Azalea frowns, but nods.

They watch him turn into his hawk form and fly off.

Vocalise says, "There he goes."

Rella sniffs. "He takes his duties seriously. I admire that."

Azalea says, "Berceuse, would you like to continue?"

Berceuse jumps. "Ah, of course, Lady Azalea. If I may, is my Captain all right? What Fierce just said ... "

Azalea raises an eyebrow at his title for her grandson. Then she smiles and pats his hand. "Yes, he will be all right."

Berceuse looks relieved. "Thank goodness." He gathers his thoughts. "Penelope has rightly said that our brother, Ara, is the only one who can truly stop this storm." He winces. "Yet, I am not sure what we can do in that case. Besides him, it would fall to Merp, wouldn't it, as the ruler of this world? Do we know if Merp has? Or will?"

Azalea sighs. "It is likely best that he does not." She pauses to take a sip. "If one of you were hurting, what would you do?"

Oracle answers, "Go to help them, of course."

Berceuse says, "That is what my dear ones have always said to do as well."

They all pause, then look at one another, suddenly quiet. Even Vocalise looks nervous.

"Hm," is all Azalea says as she takes another sip, then sets down her teacup. "Well, whatever your decision is, I think it would be best to consult Elvin on it. He was directly affected by Ara's Storm, after all, and should have some input on the decision."

Marchand swallows. "Elvin has always been the most tactful of us all." The others nod.

Berceuse says, "I-I am willing to go to Pica Pica to discuss this with Elvin."

Oracle says, "As am I."

Vocalise leans back in his chair. "I mean, I guess I could go, too."

"I cannot leave Cunica," Rella says with a frown. "Not if the storm progresses. Too much could be lost."

Penelope says, "I can't imagine leaving my people if it does come this far south."

Marchand says, "Then, you don't need to go." He looks around the table to Vocalise, Berceuse, and Oracle. "The four of us will. Thank you, Lady Azalea."

"You are all welcome any time," she says. "Before you leave, Berceuse, why don't we take a walk through my gardens? I don't believe you've ever seen them before?"

"No, I have not. I would truly love that, Lady Azalea. Thank you."

After they do, they join the others on the south beach.

Berceuse says, "They are wonderful, Lady Azalea! I find the plants that my Captain chose this past year to be absolutely adorable."

Azalea beams. "I believe they are perfect."

Berceuse looks at his siblings, then takes Azalea's hands. "I will most certainly visit this island more often, with your permission, of course."

"It is open for you whenever you need."

"Thank you." Berceuse walks over to Penelope, "Will you be all right on your journey back to Campi?"

"Oh! Um ... " She nods boldly. "Yes! It is not a long way and I will focus on how happy I will be to see my own when I arrive!"

"Exactly!"

With a few hugs and a little wave to her siblings, Penelope turns into her seahorse form and swims off. In her bird form, Oracle bends to allow Rella to climb onto her back so she can be taken back to Cunica on their way to Pica Pica.

Once they are all ready, Oracle lifts off, Vocalise – now in his chimpanzee form – leaps to the nearest rock in the ocean, Marchand dives into the water, surfacing in his dolphin form, and Berceuse joins him, turning into his octopus form.

They all travel east.

24

High above the dark clouds and storms in the Phoenae Sea, the floating island of Phoenae rests. Its golden buildings shine in the bright sun and the Phoenae airships glint as they fly around the country. A large city entirely populated by those born in Phoenae covers much of it and in the center is a large, multi-winged building – the Council Building.

Inside, Georgio, Rath's father and the Councilman of Delphy, walks with Fenrir, Rath's former first mate on *PearlHeart* and now the Councilman of Sudines.

They enter a large, circular room with seats on different tiers and a balcony above them, where several children of the councilpeople are seated to listen and take notes during the meeting. Georgio and Fenrir sit down next to each other in front of name plates stating their country of origin while others do the same. Once all are present, the meeting begins.

Councilman Prillek of Phoenae stands at the podium in the front of the room. "As Councilman Hailcorn of Haliae has deigned not to appear once again, I shall take his place in the rotation of those who will preside over our meetings." He picks up the first paper in front of him. "We shall begin with … "

They start with updates from each of their respective countries, then any proposals submitted by the councilpeople. Most are about Ara's Storm and its impact on different countries and what aid can be offered to them. Forty minutes later, the stack of papers has diminished to the last three items.

Prillek writes notes on one, saying, " ... so the proposal to continue to provide aid to the Paradi Messengers who have lost or greatly had their work reduced due to Ara's Storm has been approved."

Councilwoman Isis of Paradi nods. "Thank you, everyone." Her bird partner, Micah, looks grateful.

"Next, we have ... " Prillek frowns when he sees the last two items are letters. He looks at the first. "An update from Councilman Hailcorn, who is still on Pica Pica. I shall read it now."

"Hello to everyone in the Council and thank you for your understanding of my not being present during this season. Things are progressing here. If the move was startling for everyone, no one shows it much now. The people of Pica Pica and their goddess, Liette, have been continually welcoming and open – they even want to incorporate some of our customs into their daily celebrations! A merging of cultures is never a bad thing, in my opinion." Prillek's lips twitch as he reads the last sentence. *"The storm to the north shows no signs of stopping. Elvin's Spirit Eagles report that it has moved further south by another one hundred miles as of this Summer and the Selachuu Military has confirmed this with their Spirit Sharks. We do not expect to be able to return to Haliae for some time. In regards to the additional letter I have forwarded, I wish to clearly state my and Elvin's complete support and approval of the request it contains and I look forward to the final decision on it, as determined by the Council. Thank you, Councilman Hailcorn."*

Prillek sets down the letter and picks up the second envelope. As soon as he opens it, he freezes. "This is ... " He looks around the room, then folds it up briskly. "I must – I am calling an emergency recess." Then, without anything further, he leaves through the door behind the podium, letter in hand while Georgio and the other members of the Council watch in surprise.

Inside a small, brightly lit office, Amara speaks to a man in golden clothes with blond hair tied back in a long braid.

The man says, "The Three Dragon Guardians would not let you pass?"

"No. They have never disallowed my visit since the beginning of this world."

"Ara must truly be upset then," he says. Amara watches as he rises and looks out the window. His golden eyes flick around the bright blue skies. "With this Summer, Ara's Storm will have lasted over eight months. By Fall, it will be a year." He thinks.

There is a knock on the door. He walks over swiftly and opens it. Prillek is there, holding up a letter. "Merp, this – " His breath catches when he sees Amara.

Merp, the Elder God of Phoenae and Ruler of the Fourth World, frowns. "I am in a meeting, Prillek"

"I am sorry."

Merp glances at Amara, then shuts the door behind him so he and Prillek are out in the hallway. "It is fine. What is it?"

Prillek hands him the letter. "This was received today, along with a letter from Councilman Hailcorn on Pica Pica."

Merp nods. He takes it and reads quickly. His eyes flare for a moment, then narrow. "Does the Council know about this?"

"No. I called an emergency recess before they could."

Merp rubs his eyes. He hands the letter back. "You must read it to them."

"But – "

"We will discuss this more later. Resume the meeting, Prillek."

"Yes, Merp." Prillek speed walks away.

Merp enters his office.

Amara raises an eyebrow. "Ill tidings?"

"Disruptive." Merp sits down. "Pantha. It remains unpredictable."

"This disturbs you?"

"It is proving how they have always been. Before, Pantha was ruled by its royal family, then King Neihr chose not to share the food gathered by his people, resulting in them becoming bandits and pirates. The Council responded by sending the Selachuu Military to the North to protect the immediate area – Haliae and Pantha's border with Daerce – and their presence there is what makes it necessary for the Butej Guard to remain in the South." He rubs his right temple. "Now, it seems their new royal – King Faerohr – wishes to join the Alliance."

"Truly?" She nods. "Such aid that would be provided to them is assuredly needed during this time." She studies him. "You do not approve of their action?"

Merp frowns. "As I said, they are unpredictable. I do not fully trust them joining the Alliance, however" – he sighs – "that decision will remain with the Council. I will not interfere," he says. "Nor will I with Ara. He has had storms such as this in the past – they have always ended. I see no cause to act at this time. I am sorry to hear of Haliae and will request Prillek to suggest more provisions be brought to Pica Pica."

Back in the Council Room, Prillek has resumed the meeting.

He stands at the podium. "We will now read a letter from the King of Pantha, as forwarded by Councilman Hailcorn." Eyes widen around the room. Some look hesitant, but most seem interested in what it might entail.

"To all in the Alliance's Council," Prillek reads. *"As King of Pantha, I formally request Pantha's acceptance into your Alliance. Ara's Storm has affected my country greatly and we are in need of provisions, including food, clothes, and medical supplies. We do not seek evacuation – we shall remain in Pantha for the duration of this storm. I seek to be in the Alliance for Pantha's current state, however, I assure you that once Ara's Storm has ended, Pantha will contribute fully to other countries. We have abundant land, which in the coming years, I have plans to turn"* – Prillek chokes – *"into farmland, so that we may provide for others. I thank you for your consideration. King Faerohr of Pantha"*

After he finishes, the room is completely silent. Prillek sets the paper down, his eyes darting around to those in the Council. "As is customary for a request to join the Alliance, we will now put the matter to a vote." He frowns. "Unless any have a discussion that they would like to begin?"

The Councilman of Pantrog, Nex, speaks, "Yeah. Sounds good to me." He leans forward. "Listen, we've had Lionel's people on Pantrog for years – an' they're not even asking to go evacuate to another country or anything. Just some supplies while they stay in Pantha."

The Councilwoman of Cunica, Sophie, says, "They are only asking for basic necessities with the promise of providing for others in the future. Quite reasonable. My goddess will be very interested in Faerohr's plans for farmland, as well."

Georgio nods. "I agree. King Faerohr speaks well and he seems to have a very realistic view of the situation — as well as how we may react to his request."

Prillek turns to the Selachuu Councilman, Lane. "How have the borders been?"

"Fine. Quiet. For almost a year now."

The Councilman of Pertes, Venti, picks his nails. "Almost as long as King Faerohr has been in power, it seems." He grins. "It would open up more trade routes, which my goddess would most certainly approve of."

Fenrir speaks. "It seems fair. I do not see any cause for alarm."

The Councilwoman of Campi, Marcia, ducks her head, "Well, if everyone seems to think it's all right ... "

Prillek turns to her. "You will make your decision on your own opinion, Councilwoman Marcia."

"Y-Yes, Councilman Prillek!" She thinks. "I'm not sure. I heard piracy went up two years ago ... "

Charon, the Councilman of Lotinx and Estival's father, says, "That's true, but it's since gone down. Belle has been moving his soldiers back to their customary posts since last year. King Faerohr is doing much good for the country."

The Councilman of Ullia, Rittel, is quiet, only listening.

Prillek looks around the room again. "If there are no other comments to be made, we will begin the vote." He raises his hand. "All who *reject* the King of Pantha's proposal for Pantha to join the Alliance, raise your hand now."

The councilpeople of Ullia and Campi raise their hands.

Prillek frowns. He lowers his hand, saying, "All in favor of Pantha joining the Alliance and all that doing so may bring for the countries involved, raise your hand now."

The rest of the councilpeople do — Georgio, Fenrir, and those from Pertes, Cunica, Pantrog, Selachuu, Paradi, and Lotinx.

After a moment, Prillek gestures and they lower their hands.

"A majority," he says. He takes up his pen and begins writing on the letter. "By the ruling of the Council, *Pantha* is now officially a member of the Alliance as witnessed by I, Councilman Prillek of Phoenae." He swipes up the paper. "I call this meeting adjourned," he says, then enters the door behind the podium and shuts it firmly behind him.

25

Meanwhile, in the Southern Seas, Marchand, Berceuse, Oracle, and Vocalise are traveling to Pica Pica. They make it past Paradi and are continuing on when Vocalise pauses on a rock.

Marchand stops beside him. "What is it?" he asks.

Vocalise looks at three long, flat isles in the distance. Then he hops toward them, going south instead of east. "I'm gonna go check something!" he calls behind him. "I'll meet ya' at Pica Pica!"

"Vocalise!" Marchand says, but his brother is already miles away. He sighs.

Oracle flies lower. "What should we do?"

"Continue on, I think. I'm sure we'll meet up again." He swims on, Oracle and Berceuse following.

"Those isles are Xiphi, aren't they? Our brother Ran's country?" Berceuse asks.

"That's right!" Oracle replies. "Every year, Ran holds his Xiphi Races there. They're quite popular!"

"Oh! My dear ones have told me of them! They say they are very exciting!"

PearlHeart arrives on Xiphi the evening before the Xiphi Races will begin. Preparations are going on all over the three isles and other Pan ships bringing supplies are docked with *PearlHeart* on the northernmost of the three. Rath's crew is currently carrying crates down the gangplank under his, One-Eye, and Well-Pagu's direction, after which race organizers guide them to where they need to go.

It does not take long for them to finish, and afterward the crew is gathered on the main deck. Rath says, "Excellent work, everyone!"

"Thank you, Captain!"

"We have been asked to stay for the races. All who have helped provide supplies have been given a pass to see or participate in them without any additional charge. Meals are included with this and there is a reduced rate at all gift shops. I hope everyone enjoys their time here, however you choose to spend it."

"Yes, Captain!"

Everyone goes to bed, talking excitedly with each other, wondering what the next day will bring.

In the morning, the isle is already crowded with people who have come to the races. Many in the crew of *PearlHeart* are going down the gangplank to join in the festivities as well.

Isaac says, "I'm totally going to join a bunch of races!"

Oren follows him. "I'll go with you."

Perri skips down. "Me too!"

William and Phobos come after her. "We'll watch you guys!" William says and Phobos gives a happy "Caw!"

Franz and Charles go next. Charles says, "I heard there's vendors from all over the Southern Seas here."

"Let's go check them out!" Franz says.

Velt, Felix, and Triphonius go after them. Velt asks, "So, is Triphonius joining any races?"

Felix says, "He won't let us leave until we do!"

On his shoulder, Triphonius puffs with pride. "Caw!"

Carlos and Phillip go down the gangplank. Phillip says, "I'm curious about some of the food booths they have."

Carlos asks, "Would you like to eat together?"

"Definitely!"

Melody, Demeter, and Evermore choose to stay on

PearlHeart. They stay in the shade of the upper deck and Melody plays her harp while Demeter sings and Evermore listens peacefully.

Rath, One-Eye, Well-Pagu, Bucket-Pagu, and Flower-Pagu go down last. As Rath looks around, Flower-Pagu says, "There's so many people!"

"Indeed," Rath says. "I find it very exciting."

Bucket-Pagu shifts. "It's a little much for me, but ... if I'm with everyone here, I know I'll be okay!"

Well-Pagu says, "Yes!"

Rath turns to One-Eye. "I hope that you enjoy the races. I" – he flushes suddenly – "I would like to see you in one of them, if that is all right."

"Sure." One-Eye looks at the four of them. "Are you all going to the gift shops?"

"Yes. Flower-Pagu wished to see them. May we meet you later?"

One-Eye nods.

While Rath and the Pagu head to the left, One-Eye and his Spirit Lion go right, toward the races.

As they are looking at a race that seems to be suited for those with aquatic traits, Isaac suddenly calls out to them. "Hey! One-Eye!"

When One-Eye turns, he sees Isaac and Oren run up to him.

Isaac says, "We were thinking of joining the race ahead. You don't need to be able to breathe underwater for it."

"Sounds good."

They walk beside one another. Oren grins at One-Eye. "I don't think I've ever seen you run. Heard Lionel's people have pretty good endurance from his traits."

One-Eye frowns.

Isaac says, "It'll be fun. Oren, you and me have raced on Pantrog before. I'm glad One-Eye's joining us."

Near the gift shops, Rath is looking at some books. Flower-Pagu twirls around some blown glass bobbles. "Oh! Captain, these are so pretty! Look!"

Rath smiles. "They are beautiful."

Flower-Pagu flies up to the proprietor. "May I have the

small pink flower? It's so pretty! I helped out with the crew on *PearlHeart*."

"Of course," she says. "Thank you for your help. The price with the discount is just one gold piece."

Flower-Pagu nods and pulls out their little money pouch. They exchange a little golden coin for the bobble.

"Thank you," the woman says. Then she unhooks the glass flower and hands it to Flower-Pagu. "Here you are!"

"Thank you so much!" Flower-Pagu beams at their new purchase.

Bucket-Pagu, who is over by the books with Rath, says, "Have you seen anything you would like, Captain?"

Rath shakes his head. "No. I thought of purchasing this book, however, I was not sure. I told Carlos that I would try to buy something for myself today. He said it was a good idea."

Flower-Pagu flies over. "You should, Captain!"

Bucket-Pagu says, "I'm sure you'll find something!"

Well-Pagu says, "Happy!"

Bucket-Pagu looks around, then points. "There's another booth with books there. Maybe you can find one you like!"

"You're right!" Rath says. They go together.

Meanwhile, Isaac, Oren, and One-Eye – with his Spirit Lion running beside him – finish their first race. One-Eye crosses the finish line first, then his Lion, then Oren, then Isaac. The latter two pant at the end, but One-Eye barely looks winded.

Oren says, "Nice, One-Eye."

One-Eye smiles. "Thanks."

Recovering his breath, Isaac says, "You're really good at this. I'm definitely going to do better next time."

Oren tells him, "You've always been a lot more skilled at acrobatics. I'm interested to see how One-Eye does with that."

One-Eye starts to frown, but his Spirit Lion butts his legs. "I'll try it," he says as he pets his Lion, who is still exhilarated from the race.

As they exit the racing area, Carlos and Phillip walk by. Phillip is holding some treats made from the local fruits. He sees One-Eye and the others and waves, "Oh, hey guys! You all doing the races?"

One-Eye replies, "Yeah."

Isaac says, "You wanna join?"

Phillip shakes his head. "Naw, not really my thing. Or my Spirit Rabbit's." He pets her as she sits on his shoulder.

One-Eye's Spirit Lion pricks up his ears and One-Eye says, "There are races for Spirit Animals?"

Carlos answers, "Yes. Xiphi's God, Ran, personally runs them."

"Great." One-Eye's Spirit Lion looks up at him. "You don't need my permission." The Lion gives a roar of triumph and runs off through the crowd. One-Eye smiles as he watches him go.

As he does, William, Phobos, and Perri – who is now drenched from an aquatic race – join the group. William says, "Perri just got first!"

Perri laughs. "It was a lot of fun!"

Isaac blushes, smiling, "That's really great. Good job, Perri."

"Thanks, Isaac!" She shakes out her hair.

William pets his bird partner. "Phobos and I were going to find a race for aerial traits. We're sure that Felix and Triphonius are at one of them. Anyone want to come with?"

Most of the group nods, however Carlos says, "I believe I will return to the ship."

Phillip says next to him, "Me too. It's almost time to make lunch."

Perri waves. "Got it. Bye Carlos, Phillip!"

"See ya!'

As Carlos and Phillip walk together, Carlos asks, "Will Flower-Pagu be helping you?"

"No. I told them they could have the morning off. They said they wanted to spend it with the Captain."

Carlos nods. "Bucket-Pagu said the same thing. I am sure Well-Pagu is with them as well." He sighs. "I do hope Master Rath found something for himself."

Rath and the Pagu are still looking in the gift shops. Bucket-Pagu has purchased a book and Well-Pagu has bought a new notebook.

Bucket-Pagu says, "I don't think I've ever read this one before! It must be new."

"That is exciting," Rath says.

Well-Pagu flips through their notebook. "Many."

"That is good. You will be able to write in it for long time."

Well-Pagu nods.

As they pass by another shop, the man seated in front of it calls out, "Hey! Any of you interested in playing?" The man is sitting on a stool in front of a game board with small pieces carved out of wood.

Rath walks over and the Pagu follow him. He studies the pieces. "These are wonderfully made."

The man grins. "Thanks. Made them myself. Now, are you interested? We need at least two to play."

"I see. And, I am afraid that I do not recognize this game."

"No problem with that. I can teach you."

Rath looks surprised, then grateful. "Thank you." He takes a seat on a wooden stool opposite the man.

The Pagu sit on the game board. Flower-Pagu asks, "May we play, too?"

Bucket-Pagu says, "I think I've played this before."

"Long," Well-Pagu says.

"Of course you can," the man says. "Don't know what you mean by 'long,' though, little one."

Well-Pagu looks up at Rath, who explains, "I believe what Well-Pagu means is that it has been a 'long' time since they have played it."

Well-Pagu beams. "Understand."

The man's eyebrows go up. "You get all that from just one word?" Rath nods and the man laughs. "I suppose you must be friends then." He holds out his hand. "Eben, of Ursi."

Rath takes it. "Captain Rath of Delphy."

The Pagu introduce themselves.

"I'm Flower-Pagu!"

"I'm Bucket-Pagu. It's nice to meet you!"

"Well ... Pagu."

Eben smiles. "Good to meet all of you. I'll have to give you a discount, too — if you decide to purchase anything. I take it you're from one of the ships that brought supplies?"

Rath says, "Yes, that is true. We are from *PearlHeart*."

"Thanks for your help." Eben flexes his fingers. "Now, on how to play ... "

He explains the rules and afterward, the five of them begin. The game involves spinning a wooden piece with four faces with symbols on them and a point. The symbol that it lands on determines how to move the other pieces across the board. The Pagu have smaller versions of each for them to use. When Rath wins, Eben says, "Well done! Not bad for a first time. Shall we play another?"

"Yes, please."

They play through the morning. Rath spins the piece. He reads the symbol and nods. "I will move here."

Eben studies the board. "Hmm ... "

They are busy playing when Charles and Franz pass by, having just come from the food booths. Franz says, "Oh! It's the Captain."

"And the Pagu, too," Charles says.

They walk over and Franz asks, "What are you all playing?"

Rath replies, "It is called Ursian Checkers. I find it very fun."

Eben says to them, "You're all welcome to join. We can have seven players easily."

Charles says, "Sure!"

They all gather in a tight circle around the board and continue to play. At the end of the third game, Franz has won and Eben asks, "Anyone up for another?"

Rath begins to say, "Yes, please," when his stomach growls. The Pagu's do, too. Rath flushes. "I do not believe I have had lunch."

Bucket-Pagu says, "I'm really hungry, too!"

They rise up to leave and Rath says, "May we come back later?" The Pagu nod in agreement.

Eben pats his knee. "Absolutely. I'll be looking forward to it."

"Thank you very much."

Franz puts in, "We found this really good booth over there. They sell Ursian food, if you're interested, Captain."

"That sounds wonderful. I have never tried it before."

Bucket-Pagu says, "I have. It's really good!"

Eben says, "You must be talking about the booth my friend is running – we sailed here together from Ursi. He's a great chef. I think you'll enjoy."

Rath says, "I am looking forward to it." They find the food booth quickly and order pocket pies from it – one larger one for Rath and three small ones for the Pagu. They eat together underneath a tree, away from the crowds.

Afterward, they start toward the races.

Rath looks around. "Do any of you see One-Eye?"

Flower-Pagu flies a little higher. "I don't think so ... "

They keep moving. As they do, familiar clothing catches Rath's eye and he looks to his right, down a hill, to see One-Eye dash past, in the middle of a race against Isaac, Oren, and Perri. One-Eye leaps over a barrier, tumbles, and makes it to the finish line in third, behind Oren in second and Isaac in first. Perri finishes in fourth. William and Phobos, who are at the gate where the racers exit, see Rath and the Pagu. William waves, "Captain! Everyone! Over here!"

They join them just as the others are exiting the race.

William says, "You did good!" to Perri.

Perri says, "Thanks!"

Oren says to Isaac, "Told you you were better with the acrobatics."

Isaac replies, "You guys did really good, too!"

One-Eye says, "It was fun." He looks over and sees Rath and the Pagu. "Hey. Did you find anything to buy?"

"You are very fast." One-Eye's eyebrows go up. "Th-That is, ah, no. However, I believe I may go back for a game I tried." One-Eye smiles and Rath continues, "It was wonderful to watch you, One-Eye."

He flushes. "Thanks."

Rath says to all of them, "I'm glad to see that everyone seems to be having fun."

Isaac asks, "Do you want to race with us, Captain? I bet you'd do great."

"I am not sure. I am not very competitive."

Isaac shakes his head. "You don't have to be, I don't think. It's just about having fun with everyone."

Oren lifts his hands. "I dunno, I also like winning."

One-Eye nods in agreement.

Rath says, "Perhaps. Is there a ... together race? One that is done in a group?"

Isaac says, "I think I saw some relay races over there."

However, Oren suddenly sees something and madly nudges Isaac's shoulder. Isaac turns to him. "What is it?" Oren jerks his chin forward.

Isaac looks and his eyes widen. "Vocalise!"

Vocalise, who had been walking, enjoying a pocket pie like Rath and the Pagu were earlier, stops. He quickly walks toward them. "Hey, Isaac. I don't really want anyone to know I'm here."

"Oh! Sorry!"

Vocalise looks at the group. "Thought you might all be here. I saw *PearlHeart* when I arrived." He eats the rest of his pie. "You enjoying Ran's races?"

Isaac says, "Totally!"

Oren asks, "You wanna race with us?"

Vocalise grins. "Definitely." He asks One-Eye, "Your Spirit Lion doing the Spirit Animal races?"

"Yeah. That's what he says."

"Good for him. It's good of Ran to hold those for them. No one can see all of the Spirit Animals except us gods – and some others – so it's nice for them to have an event, too."

Rath says, "That is wonderful."

"What about you, Captain? Any races for you?"

"No, not yet. I am considering participating in a group race – a relay race, Isaac said."

Vocalise's eyebrows go up. "There's a thought." He pauses, then nods. "Yeah. Sounds good to me." He walks forward, waving an arm. "There's a good one up here. Come on!"

Isaac and Oren grin at each other and follow eagerly, with the rest behind them. They meet up with Velt, Felix, and Triphonius on the way and Perri tells Velt, "We're doing a group race – want to join?"

Velt says, "Absolutely!" and Triphonius "Caws!" with anticipation.

Felix says, "Triphonius, we've already done like five races!" He smiles a little. "But, I guess it does sound fun."

Triphonius stands up taller.

Whent they reach the race, it looks to be broken up into different sections based on the traits of the racers.

Vocalise looks at the size of the groups and scratches his chin. "Oh, right. Looks like we'll need one more to join."

Flower-Pagu says, "What about Ran? We could go check if he's done with the Spirit Animal races."

"Yeah. Thanks."

However, before they can fly off, One-Eye's Spirit Lion

returns. He licks his paw smugly. One-Eye listens to him say something, then ruffles his mane. "Congratulations."

The Lion puffs up his chest with pride.

Vocalise, having heard as well, says, "Good job. You know where Ran's off to now?"

The Lion points his nose behind them. Vocalise turns and shouts, "HEY! RAN!"

A man with long dark blue-green hair and a sleeveless shirt jumps. He looks over. "Vocalise?" He walks over to them. "What in the world are you doing here?"

"Joining your races."

"You could have let me know that."

Vocalise shrugs.

Ran, the God of Xiphi, looks at the group assembled. "Are you all enjoying?"

Rath says, "Yes. Very much so. Thank you." The others agree and Perri says, "Definitely!"

One-Eye gives a short nod, frowning.

Ran sees him and gestures to his Spirit Lion. "Good runner you have there. It was an honor to see him at my races."

One-Eye seems conflicted. "Sure."

Vocalise says, "Sooo, I was thinking we all do a group race together." He asks the Pagu, "Although, do you all want to join?"

The Pagu shake their heads. Flower-Pagu says, "No, but we'd love to watch!" Bucket-Pagu and Well-Pagu nod in agreement.

Ran grins. "Fabulous idea. I will be a Team Captain – "

Vocalise cuts in, "Captain Rath and One-Eye will be the captains."

Rath and One-Eye look at each other.

Ran frowns, tapping his foot. "Well, I suppose."

"I am afraid I do not know the meaning of this, ah, type of captain," Rath says.

Vocalise puts an arm around Rath's shoulders. "It just means you pick who you want on your team."

"Everyone."

Vocalise pauses, then grins at him.

Ran says, "I'm afraid that wouldn't work if we are to have two teams. You may pick four others to race with you."

Rath looks disheartened. "Oh."

"Why not you take turns? One-Eye will pick first."

One-Eye says, "Isaac."

Rath says, "Oren."

"Perri."

"Velt."

"William and Phobos."

"Felix and Triphonius."

One-Eye hesitates. The last to be chosen are the gods. Finally, he says, "Ran."

"Good choice."

Vocalise says, "An' I've got you, Captain!"

Rath laughs. "Indeed!"

Ran begins stretching. "I am looking forward to this. Now, let's go down there – they're just beginning a new race. We'll have time to hear the rules and be ready to participate afterward."

The Pagu go to the stands, where they join Carlos, Phillip, Franz, and Charles, who come to watch the race as well. When Rath and the others arrive, two medium-sized Xiphi boats with a single sail wait for each team to travel through the course. The race has several checkpoints with platforms floating on the water that lead to different obstacles that team members will go through, at the end of which there is a flag to collect. Once the previous teams have finished and their race is ready to begin, Rath and One-Eye take up the lines on each of the boats and the other members of their teams board them.

A race official stands on a platform between the two water lanes looks at both teams, ensuring that they are ready, then shouts, "Three ... two ... one ... GO!" The crowd cheers as both boats take off. Rath's picks up speed quickly while One-Eye's starts slower.

They arrive at the first obstacle. Isaac and Oren get off their respective boats.

"Please be careful, Isaac!" Rath says.

"Yes, Captain!"

They both climb a series of ropes like the lines on *PearlHeart,* traveling across them as the boats continue to sail beneath them. At the end, they grab a flag and swing down a longer rope back to a platform where they can meet their teams again.

Rath and One-Eye slow as Isaac and Oren rejoin them, then pick up speed on their way to the next checkpoint. There, William and Phobos, and Felix and Triphonius leave.

William says, "Good luck, Phobos!"

Phobos "Caws!" as she flies up into the air.

Both birds swirl up to the top of a tall tower to retrieve a flag as their human partners race up and down a hill. They reunite with their birds, then return to their boats.

Afterward, they enter an area with water obstacles and Rath slows, but One-Eye keeps their speed up.

However, it causes him to reach a turn a little too quickly and hit one of the barriers. "Sorry," he says, then rights himself and they continue.

Rath reaches the next checkpoint first.

Velt dives into the water. "See you there, Captain!"

On the other side, One-Eye arrives and Perri dives in. Velt and Perri both swim underwater through rings while the boats sail above them, their Delphaen tattoos glowing as they do. Perri reaches the flag at the end faster and rises to the surface, where Oren helps her up.

"I got it!" she says, holding up the flag. Across from them, Velt has just surfaced.

Once both are back in their boats, Rath and One-Eye sail through more obstacles. One-Eye goes slower, being more careful. Rath catches up to him and they are even at the last checkpoint. Right before they reach it, Vocalise says, "Ya' ready, Ran?"

"Of course!" Then, to the surprise of the others, Ran steps down onto the next platform and becomes a streak of dark blue-green using his traits to travel up the ladder in the blink of an eye. On the other side, Vocalise climbs up in leaps.

Vocalise arrives at the top and looks across at Ran, who is now running across the raised runway. Vocalise shouts, "That's no fun!"

Ran disappears into another streak, reappearing to do a flashy flip or a jump. "I think it is! Why not use more of your traits?"

Vocalise runs, hopping on top of the safety railing and continuing on without missing a beat. "Eh, don't feel like it."

"You never do! It makes me wonder if I'm ever truly winning

when we're racing."

They reach the rope maze and Vocalise jumps into it. He continues running along one rope, then up onto another. He shrugs. "Don't worry, you do."

Ran frowns at him. The rope he is on turns bright blue-green as he travels across it with his traits, then he leaps up to the same one Vocalise is on. He reappears running backward, just in front of Vocalise. "Come on, just this once."

Vocalise grins, but for the first time he looks a little annoyed. He suddenly drops, catching the rope with his hands so he can swing himself along it below Ran. "Naw."

Ran turns around, running above him on the same rope. They are nearly matched in speed. They leap and swing off at the same time, grabbing their flags before rejoining their boats.

"Hey, Captain Rath," Vocalise says.

"Hello, Vocalise. Wonderful job."

On the other boat, behind One-Eye, Ran mutters, "Tie."

Both boats reach the last stretch. Rath adjusts his sail as the wind picks up, bringing their boat just slightly ahead of One-Eye's. The distance increases and the crowd cheers louder. Then Rath's boat pulls across the finish line, One-Eye's just two seconds behind.

As Rath and One-Eye bring them both to shore, Vocalise and Ran get out. Vocalise says, "Fun, wasn't it?"

Ran just crosses his arms and huffs.

After the rest of their teams exit, Rath and One-Eye hand their boats off to race officials to be sailed back to the starting line. One-Eye says to Rath, "What did you think?"

Rath is flushed. "It was very fun. Although I felt nervous. I do not believe I have ever seen everyone move so fast."

One-Eye smiles. "You did good."

"Thank you. Everyone did, I believe."

One-Eye starts to reach for his hand, then does not. He coughs. "Did you want to show me that game you liked?"

Rath brightens. "I would love to." He nods to the group. "Perhaps everyone would like to as well."

They walk over and Rath asks them. They all agree and meet with Carlos and the others, who wish to go as well. In a group, they travel back to Eben's booth, picking up food for dinner on the way. When Eben sees them, he raises his eyebrows, then laughs. "Brought friends, I see!"

"Yes!" Rath says.

They start to gather themselves around the board, but Eben says, "With this many, we'll need to break up into a few groups. I've got some more boards over here." He goes back into the storage area of his booth.

Once he returns, he hands out two more boards and they play in groups of six around them. Rath, One-Eye, Vocalise, Ran, Phillip, and Carlos on one and Velt, Franz, Charles, William, Phobos, Perri, Felix, and Triphonius on another. The Pagu play with Eben on his board.

They play until the sun starts to go down. As they are leaving, Rath purchases a game. Eben says, "Thanks for your business! And for playing."

Rath holds the board to his chest. "Of course. I cannot wait to play this again with everyone." The crew nods.

Isaac looks around. "Hey, where'd Vocalise go?"

Carlos frowns. "Ran is gone as well."

However, One-Eye's Spirit Lion yawns and One-Eye says, "Is everyone ready to go back?"

The others agree and travel in a group, talking about the day.

Ran and Vocalise are walking over by the beach.

Ran says, "Come off it, Vocalise. You didn't just come here for my races and tie with me again because you felt like it." Vocalise raises an eyebrow. "So, what's the other reason you came?"

"I dunno. Wanted to see how you were doing. Wanted to know what you thought of Ara's Storm."

Ran's mouth twitches. "At the moment, I don't care. Ara makes his people miserable enough in Draconi. I see no reason why I have to make that my problem here. I'd rather focus on making people happy with my races."

"Yeah, they are." Vocalise pauses. "Marchand, Oracle, Berceuse, and I are going to Pica Pica to talk with Elvin about it."

"I heard about Haliae. It was unfortunate. As well as Berceuse's sudden reappearance." Ran crosses his arms. "Why tell me?"

"Just wanted to know if you wanted to come with."

"And do what? Talk about the storm?"

"Naw. Talk to Ara, I think."

Ran gapes. "Absolutely not."

Vocalise looks at him seriously. "The Pagu don't think his storm is going to end this time – they think it's going to grow."

"Well, that's ... " Ran glares. "Not my problem."

Vocalise looks mildly disappointed. "Got it. Thought I'd ask. Well, see ya."

"You're leaving already? What about another race?"

"Don't really have time for that. Kinda got a feeling I should meet the others on Pica Pica. Had fun with everyone, though." He glows and turns into his giant chimpanzee form. He leaps to the nearest rock in the ocean, heading northeast.

Ran shakes his head, watching him. "*Now* he uses his traits."

At the same time, the crew of *PearlHeart* returns. Isaac and Perri tell Evermore, Melody, and Demeter about what they all did while everyone else talks excitedly with one another. At the same time, Rath sets down his game carefully in a cabinet in his cabin and the Pagu talk to each other as they get ready for bed. One-Eye hears more about the race his Spirit Lion did with the other Spirit Animals and congratulates him again, scratching the Lion's ear. Then everyone goes to sleep.

26

PearlHeart leaves the next day, traveling northeast toward the Southern Selachuu Military Base. During that time, Rath teaches Melody, Demeter, and Evermore how to play the game he bought on Xiphi. They sit in a dim area of the galley so that Evermore can see comfortably. All enjoy it greatly.

Two weeks later, they arrive at the base. Rath and One-Eye are talking with Captain Farbourne and Sir Ronan. Opal Starlight is sparring with some Selachuu soldiers behind them.

Farbourne is saying, " ... evacuations went smoothly. Also got the supplies sent to – " He stops suddenly. He looks at them both. "You don't know." He grins. "Pantha's just joined the Alliance. As per King Faerohr's request, emergency supplies have been sent there." Seeing their expressions, Farbourne nods. "Surprised us, too. Turns out Belle delivered a letter from their king to Councilman Hailcorn and Fritz on Pica Pica not long ago. Hailcorn sent it on to the Council and it was agreed upon with a majority. All the bases were notified recently." Farbourne hands a packet to One-Eye. "This is for you. Elvin drafted one for every one of Lionel's own so they'd know what it means for their country. It's a dense read, but probably useful for you to know."

One-Eye takes it. "Thanks."

Ronan speaks. "It was a surprise to us as well. I can only imagine what Lady Amara may think." He smiles at Rath. "Captain Rath, if I may put in but a few words to express how much your letter meant to me and that I would wish to – platonically – continue such correspondence with you. It brings me much joy."

Rath looks touched. "I ... It does for me as well. Thank you for your kind words, Sir Ronan. I would be happy to."

Ronan beams.

They leave the base and travel on to Pica Pica. After they are on their way, Rath and One-Eye sit in the captain's cabin, eating lunch with the Pagu.

One-Eye finally sits back. "I can't believe it. Pantha joining the Alliance – or the Council accepting. Mostly, that Pantha accepted help." His Lion looks equally stunned beside him.

Rath says, "I think it is very good that they asked for supplies. However, I cannot speak, as one who is not from Pantha."

"It's weird. I don't trust it fully." One-Eye shakes his head. "I glanced through Elvin's paperwork, but I don't understand half of it."

"May I see it? We could go over it together."

One-Eye nods, pulling it out.

Rath moves to sit in the chair closer to One-Eye and they begin to read through it, the Pagu sitting happily across from them.

Once they finish, One-Eye says, "Sounds like a lot of it doesn't matter much for me if I'm not living in Pantha. You're good at explaining this. Thanks."

Rath smiles. "Of course."

As One-Eye gathers up the paperwork, he says, "You would have learned about all of this before, right?"

"Yes, when I was training to be councilman. My father and grandfather helped me with it as well."

One-Eye nods to the papers. "It mentioned that usually the councilpeople are descended from their god's First. Rif said the same thing about you on Cunica, too."

"That is true. Delphaen councilpeople customarily are."

The Spirit Lion says something and One-Eye says to

Rath, "My Lion always told me that the royals in Pantha were descended from Lionel's First."

"Really?"

"Yeah. He doesn't think Faerohr is, though." Rath nods and One-Eye continues, "Are there any in the Council that aren't from that bloodline? I doubt anyone in Pantha would want the old king to be councilperson." He frowns. "I still can't imagine Pantha even *having* one."

"I know the Councilman of Selachuu, Lane, is not from the line of Belle's First. Most are, however."

One-Eye sighs. "Doubt they'll do anything right now about it." He suddenly has a thought. "The Council's in Phoenae. Did you ever go there?"

"I did, from when I was fourteen until I was sixteen. I sat in the balcony in the meeting room to listen and take notes that my father and I would talk about afterward. Sven and Pema did, too, as well as others who would become councilpeople in the future – often children of the council members."

"Georgio's councilman right now – was Garreth, too?"

"Yes. My father succeeded him not long after I was born."

One-Eye hesitates. "Can I ask why your grandfather stays on Delphy? Seems like … " He does not finish.

Rath shifts uncomfortably. "After the new law allowing councilpeople to marry whoever they wished was passed, Councilwoman Heylin of Phoenae, who had presided over the meeting, insisted that my grandfather handle every marriage request thereafter. They will only send them to Delphy." One-Eye looks surprised, then glares down at the table. He glances up when Rath says, "I wish very much that he would come to Grandmother's island with Mother, Father, and me."

One-Eye is quiet, then nods.

On the day *PearlHeart* is set to arrive on Pica Pica, Vocalise makes his last leap to the shore. He turns into his human form and is merging with the crowd when he hears a voice.

"Vocalise! Vocalise! Over here!"

He looks up and sees his sister, Liette, the Goddess of Pica Pica, using her traits to stand above the crowd as if on an invisible platform.

Vocalise grins as she leaps down to meet him. They hug

each other and he says, "Hey, Sis."

"Hey, hey!" When they pull away, Liette says, "I was told to expect you! Elvin wishes to talk right away!"

They walk through the crowd together. Liette continues, "Honestly, it sounds super scary – I mean, talk to Ara when he's like this? I can't imagine doing that."

When they arrive at the clock tower, they go inside and up to the set of rooms where Hailcorn, Fritz, Sven, and Pema are staying. Hailcorn and Sven wave to Vocalise and Liette when they enter, greeting them, but remain in the sitting room while the gods go out to the balcony. Outside, Elvin, Marchand, Oracle, and Berceuse are seated at the table.

Liette gestures. "I brought Vocalise!"

Vocalise waves. "Hey." He sits down in an open chair.

Oracle asks Liette, "Are you sure you don't wish to join us, my dear?"

Liette steps back and up as if on stairs. "Ohh, no no no. That's too scary for me. But, good luck with everything! Byeee!" She skips off, leaping through a cloud of pink smoke that just exploded.

Oracle sighs.

Berceuse asks Vocalise, "Did you go to the Xiphi Races? That's where Marchand believed you went."

"Yup."

Oracle asks, "Did you speak with Ran?"

"Uh huh. Raced, too." He grins at Marchand. "*PearlHeart* was there at the same time. We all got to do a group race together."

"That's – " Marchand's smile fades. "With Ran, too?"

Vocalise nods.

Marchand frowns. "I see."

Berceuse asks, "Was he, ah, willing to help?"

Shaking his head, Vocalise says, "Nope. Said it wasn't his problem."

Marchand flips his hair back. "I suppose it isn't. But, even if Ara's Storm has not directly affected our countries, we are still here to help."

Elvin nods. "And I greatly appreciate it. While I would gladly accept help from Ran, he is also not part of the Alliance and has no obligation to."

"I'm not here on obligation. I want to help you, Elvin. Ara, too, if we can."

Oracle nods. "Me, too"

Berceuse says, "I as well."

Vocalise says, "So, what are we gonna do?"

Elvin looks around at them. "That is what we are here to discuss!"

Marchand begins. "We believe we should consider speaking with Ara ourselves."

Elvin's mouth hangs open. "I see," he manages. He fluffs his robes. "Well, it truly is the most diplomatic course of action."

Vocalise waves his foot in the air. "What about Amara?" He leans backward until his head is nearly over the back of the chair. "Or Merp?"

"Whatever course of action we take, we should notify them. Actually, we really should not be having this meeting without them."

Suddenly, Belle walks out onto the balcony and sits down. "Merp won't do anything. Amara tried and couldn't get past Ara's Three Dragon Guardians."

Another man also walks out – a shorter man with a kind face. Belle waves his hand to bring another chair and the man sits a little uncomfortably. "I am unfortunately not surprised she could not," he says.

Vocalise's head reappears. "Maro! Heeeey."

"Hello to you as well, Vocalise," Maro, the God of Tecla, says. He looks around at the assorted group. "I thought I would check on everyone. I must have arrived at Lady Azalea's as soon as all of you left. She said you would be here having a meeting about what to do regarding Ara's Storm."

Oracle nods. "I see. What about you, Belle?"

"Same thing. Talked to Azalea and decided to come here." He looks at Berceuse. "Good to see you again. What do the Pagu say about all of this?"

Berceuse, who had smiled at Belle's greeting, suddenly looks nervous. "They have not spoken directly on this situation, but they have always said if one of us were hurting, that it was always best to go to help them. Lady Azalea implied the same."

Frowning, Belle says, "Most of us have enough sense to know when our mood affects the world in a negative way."

Vocalise stretches. "Ara's always been like this."

Marchand says, "But not this upset. Especially if the Pagu don't think that this storm will end without us intervening."

Elvin sighs. "Which brings us back to the initial matter – we cannot intervene without Merp's permission. Perhaps our first step is to petition him and ask what we must do."

Belle takes the toothpick out of his mouth. "We don't have time for that, Elvin," he says, not unkindly. "He won't do anything about Ara unless it changes a precedent."

Vocalise raises an eyebrow. "Huh?"

But Marchand nods, understanding. "I see. Ara has had storms like this before, so Merp doesn't see any reason to intervene. But, if it went longer or grew to be larger than it ever has ... "

Belle says, "He would do something. Not before."

Berceuse hesitates. "But, that ... Well, doesn't that seem rather unfair? The storm has already caused so much pain. For Elvin and Haliae and his people ... My dear ones are deeply troubled as well."

Vocalise nods. "So, we wait until it's really bad. Got it."

With a cough, Maro says, "From what I recall, the largest that it has ever been was halfway down Pantha and the longest it lasted was through the Summer."

Belle says, "You're right. That's where it is now."

Berceuse tugs on his hair. "I don't quite agree with waiting until Fall."

"Neither do I. But, if I'm honest, even with all of us combining our barriers, we likely wouldn't reach Draconi."

They are all quiet for a moment.

Oracle says, "But, Amara could, couldn't she? Although you said the Three Dragon Guardians wouldn't let her through. But maybe Merp ... "

Elvin rubs his eyes. "Then, we are back where we started. Our first step is to petition Merp and ask that he act before the storm gets any worse."

Oracle, Marchand, and Maro nod. Vocalise scratches his chin. Berceuse looks deeply uncomfortable. Belle chews on his toothpick.

Finally, Berceuse speaks up. "I may have an idea." He turns to Marchand. "I would deeply not wish to involve our Captain in any way, but well ... " He takes a deep breath. "When I was on *PearlHeart,* Captain Rath's ship, it was far easier to maintain my barrier. I believe it was because I could focus completely on it – not on swimming or my surroundings." He frowns. "Or the very cold ocean ... "

Marchand says, "That's a thought." He looks hesitant, however.

Belle says, "It would work."

They all turn to him.

He continues, "It would make sense that you'd have an easier time while on the Captain's ship. The Pagu are there, too."

"Oh, most assuredly," Berceuse says.

Oracle says, "Then, if we were all on Captain Rath's ship and able to focus on our barriers, could we reach Draconi without Merp?"

Belle nods. "Should."

Elvin strokes his nose thoughtfully. "It does address another concern of mine – it allows us to have human representatives with us. They are just as affected – if not more so – by Ara's Storm."

Vocalise says, "Fine with me. I kinda like ships. Pan ships are neat." He grins. Maro snorts beside him.

Marchand runs a hand through his hair. "That's all not ... I think we should speak with Rath before we make any final plans." He sighs. "He has been to the waters around Draconi before, with myself and his father – as a passenger, but he knows the area. And he's introduced himself to the Three Dragon Guardians like everyone who has trained to be in the Council. He knows the etiquette. Not many can say they do."

Nodding, Elvin says, "Then it sounds like speaking with Captain Rath is our next step."

Sven and Pema comes out to the balcony. "Um, Elvin?"

"Yes, Sven?"

Petting Pema, he says, "We were just informed that *PearlHeart* has arrived. Your ink and paper should be here. Pema and I thought of going to meet Rath and the others."

Elvin stands. "Brilliant! That is all right, I told him I would retrieve it. I also need to ask Captain Rath if he will meet with us here."

Sven looks surprised and Pema, curious. "Oh. All right. We'll stay here, then." They return to the sitting room.

After he does, Maro frowns. "We do not wish to overwhelm the Captain."

Vocalise waves his hand. "Aww, he knows us."

Oracle smiles. "And we, him."

Maro looks around. "Really? All of you?"

Berceuse says, "My Captain is who helped me leave my Isles."

Vocalise says, "He's pretty neat. Good sailor, too."

Elvin says, "I've worked with him and his family for years."

Oracle says, "He always spends so much time on his letters and he's so kind to my dears."

Belle says, "He's been through a lot, but hasn't let that hinder him. I don't think he'll be overwhelmed by us."

Marchand says, "Rath has and always will be my own. No matter what has happened to him."

Maro blinks. "Well." He smiles. "I suppose I have missed quite a bit over the centuries. I know him as a kind young man and the grandson of Lady Azalea's. Very caring toward plants as well."

They all smile.

Elvin rises and goes to the door. "I shall return with the Captain immediately."

Marchand says, "Thank you, Elvin."

After he leaves, Vocalise puts his arm over Maro's shoulder. "So, where've you been?"

"Oh, working on my garden. My plant shop. Lady Azalea's recently – her gardens are *wonderful.*"

"Yeah, they're pretty nice."

At the same time, *PearlHeart* has just finished unloading their cargo and delivered part of it to Pica Pica. They are docked at the South Port. One-Eye and Well-Pagu are with Rath.

One-Eye asks, "Is that everything?"

Rath replies, "Almost. Only Elvin's ink and paper is left. Elvin said in his letter that he would come retrieve them himself."

Up above, they suddenly hear a call. "Greetings!"

They look up and see Elvin, in his giant eagle form, flying

toward them. He descends and carefully lands in a gap in the crowd in front of them.

Elvin grins. "It is good to see you, Captain Rath, One-Eye, and Well-Pagu!"

Rath bows. "It is wonderful to see you, Elvin." He gestures. "Your ink and paper are here."

"What? Oh, yes. Thank you very much for bringing them. And the provisions for everyone on Pica Pica." He pauses. "There is something that I, my brothers, and sister would like to discuss with you, Captain. Would you be available to meet with them now? It should not take long."

Rath blinks. "Yes, I believe so."

One-Eye says, "We'll watch the ship." Well-Pagu nods beside him.

"Thank you, One-Eye, Well-Pagu"

Elvin beams. "Perfect! Please, climb on my back. It will be far faster that way."

One-Eye and Well-Pagu watch as Elvin dips his head and Rath climbs on top of his back. Elvin gives them one more nod, then takes the crate with his ink and paper in one talon and lifts up into the air. They fly in between the tall buildings, confetti flitting by them and cheers erupting from the crowd below. They approach the large clock tower with a fountain in front of it. Instead of landing there, Elvin flies straight to the balcony with the other gods. Once they arrive, he lets Rath down. "Here you are, Captain!"

"Thank you, Elvin." Rath's eyebrows raise as he looks around. "Hello, everyone." Then his eyes settle on his god. "Marchand."

Marchand smiles warmly. He stands up and wraps Rath in a hug. "How are you?"

"I am well. How are you?"

Marchand hesitates. "I am, too." He takes Rath's shoulder and squeezes it. They walk over to the table and Marchand waves his hand to make another chair appear.

Rath thanks him and sits, however, when he sees Maro, he seems surprised.

Maro coughs. "I apologize for not telling you who I was when we first met. Compared to some of my brothers and sisters, I prefer to be ... quiet about my godly nature. I am Maro, the God of Tecla."

Elvin, now in his human form, sits down in the chair to Rath's left. He clears his throat. "Now, before you arrived, we had all been discussing our current situation."

Vocalise says, "We were at Lady Azalea's, too."

Rath says, "Really? How is Grandmother – " He flushes. "I apologize. This is not the time to ask."

Marchand says, "It's all right, Rath. I think she was good. If direct with us."

"Grandmother can be that."

Elvin says, "She – as well as the Pagu, from what Berceuse has said – believe that we must journey to Draconi to speak with our brother, Ara, regarding his storm." He clears his throat. "We wished to know if you would allow us to board *PearlHeart* to do so."

Berceuse quickly says, "I brought it up, my Captain – I wish to say that. When I was on *PearlHeart*, traveling to Haliae, it was far easier to uphold my barrier. I did not have to worry about swimming or knowing where I was going."

Belle says, "All of us can't reach Draconi if we traveled there the way we're used to. But, aboard your ship, we should reach it."

Marchand says, "You've been to Draconi as well. With Georgio and I."

Rath says, "Only as far as the Three Dragon Isles."

"Not many have reached even that far."

They all wait as Rath thinks.

He says, "Well-Pagu tells me that they have been to Draconi. I believe they would be able to navigate." He looks to the gods. "May I ask when we would leave?"

Elvin says, "As soon as possible." He blinks suddenly. "You agree?"

Rath shifts uncomfortably. "I would like to do something to help those affected by Ara's Storm and Ara, too, if that would not be inappropriate to say. From what Hep, the Pagu, Grandmother, Carlos, Berceuse, and Marchand have told me, this storm would mean Ara is very upset." He nods. "Yes, I agree to have everyone board *PearlHeart* to travel to Draconi."

Elvin looks relieved. "Brilliant! We do need to notify Merp before we go, but after that, we may leave. When would your crew be ready to depart?"

"This evening."

Elvin looks at his siblings. "We shall be there then!"

They discuss a few more details, then Elvin carries Rath back to *PearlHeart*. After the god returns to the clock tower, Rath gathers his crew on the deck to speak with them. Rath finishes, saying, " ... we will go to Draconi so that the gods may speak with Ara regarding his storm."

"Yes, Captain!" The crew looks concerned, but most look relieved to hear the gods will be with them.

One-Eye is not. As the crew is dispersing, he says, "How many?"

"I'm sorry?"

"Gods."

Rath's eyes light with understanding. "Seven, I believe."

One-Eye stares at the horizon. "Right."

At that moment, Rath hears Vocalise call up from the gangplank, "Captain Rath! Permission to board? For all of us, I mean."

"Yes, permission granted. Thank you for asking," Rath replies.

Vocalise, Maro, Elvin, Belle, Oracle, Marchand, and Berceuse step onto the deck. Almost immediately, the people from Paradi run to their goddess, saying, "Oracle!"

"My dears!"

Vocalise walks up. "Hey, One-Eye."

One-Eye just glares at him.

When Berceuse joins them, Well-Pagu, Bucket-Pagu, and Flower-Pagu fly up to him. "Hello, Berceuse!" Flower-Pagu and Bucket-Pagu say.

"Welcome!" Well-Pagu says.

Berceuse immediately relaxes. "Hello! Thank you, my dear ones. It is so good to see you again. I only wish that the circumstances were better. Again."

Elvin walks up to Rath. "I sent one of my Spirit Eagles to Merp before we left." He frowns. "Truthfully, he would prefer a Phoenae message, but doing so would take far longer than I am comfortable with. However, if I do not hear back by tonight, we will have to delay our departure – hopefully only until tomorrow."

"That is all right. Please let me know when you receive a reply."

"Yes, Captain."

Belle comes over. "Captain, you'll have to decide where you want us for the barrier – around the ship, I mean."

"Of course."

While Rath thinks, Carlos says to the gods, "Tea?" and all of them readily agree, following him below.

As they do, Rath talks through his decisions with One-Eye and Well-Pagu about where the gods will be. " ... and I thought Marchand and Oracle could be on the port and starboard rails. That would be" – he counts – "yes. All seven of them."

Well-Pagu nods. One-Eye does not say anything.

"We will need to prepare the guest cabin, too. Elvin told me that they will not need their barrier until we enter the storm and wish for somewhere to stay. I believe we would be able to fit seven hammocks in it."

One-Eye exhales. "I'll help you with it."

They go below to retrieve the supplies, then to the guest cabin.

One-Eye holds in a hook while Rath pounds it into the ceiling. They have already hung four hammocks and are on the last three. One-Eye glares at nothing in particular.

Rath says, "There. You may let go now."

"Right."

They do two more, for a total of seven. After they are finished, Rath says, "Thank you for helping."

"Yeah." As Rath puts away his tools, One-Eye says, "Have you been to Draconi before?" Beside him, his Lion looks curious.

"Only to the Three Dragon Isles. It was when I was training to be a councilman. My father, Marchand, and I went on a Selachuu ship. When you turn sixteen, it is considered most respectful to start your journey meeting the gods in the Alliance by starting with the Three Dragon Guardians and introducing yourself to them."

"Did you meet Ara?"

"No. No human outside of Draconi has, to the best of my knowledge. Draconi is not an active member of the Alliance. They are a Protected State, like Daerce, and are able to call on the Alliance for aid, but are not required to provide for other countries beyond keeping their communication open to the Council. They do not have a councilperson that travels to Phoenae." He continues, "I met the Three Dragon Guardians, but I did not formally meet any of the gods that I would have that year. That Winter, when I was traveling to my grandmother's island, was when I lost my traits."

That evening, Elvin finds Rath out on the deck. He sighs. "I am afraid I have not heard back from Merp yet. I am certain we will hear a reply in the morning, however."

Rath says, "Thank you for letting me know."

"Of course. And I do wish to thank you for the accommodations you've provided for us during our stay. The hammocks were very thoughtful."

"I am glad to do so. Please let me know if there is anything else that you may need."

"Yes, Captain." Elvin bows, then returns to the guest cabin.

Rath stays outside and the Pagu join him. They look up at the stars together in a peaceful silence.

One-Eye comes up from below and sees him. As he walks over to join them, he sees Rath smiling softly as he traces a constellation with his finger. Rath notices One-Eye and flushes. "Ah, I apologize. Is there something you need, One-Eye?"

"No. I thought – "

Marchand comes out to the deck. "Rath!" He walks over and hesitates. "I'm sorry. Am I interrupting?"

Rath turns to One-Eye, who says, "No."

"All right." He turns back to Rath. "We're all settled in the guest cabin. Thank you for having the hammocks prepared."

"Of course. And I am very glad to hear that. One-Eye helped me put them up."

"I see. Then, thank you as well, One-Eye."

"It's fine," One-Eye says.

Marchand extends his hand. "I don't believe we've ever formally met. I'm Marchand, Rath's god and the God of Delphy."

One-Eye does not shake it. "One-Eye. His first mate."

Marchand takes back his hand. "Right. Are you both looking up at the stars? They're rather clear tonight."

Rath nods. "Yes. Or, rather, I was. I cannot speak for One-Eye."

One-Eye says to Rath, "I was watching you," but as soon as the words leave him, he shuts his mouth, reddening. His Spirit Lion flops down on his feet. "Tracing a constellation, I mean. *Marchand's* – " He glances at Marchand, then just frowns.

The god says, "*Marchand's Message?*"

One-Eye grits his teeth. "Yeah."

Rath says, "It has always brought me great peace."

Marchand settles on Rath's left. "I'm truly glad to hear that. Would you mind if I stayed with you a while? Pagu, One-Eye?"

"I would love that."

One-Eye glares at the deck. "Sure."

Flower-Pagu says, "Of course, Marchand!"

"What if the Captain told the story of your constellation?" Bucket-Pagu says.

Well-Pagu says, "Tell?"

Marchand laughs. "Well, I certainly wouldn't mind."

"I would like to," Rath says. He turns to One-Eye. "Would you like to listen?"

"He's right there," One-Eye says. To Marchand, he says, "Why do you need to hear your own story again?"

Moving his hair back, Marchand says, "I do like hearing my own tell it. Especially, because it tells of Rath's ancestor, the origin of Delphy, and all those I protect. It has always been a very happy memory of mine."

Rath says, "I as well." He waves his hand suddenly. "Ah, not as a memory – I was not present. But, as a story."

Marchand chuckles, fondly taking his own's shoulder. "I know what you mean, Rath."

Rath smiles, grateful.

One-Eye sees his expression and coughs into his hand. "I'll stay." He looks at Marchand once more, then settles his eye up on the constellation in the sky.

Rath brightens, then looks up, too.

"Marchand's Message is the longest constellation to extend in a single row of stars. Even so, most" – Rath holds up his hand and spreads his fingers, making his thumb and pinky the furthest points – *"can use their thumb and pinky to trace the constellation from beginning to end. Family and friends are often not as far away as they seem and may always be reached.*

"As the Third World was coming to an end, a group of people tried to escape the destruction traveling by sea. The waters were very dangerous and the winds made it very difficult for them to keep their sails set. However, together, they braved the storm and traveled steadily away from its origin.

"When they were approaching a distant island – their goal and what they hoped would offer them shelter – a strong wind hit them, dismasting their ships and tearing their sails apart. Many people fell into the water and all were separated.

"Not far from them, Marchand and his dolphins were trying to stay safe in the storm. However, upon seeing the ships destroyed, Marchand wished to help. He told his dolphins to search for any humans that had gone underwater while he sought out those that were still above.

"The first human he came to was a young man. He was not afraid for his own safety, but terrified for his mother. He pleaded to Marchand to find her first and return to him. Marchand could not leave the man, but he heeded his request. Carrying the man through the water on his back, Marchand asked that he think very strongly of his mother and the love he held for her. The man did and Marchand began to glow. A Delphaen message was sent across the water ahead of them and soon, to the man's mother. They rescued her and Marchand carried her as well on his back. But the mother was fearful for her sister, from whom she was separated. Marchand told her to think strongly of her sister and another Delphaen message was sent. Marchand followed the trail and found the mother's sister. The sister pleaded for her friend and that friend pleaded for their grandmother. Soon, all of them were connected – they had found each other and were together, every friend and family member.

"Marchand and his dolphins carried them to the island that had been their original goal and what would become Delphy, where he gave them his protection. Their traits became Delphaen messages that they could send to those who are dear to them and the ability to breathe underwater. He started with the man he initially found, who became his First and who would later represent him and their people in the future."

They all pause after Rath finishes.

Marchand closes his eyes, thinking. Finally, he opens them and says, "Thank you, Rath." He smiles, a little sad. "You remind me of that first man greatly, you know – Meridan was his name."

One-Eye glances at his Lion – his Lion is quiet – then repeats, "'However, together, they braved the storm and traveled steadily away from its origin.' I've heard about that a lot in the constellation stories I've heard. No one seems to know what that origin was." He looks at his Lion again. "Or can't say."

Marchand sighs heavily. "It is a very unhappy memory for all of us. Some of us more than others." He steps away from the rail. "Thank you again, Rath. I always enjoy speaking with you. And it was good formally meeting you as well, One-Eye."

Rath says, "You too, Marchand."

One-Eye nods.

Afterward, Marchand goes to the guest cabin. One-Eye stands beside Rath, petting his Spirit Lion. The Pagu are quiet. One-Eye finally says, "He's nice. Your god."

"I love him," Rath says without hesitation.

One-Eye pauses. He hums in a noncommittal answer.

The next morning, One-Eye leans on the rail, watching Elvin pace the deck. After a few more minutes, One-Eye walks to the galley with his Spirit Lion.

Inside, many crew members are sitting and talking. One-Eye and his Lion join the table where William, Phobos, and Isaac are. William says, "What do you think of all of this, One-Eye?"

"The Captain thinks it's the right decision. I'll follow him." He pets his Lion. "I'd like the storm to end, too. My Lion says it's causing a lot of problems in Pantha."

William and Isaac nod. William raises his hand up to Phobos. "Oracle is worried about Ara. I'd like to do this for the people of Haliae, too – so that they can finally go home."

Isaac says, "From what the Captain said, it sounds like this storm is just going to keep on getting bigger. That's kinda scary. But, Vocalise is here – and the other gods – so I'm not as worried about going."

That afternoon, Sven, Pema, Hailcorn, and Fritz visit *PearlHeart*. Hailcorn and Fritz greet Rath, then speak with Elvin.

"No, I still have not heard a reply," Elvin tells them.

While they talk, Sven speaks with Rath.

"Elvin told us what you would all be doing – I still can't believe it. Do you remember going to the Three Dragon Isles to meet Ara's Guardians before?" Rath nods and Sven says, "It's hard to imagine they have more power than the Gods." He pets Pema for a moment, then takes Rath's hand. "Well, if Merp does accept and you all go on this journey, I hope everyone will be safe."

"I do as well."

That evening, Elvin approaches Rath again. "I sincerely apologize. I do not know what is delaying him."

"It truly is all right, Elvin."

Elvin, frowning, nods and goes to the guest cabin to pace.

Rath turns, looking out at Pica Pica. The festivities go on late into the evening – and sometimes through the night – and he watches the confetti and explosions of colored smoke drift through the air. A small family is just walking past the docks, looking up at the different ships and even pointing up at *PearlHeart's* masts. Rath smiles.

Suddenly, he hears a rushing sound, then what appears to be smoke races through the city. A cold wind hits him and then he hears the shouts of people below. Rath runs down the gangplank.

He reaches the family just where they stopped, stunned to see a wall of snow and ice coming their way. Rath runs in front of them and takes the parents' shoulders, who are in turn shielding their children. They crouch down together, eyes shut as Ara's Storm passes over them.

It takes all of them a moment to realize that it has not hit them.

Rath opens his eyes and sees something white glowing in his waist scarf. When he pulls it out, he sees it is the small woven grass charm that Sir Rif and Amethyst Rose gave to him on Cunica. Its white light surrounds him and the family, preventing the storm from touching them.

The father looks at it, then at the white glow in amazement. "What is that?" he asks.

"An Amaran charm." Rath studies the barrier then nods, handing it to him. "Please have this. I believe it will keep you safe. I need to check on my crew."

"O-Of course."

Rath takes a deep breath, then runs out of the white glow and into the storm. His boots skid on the dock as he is pulled across by the force of the wind. He reaches the gangplank just as seven different colors rise up in front of his eyes, encasing *PearlHeart* in a rainbow barrier.

He can just see Marchand, at the starboard rail, look down at him and shout, "Rath! In here!"

Rath leaps up the gangplank, through the barrier, and into One-Eye, who catches him.

"Are you –" One-Eye starts to say.

"Is everyone all right here?"

"They are." One-Eye releases him. "What were you doing down there?"

Rath shakes out his hair – there is snow on it. "There was a family there that was taken by surprise by the storm." He looks through the colors and can just see the bright white light shining through, protecting the family.

One-Eye sees it, too. "What's that light?"

"The Amaran charm Sir Rif and Amethyst Rose gave me. I am glad that it still seems to be keeping them safe." Rath suddenly frowns. "Perhaps we should try to get them and everyone else aboard *PearlHeart*."

"All of Pica Pica?"

Rath hesitates.

Marchand hears them and says, "We may be able to help." He looks toward the other gods, who nod.

They all concentrate. Slowly, the combined barrier grows past *PearlHeart* until it is as large as the docks and continues to expand, reaching the city. Groups of people, including the family Rath helped, who were clustered together stand up and look in wonder as the light spreads over Pica Pica and the snow appears to stop. The barrier grows taller, rising above each tower and – finally – over the largest, the clock tower. There, from within a small orb of turquoise – the Goddess of Pica Pica, Liette – looks up into her siblings' barrier.

"Whew," she says, then adds her power to it. The barrier grows more quickly afterward, arcing over the clock tower and to the North Port. There, it spreads into the ocean, calming the water on the surface. The gods on *PearlHeart* concentrate to keep it up while Ara's Storm pounds on it from outside.

Far above, in Phoenae, Merp paces on a balcony with a small fountain. A Pagu in a yellow sundress and hat is cooling their feet in the water while they watch him.

"Elvin says Captain Rath of *PearlHeart* will be taking them. What right do they have to even propose such an idea without my permission? And why would they think a man like that would be fit to take them?"

Fountain-Pagu looks at him calmly. "Merp, you do need to reply."

Merp stops. He takes a deep breath. "I understand." He glances at the Spirit Eagle fidgeting on the balcony. "Tell them – "

However, at that moment, a Spirit Phoenix lands beside the Spirit Eagle. She talks to Merp. He listens carefully.

His eyes widen. "What?"

Below, on Pica Pica, the gods have continued to uphold the barrier for the whole afternoon.

The partying that was interrupted by the storm has tentatively continued by the next hour and now is as loud as it was before.

One-Eye gestures at it. "They're doing that while this is going on?"

Rath replies, "Yes." He turns toward the gods, looking concerned.

One-Eye faces them, crossing his arms. "So, we can't leave at all now."

"I do not believe so."

The Pagu, who are on the railing next to them, look up into the sky. Bucket-Pagu says, "Captain, One-Eye, look!"

Up above, a bright white light similar to the light from the Amaran charm descends from the sky. As it grows closer, they all see a unicorn gallop down to them on a glowing white ramp that curves like a ribbon as it travels toward *PearlHeart.*

The unicorn pauses just above them. "Captain Rath, if I may ask permission to board your vessel. As captain, this is your authority to allow or deny. I am Amara, Elder Goddess of Unys."

"It is. And permission granted."

She gives a brisk nod, then steps down. She reaches the deck in her human form and looks around before turning to Rath. "What is the meaning of this? Why do my siblings gather here so?"

"They have asked that *PearlHeart* take them to Draconi so that they may speak with Ara and ask that he end his storm. However, currently they are maintaining a barrier so as to protect Pica Pica from it."

"I can see that!" Amara snaps. She raises her chin, looking at the docks, where the white light still is around the family. She points. "And that. I had felt the energy of one of my Amaran knights, yet not their presence. I now see that it is a Knight's Charm. I will retrieve it, for it is not truly for them."

"Please do not," Rath says and a few gods open their eyes in surprise. "It was given to me by Sir Rif and Amethyst Rose and I gave it to the family there so that they would be protected from the storm."

Amara looks startled. "That was rather appropriate." She clears her throat. "I will excuse it given the present circumstances." She looks at the docks again. "It will lose its power soon – it shall not work again. And if it protected you and the good people of Pica Pica from my brother's storm, then that would be a noble duty accomplished. As such, I will allow them to keep it as it would be dishonorable to demand the return of a gift that could have only been given freely, first by my knight, then by you."

Rath dips his head respectfully. "Thank you very much, Amara."

Her expression tightens. "You say that my siblings have asked you to take them to Draconi to speak with Ara. Why is it that you were chosen for such a task? My Amaran Knights would be far more suitable and worthy."

One-Eye grits his teeth. Rath calmly responds, "I am told that it would be easier for everyone to focus on their barrier while aboard my ship."

Amara narrows her eyes. "Does Merp know of this?"

"I do not know. Elvin sent one of his Spirit Eagles to him asking if we would be allowed."

"A most appropriate decision and one necessary in such a

situation." She falters. "Then, he has not replied?"

"No. Elvin says he has not."

Amara looks concerned for a moment. She hesitates, turning her eyes toward the sky and the storm raging beyond the barrier. She looks at her siblings and the dim glow of Liette on her clock tower, then all of the people underneath their protection. Finally, she says to Rath, "It is not your place to speak with my brother or everyone here to protect those of Pica Pica from Ara's Storm. It is ... Someone must go to Draconi. I am not welcome. As well, someone must protect Pica Pica. Before I find cause to act, I will take the latter as my task. You, Captain Rath, will go to Draconi with my siblings and pray speak to Ara so that his storm may end and I do not – " She swallows. Then her eyes flare. "Go, Captain! Make haste!"

"Yes, Amara."

Amara nods to him once, then races off the deck on a glowing white path and gallops away as a unicorn.

While Rath organizes his crew to cast off, Amara travels over Pica Pica, just outside of the gods' barrier. Her white light protects her from Ara's Storm. Beneath her hooves, that light spreads, slowly covering her siblings' barrier during her journey. She passes the tall buildings and the clock tower in the center, where Liette still is, until she starts to descend on the northern side of the island.

That evening, when she reaches the water, she steps out onto it in her human form and sits. She closes her eyes and concentrates. Immediately, the white light she had spread on her way there intensifies and fully encases the rainbow barrier, muting the colors from the outside.

On the deck of *PearlHeart*, the gods feel the change. Belle says, "Release it now."

The others do and the rainbow fades away. Up on her clock tower, Liette releases hers, too, and flops down on her back, exhausted. The gods all sigh, relaxing. Vocalise rolls his shoulder. "Well, at least we know we can do it."

Maro nods. "And it will not be over anything as large as Pica Pica, either."

Belle says, "It still won't be easy." He looks past them, to Rath, who is now at the wheel. "I heard your talk with Amara, Captain."

Elvin sighs. "We truly should wait until Merp's reply, however Amara has given a direct order."

Vocalise shrugs. "I actually agree with it."

Rath says, "I do as well."

Marchand leans on Oracle. "We'll be able to rest while we're under Amara's barrier, but we'll be back out to create ours around *PearlHeart* as soon as we leave it and enter Ara's Storm."

Rath looks concerned for a moment, then nods. "Thank you, everyone."

They smile at him, then make their way to the guest cabin to rest.

Soon, *PearlHeart* is sailing around the western side of Pica Pica, heading north toward Draconi.

27

In the North, past Haliae and Ara's Sea, the Three Dragon Guardians rest on their Isles. Each isle is just big enough for their enormous forms to stand on. Even though their wings are folded, their overall size still obscures the far larger landmass behind them – Draconi. Their glowing eyes – all an icy blue – look south, unfazed by the storm that Ara has created.

In Draconi, the winds blow over a wide field and beyond that, hills and valleys for many miles. On the other side of one of the hills lays a well-lit city – the City of Draconi. There is a thick, stone wall around its perimeter and small ice dragons sit on top of it, watching the outside world.

The city is full of people wearing sleeveless garments with an unusual sheen and boots that appear to have a layer of metal over them, all walking between stone buildings with stained glass windows and smoke rising out of their chimneys. All do not seem to be bothered by the cold. Any snow that comes near the city immediately melts due to the heat.

One large building stands in the center of the city, shining in the bright, wintry sky – a cathedral that appears to be made out of solid ice. The people know it as Ara's Cathedral.

It has five bell towers, two on either side of a far taller one, each with stained glass windows. The bells at the top of all are frozen.

Behind the cathedral is a walled-in garden and within it there is little else but Frost Flowers.

Besides a path to walk on and tend to them, the ground is covered in the species native to Draconi. They have five petals, each looking as fragile as glass, but pliable, swaying in the breeze as a man walks next to them. He has long dark blue hair done in four long braids at his back and one shorter one on the right side of his face. He kneels and studies the ground, placing his hand carefully around the stalks of the flowers.

"No ... " he mutters. "Still none. Where are they?" He rises and continues on.

An older man and a younger one, standing and sitting on the covered patio leading into the back of the cathedral, watch him walk further into the garden.

The younger man says, "What is he looking for? If he'd tell us, perhaps we could help."

The older man sighs. "Ara will not. I asked him last year and several times since. He says only he must find them." He watches his god, the Elder God of Draconi, Ara, get on his knees again, searching the ground.

Later, the three of them are in a long dining hall with a chandelier made out of ice. It glints dully. Ara sits at the head, looking distracted.

The older man has a tea trolley set out. He lays a stone cup in front of his god. "Tea, Ara."

Ara glances over. "Thank you, Niven." After a moment, he takes a sip.

Niven nods, then serves the younger man – Krir – and himself before sitting down with his own cup. Both have Ara's Traits and even the stone cups turn red from the heat of their hands.

Krir says to Ara, "What is it that you are looking for?"

Niven coughs and Ara, who had been turned toward the window behind him, whips his head back. He narrows his eyes. "I will tell you when I find it, Krir."

"But – "

"It is what I would prefer at the moment." He rubs his

temples, thinking.

Krir takes another sip. "But, if you would tell us, perhaps we could help."

"No. No, because ... " Ara falls silent. He finishes his tea, then stands up. "I am going out to the garden. Thank you for the tea, Niven, and the company, Krir." He leaves the room.

Niven and Krir watch him. Niven sips calmly, but Krir says, "He cannot keep going about like this. It's been nearly a year."

"That amount of time would seem like a blink to one such as him."

"Perhaps. But, I truly do not think I can handle another outburst like last week. And what of the world outside? You told me people outside do not have traits like ours. Surely this storm is affecting them more than us."

Niven sighs. "I cannot say." He frowns. "I do hope that Wagon-Pagu returns from visiting the Three Dragon Guardians soon. Ara needs them. They may know more about how those outside of Draconi are."

"From what they said last, this storm had covered much of ... Haliae, was it? And ... " Krir struggles.

"Pantha, which is a very large country." Krir nods, listening. They finish their tea, then Niven says, "Now, shall we go out with Ara again?"

"I suppose so."

They put their stone cups on the tray. Niven carries it into the kitchen with Krir holding the door open for him. Afterward, they go out onto the covered patio again and watch Ara search among the flowers.

28

In Pantha, Faerohr is handing out food to his people when the front doors of the castle open, letting in the storm, and Lionel walks in. He shuts them behind him, then turns into his lion form and shakes the snow off of his fur.

Faerohr asks, "How is it?"

"A lot worse. Don't you remember that yell?"

Faerohr sighs. "Of course, I do. It took the better half of the afternoon to convince everyone that it wasn't Ara challenging them to a match."

"Might as well have with the mess he's making." Lionel turns back into his human form. He stands next to Faerohr and starts handing out food, too, from the crates the Selachuu Military brought.

"Thanks!" a man says.

"Yeah," Lionel says. "Stay warm."

Faerohr glances at his god curiously, but says nothing as he continues to pass out the provisions. Once everyone is seated and eating and they have gotten their own food, Lionel says, "It's definitely gotten bigger. The storm, I mean."

"That is concerning. Has anything ever been done about it

in the past?"

Lionel snorts. "'Course not. Before, they always ended." He takes a bite. "Eventually."

Faerohr hums in response. He looks at the crates, two of which are empty. "We haven't been able to find much food, either, or travel very far in the storm ... "

"We'll be fine," Lionel says. "So, don't worry about it. I'm not."

In the South, Fierce is sitting on top of his mountain on Butej in his hawk form, thinking.

Something catches his eye far below and he looks down to see a flash of yellow in the ocean. A second later, he flies down.

When he is just above the water, he slows his fall and flaps in the air, stationary. "Erole. What is it?"

A giant electric eel curves beneath the waves, sending out errant sparks.

Fierce says, "And stop sending out electricity near my people."

The eel stops and glows, turning into Erole's human form. He climbs up and sits on a small outcropping of rock in the ocean. The God of Ullia has thin pale blond hair tied over one shoulder and dark clothes. He grins underneath his hood. His eyes are a luminous pale yellow. "I can't help it. I'm too excited."

"About?"

"Ara. This storm of his." His eyebrows raise impossibly high. "It's grown. Did you know?"

"Yes." Fierce flaps twice more. "This is not a good event, Erole."

"No, but it's interesting. That's what's important." He studies the water. "What could have made Ara so upset? Do you know, Fierce?"

"I do not. I have not been to the North."

Erole hums. "The South is your jurisdiction." He leans back. "But, you can travel fast, can't you? Why not just take a quick trip there? Why is it you're so determined to stay in the South?"

Fierce does not say anything.

"Does it have something to do with Captain Rath? I know you're always checking in on him. Or is it because Corxae is down here? After that one person – "

Fierce's expression tightens. "I will not answer any of your questions, Erole."

Erole stands up, brushing off his pants. "That answers more than enough for me. I can't wait for the reports from my own this year." He grins up at Fierce. "I have a feeling it's going to be SO interesting."

Fierce stares at him, saying nothing.

His brother dives back into the water, disappearing beneath the waves.

Near Phoenae, a bright form flies.

Merp, now in his phoenix form, plunges through the crowd cover and emerges from the bottom.

He immediately encounters Ara's Storm.

Testily, he looks around at the ice and snow. His golden glow easily evaporates any parts of the storm from reaching him. To the east, he sees three things – a small rainbow barrier heading steadily north, a large white barrier encasing the island of Pica Pica, and a yellow and green barrier over the country of Daerce. He flies toward Pica Pica first, aimed for the North Port where the white glow is the brightest.

When he arrives, a path of white light is sent out to him over the ocean that he can walk on in his human form. He follows it to his sister Amara seated on top of a white disc. When he reaches her, he stops, arms crossed.

Amara opens her eyes. "Greetings, Brother."

Merp snaps, "What are you doing? Why is *PearlHeart* – I can only imagine it must be given Elvin's message – sailing to Draconi without my permission?"

With a level look, Amara replies, "I am protecting my sister Liette's land of Pica Pica as suiting my Knightly Creed. *PearlHeart* I have deemed more suitable for the other task. I commanded them." He frowns and Amara says, "I am sorry, Merp. Such is your duty to make this decision. I was assured they sought your permission, but you had not yet responded and the people here could not be left unprotected, nor our brother not spoken to for what he has caused."

Merp shifts, uncomfortable. "I did not reply. I did not deem Ara's Storm to be ... " Suddenly, the barrier over Daerce wavers as a gust rails against it. Merp swallows. "I cannot see any of this from Phoenae."

Amara does not say anything. She turns toward the other barrier. "Sevran and Feep are currently protecting Daerce – such is only right – however, surely, if Ara's Storm reaches further south, Sevran will need to return to her country of Pertes to protect it and her own."

"Feep likely cannot maintain his on his own. And Pantha?"

At this, Amara's eyes narrow. "Despite accepting aid from the Alliance, Lionel himself has still not acted. I pray his own are safe."

"They are strong ... " However, Merp sounds unsure. He shakes his head. "I will go to *PearlHeart.*"

"Will you stop them?"

Merp takes a breath. "No. However, I would speak with all of our siblings – and Captain Rath." He steps away, glows, and turns into his phoenix form, flying north toward the rainbow barrier.

PearlHeart sails north through Ara's Storm.

As soon as they neared the edge of Amara's barrier, the gods had returned to the deck to be ready to begin their own. Now, they are all in their positions, concentrating, and Rath and the Pagu watch them by the port rail.

Franz comes down from his watch at the wheel and looks at the gods, too.

Below, in his hammock in the crew's quarters, Evermore touches the wall. His hand glows a pale yellow with Erole's Traits as he uses them to check who is currently aboard *PearlHeart.* He sighs, still uncomfortable with so many gods.

In the galley, Melody, Demeter, and Velt are talking. Melody says, "I'm scared about this, but Oracle and Demeter say it'll be okay. I trust the Captain, too."

Velt nods. "We all do. I didn't like how Amara talked to him, though."

"Velt! She's a goddess." Melody turns to Demeter as she gives a short "Caw," then Melody says, "Well, yes, I suppose that they can be rude, as well."

Rath is still on the deck when they all hear a piercing call. He turns and sees a great golden light approaching them from the stern. It flies through the barrier and flaps in place. Merp, in his phoenix form, glares down at them, then focuses on Rath. "Permission to board, Captain Rath?"

Rath bows. "Yes, permission granted."

Merp lands and turns into his human form. He addresses his siblings, "All of you – I would speak with you."

The gods do not reply. A few open their eyes to look at Merp, but shut them again.

Merp looks incensed.

Rath says, "Please do not speak to them. I am told that they need to concentrate to maintain their barriers."

"I know that, Captain Rath. I am a god. You are not." He takes a deep breath. "Then I would speak to you. Now."

Once they reach the captain's cabin, Merp goes to the table. "Shut the door firmly behind you."

"Yes, Merp." Rath does so, then sits in the chair across from him.

Merp studies him for a long moment. "For what reason are you undertaking this voyage?"

"To help Ara. I was also asked by the gods."

"The first is new to me. The second I already knew from Elvin's Spirit Eagle." He sits back. "Why would you wish to help Ara? You've never met."

Rath shifts uncomfortably. "That is true."

"But, he has hurt others around you – Haliae? – is that why you wish for his storm to end?"

Rath looks startled. "No. I do wish for this storm to end. I would also like for Ara to be well." Merp blinks, surprised. "From everything that I have been told, the reason for this storm is because he is upset. As you said, I have never met him. However, if bringing his family to him would help, then I wish to do what I can to aid in that."

For a moment, Merp says nothing. Then, very slowly he says, "Ara has been upset for a long time. I am not sure that a venture such as this will change that. Will you still insist on going, knowing that?"

"Yes."

Merp thinks. "The Pagu approve of this?"

"I believe so."

Merp sighs. "And your grandmother ... She does as well?"

"I am told she suggested it."

Merp's mouth drops open for a moment. He coughs, raising his hand to cover it. "I see." He studies Rath again. "I will not disallow this voyage, nor will I offer you any aid. Know that whatever the outcome, it is your responsibility, Captain Rath."

"I understand, Merp."

They return to the main deck. The Elder God of Phoenae looks around at his siblings one last time, then Merp leaves, leaping off in his phoenix form. He exits the barrier, becoming a golden light within the storm outside.

Later that night, Rath sits at his desk in his cabin, writing in his logbook. He looks up and out his windows. The rainbow barrier swirls around *PearlHeart*, but beyond, nothing can be seen but white.

There is a knock on his door.

Carlos comes in. "Master Rath?"

"Yes, what is it?"

Carlos frowns and sets a bowl of food down on his desk. "Phillip and Flower-Pagu told me you did not arrive for dinner."

"For ... " Rath flushes as he looks at the meal. "I apologize. I will tell them as well. Thank you for bringing this, Carlos." He takes the warm bowl in his hands and begins to eat.

"Of course." Carlos studies him. "How are you?"

"Well. May I ask how you are?"

Carlos looks out at the storm. "I am all right."

"I am very grateful to everyone for what they are doing to help us reach Draconi."

Carlos listens, then says, "You are doing well, too, Master Rath. Both the gods and your crew trust you deeply."

Rath nods, eating his soup.

They travel on under the barrier. Almost a month later, Rath is with One-Eye near the rail with a map spread between them. Rath lays his finger on an area to the northwest. "We are currently sailing past Haliae."

One-Eye frowns. "You can't see it."

"No, you cannot."

They continue for the next four days and on the morning of the fifth, Berceuse, who has been standing near the upper deck, stumbles.

Rath, who had just been walking out to the main deck, sees and steadies him. "Are you all right?"

Berceuse says, "Yes, thank you, my Captain. I do apologize." He sighs. "It is far easier with everyone, but ... " He shakes his head. "I only need a moment – then, I will be all right. Would you stay with me? It feels like so long since I've been able to speak with you."

"Of course."

They lean against the wall. Berceuse notes what Rath is wearing. "Are the gloves I made for you warm?"

"Yes, very." Rath smiles. "Thank you very much for knitting them."

"Most certainly, my Captain!"

They stand for a while longer, then Berceuse takes a deep breath. "Thank you, my Captain. I hope we may speak again soon."

"I do as well. You are welcome, Berceuse."

Rath steps back as Berceuse clasps his hands together again. He begins to glow purple, adding his power to the barrier.

The next day, Oracle and Elvin begin to weaken. Belle notices and says to them, "Rest for a while."

Oracle sits against the rail. "Yes, Belle!"

Elvin leans heavily on the mast. "Yes, Brother!"

Oracle waves to Elvin, saying, "Come over here a moment."

When he joins her, they sit next to each other by the rail. Oracle says, "Ara's Storm seems far stronger than it was when we evacuated Haliae, doesn't it?"

Elvin tucks his robe more firmly around himself in the cold. "I was thinking the same thing. All the more reason why we need to help everyone reach there and ask that Ara end it."

"I still wonder what has caused it."

Elvin hesitates. "Ara has been upset for a very long time."

Oracle lowers her eyes. "True."

"Perhaps if we had ... " Elvin sighs.

Oracle takes his hand, nodding.

They sit for a while longer, then return to their positions. They glow magenta and light blue, strengthening the barrier again.

Maro and Vocalise take a break two days later. They sit, talking by the stern. The day after that, Marchand takes a break and speaks with Rath by the port rail and the same day, Belle takes a standing break at the prow. Carlos brings him tea.

After he finishes, Belle hands him back the teacup. "Thanks."

"Certainly." Carlos looks out into the storm. "Master Rath says that we are to arrive at the Three Dragon Isles within the next week."

"Sounds right to me." He studies it himself. Then he says, "Take care," and adds his energy to the barrier.

Carlos smiles briefly, then walks below to return the teacup.

The next days grow darker. Even the barrier seems to not cast as much light and Rath asks that the lanterns are lit to help everyone.

Berceuse takes another break. He rubs his face while he is speaking with Rath. "We are almost there, yes?"

"Indeed. Well-Pagu says that within a day, we should arrive at the Three Dragon Isles."

Berceuse shivers. "And I am sure their Guardians are there. They are – "

Suddenly, a rush of wind screeches toward them. Berceuse takes Rath's hands, glowing a bright purple as – even with the barrier – an icy wind cuts through *PearlHeart.*

Then, above them, they hear something shatter. They look up and see Melody climb down from the nest and run to the starboard railing, where Oracle is slumped, exhausted. Magenta sparkles from Oracle's barrier rain down and fade when they hit the deck. Melody kneels next to her goddess.

Oracle says to her, "Do not worry, my dear. I will be all right in just a moment."

"But – "

Another wind screeches through. Two more barriers break up above – light blue and orange. Vocalise shouts, "Maro!" and runs toward him.

But Maro raises his hand and says, "I will be okay."

Vocalise hesitates. He goes to Elvin instead and helps him up, but releases his barrier in doing so. "You good there, buddy?"

Elvin rubs his face. "I will be."

Belle switches his toothpick to the other side, staring out into the storm. He, Marchand, and Berceuse are the only three left. Marchand visibly struggles to maintain his own while the others recover and Berceuse's purple begins to fade. Finally,

Berceuse leans against the wall. "I am sorry, my Captain. I need to rest."

Rath shakes his head. "Do not worry, Berceuse."

Around them, Oracle's barrier begins to glow again. William, Phobos, Felix, and Triphonius are now with her, too. Franz and Charles are near Maro on the upper deck. Velt and the Pagu are with Elvin and Vocalise. Slowly, Maro begins to glow, then Vocalise, then Elvin. Marchand finally releases his own barrier to rest and nearly falls over, but Rath makes his way over quickly and holds his god up. "Are you all right?"

Marchand smiles at him. "Yes. Thank you." He holds Rath tightly, but Rath can feel his arm shake.

Up above them, the colors from the other gods begin to join Belle's gray-blue, covering it in layers as they reach for one another.

However, just before they can connect, one more howling wind hits them, making the mizzenmast creak. Rath and Marchand brace themselves.

As the gods struggle, Belle grits his teeth. He increases the strength of his barrier, but *PearlHeart* begins to move backward from the force of the wind. When Belle sees this, he throws away his toothpick and dives overboard. Marchand sees and shouts, "Belle!"

They all see a gray-blue glow swim toward *PearlHeart's* stern and disappear. Then, very slowly, they start to move forward again. A topsail tears and flies away. *PearlHeart* gains speed and the other gods try to piece together their barriers again. The snow grows heavier around them and the wind continues. All of them start to skid backward on the deck.

Then all of it stops.

Suddenly, there is only black around them. They can still hear the wind outside, but none of it reaches them.

On the port side, someone climbs over the rail, dripping water.

Breathing heavily, Belle says, "We're here."

Rath sees a bobbing blue light on the deck and realizes that it is One-Eye's eye, glowing with Lionel's Traits. Next to Rath, Marchand puts his barrier back up, casting a weak blue-green light on everything. It illuminates One-Eye standing next to Belle and other members of the crew by each other or the gods.

From above, a giant snout, eyes, and horns appear until a dragon head breathes over *PearlHeart.* His wings – the black that they saw before, but now can see are truly an icy blue, made darker by the storm – are stretched out around them, easily encasing *PearlHeart* and protecting them from the wind outside. Two bright blue eyes look down on them. A deep, but warm voice says, "You were nearly lost. Who are you and what business do you have in Draconi?"

Rath steps away from Marchand and speaks. "I am Captain Rath of Delphy. My ship is *PearlHeart.* I have heritage with the Gods Marchand, Penelope, Hep, and Fierce. We ask that the gods here may speak with Ara."

"Well-spoken. I am South, one of Ara's Three Dragon Guardians. I recall you, Rath, but you held a different station then as a future member of the Council."

"That is true. I will no longer be succeeding my father."

South studies him, then his eyes widen briefly. "I see." He then says, "To your request – why? What do you hope for by speaking with our god?"

Elvin, recovered now, says, "We have been greatly hurt by his storm. We wish to ask if he may end it."

South's eyes narrow. "Then you speak for your own and not for Ara."

"I would ask that we speak for both."

Another voice – vibrant – says, "South – create a barrier for them. They are too tired to do one for themselves. West and I would also like to speak with them."

South pauses. "Very well." Then he leans forward and blows. The wind is not cold, but warm, and as it spreads, a yellow glow envelopes *PearlHeart* – bright, like a Summer sun. All of the gods relax. Belle and Marchand release their barriers.

The dragon removes his wings from around *PearlHeart.* When he does, two other dragons are revealed on either side of him, all of similar stature. Ara's Storm swirls around them.

South's eyes move to each of the gods. "Marchand, Oracle, Berceuse, Elvin, Vocalise, Belle, and Maro." He breathes out frost. "This is surprising."

Vocalise grins. "Just thought we'd stop by."

Belle gives him a sharp look and Vocalise snaps his mouth shut.

The dragon to the left of South gives a short laugh. She leans forward. Her breath blossoms in crystals over the barrier. "Ha! Since when has it been customary for you to stop by, God of Pantrog?" To the humans, she says, "I am East, one of Ara's Three Dragon Guardians."

The dragon to the right of South leans forward then. He snorts and a flurry of snow blinds them all for a moment. "It has been a very long time since you have even been within eyesight of Draconi. We would know. I am West, one of Ara's Three Dragon Guardians."

Marchand says, "We realize that. As Rath said, we have come here to speak with Ara."

East narrows her eyes. "Of course you do. We have watched his storm grow with each year and the problems that it has caused. We are regretful for what happened to Haliae, Elvin."

Elvin can only nod.

"But, that does not excuse the fact that it is only when it has become an inconvenience to you that you decide to arrive. Do not claim it is out of kindness for Ara."

Belle speaks. "Ara's always been distant. He prefers it that way."

West snorts again. "Belle is right."

South says, "Even so ... " He studies them all. "Why bring humans into the matter? They have no place here, especially those without Ara's Traits to survive the cold."

Oracle says, "We could not arrive here without Captain Rath's ship. The storm was too strong for us to travel as we normally do."

South looks surprised. "And it took all seven of you even so?" They nod. The dragon hesitates and murmurs, although it is loud enough to be heard by everyone on *PearlHeart*, "I did not know that it had grown to be so great."

Elvin says, "May we ask if you would know, being Ara's Guardians, what has made him so upset to cause this storm?"

Immediately, they all narrow their eyes. South says, "No. We do not."

West says, "He will not tell even us."

East says, "All he does is continue to search his garden."

Maro says, "Then, perhaps it is something that he has lost

that is connected to that. We could help him find it."

Marchand says, "Whatever it is, we would like to help. I understand that our coming may not seem to be in kindness but due to our own inconvenience, like you said. However, we also cannot allow Ara to continue this for the safety of our own people."

East and West are silent, but South says, "Well spoken, Marchand. I will forward your request to Ara." He studies *PearlHeart* with some concern. "However, I do not wish to endanger any humans. I also do not believe any of you are strong enough to travel through his storm on your own to meet with Ara in his city." He pauses for a long moment, then says, "I have told Ara of your arrival and who is with you. He has accepted you coming to Draconi on one condition – that Captain Rath accompany you."

Rath's eyebrows go up. "Of course."

Marchand frowns. "Did he say why?"

"No. Just that he believes the Captain may be able to help him with something. I will carry the gods and Captain Rath to Draconi. East and West will protect *PearlHeart* from the storm. Is that acceptable?"

Elvin replies, "It is. Thank you very much for your considerations."

"You are welcome." To Rath, South says, "I will protect you in my barrier while we travel there, however I will need to leave all of you at the gates to the city. Draconi is not as dangerous as it is out here. The people make it warm, so you will be safe in what you are wearing currently."

"I understand. Thank you."

While the gods gather on the deck, One-Eye, the Pagu, and Carlos approach Rath. One-Eye says, "You sure we're safe with them?"

"Yes. They will do as they say."

Carlos nods as well.

Flower-Pagu says, "Be careful, Captain and everyone."

Bucket-Pagu says, "We hope you're able to speak with Ara."

Well-Pagu says, "Soon."

"We will and I do as well," Rath says. In answer to Well-Pagu, he says, "Yes, I will see you soon." They hug him and he hugs them back gently.

When they pull away, Flower-Pagu suddenly gasps. "Oh! That's right! Would everyone wait for just one moment, please?" Everyone nods. Flower-Pagu flies to the galley, where Phillip is standing in the open doorway, watching what is occurring outside. They talk to him and both go inside. When they reappear, Flower-Pagu is flying in front of Phillip, who is carrying a travel bag sewn specifically to insulate a large dish.

Flower-Pagu asks Rath, "Captain, would you bring this to Ara and everyone? It's a nice, hot meal!"

Rath takes it, putting it over his shoulder. "Yes, I will do so. Thank you very much."

"Of course!"

South sees them. "My ... " All three dragons bring their heads down close. They seem to bow. "I had not known the Holy Pagu were here. It is a pleasure to see you."

East says, "May we ask for your names?"

West says, "It would be our honor to know."

"Of course! I'm Flower-Pagu!"

"I'm Bucket-Pagu!"

"Well ... Pagu!"

The dragons look thrilled. They grin at each other. Then South clears his throat and addresses Rath and the gods. "Is everyone ready to depart now?"

Rath looks to the others and says, "Yes!"

South dips his head until his chin is just above the railing. The gods climb up. While most do so normally, Vocalise makes it in one leap, landing next to South's left horn. Marchand and Rath are last and the God of Delphy helps his own up to the top.

"Thank you, Marchand," Rath says.

He nods, still looking nervous.

Elvin says, "We are ready, South."

"Very well." He glances to his right and left at East and West.

They nod and both concentrate on *PearlHeart.*

For a moment, East's eyes look green and West's eyes look orange. Then they lean forward and blow at *PearlHeart.* East's wind swirls over them and Rath smells rain and grass. West's blows over cooler, and encases *PearlHeart* with a dry crackle. The green and orange combine, protecting them with a greater power than that of the gods.

Elvin says, "Thank you very much, East, West."

East says, almost longingly, "It has been some time since I've smelled such things ... "

West says, "The sounds of that time are like none other."

South raises his head, carrying the gods and Rath up with him. He blows around himself – yellow, again – and Rath feels the warmth of it and the faint scent of a sea breeze.

South says, "Go down to my back – not as far as my wings – yes, there. You'll get less wind there than on my head."

Once they are all settled, South leans back and raises his great wings. He flaps them once and the gods and Rath hold onto each other. With each pump, they ascend and *PearlHeart* grows smaller. When they are high enough, South turns around and begins flying north, toward the City of Draconi.

29

Rath watches the bright white snowfields run by from within South's yellow barrier. He is wearing the gloves that Berceuse made for him the previous year. Marchand looks over at him, then goes to join his siblings, who have gathered together a bit apart to speak with each other.

An hour into travel, South says to Rath, "Does Draconi interest you, One of Marchand's?"

"Ah, yes."

South chuckles. "I thought so. While the gods chatter, you have remained silent."

The gods pause in their discussion. Vocalise says, "So, you can hear us?"

"Every word, Vocalise."

Belle looks at his brother and Vocalise throws his hands up. "Yeah, I know. You told me!"

South continues, "I suppose an outside human has never seen Draconi before. I would have liked it to be in better times. Although it is not my preferred Season, I will admit that Ara's Winters can be very beautiful. We Dragon Guardians do not have complete control of the Seasons anymore – that was a role we left in the Second World. However, we still bear a connection to them and can influence them. I with Summer, East with Spring, West with Fall, and North – our sister – with Winter. She and Ara were together for many centuries. When she disappeared, Ara inherited part of her ability for creating Winter." He sighs. "Gods and Guardians do not die. However, they can lose too much energy and be unable to manifest in this world. That is what happened to my sister."

Rath's eyes lower. "I am sorry to hear that. I did not know."

South glides. "None would have told you. North's disappearance was before you were born. And, not many wish to discuss what happened in the Third World, the one previous to this. But, you are Lady Azalea's grandson. Her parents, your great grandparents, were surely alive during that time. Has she not told you?"

"No. I know many of the constellation stories that occurred during the Third World. However, Grandmother says that there is much her parents did not tell her."

South is quiet for a time. "I cannot fault them for that." He continues to fly and in the distance, Rath sees the lights of a city on the opposite side of a hill. "But that does not mean we should not acknowledge what has happened. Forgetting such things is not laying them to rest but making them *restless*. All of the Gods in this world – the Fourth, ruled by Merp – have abilities strongly driven by their emotions. Although born in a previous one, Ara is the same and how he is feeling affects what goes on around him – positively or negatively. The reason for that, I do not believe is my place to say, nor is it my expertise. That is what is causing this storm."

"The Pagu told me it was Ara's emotions as well."

The scales over South's eyes raise for a moment. "I see." He continues, "As I said, Ara's Winters could be very beautiful. Over the decades since North's disappearance, they have become far more cold, treacherous, and dangerous than my sister would ever have allowed." He inhales suddenly, then exhales more peacefully. He pauses for a moment, thoughtful. "Now, why it is this past year that he has extended Winter far beyond what the Seasons of this world should allow, I cannot say." Then he flies on, saying nothing more.

They travel for several more hours. Rath watches the bright

landscape darken, then closes his eyes.

He does not realize he has fallen asleep until he wakes up and feels something warm beneath his head. He opens his eyes and looks up to see he has been resting against Marchand's shoulder, who has his arm around him. Marchand smiles. "Did you rest well? I'm glad that you were able to."

Rath frowns. "I do not remember falling asleep." He flushes, then sits up. "That is, I did rest well. Thank you for asking."

Marchand sobers as he looks north. "We're nearly there. Are you warm enough? South has said you'll be all right in Draconi, however ... "

South says, "He will be fine, Marchand. You know Ara's fondness for humans. Regardless of how he is feeling right now, he will not let any harm come to Rath while he is there."

Marchand opens his mouth to protest, but exhales instead. He studies his own, then pulls up Rath's scarf.

Thirty minutes later, South begins to descend. Rath can see a tall wall protecting a large city. The wind rushes toward them and he closes his eyes. He hears South pump his wings, slowing them down.

South reaches out his long legs to plunge into the deep snow just outside of the wall and once he is settled, they all climb off. Being much lighter than the dragon, they can stand easily on the snow, stiff with layers of ice.

The small ice dragons on top of the wall eye Rath and the gods suspiciously.

South tells them, "I have brought seven gods of the Fourth World and one human to represent others outside of Draconi. Please raise the gate so that they may enter and ask to speak with Ara."

The ice dragons glance at each other without moving. One shrieks.

South sighs heavily, sending a plume of snow up from the ground. "I realize that the time of their arrival does not express good intent. However, I believe they ultimately act, if not for Ara, for the protection of their own people."

The ice dragons shift, understanding the sentiment.

Then, as one, they rise up into the air and take up an ice encrusted chain in their mouths. Their sharp teeth glisten as they flap backward, pulling. From inside the city, the sounds of talk grow louder, then quieter as the people see the gate open for the first time in many years.

South says, "Thank you." To the gods and Rath, he says, "I will release my barrier once you are inside.

"Thank you very much for carrying us, South," Rath says.

South seems to smile. "You are welcome, Captain. Do be careful. All of you."

As they enter the city, the ice dragons watch their every step. It is far warmer inside and many of them take off layers and gloves. Behind them, the gate is lowered again. As Rath and the gods move forward, most of the people seem curious, but none step toward them.

Ahead, the crowd begins to part as an older man politely moves through. "Excuse me. Pardon me." He reaches the front, assesses the group, then says, "Ara's siblings and Captain Rath, I would presume?"

Elvin says, "Yes. Have you been sent for us?"

"I have. Wagon-Pagu told me that Well-Pagu, Bucket-Pagu, and Flower-Pagu told them that you would be arriving soon and that it would be only appropriate that I meet you." He nods to them all. "I am Niven, the keeper of Ara's Cathedral. I will escort you there."

Rath and Niven walk in the front while the gods follow. Niven says, "Do you often find yourself in the company of so many gods?"

"No – " Rath pauses. "Actually, I am finding that I do so more recently."

Niven chuckles at his response. "I have known and been with Ara my whole life. I rather think that they are quite like us."

"I agree."

They are led past tall stone buildings with chimneys whose smoke rises up into the snowfall far above. Stained glass windows glint on many of them, mostly in shades of blue, but also green, orange, and yellow. Rath looks at one shop – a bakery – and its yellow window with a symbol of a sun beneath it reminds him of South.

Niven pauses and the group gathers behind him. In front of them is an enormous building.

Ara's Cathedral appears to be made entirely of ice with

stained glass windows on each of its five bell towers, four of which seem to have a symbol right beneath their belfry. Rath can barely see a flower on one of them, but the others are covered with frost. The tallest one has no symbol, but a statue of a dragon is perched on the top. All of the bells are frozen and the largest one in the center glints.

Niven asks Rath, "What do you think?"

"It is beautiful."

Niven pats his shoulder gently – he is wearing metallic gloves, but Rath can feel his hand is very warm – and says, "Ara would be pleased." He looks at the cathedral himself, then starts up the stairs. "Let's go inside."

They go up the steps, passing balustrades with dragons sculpted out of ice curling around them to a set of double doors with blue stained glass windows. Niven opens one and they enter.

Inside is a large central area whose ceiling rises up two-thirds of the cathedral's total height. Rath sees an elaborate skylight above them depicting a dragon in the center of four symbols he can now see clearly – a leaf, a flower, a sun, and a snowflake. Directly in front of them, a large statue of a dragon is in a circular room where ice dragons sit on perches all around it. There seem to be more doors behind the statue leading to the back courtyard of the cathedral.

To the left and right, hallways lead to staircases going up to the second floor. Stained glass windows are set at intervals, letting in light, but the cathedral itself seems to glow from within.

Niven says, "Ara is upstairs in the room below the main bell tower. I will guide you there."

They go to the left and up the staircase at the end of the hall.

At the top, another hallway extends to the left, but to the right, it opens out into a large square room with a patterned ice floor and stone furniture. A cold, dark fireplace rests against one wall. A small Pagu sits on a blue cushion on top of the mantle. Next to them, a tall man with dark blue hair in braids and a thick, heavy cloak is seated on a stone bench in front of a stained glass window. His blue eyes are currently fixed on the group that has just arrived. They look tired and pinched around the corners. When he speaks, he projects easily. "Sit."

The gods around Rath tense, then take seats on the cold benches and chairs, looking to be in various states of discomfort.

However, as Rath and Niven go to join them, Ara's gaze softens and he says, "Wait." He waves his hand and two cushions appear on the bench they were approaching. "Now."

After they sit, Ara turns his eyes on his siblings. "Well? What is it? South told me that you all wished to come here." His eyes narrow. "For interests that suit more yourselves."

Elvin chokes. "That is ... that is true. We are concerned about your storm, Ara. It has caused much disorder outside of Draconi."

Ara's eyes flare. "A fact that I regret, but ... " He rubs his temples as if nursing a headache. " ... one that I cannot avoid currently."

Maro says gently, "We had heard from South that you may be looking for something. What is it? Perhaps we could help."

"I would prefer you did not." Maro looks taken aback and Ara sighs. His eyes go to Rath. "May I ask if you are Captain Rath?"

"I am."

"I am Ara, Elder God of Draconi." To his siblings, he says, "Truthfully, the only reason I accepted you coming to Draconi was for the captain that may be with you and his ship that has been able to travel through my storm." He says to Rath, "What sort of vessel is it? What is your trade?"

"*PearlHeart* is a Pan ship. We carry people and cargo to where others wish for them to go."

Ara nods slowly. "Good." He sits up. "I have lost something very dear to me. I would like you to find it and bring it back to me with your ship."

Rath looks startled.

Marchand says, "You cannot request that of him." Elvin puts a hand on Marchand's arm, but he continues, "He does not ... *None* of us know what it is you are looking for."

Ara says, "Belle, would you be able to find something of mine if it left Draconi?"

They all turn to the God of Selachuu, who says, "Likely. Not much has left Draconi over the years."

Ara relaxes. "No, very little has. Except ... " He shakes his head. "I've searched all over Draconi. The only alternative is that" – he swallows – "it's left somehow."

Belle pauses, then takes out his toothpick. "It may be more difficult with your storm."

"How?"

"It's yours. It has your energy with it – just like what you're looking for." He puts his toothpick back in his mouth and crosses his arms. "If it's in your storm, I can't guarantee that I'll be able to pick it out."

Ara pales.

Berceuse says, "Perhaps if you ended your storm, then – "

"Enough," Ara tells him and Berceuse flinches, falling silent immediately.

In the silence, Rath says, "Please do not speak to Berceuse in such a way."

Ara's eyebrows go up and he frowns, but he says nothing.

Rath gestures. "Berceuse – everyone – is trying to help. I am willing to carry your object if it is able to be found."

"It *has* to be found. If – " Ara falters. "If it is to be found outside of Draconi, you *will* find it for me and bring it back here. I will not end my storm until then. You may remain here until this evening, when South will carry you all back to Captain Rath's ship. Niven, would you please provide lunch and dinner for them?"

"Of course, Ara."

To the rest, he says, "We will not discuss this further." He leaves the room, walking around the left corner and down the hallway.

After he does, Marchand says, "Rath, that was very dangerous to do."

Belle immediately says, "Ara would never hurt him." He looks directly at Rath. "And nothing you said was inappropriate."

Rath listens to him, then nods.

The small Pagu on the mantle speaks. "I would agree." Everyone looks over at them. They slowly stand up and adjust their warm dress, fitting their hands in their muffler. "Ara has been very upset since this event began. I appreciate all of your patience with him." They look at Rath and their eyes glitter. "I am told that Well-Pagu is your navigator, Captain Rath. They are very talented at what they do. I am happy that they are to be on this journey with you."

Rath relaxes. "They are wonderful. I am very grateful to have them."

The Pagu flies off of the mantle, nodding to all the gods they pass saying, "It has been some time," and "Are you well?" and the gods reply to them, all looking far more at ease. When they arrive at Berceuse, they pause. "You have left your Isles. I am very proud of you."

Berceuse is overcome. "Well, I ... " He swallows hard. "Thank you."

They beam.

They fly up to Niven next, greeting him, then face Rath. They extend a little hand. "I am Wagon-Pagu. I have been with Ara for over five hundred years, living in Draconi with him and his own. It is a pleasure to meet you, Captain Rath." They smile. "I have heard much about you from my friends and family."

Rath extends his pointer finger for them to shake. "I see. I am very happy to meet you as well, Wagon-Pagu."

Wagon-Pagu's smile grows. Then they look at the satchel over Rath's shoulder curiously. "What is this?" They sniff. "It smells wonderful."

"A meal that Flower-Pagu and Phillip, the cooks aboard my ship, made for everyone."

"Oh, how lovely!"

Vocalise says, "Should we go ahead and eat it now?"

Rath shakes his head. "I believe Flower-Pagu intended for it to be with everyone. I do not think we should if Ara will not be joining."

A few of the Gods look surprised, but nod.

Wagon-Pagu says, "I think that would only be appropriate." They pause. "Although, it does smell wonderful. Niven, would there be a safe place this may be kept?"

Niven nods. "Certainly." He takes the bag from Rath, saying to the others, "It is nearing lunch. We often have traditional Draconi fare – we've known nothing but – however, I did promise Krir that he could go out into the city and bring back one of his favorite dishes for us all."

Marchand says, "Krir?"

"Yes. My apprentice. He will one day take over my role as caretaker of Ara's Cathedral." He turns to Rath. "Why don't you go with him? You could see more of Draconi. I'd imagine being a sailor who travels, you may enjoy that."

"I would."

Niven gestures. "Krir should be in the study – he often is. It is just down that hallway and to the left."

While Niven carries the meal away and the gods stay in the room to talk with each other and Wagon-Pagu, Rath goes in the same direction as Ara did before. Windows along the wall look out on Draconi and pour in gray light from the snow clouds above. Up here, this far away from the people of Draconi and their warmth, a few snowflakes drift down.

Rath walks past several closed doors until he finds one that is open. He looks inside.

The room is small, with bookshelves to his right, a desk across from him below a large window, and a table in the center. All of the furniture is made out of stone and the scrolls in the bookshelves seem to be made out of a thin metallic material. A stack of what appears to be paper lays on the desk, carrying a similar sheen.

A young man with dark brown hair bound in a short braid down his back and another hanging past his left ear is leaning over the table in the center of the room, looking over something. He is muttering under his breath.

He straightens abruptly – Rath starts – and says to no one, "Ur ... shi? What kind of name is that? I don't recall Niven telling me about some place called Urshi."

"Ursi?" Rath says without thinking. He puts his hand over his mouth.

The young man turns, glaring over his shoulder. However, it suddenly disappears and he abandons the table to walk up to Rath, looking him up and down. "You're ... You're not one of the gods, are you? Niven said gods would be here and I'd best not be there when they're meeting with Ara."

"No, I am not."

"Then, you are human, like me." He squints. "And you're certainly not from Draconi."

"I am from Delphy."

"Really? Then ... " The young man's eyes slide over to the table. He takes Rath's arm, pulling him over. He is wearing gloves much like Niven's. "Read this for me."

"Y-Yes." When they arrive at the table, Rath sees that what was laid on it was a map. It seems old and he looks at it with interest.

The young man tugs off his right glove and points at a large country to the east bordering Pantha. Where his finger touches, the metallic map turns red. "What is that country? Some of the letters are scrubbed off."

Rath leans over. "Ursi."

"Ursi ... Oh." The young man flushes. "That's what you said earlier. You were correcting me."

Rath says, "Are you Krir?"

"That's me. Does Niven need something?" Before Rath can respond, he suddenly says, "That's right. Lunch is soon." He hastily puts his glove back on and rolls up the map. "Niven promised me something different from what we're used to, though it's not as if I haven't had it before. I've probably eaten everything you can have here." He looks up. "What is your name?"

"Rath."

Krir grins. "Well, it may not be new to me, but it certainly will be for you. Niven and Ara both say no human from outside Draconi has ever been here before." He walks over to replace the map in the bookshelf then he and Rath leave. "So – expect many, many questions. I don't get much from in there." He gestures back at the study. "Most of it's old or hard to read, anyway."

"What would you like to know?" Rath asks as they start down the hallway.

Krir gestures with both hands. "Everything. You can give that, can't you?"

"Ah – "

Krir grins again. "Then, let's just start with what you know. And my questions. Would that be all right?"

Rath smiles. "Definitely."

Once they reach the first floor, Rath says, "Niven had said this dish was one of your favorites. I am excited to try it."

Krir's eyebrows raise. "Oh. Well, yes it is." He hesitates. "But, I've had it many times. Don't you get tired of your favorite dish sometimes?"

Rath thinks. "No."

As Krir opens the front doors for them, he says, "Ah, but you likely try lots of other things in between – and new things, too. You must be a traveler to have come as far as Draconi."

"That is true – and I do very much enjoy trying new foods. I am a sailor, the Captain of *PearlHeart,* a Pan ship."

"I knew it! You must have all sorts of stories. I want to hear all of them." He trots down the outside steps. "Shall we start with my questions?"

"Of course."

Krir begins, but as they walk down the streets, he instead listens far more as Rath tells him about his journeys on *PearlHeart.*

Suddenly, he stops and Rath does as well. Krir points behind them. "The bakery. We've missed it."

"Oh dear."

As they go back, Krir says, "I was too busy listening! Delphy and the Isles of Oct and Xiphi ... I want to see those races some day."

"They are very fun. May I ask if you had heard of the Isles of Oct before? I had not."

"A few times. Ara has sometimes spoken of a brother who hid himself away at the end of the previous world on his Isles of Oct with the Pagu. I'm not sure he approved of the decision." When they reach the bakery, Rath sees that it is the one that he saw on his initial walk to Ara's Cathedral, with the symbol of the sun.

When they enter, Rath says, "If I may ask a question?"

"Definitely. That seems only fair given how much you've answered for me."

"Thank you." They join a crowd bustling around the front counter. Wonderful smells come from the kitchen behind it. "I have seen four – no, five – of the same symbols in Draconi. A sun, a flower, a leaf, a snowflake, and a dragon."

Krir nods. "The Seasons and Ara. It is very important here. You know of the Three Dragon Guardians?"

"Yes. South carried us here."

"I love him. He visits us sometimes, though he never enters the city." Krir sobers. "There used to be a fourth – North, Ara's wife. Niven tells me that she disappeared several decades ago."

Rath's eyes lower. "South told me she had. I am very sorry

to hear of it."

"It pains Ara still." Krir continues, "My parents died not long after I had been born – disease – and Niven took me in as his apprentice to be the caretaker of Ara's Cathedral. Ara, too, has cared for me like he does all of his own, even through his grief. I am immeasurably grateful for what I have, which sometimes makes me feel guilty for thinking – "

Suddenly, the hand of another patron brushes up against Rath's and he hisses in pain. When he looks down, the back of his hand is red with a burn.

Krir immediately takes off his gloves. "Oh dear." He hands them to Rath. "Best you put these on. Just don't touch my hands when you do. Ara's Traits make our skin far hotter than others', I'm told. We can even start fires. Fine for us, but dangerous for you."

Rath's eyes widen. "I see. Thank you, Krir." He takes them carefully and pulls them on, wincing as they go over the burn.

"Niven should have something to put on it when we get back." Krir looks ahead at the crowd, then says, "Perhaps you should stand a bit away. *I'm* aware you don't carry Ara's Traits, but these people will not. I'll get our food, then be right back."

Rath nods and steps away as Krir goes forward. He stands by the windows displaying different pastries and looks at them while he waits, wondering if one is Krir's favorite.

When Krir returns, he is carrying two boxes. "Do you think that you can take the top one?" Krir's bare hands are making the metal casing of the bottom one bright red with heat.

"Of course. Thank you for lending me your gloves."

Krir shakes his head. "I should have from the start. Niven, Ara, and Wagon-Pagu will be most disappointed when they find out."

As they walk back to Ara's Cathedral, Krir says, "That's one of the reasons why Ara doesn't want any of us to leave Draconi. He doesn't think that our traits would be compatible with the world outside. You use a lot of wood, right? And cloth?"

"Yes. I've noticed that much here is made of something different. Is it a type of metal?"

"That's right. A special alloy from Grist, made by Ara's sister, Polly." Krir looks down at his own clothes. "These, too, are made from it. Otherwise, they would burn off our very person."

Rath reddens.

"Come now, the cathedral is this way," Krir says brightly.

As they approach it, Rath says, "Is Ara's Cathedral made out of ice?"

"It is. It was created by North and Ara both. North formed the ice and Ara used his fire to shape it, but he's the only one that could. Niven says that even with how strong our traits are, we would never be able to melt it. The only reason Niven and I have these gloves is because Wagon-Pagu thought it would be prudent. They were right. I wonder if they knew we would meet you or someone outside Draconi soon?" As they walk up the steps, he asks, "Have you been told what is behind the cathedral?"

"I have not."

Krir smiles. "There are Frost Flowers. A whole garden of them. Ara created them for North. Niven says she loved them greatly and tended to them daily. Maybe you will see them while you are here. They are beautiful."

"I would love to, if I am allowed."

Krir hesitates. "Normally, I think Ara would like that, too. But, he's been so upset recently ... " He leaves it at that and opens the door with his free hand. When they get to the room below the main bell tower, they see that the gods and Wagon-Pagu are no longer there.

"They're likely already in the dining room," Krir says. "It's over here."

Niven meets them at the door. "Ah good. You're here." However, then he says, "Krir! Where are your gloves?"

"Rath has them." He winces. "Someone burned him at the bakery."

Niven frowns deeply. "Set those down on the table – Krir, would you serve? – and I'll tend to the Captain."

They walk inside and Rath sees that all of the gods are seated at a long table with Ara at the head and Wagon-Pagu to his left. A chandelier made out of ice hangs over them and a large window depicting a dragon looks out on the area behind the cathedral.

Ara seemed to be in the middle of a discussion when they entered. He looks nervous as he says to Belle, "Pagu? You did not tell me that they were aboard the Captain's ship." His eyes flick up toward Rath, Krir, and Niven. "Niven, I ask that you, Krir, and Captain Rath leave for a moment. There is clearly more about this situation I did not know."

Niven clears his throat gently. "Krir and Rath have brought food for lunch, Ara."

Ara pauses. After a quick look at Wagon-Pagu, he says, "Very well." He frowns suddenly. "Captain, what happened?"

Rath, who had returned the gloves to Krir, revealing his reddened hand, says, "I was burned while we were at the bakery."

"By one of my own?" Rath nods and Ara looks pained.

Niven says, "I was just about to tend to it myself. Krir has agreed to set the table."

Ara stands. "No. Help Krir. Captain, if you would join me for a moment, I would ask you a few questions given what I have just learned. I will tend to your burn."

"Yes, Ara. Thank you," Rath says.

Niven and Krir exchange a look, but begin setting the table with dishes from tall, stone cabinets.

While they do, Ara joins Rath. The Elder God of Draconi stands nearly two feet taller than him. They go into an adjacent room with seats around small tables and a window on the far wall.

They go to the chairs and Ara waves his hand just before Rath sits, causing a cushion to appear.

After they sit, Ara says, "Your hand?"

Rath nods and holds it out.

Ara's expression tightens as soon as he sees it. Then he puts one hand beneath Rath's and the other above. He concentrates and it glows blue. Rath feels something cold but gentle press on the burn. He watches as the red fades and the pain eases.

Ara speaks. "Unlike my own, I have the ability to create cold as well. It came from my wife." He sighs and lets go of Rath's hand. "Is that better?"

Rath flexes it. "Much. Thank you. Is it similar to Pertan healing?"

"No. Are you familiar with it?"

"I know of them from my doctor, Carlos. My first mate, One-Eye, also has them."

However, Ara's eyes had widened at the first name. He

leans forward. "Carlos. It has been a very long time since I have heard that name. Does he have heritage in Sudines as well?" Rath nods and Ara says, "And Lady Azalea. Has he mentioned her?"

"Lady Azalea is my grandmother. She is how I met Carlos."

For a moment, Ara says nothing. He clears his throat. "I see." His expression changes and he seems thoughtful. "Perhaps you could help me with something – at my cathedral, I mean."

"I would like to."

Ara's eyebrows go up, then down in disapproval. "Do not agree to things so readily, Captain, before you're told what they are."

Rath flushes. "Y-Yes, Ara."

Ara smiles faintly. As he rises, he says, "I will tell you more after this meal."

While they were gone, Niven and Krir served everyone. As he and Ara return, Rath looks at what is on the stone plates. He brightens. "I remember seeing that in the window!"

Krir, already seated, smiles. "I wondered if you were looking at those."

As Ara goes back to the head of the table, Rath sits in the open seat next to Krir.

Krir says, "Do you like sweets?"

"Very much so. Fruits, especially."

"Then, you'll like this a lot." Krir asks his god, "Erranin Fruit is only in Draconi, right, Ara?"

Ara, who has not started on his meal yet, glances over. "Yes. I do not believe the climate would be suitable anywhere else." Wagon-Pagu gives a delicate cough next to him and Ara begins to eat.

Krir says to Rath, "So this will really be new to you!"

"Indeed!"

After they begin to eat, Krir asks Rath, "What do you think?"

"It's wonderful! It's very different from Delphy Fruit, which is my favorite."

"How so?"

"Well, this is a little less sweet. Delphy Fruit has more water content in it, too. Are these seeds?" he asks, looking at the pastry.

"Yes! They're my favorite part!"

"They are very good."

As they continue to talk, Niven, Wagon-Pagu, and the gods around them smile.

Belle, who is seated at Ara's right, says, "Good to see them getting along."

Ara, looking more relaxed, says, "Yes. Krir often stays at the cathedral all day with me and Niven. I am glad to see him interacting with someone more close in age to him." Then he asks, "Do you really believe you could not find my object if it was in my storm?"

"It would be unlikely. Are you sure it's not here?"

"Of course I am. I've looked every day."

Belle stares at him. "It might help if we knew what it was."

Ara glares at him, but does not say anything.

"If I can ask something else."

"You may. I hold no irritation toward you personally, Belle."

"I know. If this object is so important to you, who would you be comfortable carrying it? I don't mean delivering it back – I mean, *physically* carrying it." Belle nods toward Rath. "I have no doubts that the Captain would see it here safely and all of us would, too, but I wanted to know what your thoughts were."

While Belle spoke, Ara stopped eating. Setting the pastry back down on the plate, he clears his throat uncomfortably. "I ... hadn't thought of that. I'm not sure."

"One of your own?"

"Absolutely not." Even Wagon-Pagu looks startled and Ara lowers his voice. "No. I would prefer they not leave Draconi."

Belle sighs. "Right. Think on it. We'll need to know before we leave."

After they all finish eating, Ara says to his siblings, "If you would all join me so we could discuss what we were going to earlier." To Rath and the others, he says, "I would like to speak with my siblings privately. We will not plan to meet again until dinner."

Niven says, "I understand, Ara."

Beside him, Krir says, "Could I show Rath your garden, Ara?"

Ara shakes his head quickly. "No – that is, I would prefer it if I were there when you did. I am sorry. Not right now."

Krir looks disappointed, but nods. "Yes, Ara. Then, could I show him more of Draconi?"

Ara hesitates.

Wagon-Pagu says, "I would be willing to go with them. An outing sounds very fun."

Ara pauses for a moment, then exhales. "Very well. Please be careful and return before dinner."

More happily, Krir says, "Yes, Ara!" and all but drags Rath out of the room. Niven smiles at their departure, then nods respectfully to Ara and the other gods and leaves.

Once all of the gods are settled in the adjacent room, Ara opens his mouth to speak, but before he can begin, Marchand says, "What did you talk to Rath about?"

Ara turns to him. "I meant to speak to him about the addition of the Pagu on board his ship, but instead I learned about his connection to Carlos, and – more directly – to Lady Azalea." He glares. "None of you told me this."

Maro says gently, "Would it have changed your opinion of him?"

Ara considers, then shakes his head. "No, I suppose not." To Marchand, he says, "You've raised someone very kind, if too willing to help at times."

Marchand opens his mouth, shuts it, then can only nod.

"I will tell you I've asked his help in something else while we are still in Draconi, but have not told him what yet." His expression tightens. "What is my storm like outside of Draconi? Are the conditions truly so extreme that you all have made the journey here and brought humans as well? East and West tell me that they are watching the Captain's crew and ship near the Three Dragon Isles."

The gods exchange an uncomfortable look. Elvin says, "Haliae is frozen. My people cannot go home. They have been on Pica Pica for the past six months, I – " He stops and merely frowns, his glasses icy in the silver light.

Ara looks startled. "I thought it was just high winds. I always told you that having such a high peak was dangerous for humans."

"No, it was not – not for my own." Elvin smiles. "They are brilliant. They keep one another safe even ... even when I am terribly distracted and not doing what I should for them."

Ara glances around the room. "Who else is affected by this? By my storm?"

Belle says, "Pantha. But, they have a king now that understands their limits. He's teaching Lionel, too."

Ara makes a sound half between relief and incredulity. "Impossible. Lionel doesn't listen to anyone."

"He's learning," Belle says, smiling a little. "The Alliance has been providing support for them — supplies and food during the storm."

"They would never accept that." Ara pauses. "The Alliance? Why would they have cause to aid Pantha?"

He turns to Elvin, whose eyes brighten. "Because they have officially joined the Alliance. I think it is wonderful — a true bright spot within all of this."

Ara does not say anything. Looking at nothing in particular, he says, "My storm has caused Pantha to join the Alliance."

Belle says, "Ara, they're human. They don't have traits like your own either to keep them warm no matter how strong Lionel says they are. They — like Captain Rath — can't handle temperatures like in Draconi or conditions created by your storm. It took all seven of us aboard *PearlHeart* to travel here."

"South told me before. I assumed that you were being overly cautious because you were with humans."

"That's a part of it. Berceuse suggested it. He traveled with Captain Rath and his crew on *PearlHeart* through your storm last year to reach Haliae and found that it was easier to maintain his barrier while he could focus on it instead of traveling on his own."

Ara's eyes go to Berceuse. "That is why you left your Isles."

"I needed to see how Elvin was — and his people." Berceuse combs his fingers through his hair. "My dear ones were so worried as well."

Oracle says softly, "Pica Pica has also been affected. Amara is currently there protecting the island."

"She is?" He sighs. "She tried to come here before. South, East, and West disallowed her passage." To them all, he says, "I deeply apologize for what my storm has caused. It clearly has affected far more than I realized. Even so ... I cannot let it end. Not until I find what I lost."

The gods look at one another. Elvin says, clearing his throat,

"We are happy to help you do so. Truthfully" – he glances at his siblings – "I believe we have been remiss in these years. We know how North's disappearance affected you." Oracle nods beside him. "Since then, we have hardly spoken. I feel I am mostly to blame for that and I am sorry. Haliae is very close to Draconi and – well, it would not matter. I have not made the effort to reach out to you in all of these years."

Ara seems uncertain. "No, you have not."

Berceuse says, "I haven't been the best either and it was entirely my choice. I closed myself off from everyone except for my dear ones." He smiles. "But, reconnecting to all of my siblings – although terrifying at first – is something that I wish I had done far, far sooner."

Ara quietly nods. "I was greatly surprised to see you, Berceuse." He leaves it at that.

Oracle joins in. "It has been far too long for me as well. The least I could have done was send a letter."

"Your birds could not have reached Draconi."

"With my help – and, perhaps, without your storm – I am sure that they could. Or one of my Spirit Birds. They love to help."

Vocalise raises his hand. "Does this mean I can visit when all of this is over?"

Ara does not hesitate. "No." He thinks. "The last time I recall you in Draconi was over eight hundred years ago and I banned you ever since. North believed your intentions were good, however."

"I just wanted to challenge a few of your people to a race or two – have fun, ya' know?"

Ara gives him a hard look. "My people are not allowed to leave Draconi. This world is far too dangerous for them and their traits are not compatible with it." He looks sad for a moment, then says, "You are lucky I allowed you into Draconi today."

Vocalise shrugs. "Yeah, but I dunno, those ice dragons gave me *quite the look* when I walked in."

"As I ordered them to." Ara turns to Maro. "Did you ever begin that garden you spoke of? One to be like Lady Azalea's. North thought it was a beautiful idea."

Maro's eyes shine. "I did. It's become ... Well, I won't say finished. It is always growing."

Ara smiles a little. "Is that so?" He says to Belle, "My Three Dragon Guardians tell me you have been near Draconi a few times."

Belle nods.

"I thank you for your diligence. Does Fierce still do the same in the South?"

"He does."

Ara looks at Marchand last. "I don't believe we've seen each other since this world began. I would assume my waters are far too cold for your people."

Marchand moves his hair back. "A bit. But, Elvin and everyone are right – the Three Dragon Guardians are, too – we should have made more of an effort to see you, especially when we knew from your storm, from everything before, that you were hurting. I am sorry, Ara."

Ara listens to him. Then he says, "I will think on all of this." He rises. "Dinner will be served at six. I expect everyone will be present for it."

He leaves and the gods remaining take a collective breath.

While they spoke, Rath, Krir and Wagon-Pagu had exited the cathedral and started down the street, heading north.

Krir says to Rath, "I know exactly what I want to show you. This way."

"All right."

As Krir leads them, Wagon-Pagu smiles, happy to see him so excited.

Before they left, Krir had given Rath a cloak made of the same thin metallic material as his gloves.

"I don't need it," Krir had said, shrugging. "But, it should help you from getting burned again."

"Thank you." Rath took it, brushing his hand over the fabric.

It seems to work and every time Rath passes by another person in the crowd and they touch, the material glows faintly red and he feels heat, but is safe beneath it.

After a few minutes, Wagon-Pagu says, "Rath, if I may sit on your shoulder? Or would that be inappropriate?"

"Not at all. You may."

"Thank you."

Wagon-Pagu flies down and settles on the fabric. They look at it themselves. "Polly did a very fine job with this," they say. "I wished to tell you, Captain Rath, I have been in communication with Well-Pagu, Bucket-Pagu, and Flower-Pagu."

Rath stops and Krir looks back at them curiously. Rath says, "M-May I ask ... "

"Yes!"

"How are they?"

"Good. They miss you, but East and West are protecting them and they are very much enjoying speaking with them. It has been a very long time since they have. Well-Pagu wishes to inform you that the rest of the crew is well, too."

Rath exhales. "Thank you very much for telling me."

Wagon-Pagu pats his shoulder. "Absolutely." They laugh. "Now, I believe Krir is quite excited to show you his surprise. Shall we go?"

"Yes."

They rejoin Krir, who smiles when he sees Rath's happy expression, then they all continue through the city.

On *PearlHeart*, One-Eye eats dinner in the galley. As he stands up to take his empty bowl to be washed, he passes his Spirit Lion, who is trotting over to Phillip's Spirit Rabbit.

One-Eye says, "Gossiping again?"

The Lion whips One-Eye's legs with his tail and One-Eye grins.

While the Lion and the Rabbit talk, One-Eye walks over to Phillip and Carlos, who are speaking near the warm stove. One-Eye says, "Thanks for the meal."

Phillip says, "Sure!" He nods to Carlos. "We were just talking about my goddess, Rella. I don't think she would be happy at all if she knew what was happening."

Carlos sighs. "I am certain she does."

One-Eye says, "Why isn't she here to help then?"

In response, Carlos looks to Phillip, who says, "She might think that it'll sort itself out on its own."

"It hasn't for almost a year."

Phillip rubs his arm. "Yeah. I just hope things do go back to normal soon. Who knows how far Ara's Storm will reach if it doesn't?"

Carlos says, "It is difficult to say."

"It'll be all right!" a little voice says. They all turn to see Flower-Pagu. One-Eye can see that they are sitting on top of One-Eye's Spirit Lion, braiding his mane. Phillip's Spirit Rabbit already has a flower next to one ear. Phillip and Carlos, unable to see the Spirit Lion, only see Flower-Pagu sitting in the air. "The Captain and the gods are doing what they need to! I'm sure that they'll all be back soon and we'll be together again!" They tie a bow at the end of the braid, then pat the Spirit Lion's head. "You look wonderful!"

The Spirit Lion's eyes sparkle.

Flower-Pagu flies off. "We – Bucket-Pagu, Well-Pagu, and I – just heard from the Captain, too!"

They all look surprised and Carlos says, "Truly?"

One-Eye says, "How?"

Flower-Pagu says, "Wagon-Pagu is there! They're currently with the Captain and a man named Krir who is showing them both something in the City of Draconi. The gods are talking at Ara's Cathedral."

Carlos sighs. "I had heard Wagon-Pagu was still in Draconi. I am happy for it – especially right now – however, it has been a very long time for them to be there."

Flower-Pagu is quiet for a moment. "It has. But, they know that Ara needs them right now and they really do love him and the people of Draconi."

One-Eye clears his throat a little awkwardly. "Did he – did the Captain say when he might be back?"

"Wagon-Pagu says Ara has told them to leave by this evening. Anything else they thought it was more appropriate that the Captain tell us when he returns."

They all nod, looking relieved.

In Draconi, Krir abruptly stops. "Here," he says, then ducks into a small crevice between two buildings.

Rath and Wagon-Pagu peer inside. Wagon-Pagu frowns. "Krir, this is a construction area."

However, Krir is already climbing a tower in the process of being built. An open doorway at the bottom reveals a spiral staircase leading to the top, which only has half of the parapets finished.

"I know," Krir says. "But it's sturdy" – he stomps his boot twice – "I'm sure." He colors. "Also, I was already yelled at by the builder a few days ago. But, when I told him why I wanted to go up, he said it was all right as long as I was careful."

Wagon-Pagu continues to frown, but says, "Very well."

With them on his shoulder, Rath carefully enters the narrow area and climbs up the steps.

They pass by small holes that will one day be windows, letting in shafts of gray light.

When they arrive at the top, stray snowflakes that have not been melted yet by Ara's Traits drift around them. Rath walks forward to stand next to Krir.

Krir says, "Well, what do you think?"

All around them, Rath can see the City of Draconi stretching out south, east, and west of where they are. There are other similar towers being built to the one that they are currently standing on, some finished with ice dragons roosting on them and others with workers laying down stones. Thick smoke rises up from chimneys from the surrounding buildings and above all, Ara's Cathedral seems to glow with its frozen bell towers.

"I have never seen anything like it," Rath says. "It is amazing."

Krir smiles. "I want to go somewhere else one day, but I do really love Draconi and Ara. This isn't exactly what I wanted to show you, though."

"What is?"

Krir takes Rath's shoulder with his gloved hand and points him due north. "That."

Rath gasps.

In front of them is the largest mountain he has ever seen, covered in white so bright it stands out sharply against the gray sky and even the snow from Ara's Storm still going on outside the city.

Wagon-Pagu looks, too, their expression very respectful.

Krir explains, "That's the Mountain of the North. Ara says it's where Winter began – where North was born."

Rath looks at him in surprise. "Really?"

"Yes. Both he and Niven say that the Seasons were created in the Second World, by North, South, East, and West. It's where they were all born. Ara was, too, but he says it's best he not say what his role was there."

Rath nods. He continues to study the mountain. "It is beautiful."

Krir laughs. "Isn't it? It has always made me feel safe." He looks thoughtful. "Ara ... Well, before, he would tell me about North. She sounds wonderful. Even if she's no longer here, her mountain still looks so bright."

"It does."

Krir stretches and sits on the side of the tower, where no stones for parapets have been laid yet and Rath joins him. Krir says, "Actually, the view is a lot better from the North Gate, but if we were to be back by dinner ... "

Rath understands. "It would have taken too long to get there."

"Exactly. But, this spot is definitely second best. I'm glad that I found it."

"I agree. Thank you for showing this to me, Krir."

"Of course."

They are quiet for a moment before Rath asks, "Are there other mountains? Like the Mountain of the North. There are Four Seasons."

"Niven says there are. I asked South, but he just laughed – in a kind way, I mean – but he didn't exactly give an answer either. All I've ever gotten him to say is, 'Well, why wouldn't there be?'"

Rath thinks. "I am not sure that I have seen them. Or heard of them."

"Really? In all of your travels? You've been so many places."

"Not everywhere. I would" – he flushes, thinking of One-Eye – "I would like to, though."

Not noticing Rath's reddened face, Krir sighs. "That does sound nice one day. But, if I become caretaker of Ara's Cathedral, I don't know if I ever will go anywhere else. That's, um, what I was trying to say before. Sometimes I felt guilty about wanting to leave Draconi when Ara and Niven have been so kind to me. They're my family." Krir stands up. "Anyway, we should go back." He tilts his head to the side, thinking. "Niven didn't tell us to get food. I wonder if he's cooking tonight."

Rath joins him, Wagon-Pagu still on his shoulder. "I brought a meal from *PearlHeart* we could all have."

"Really?"

Wagon-Pagu claps their hands together. "It smelled most wonderful!"

Suddenly, Krir grabs Rath's hand, tugging him down the stairs while Wagon-Pagu holds onto Rath's shoulder. "Come on then! If you brought it from your ship, it must be food from another country! What kind of food is it? Is it from Delphy?"

"I am not sure. I did not ask before we left."

"Well, it certainly won't be from Draconi, which means it's something new!" They reach the bottom and Krir abruptly hugs Rath – safely, due to Rath's cloak. "I'm going to try something new!"

Rath laughs. "You are!" As they start to walk back to the cathedral, he says, "I am very much looking forward to it. Phillip and Flower-Pagu, our cooks aboard *PearlHeart*, always do a wonderful job."

"I cannot wait!"

Wagon-Pagu says, "Neither can I!"

They continue toward the high towers of Ara's Cathedral at a faster pace, eager to get to dinner.

30

When they arrive, Niven meets them at the door.

Rath says, "We had thought to have the dish Flower-Pagu asked I bring for dinner."

Niven smiles. "That is a wonderful idea. Krir, would you help me warm it up?"

"Yes, Niven."

As they go up the stairs together, Niven says, "The others should already be in the dining room."

However, when they reach the top, Marchand is there. He relaxes a little when he sees his own with Wagon-Pagu on his shoulder.

While Niven and Krir leave to prepare dinner, Marchand says to both Rath and Wagon-Pagu, "Did you enjoy yourselves?"

Rath says, "Very much so. I was able to see more of Draconi and Krir showed me the Mountain of the North."

"Really? That's quite a ways from here, from what I remember."

"It is. But, it is enormous and you can see it from the city. Krir, Wagon-Pagu, and I went to the top of a tower under construction to see it."

Marchand looks a little concerned, but Wagon-Pagu says, "I was similarly hesitant. However, Krir had been assured by the builder that the structure was secure."

They go to the dining room together. As Rath and Marchand sit down near the end of the table and Wagon-Pagu flies to the head, Ara says, "If I may have some of your time after dinner, Captain."

"Definitely."

Niven and Krir come in not long afterward. Krir is ecstatic. As they carry around bowls of stew for everyone, he says, "It smells so good! I can't wait to try it."

Niven laughs. "You will soon."

Ara, however, frowns when his bowl is set in front of him. "This is not our traditional fare. Where was it acquired?"

"I brought it with me," Rath says. "Flower-Pagu asked me to."

Ara's eyes widen for a moment. "I see." He takes a tentative spoonful. Wagon-Pagu starts as well, looking to be in pure bliss.

Krir sits down next to Rath. "What kind of food do you think it is?"

"Ursian, I believe."

"Really!" Krir takes his first bite, then a few more quickly.

Across the table, Niven says, "Krir, slow down."

"Yes, Niven! But, this ... I mean, Draconi food is good, too, but ... " He glances at Ara guiltily.

Ara is quiet. Looking at his siblings, he says, "I realize that I, too, have caused Draconi to be rather distant." The other gods seem surprised by his admission. Ara turns back to Krir and his expression softens. "I am glad that you are enjoying it."

"Thank you, Ara!" Krir continues to eat more slowly, but happily.

After they are all finished, Krir gives Rath a hug then goes to help Niven clean up. Ara meets with Rath afterward and they both go downstairs.

When they reach the first floor, Ara says, "That was very kind of Flower-Pagu to provide."

"I think so as well. They work very hard on *PearlHeart* and are a wonderful friend."

Ara smiles for a moment, but it fades and he grows quiet.

He guides Rath down the center hallway to the circular

room with the large statue of a dragon. They walk past the ice dragons sitting on perches along the wall to a set of eight doors leading outside. Each has a stained glass window that connects directly to the next, depicting a great dragon standing on a large country with its wings spread out protectively. Ara opens one of the center doors, then gestures for Rath to go before him.

Rath does so and gasps.

Outside, everything seems to sparkle. Flowers that appear to be made out of ice cover the entire back courtyard, their petals gently swaying in the night breeze.

Rath looks up at Ara. "Frost Flowers?"

Ara raises an eyebrow. "Yes. Did Krir tell you?" Rath nods and Ara sighs. They walk together until they are at the edge of the covered patio, quietly looking at the flowers.

After a time, Ara looks over, sees Rath's expression, and asks, "Do you like flowers, Captain?"

"I love them," Rath says immediately. "That is ... I do. Very much so."

Ara smiles in full for the first time. "I do as well. These in particular are very important to me." His expression falters for a moment. Looking forward, he nods to the path. "Let us go."

As they walk, Rath looks at the flowers glittering on either side of them in wonder.

Ara says, "Does your grandmother still have gardens?"

Rath turns to him. "Yes. She has many on her island."

"Island." Ara pauses. "Yes, I do recall Marchand and Belle telling me of its creation." He continues, "Before, when your grandmother lived on Sudines, my wife, North, visited her and her gardens. Are you very familiar with your grandmother's island?"

"I am. I was raised there."

"Did you ever see my siblings there? Many of them have sought her counsel over the years – even Amara."

"I have not. Carlos told me that he and Grandmother thought it was best I was not present while they were."

Ara exhales. "Very wise of them." He moves on, "North, too, sought her counsel. I have not. I have not even met Lady Azalea." He adjusts his cloak. "North asked me many times to come with her. She thought Azalea would be delighted by my Frost Flowers. But, I could not leave Draconi or my own."

They walk for a while longer until they come to a stone bench. Ara waves his hand and a cushion appears on Rath's side only.

As they sit together, both are very quiet. Ara glances at Rath as if assessing him, then back out at his garden.

After fifteen minutes, Rath shivers and Ara notices. He waves his hand again. A cloak thicker than the one Krir gave him appears. "Put this on."

"Thank you." Rath does and sighs, his breath making a cloud in front of him.

"You are welcome. Thank you for bringing that dish for dinner. Krir enjoyed it greatly."

"Of course. May I ask if you did?"

Ara seems surprised. "Yes. I did. I have never tried my brother Forte's food. It is much like him from what I remember."

"Have you seen him recently?"

"No. I have seen none that have not gone to Draconi themselves. They did, centuries ago, to visit North and I. Afterward ... " He sighs. "Until today, it had been a very long time since I had seen them."

Rath nods.

"Tell me about your grandmother's gardens. What are they like?"

"Warm." Ara raises an eyebrow and Rath flushes. "Th-That is, I do not mean the temperature, however, that is true as well. It is more ... " He waves his hand in front of his chest in a circular pattern. "A warm feeling. I feel relaxed and safe."

"That is very good. Are there many of them?"

"Grandmother has three main gardens. The South Garden was started just last year."

Ara – who had been listening calmly – suddenly pauses, an odd expression on his face when Rath mentioned the South Garden.

Rath continues, "Everyone aboard *PearlHeart* helped plant it and we added more plants to it this past year. It was wonderful to see. She also has her West Garden, however, it is Grandmother's private garden. I have not seen it. The East Garden is beautiful. Grandmother and I started it together when I was very young. It has flowers in every color of the rainbow."

"Those all sound beautiful." Rath looks up at him happily

and Ara says, "I hope it continues to bring you joy."

"Thank you, Ara."

Ara turns toward his own garden. "The peace you have there ... I have a similar feeling here. North began this garden. I do my best to tend to it, but ... " For a moment, he looks deeply sad. He shakes his head and says instead, "Your grandmother. Has she ever told you about Sudines Philosophy?"

Rath blinks in surprise. "No. She said that she and Carlos were not the ones to tell me."

"Then, I will." He faces Rath fully. "In Hep's Philosophy, the different cardinal directions are representative of the different phases of life. Draconi Philosophy is rather similar. I have always liked Hep." He creates a cross with his hands. "West is associated with grief when a new path is needed – I have no small surprise that your grandmother prefers to have that garden private." He looks to his left. "East is often associated with the joy after beginning that new path – you said you and your grandmother started it together. The South ... is auspicious."

"Grandmother has said the same. As well for me beginning my fifth year of journeys on *PearlHeart* last year."

"I see. Five ... Yes, I recall the number also having importance. However, I also feel that I am not the one to share that piece of Hep's Philosophy with you. I am sure it will be in the future." Ara goes on, "The South is auspicious – it represents the preparation before a new – and good – beginning. The North ... where is your grandmother's home in relation to her gardens?"

"To the north."

"The New Beginning. It likely also includes the creation of her island." He puts his hands in his lap. "Has all of this made sense to you, Captain?"

Rath thinks for a moment, then nods. "It has. Thank you for teaching me."

"Of course. It is part of your heritage." He looks up at the sky. "It is growing late. I had said you would all leave this evening, however ... I would wish to speak with you again. I will ask that all remain until tomorrow morning. Then, South will take you back to your ship."

They go back inside and join the gods in the room below

the main bell tower. Niven, Krir, and Wagon-Pagu are there as well. Ara says, "You will stay here for the night. In the morning, I will decide what needs to be done."

The gods look startled, but nod.

Ara turns to Rath and waves his hand. A thick blanket appears, which he presses into Rath's hands. "Use this. My own are comfortable with their inherent warmth, however, I would assume that it is rather cold here for you."

Rath accepts it. "It is. And thank you, Ara, for *Whooshing* this for me."

Ara pauses. "'Whooshing?'"

"Yes." He waves his hand. "*Whoosh.*"

Ara repeats the gesture. "*Whoosh*," he says. "I see. I do not believe my siblings or I ever determined what to call it – your term is very apt."

After Ara leaves for his own room, Vocalise walks over to Rath and swings an arm over his shoulder. "I never knew you had a term for that – *Whoosh.*" He waves his hand. The other gods join them, smiling as well.

Rath says, "I thought of it while I was on Berceuse's Isles of Oct. One-Eye had been speaking of how Berceuse made a fire appear by waving his hand."

Berceuse claps his hands together. "I remember hearing of it! My dear ones were absolutely delighted by the term."

Wagon-Pagu laughs. "Hearing of it now, I am absolutely delighted as well." Their eyes sparkle up at Rath.

Belle says, "Captain, what did you and Ara talk about?"

Beside him, Elvin says, "I was rather surprised that he wished to speak with you alone."

"And that he took you to his garden!" Krir says. When the others look at him in surprise, he flushes. "I may have looked out the window."

Niven huffs good-naturedly.

Rath says, "He did. It was absolutely beautiful. Then, he asked that I tell him about Grandmother's gardens and he explained Sudines Philosophy to me."

All of them look startled. Marchand says, "I'm very glad that he did. I always hoped that you would learn about it one day."

Oracle sighs. "I haven't seen Ara's Frost Flowers in so long. North loved them."

"I'm not sure any of us have since her disappearance," Marchand says. "We'd best rest if we'll be traveling back with South tomorrow. Then ... finding Ara's object and returning it to Draconi."

Niven leads them down the hallway to where the bedrooms are. The gods, having some familiarity with the cathedral, go to different doors after saying good night to the others.

Krir, next to another door, says, "Good night, Rath. Thanks for everything today."

"You as well."

Wagon-Pagu nods to Rath's blanket. "I hope that helps you be very warm tonight."

"Thank you. I think it will. I hope you are warm as well."

They beam up at him. "Thank you, Captain Rath." They give a respectful nod to him and Niven, then fly down the hallway in the same direction Ara went earlier and up another set of stairs to the third floor.

After they do, Rath opens the door to the bedroom he will be using.

The small room has a window, a wardrobe, and a bed. All appear to be made out of stone, but the bed does have a mattress, a blanket, and a pillow in the same material as Krir's cloak and gloves.

"It is good that Ara provided you with another blanket," Niven says. "I would imagine people without Ara's Traits would get too cold with only a light one. Rest well, Captain."

"Thank you. Rest well, Niven."

Inside, Rath prepares the bed and very soon is under both blankets. He closes his eyes and falls asleep.

On *PearlHeart*, everyone is getting ready to go to bed, too.

Carlos, standing next to One-Eye, says, "The fact that they are not leaving tonight is a good sign."

One-Eye glares at him. "How?"

"Because it means that Ara may be willing to consider their words."

"He shouldn't have to consider anything given what he's caused."

Carlos sighs. "Even so, he has accepted Master Rath and the gods entering Draconi, which is not something I would have expected. Regardless, we will not know more until morning."

"Yeah." One-Eye pets his Lion who is sitting beside him, then they all go to sleep while East and West watch over them.

That night, outside of the City of Draconi, Ara's Storm worsens.

Early in the morning, in Ara's Cathedral, Niven knocks on Rath's door. When Rath opens it, he asks, "Did you sleep well?"

Rath is hugging the blanket given to him, now neatly folded. "Yes, I did. Ara's blanket is very warm."

"I am glad to hear that," Niven says. "Ara told me he has asked that he wished to speak with you this morning. Would you come with me?"

"Of course."

They walk further down the hallway until they reach the stairs Wagon-Pagu flew up the night before. Niven says, "I have already brought Ara something to drink. There is another cup there for you. I pray it is still warm when you arrive. Ara was very adamant that he speak with you alone."

"I understand. And thank you, Niven."

Niven nods, then watches Rath go up the stairs.

When he reaches the stone door at the top, he gently knocks. "Ara? I am here."

"Enter, Captain."

When Rath opens the door, he sees Ara is sitting at a small stone table placed by a window on the right wall. The furniture is sparse, with only a bed and a bookshelf similar to the one in the study.

Ara gestures to the empty chair. "Here." Rath sits and Ara looks at the steaming cup on the table. "I hope it is still warm."

Rath touches it. "It is."

"I am glad," Ara says, relieved. He holds out his hand. "Give me the blanket. Did you sleep well?"

"Yes. Very. Your blanket is very warm."

Ara hesitates, nods. "I see." He *Whooshes* it away.

Rath asks, "Did you sleep well?"

"No. I did not," he says sharply and Rath's eyebrows go up. "I have thought much about our situation. Belle had asked me yesterday who I might wish to physically carry this object aboard your ship. I currently cannot think of anyone."

"I am sorry to hear that."

"I have thought of my siblings, of course, but I do not trust them to, or – and I truly apologize – you, either, Captain. I have not met your crew, so I would rather they not do so. I have thought of the Pagu that are on *PearlHeart*, but Wagon-Pagu is certain that they all have roles that carrying the object would take them away from." He looks at Rath. "I need it returned to me."

"I understand." Rath takes a sip, thinking. Then he asks, "Would you be amenable to boarding *PearlHeart* to carry your object?"

Ara's eyes widen. He opens his mouth. "I ... " Shutting it, he shakes his head. "Absolutely not. I cannot leave here – my own need me. But ... " He clutches his cup. "Your crew – they are much like your family, are they not?"

"Yes. I feel truly grateful to have met all of them and that they have chosen to sail *PearlHeart* with me."

"Is *PearlHeart* your home?"

"It is."

"Yet, you left it. And them. Berceuse, too, left the Isles of Oct and his dear ones there to help Elvin." He frowns. "Why did you agree to come to Draconi and leave those you care about?"

"Because I wish to help you, Ara."

"Do you not worry about what occurs on your ship in your absence?"

"No. I trust One-Eye and Well-Pagu – my first mate and navigator – and the rest of my crew that they will be safe. As well as East and West to keep them protected from your storm with their barriers."

"South is already here, too. He could ... " He takes a long sip. When he finishes, he says, "I will consider what you have said. It seems to be the only option, but not what I would prefer. I will need to speak with East, West, and South before I make my final decision. I will give it to you within the hour, if you would allow?"

"Of course."

Ara gives a shaky nod. "I will meet all of you on the first floor. You are excused, Captain. Thank you for speaking with me."

"I understand. Thank you, Ara." Rath stands up and walks

to the door. Ara watches him then looks out his window, his hand trembling on the table.

Rath meets with the gods in the foyer. He briefly tells them about his and Ara's conversation. "Ara says he will give his final answer by the end of this hour," he finishes.

The gods appear shocked. Niven and Krir look equally startled. Elvin finally says, "Well! That is ... " He pushes up his glasses.

"Good," Belle says.

"I was going to say, 'highly appropriate,' but it seems not, well, appropriate to say."

Berceuse frowns. "My dear ones told me that Ara has not ever left Draconi in this world."

Marchand says, "That's true. He wished to stay with North. Then, with his own."

As they speak, Ara comes down the stairs. He is wearing a heavier cloak and Wagon-Pagu flies next to the folds. He approaches them, stops, then presses his lips together. "I have thought much of what may be done concerning my object and my storm." He turns to Rath. "With your permission, Captain Rath, I will be the one to board *PearlHeart* and seek it out. Do you accept?"

"Yes, Ara."

Ara inhales deeply. Then he looks to his side and Wagon-Pagu flies forward. They say, "I ask for permission to come as well, Captain Rath. Ara has asked for my company and I accepted."

"Of course. I would be very happy for you to come, Wagon-Pagu."

"Thank you!"

Ara speaks to Niven and Krir last. "I ask that you remain here during my absence to watch my cathedral and ... my Frost Flowers."

"We will do so, Ara," Niven says and Krir says, "Yes, Ara."

"Thank you."

While Niven opens the doors to let everyone out, Krir takes Rath's hand. He clearly wished to hug him instead, but Rath is no longer wearing the heat-resistant cloak. "Take care. I hope ... " He exhales. "Well, with Ara going with you, you won't be returning to Draconi after, will you?"

"I do not believe so," Rath says.

Krir looks up at his god. "Ara, can I ... " He bites his lip.

Ara studies him for a moment, then his eyebrows raise and he nods. He waves his hand and two stone slabs appear with stone pens attached to the corner of each with a small chain. He hands one to Rath and the other to his own. "Yes, Krir."

Krir is absolutely thrilled.

Rath looks at his slab, curious. "May I ask what this is?"

"Let me show you instead." He begins to write on his, each word lighting up in a bright red.

Rath watches for a few seconds until he realizes his slab has also started to glow. When he compares both of them, he sees that the same writing from Krir's has started to appear on his, only half a second delayed. He turns to Krir quickly – Krir laughs – then writes something on his slab which quickly appears on Krir's.

Krir's smile grows, then he frowns. "Your handwriting is so much better than mine. It looks like I wrote with my opposite hand.

"Ah ... " Nodding to the slabs, Rath says, "Then, we can communicate like this?"

"Yes!" Krir stands next to Rath, holding them together. He draws a little person on his and it appears the next second on Rath's. "No matter what distance, um ... " He suddenly looks back at Ara. "Any distance, right?"

Ara actually colors. "It's never been tested." He coughs uncomfortably. "But, it should. I am sure it will. Krir, you will see Rath again."

"Yes, Ara." Krir grips Rath's hand and squeezes it with his gloved one. "Good luck."

"Thank you, Krir."

After Rath tucks the slab carefully into his side satchel, he joins the others by the doors.

Niven and Krir hold them open as they all exit the cathedral, Krir with his slab under his arm, looking brighter as he waves to them. Rath and the others wave back, then continue down the stairs. As they walk through the streets, most of the people of Draconi are surprised to see their god with them. Wagon-Pagu flies next to Ara, sending him silent strength.

When they reach the gate, South is still sitting outside.

"Good morning, Ara."

"Good morning, South." Ara turns around and faces his people. "I will be leaving to find the object which I lost. South, East, and West will protect you in my absence. Please ... be well."

The people are stunned, but many nod.

Ara says to his ice dragons, "Open the gate, please."

They do so without hesitation.

Outside, South dips his head in respect. "Ara, I will remain here by your city as you requested and protect your people."

"Thank you."

Vocalise's eyebrows go up. "We're not gonna go back to *PearlHeart* on South?"

Ara says, "No, Vocalise. South is needed here. I would not leave if he was not present." To them all, he says, "I am aware that you seven are unable to travel in your normal ways through my storm. With my help, it should be possible."

The gods look surprised.

Vocalise grins, "Sounds good."

Marchand says, "Thank you for your help."

Vocalise continues, "Sooo, does this mean you're gonna use your dragon form?"

Ara frowns immediately. "No. I ... would prefer not to at this time. I will aid you in the form I am currently using. Elvin, would you carry me as I do so?"

Elvin glows, turning into his eagle form. "Certainly!"

Everyone else sorts out their arrangements and soon, Ara, Wagon-Pagu, and Belle are on top of Elvin; Rath, Berceuse, and Marchand are on top of Oracle; and Maro sits on top of Vocalise, now in his chimpanzee form.

Afterward, Ara concentrates. Slowly, a deep blue glow surrounds the group. The gods add their own barriers to it and once the colors have merged, Ara says, "We may leave now."

Elvin and Oracle fly while Vocalise runs across the icy ground. Even within the storm, their barriers hold. South sees them disappear into the snow, then turns back to the City of Draconi to watch over Ara's people.

31

Further south, on Pica Pica, a large magpie soars down to the ocean north of the country. It flies toward the white spot there – Amara – and when it arrives, turns into Liette's human form. Using her traits, she stands on air in front of her sister, playing with something sparkly in her hands.

"Um ... Hey, Amara," Liette says.

Amara opens her eyes. "Greetings, Liette."

"So, I really appreciate you doing all this, but, does it have to be all white and stuff? It kinda takes the color out of everything."

"Such is the nature of my barrier."

"I know." Liette pauses, then leans forward. She puts a purple fabric flower dusted with sparkles in her sister's hair. "Thanks for doing this."

Amara is very still. "Such is my Knightly Duty."

Liette smiles. Then she waves a little awkwardly – Amara waves just as awkwardly back – and Liette flies off in her magpie form.

After she leaves, Amara closes her eyes again, but she is smiling.

In the North, the gods and Rath travel for the better part of the morning. Rath falls asleep in Marchand's arms. Berceuse sees and says, "He must be very tired."

Marchand says, holding him close, "I can't imagine it's easy for him to be in Draconi's environment, even with our barriers."

Berceuse nods. "But, it is far easier to do so with Ara helping."

"It is."

Near lunch time, they see the green and yellow glow of East and West's barriers come into view, surrounding *PearlHeart*. East and West sense the group first and turn. They dip their heads in respect when they see their god.

On top of Elvin, Ara says, "Thank you for your help, East, West."

East says, "Of course."

West says, "You're really going with them?"

Ara says, "Yes." They land on the deck. Rath is awake now and Marchand offers him a hand down from Oracle. Ara continues to his guardians, "I ask that you watch Draconi as you always have. Thank you for protecting the Captain's ship." Helped by Belle, Ara climbs off Elvin and Wagon-Pagu follows. He looks around at the crew, gathered for the gods and Rath's arrival. To them, he says, "I am Ara, Elder God of Draconi. I have asked your captain to allow me aboard *PearlHeart* so that I and my siblings may find the object which I have lost. He has accepted."

The crew nod, too stunned to do anything else.

Ara turns to Rath. "We depart now?"

"Yes." Rath raises his voice. "Everyone, please make ready to cast off!"

"Yes, Captain!"

As they prepare, One-Eye and Well-Pagu approach Rath. One-Eye says, "It's good to see you."

Well-Pagu says, "Return."

"You as well, One-Eye. I am glad to be back, Well-Pagu." He turns to Ara and Wagon-Pagu. "May I show you to your sleeping quarters?"

Ara says, "Yes, please. Thank you, Captain."

Wagon-Pagu says, "It is much appreciated!"

While the other gods go to their positions around *PearlHeart* so that they are ready to create their barriers, Rath leads Ara and Wagon-Pagu to the guest cabin.

Once inside, he says, "This is where the other gods currently are. Would you be amenable to staying here with them?"

Ara eyes the hammocks lining the walls. "All of my siblings?" When Rath nods, Ara says, "Yes, that would be amenable." He looks back toward the door leading out to the deck. "If I help my siblings with their barrier, not all of them will be needed. Would you inform four of them to come back here and rest?"

"I will. Thank you, Ara." Rath leaves.

Beside Ara, Wagon-Pagu looks very pleased.

Not long afterward, Vocalise, Elvin, Berceuse, and Oracle return.

Elvin says to Ara, "That is very kind of you to help."

Ara's expression does not change. "It would seem only appropriate given what I am asking. Now rest."

They nod and Vocalise says, "Y'know, we really haven't been able to stay in here much. I've already forgotten which hammock is mine."

Oracle says, "The one with the puzzles!"

"Ohhh. Right."

Ara watches them all enter, frowning. "Do remember that you will be needed later."

They turn around. Berceuse says, "We will. And we truly appreciate you helping."

Before Ara leaves, he *Whooshes* a cushion onto the table for Wagon-Pagu to sit on. "Until the Captain brings out hammocks," he explains.

They beam up at him. "Thank you, Ara!" They turn to the others. "I also wish to thank everyone for your help in this endeavor!"

Elvin says, "You are very welcome, Wagon-Pagu."

"It is very good to see you all – as my dear friend, Well-Pagu often says – together."

The gods look a little nervous, but nod.

Ara goes outside and speaks with Rath to inform him where he will be on *PearlHeart.* Afterward, he stands in between the foremast and mainmast, where Elvin and Vocalise normally are. He waits, arms crossed underneath his thick cloak. Around him, the crew finish the preparations.

Once they are done, Rath is at the wheel, One-Eye beside him, and Well-Pagu sitting on the console. East and West are in front of them. Then the gods begin their barriers.

Belle's gray-blue begins it and Marchand's blue-green slowly joins. Maro's red-orange comes next. Then, from Ara, a deep strong blue appears and glowing dragon wings wrap around all three. Ara turns and nods once to East and West, who concentrate, then release their own barriers.

PearlHeart begins to sail away from the Three Dragon Isles. East and West watch as their glowing barrier grows smaller and disappears into Ara's Storm.

For the next four hours, they sail south. Vocalise, Oracle, Elvin, and Berceuse relax in the guest cabin. Berceuse knits. Vocalise works on a puzzle, pretending not to know how to do it. Oracle and Elvin speak softly with each other at the table.

Outside, Ara helps Belle, Marchand, and Maro.

At eight in the evening, the bell rings and the other gods return to relieve those currently outside. Ara, however, tells them he will be remaining on the deck. Elvin says to him, "Thank you again, Brother," then begins to glow light blue, much brighter than before.

Ara hesitates. "You are welcome." When Belle walks toward him, Ara says, "I trust that you will inform me if you sense my object."

"I will." Belle studies Ara with a frown. "You're tired. You haven't been using your traits often?"

"I haven't had reason to."

Belle frowns, but concentrates and says, "I can't tell now, but if we exit the storm, I should be able to find it if it's outside."

Ara exhales, relieved. "Good. What is the fastest way of doing so?"

"South. I'll leave it to the Captain to decide on the route."

"Very well. Rest now, Belle."

Belle nods, then looks up at Rath, saying to him, "We'll need to exit the storm so I can sense Ara's object better."

Rath says, "I understand. Thank you."

Later that day, Rath and One-Eye are pounding in the last hook for two new hammocks – one human-sized and one Pagu-sized.

Rath tests them, nods when he finds them secure, then tells Wagon-Pagu – who has been patiently waiting on the table on their cushion – that it is ready. They fly over and their eyes grow wide as they look at the small hammock.

They carefully sit on the side and Rath asks, "How is it?"

Wagon-Pagu looks utterly delighted. "It is perfect!" They swing a little. "A hammock! One that is perfectly my size. I am very happy with it, Captain Rath, One-Eye. Thank you very much."

Rath smiles. "I am glad to hear as such." One-Eye, Marchand, Belle, and Maro smile as well.

After they put their tools back, Rath and One-Eye meet with Well-Pagu in the captain's cabin. Rath's map is on the table.

"We can either go west or east around the Phoenae Sea to exit the storm," Rath says. "We know that it has extended to Pica Pica since we left. I do not know how far south it is to the west."

Well-Pagu thinks very carefully. "Less," they say.

Rath and One-Eye look at them. One-Eye's Spirit Lion flicks his tail.

"I see," Rath says. "We will go west. Is everyone in agreement?" They all nod.

Outside, Ara is still out on the deck.

As it grows late, Wagon-Pagu flies up next to him. "Good evening, Ara."

"Good evening, Wagon-Pagu."

They study him for a moment, then settle by his shoulder. They look up at the combined barriers. "You are doing very well."

"I am exhausted."

Wagon-Pagu pats him. "That is what happens."

Ara sighs.

They travel for the next week. Ara helps, but grows more tired the longer they travel. Wagon-Pagu encourages him. By the end of the week, however, he asks to speak with Rath, who walks over to him.

"When will we arrive at the edge of the storm?" Ara asks.

"Well-Pagu says two days from now."

Ara exhales. He nods, focusing again.

The day before they are to exit the storm, Ara sits down and Wagon-Pagu joins him. They stay with him through the last night, curled up on his lap on their cushion with a small blanket Ara *Whooshed* for them.

By the next morning, the skies begin to brighten.

Ara looks up, past his dark blue and the other colors of his siblings.

They maintain their barriers until they have fully left the storm and Ara can see a patchy blue sky up above. Then he lets his barrier drop and picks up Wagon-Pagu with absolute care. He walks toward the guest cabin, stops to look at Rath once – "I am resting now," he says – but does not wait for Rath's response as he enters the door, shutting it behind him.

Within the next minute, he is in his hammock and Wagon-Pagu is in theirs. While Wagon-Pagu wakes up later that day, Ara sleeps for the rest of the week and the gods are all quiet coming and going from the cabin.

"Ara is still sleeping," Berceuse tells Rath one morning while Rath is mending and Berceuse is knitting out on the deck.

The Pagu are sitting on the rail with them and Flower-Pagu says, "He's used a lot of energy."

Bucket-Pagu says, "Leaving Draconi, too, must have taken a lot."

Well-Pagu says, "Hard."

Wagon-Pagu, also with them, says, "I fully agree. He will be all right. I am sure we will see him again soon."

When Ara does come out again, he squints at the bright, sunny sky.

Marchand meets him first. "Ara." His brother looks over at him. "I wish to thank you for helping us before. I don't think we would have been able to exit the storm without you. It was a far different experience than when we came."

"I did not know my storm was as strong as it was." Ara looks behind them at the dark clouds that are still spreading from Draconi, then turns back. "You are welcome, Marchand."

While Marchand goes to join Vocalise by the port rail, Ara walks to the starboard rail.

Ahead and to the right are blue skies. However, he can clearly see the storm to the east, where it has overcome most of the area. There are two barriers shining out from the darkness

– one pure white and one a mixture of yellow, light green, and pale yellow. He frowns when he sees both of them.

Ara remains outside until lunch is served, which he has quietly with Wagon-Pagu in the guest cabin.

"Amara is still on Pica Pica. Sevran, Feep, and Erole are in Daerce, as well," Ara says.

Wagon-Pagu says, "They are protecting everyone."

Ara frowns, then takes another bite.

He goes out to the deck later that evening. Rath and One-Eye are by the rail, talking in the warm lantern light. Rath points out a constellation and Ara looks up at them, too.

Belle approaches him and he asks, "Do you sense it?"

"Yeah. Southwest."

Ara pales. "But, nothing is over there except ... " He looks at the clear skies. "Delphy, Pantrog – even Selachuu would be too warm for it." He has a thought. "Is it in Cunica? Rella would ensure that it is a true Winter there."

Belle stares at him. "I can't tell yet. Just a general direction." He chews on his toothpick. "What exactly is it?"

"It ... " Ara shakes his head. "Then we will continue in that direction."

They travel in the direction of Delphy and Paradi. Marchand talks with a few Spirit Dolphins near the rail, who inform him of the state of his country.

The next day, Ara sits at the small table in the guest cabin, drinking tea with Elvin and Berceuse.

Elvin says, "It seems that we may be close now."

Berceuse says, "Indeed." They both look at Ara, but he is quiet.

That night, Ara is studying the barriers to the east again. The one over Daerce wavers. Finally, he grits his teeth and walks away.

Soon, he is in the captain's cabin, speaking with Rath.

Ara rubs his temple. "I ask for a course change. East. To Pica Pica and Daerce."

Rath's eyebrows go up, then he nods. "We will do so."

"I ... " Ara takes a deep breath. "It does not feel right to leave things how they are to the east ... and north." He sits back. "If Belle is sure that my object is due west, I will trust that it will remain that way."

Later, Rath tells One-Eye and Well-Pagu about the course change.

Well-Pagu looks surprised, then thoughtful.

One-Eye gestures to the map on the table. "Why? Isn't his thing to the southwest?"

"He did not say."

"You didn't ask?"

"No."

One-Eye stares at him for a long moment. "Right," he says. "Amara is still near Pica Pica, isn't she? And other gods in Daerce?"

"I believe so."

One-Eye glances at his Spirit Lion, who has attended the meeting as well. "My Spirit Lion says that they're doing all right in Pantha, but the Selachuu Military is starting to have trouble getting more supplies to them."

"I am very sorry to hear that."

"Seems only right if Ara helped them, given it's his mess."

At that, Rath chokes. One-Eye gives him a look and Rath says, "I agree that he has caused this storm. And I think it would be very good if he helped his siblings."

In between them, Well-Pagu nods.

32

PearlHeart changes course and sails east. During that time, the gods are out on the deck watching the skies, or in the galley eating and talking with their own or other members of the crew. They sit in their cabin, reading or playing cards together at their small table.

One-Eye is leaning against the railing with Oren when Maro walks up to them. "Good afternoon."

One-Eye nods and Oren waves. "Hey."

Maro looks at the ocean, then takes a breath and turns toward One-Eye. "Did you know I was a god back on Tecla?"

"Thought I did." One-Eye glances at his Spirit Lion. "My Lion told me Maro was the name of the God of Tecla. You didn't do anything, though."

Maro chuckles. "Godly, you mean?" He considers his words. "Not all of us exactly chose this path – or, perhaps it is more honest to say, we did not know what our actions would lead to." He smiles. "Not that I would not have my people with me for all this world."

Oren says, "That's a pretty good attitude to have."

"Did you know?"

"Not a clue," Oren says, stretching back.

Maro chuckles again.

As they pass the Phoenae Sea, Franz looks at it. He is eating on the deck with Velt and says to her, "With Ara's Storm all around it, you can barely see the storms in the Phoenae Sea."

"You're right," she says.

Ara, who is nearby, hears them both. Wagon-Pagu is with him.

On the upper deck, Vocalise is hanging out with Isaac. Not far from them, Elvin is with Rath, saying, "It's hard to believe that just three months ago, you were bringing my ink, paper, and provisions to Pica Pica."

"Indeed."

Elvin nods to the main deck, where Ara is at the rail with Wagon-Pagu. "Now, Ara is with us. I truly could not have imagined such a thing happening. And Amara is still there on Pica Pica. I wonder if this course change is because he wishes to speak with her?"

"I cannot say."

They suddenly hear the crew gasp. Rath asks, "Is everyone all right?"

Franz calls back, "Yeah – there's something weird going on by the Phoenae Sea!"

Rath turns toward it. He sees a crackle of pale yellow there. Evermore comes up from below and joins Rath. He faces the sea, his eyes covered from the bright sun with his scarf.

Elvin, watching sparks of electricity weave through the storm, asks, "Is that your god, Evermore?"

"Yes, Elvin."

Belle sees it too and walks up to Ara, who asks hm, "Erole?"

He nods. "He shouldn't be there." But, before he can do anything, a golden light appears with long wings and a trailing tail. It swoops down on the form in the ocean, which glows and diminishes in size until Merp is carrying Erole, now in his human form, away from the Phoenae Sea. He is flying near *PearlHeart* when Erole grins and says, "How interesting!"

Merp makes an irritated sound. He looks down and his golden eyes widen, then narrow when he sees Rath. "Why are you here? What did you learn in Draconi – " He suddenly stops. "Ara." In his surprise, his talons loosen and Erole squirms out of his grip, dropping into the ocean. He quickly turns into his eel form, curves around, and starts to go back toward the Phoenae Sea when Merp shrieks at him, "You will not go there – that is a direct order!"

The eel jolts and settles himself as he swirls in a figure eight pattern. His large head rises up out of the water. "Later, then," he says and, giggling, dives underwater in an arc, shooting out errant sparks as he travels west instead.

Merp watches him for a few moments, then follows *PearlHeart*, eyeing those on deck. Finally, he says, "Permission, Captain Rath?"

"Yes. Of course, Merp."

Merp flies down. He lands in his human form in front of Ara. The older god stands at least a foot over Merp's head even while hunched over in his bulky cloak.

Neither god says anything until Merp says, "You've left Draconi." For the first time, he sounds uncertain, but it disappears as he steps forward. "Why? Your storm has made a mess of everything – Pantha, Haliae, Pica Pica, the Isles of Oct ... "

"I am realizing," Ara says.

"What is your intent for being here?"

Ara glances behind the Elder God of Phoenae and Ruler of the Fourth World. "I have asked to go to Pica Pica." Merp looks back at the small island encased in white. "I respect your position as ruler, however I will not ask for your permission to do this." At that, Merp snaps back around, eyes wide. "If you disapproved of Captain Rath journeying to Draconi, you should have disallowed it in the first place."

"I could not."

Ara's eyebrows raise at his answer, then lower as he realizes why.

Wagon-Pagu flies forward. "It is good to see you, Merp. Might I ask how my dear friend, Fountain-Pagu is, in Phoenae?"

"They are well," Merp says quickly. "They ... " He shakes his head, then turns to Rath. "All that happens is your responsibility. I will remind you again, Captain Rath."

Before Rath can speak, Ara says, "You will not place that on him."

Rath says, "I have agreed to it."

Merp glances at Ara.

Ara pauses. "I see." He looks directly at Merp. "Was there more you wished to say?"

"No." Merp steps back. He looks once more at Rath and the Phoenae Sea, then departs in his phoenix form, flying high above them.

PearlHeart passes through the fog of Unys two weeks later. Once they exit it, they near the Southern Selachuu Military Base, where they see a bright white spot in the ocean.

"Sir Ronan!" Rath calls.

Ronan, atop Opal Starlight, looks grim. "Greetings, my friend, Captain Rath. If we may travel with you? You need not halt your ship, *PearlHeart*." Rath nods and Ronan waves his hand, creating a path of white light that rises up to *PearlHeart's* rail, staying just ahead of the unicorn's hooves. "I trust you have seen the state of Pica Pica?"

"Yes. We were there when Amara arrived."

Ronan's eyes widen. "My Lady – " He looks ahead at the white barrier. "We knew such work could only be hers. Yet" – he struggles and even Opal Starlight looks strained – "my Lady is very specific on what are her duties and what are ours." He rubs Opal Starlight's neck. "Even so, we wish to help her."

"That makes sense to me."

Ronan's eyebrows raise, then he smiles a little. However, it falls when he looks at Pica Pica again. "Pray tell – may I ask something of you?"

"Of course."

"To so readily agree! You truly are quite – " Ronan clears his throat. "That is, I appreciate your kindness," he says simply. "Are you currently traveling to Pica Pica?"

"We are."

"Then, if you are able to determine the state of my Lady and would have the time to write as such in a letter addressed to me, it would put both of our hearts at great ease."

"I will do so." Rath suddenly frowns. "However, I cannot say I will meet with Amara."

"That is all right. Even noting the state of her barrier will be enough." Ronan reaches out and squeezes Rath's hand. "Thank you very much, Captain Rath. From me and Opal Starlight both."

A flush rises to Rath's face. "Ah, you are welcome."

Ronan reddens as well and pulls his hand back quickly. "We shall depart, so that you may resume what is most assuredly a noble quest that you so readily find yourself – " He suddenly gapes. "Is that Most Holy Ara?"

Ara, who has been leaning against the opposite rail with Wagon-Pagu and Maro, says, "Greetings, Sir Ronan and Opal Starlight."

Ronan blinks at him, then at Rath. Finally, he says, "Such company you keep!"

"I have been asked to do so."

Ronan laughs heartily and it sounds more relaxed than anything he has said so far. "Such does not surprise me. Fair travels in your quest, my dear friend, Captain Rath."

Rath bows. "You as well, Sir Ronan, Opal Starlight." When he rises, Ronan extends his hand again. Rath smiles and takes it.

Afterward, Ronan and Opal Starlight trot down to the ocean's surface. Ronan waves to Rath as *PearlHeart* passes them and Rath returns it from the rail.

At the end of the week, now two months after leaving Draconi, *PearlHeart* reaches Amara's barrier around Pica Pica. Dark clouds surround it, but none of the storm has moved past the white sphere. Ara is with Rath, studying it. He says, "The north of the island, please, Captain."

"Yes, Ara." Rath directs his crew and by evening, they have entered the barrier.

On Pica Pica, the partying has continued in full despite the muted colors of their surroundings. While *PearlHeart* sails around the western coast of the island, Ara looks at the steady white glow with his siblings.

A week later, when they are due west of the island, a dark form flies toward *PearlHeart*. A few minutes later, a large magpie flutters over them, saying, "Oh! Everyone's here again! So, does that mean – " She jumps midair. "Ara!" She starts to swoop down, then stops. "That's right. Permission to board? I am Liette, Goddess of Pica Pica!"

Rath replies, "Yes. Permission granted."

After Liette has boarded, she gives a small wave to Rath – he gives one back – then moves toward Ara and throws both arms out. "You're here! Like – HERE." She shakes out her hair. "Wow!"

Ara's mouth twitches. "Yes, I am."

"So, does that mean this is over? It can all stop? Amara can end her barrier?" She leans back, following the barrier's curve as she speaks.

"I am not sure," Ara says, sighing. "However, I do intend to speak with Amara." He pauses. "Would you take me to her?"

Liette gapes. She bounces a curl in her hair like a spring. "Well, sure. Yeah." She stops and her brows furrow. "Wait, but can't you just – you know, *rawr!* And *swoop!*" She demonstrates, hopping on one foot, arms stretched out.

"I would prefer not to right now."

"Oh. All right." She settles on both feet and puts her hands on her hips. "I'm ready to leave when you are!"

"Thank you, Liette." Ara gestures for Rath to come over and when he does, says, "I will be speaking with Amara now. Liette will be taking me. May I ask if you will remain here while I do so?"

"Yes. We will."

"Thank you, Captain."

Liette turns into her magpie form and Ara climbs onto her back.

Wagon-Pagu speaks from the deck. "I hope your meeting goes well, Ara."

"Thank you, Wagon-Pagu."

Liette lifts off into the air, flying toward the north coast of Pica Pica while those on the deck watch them.

PearlHeart spends the next two days with the sea anchor dropped.

Rath, One-Eye, Franz, and Velt are playing the board game from Ursi at the table in the galley, talking as they do.

Franz says, "There's something I don't really get." The others look up from the game board. "So, if Ara created this storm, couldn't he just ... end it?"

One-Eye rolls his game piece between his forefinger and thumb. "I asked my Spirit Lion the same thing." The Lion has his head in One-Eye's lap, eyes turned up at him. "He says it isn't that simple." With a huff, he takes his turn.

"That makes sense," Rath says and the Lion lifts his head while One-Eye raises an eyebrow.

Franz looks thoughtful and Velt asks, "How so?"

"If it is being caused by his emotions – specifically, negative ones, as South told me – then I do not believe that is something that can be changed so abruptly."

Velt and Franz turn toward each other. Continuing with his turn, Franz says, "That's true," and Velt nods.

One-Eye does not say anything, but crosses his arms as he focusing on the game board. His Lion washes his face beside him.

After they finish, they all go out to the main deck.

From the nest, Melody calls down, "Captain! A Selachuu ship is approaching from Pica Pica!" and Demeter gives an affirming "Caw!"

They all look to the east, where small ripples catch the barrier's white light as they travel toward *PearlHeart.*

When the ship stops, it surfaces and Captain Farbourne climbs out of the hatch. He gives a short wave.

Rath asks Franz to lower a rope for Farbourne to board. After he does and sees at least four gods looking at him, he whistles. "Well." He nods to Belle, who is standing against the rail near him. "Sir."

Belle nods back. "Good to see you."

Farbourne approaches Rath. "Captain Rath. How are you?"

"Well, Captain Farbourne. And you?"

"Fine enough." Farbourne looks back at Pica Pica. "Been a bit of a mess here after the storm hit. We've had to carry provisions to them that other ships aren't willing to bring." Rath's eyebrows raise and Farbourne explains, "You and your crew might not be too fazed by this whole barrier stuff, but a lot of the other ships wouldn't even enter it. Sir Ronan and Opal Starlight came to inform us and we had to track the lot of them down. They still wouldn't go, so we transferred their cargo to our ships and just delivered it to Pica Pica ourselves."

"That was very kind of you to do so."

"Yeah. Ronan said it was quite noble. Think Opal Starlight looks at us a bit better now, too. Doubt she feels the same about those ships that left."

"Ah ... "

Farbourne laughs at his reaction. "Actually, we thought you might have been one of those ships that were leaving except you were already in the barrier. Then" – he points up – "I saw your flags and knew it had to be *PearlHeart.* Would you be available for some deliveries? We could use the help. You might also be able to convince those other captains there's nothing to worry about when sailing inside Amara's barrier."

"We need to remain here until Ara returns. However, afterward we would be able to."

"Great." He pauses. "Ara?" He exchanges a look with his god – Belle offers nothing – then says, "All right. We'll be at the Southern Selachuu Military Base. Probably for a while."

"I understand. Thank you."

Farbourne waves to those aboard *PearlHeart* before climbing down to return to his Selachuu ship. It submerges and travels southeast to the base.

North of Pica Pica, Liette flies with Ara on her back.

They travel toward a bright white light in the ocean. When they come close enough to see that it is Amara, Ara says, "Stop, Liette. I will meet her from here."

"Right-o, Ara!"

Ara raises his voice. "Amara!"

For a frightening moment, the white barrier wavers as if it has been struck. Then without any word from Amara, a white path is sent out from her to Ara and Liette. Ara steps down on it and walks toward his sister.

When he reaches her, Amara's eyes are closed and Ara stands in front of her, waiting.

Amara opens her eyes. She begins to raise her head to speak to him, but Ara abruptly sits down.

"Ara," Amara says.

"How are you?"

A frown crosses her lips. "I am troubled."

"I apologize that my storm has caused this."

"Then why do it?" Amara leans forward. "I have already lost one brother to destructive acts such as these. I cannot – " Her eyes catch the light, wavering. Drawing herself back, she says, "Why are you here? Why have you left Draconi?"

"I am here to find the object that I have lost with the help of

Captain Rath and those aboard *PearlHeart.* However, before that ... " He looks at the white all around them, then further to where his storm still rages outside. He faces his sister directly. "I intend to end my storm here, in the east, on Pica Pica and Daerce."

"Truly?"

"I created it. I now see what it has caused." The corners of his eyes are tight. "I still fear for my object – it will not survive in warmer climates – but Belle assures me it is to the west. I can only pray that if he senses it at all that it is safe." He continues, "If I end my storm here, you will be able to leave. I believe Wagon-Pagu would agree to this course of action as well."

Amara's eyebrows raise. "They are here?"

"Yes. On *PearlHeart.* They insisted on leaving Draconi with me." Ara hesitates. "They said ... it was time for them to do so."

Amara pauses, then nods.

Ara studies the storm outside the barrier to the north. "It will take time to end this. I have not used my traits in some time."

"You will need them to do so, if this is your intent."

Ara faces her again. "It is. Would you protect Pica Pica while I do this?"

"I would do no less," Amara immediately replies. "You would be wise to take those siblings who journeyed to Draconi with you and ask that they aid you."

Already rising, Ara says, "I am afraid it will be necessary at the start. Thank you, Amara."

She looks up at him, eyes narrowed. "I do not wish for your thanks. Only your word that you will do as you say." Despite her tone, her hands tremble.

"I promise," Ara says.

Amara is quiet. As Ara steps out onto the white path, she asks, "Do you fear me? South, East, and West would not allow my passage when I approached Draconi one year ago."

Ara turns around. "They feared you had come to make me disappear as you did our brother you spoke of earlier. I know what you are capable of and your sense of duty that compels you to do what you believe is necessary. I alone do not fear you, but I understand theirs."

She listens, nods, then trains her gaze north before closing her eyes again. When she does not say anything more, Ara leaves, walking down the path to Liette to be taken back to *PearlHeart.*

They arrive two weeks later. As Ara climbs down onto the deck, Rath meets him.

Ara says, "May I ask for your patience in remaining near Pica Pica? I intend to disperse my storm around it and Daerce. If I do so, Amara may leave and both her and those in Daerce may release their barriers before we continue west."

Rath's eyes widen and behind him, the other gods also look surprised. Then Rath bows low, saying, "Of course. Thank you very much for doing so, Ara. Would you allow that we help others during that time? Captain Farbourne of the Selachuu Military has asked if *PearlHeart* would help deliver supplies from the ships who are not comfortable entering Amara's barrier."

With a bewildered look, Ara says, "Amara's barrier is likely the strongest there is." He thinks carefully. "Would it take you far from Pica Pica, Captain?"

"No. Just to the Southern Selachuu Military Base for cargo, then we would return to where it is needed here."

Looking to the east, where the storm has yet to reach, Ara says, "You would be safe during your journey." He nods. "I will allow this. All I ask is that you be ready to depart when we return."

"We will be, Ara."

Ara's lips lift a little. While he walks toward his siblings, Rath goes to inform his crew.

After Ara explains what he intends to do, he finishes, saying, "It has been some time since I have used my traits to this extent and I will likely need your help at the start. Will you do so?"

They all smile. Vocalise says, "Sure thing, buddy."

Ara immediately frowns.

"We would be happy to help," Marchand puts in. "Thank you for asking us."

"Of course." He looks at all of his siblings, gathered around him. "Shall we depart?"

They all agree and soon, the gods fly, swim, or leap away from *PearlHeart.* Ara is on Elvin, Maro on Vocalise, Oracle flying alone, and Belle, Berceuse, and Marchand swimming in their other forms. They travel toward the eastern part of the barrier, where the green, yellow, and light yellow glow over Daerce is becoming weaker.

On *PearlHeart*, Charles and William haul up the sea anchor, Isaac helps set the sails under Rath's direction, and *PearlHeart* starts sailing to the Southern Selachuu Military Base.

That evening, Rath sits in his cabin, composing his letter to Sir Ronan about the state of Amara's barrier. He is also writing one to Captain Farbourne to inform him of their arrival. When he finishes, he asks Felix and Triphonius to deliver them. Triphonius flies off boldly, unperturbed by the barrier surrounding them, with a resounding "CAW!"

To the east, the gods have arrived at the northeastern edge of Amara's barrier. Just before they exit it, they all begin to glow – Elvin light blue, Belle gray-blue, Marchand blue-green, Oracle magenta, Berceuse purple, Maro red-orange, Vocalise orange, and Ara deep blue, which layers over all of the other colors. Once they have merged, they move together, through the white and into the storm.

Immediately, the snow swirls around them and the wind threatens to throw Elvin and Oracle off-course, but both glow brighter as they steady themselves and their siblings strengthen their own barriers to help them.

Vocalise lands on a rock in the ocean. "Sooo, how exactly do you want to go about this?"

Ara peers through the snow toward Daerce where the green, yellow, and pale yellow barriers are flickering, then up at the dark clouds that came all the way from Draconi. He rubs his temple. "We will simply need to begin." He carefully rises, standing on top of Elvin's back. He extends his arm out.

As heavy white snowflakes swirl around it, clinging to his heavy cloak and hair, he concentrates and the tips of his fingers glow red. The snow evaporates immediately with a *hiss*. He waves his hand, dragging the heat with it and the air steams. Above, the clouds reflect the motion, burning away as well. However, as soon as the pale blue sky appears, the storm covers it again as it moves steadily south. Ara pulls back his hand. To the others, he says, "Direct your energy toward the clouds."

They work slowly, Ara waving his hand, melting the clouds above while Elvin keeps his flight steady. Vocalise leaps high into the sky where he and Maro – who is on his shoulders in his lizard form – swipe at the storm, widening Ara's area. Oracle beats her wings against the clouds, with Belle supporting her with his barrier while in the water. Marchand and Berceuse do the same for all of them, swimming beneath the group as they travel toward Daerce. Slowly, the storm clouds are dispersed, revealing blue skies up above.

At the end of the day, they have moved forward with clearer skies in their wake, however further on, the storm continues. When Ara turns east, the barriers over Daerce are brighter. Sitting back down on Elvin's back, he says, "We need to rest. We will return afterward." He looks down at his hand, now cool, frowning.

They return to Amara's barrier and go on to Pica Pica. Liette meets them on the eastern beach. "I saw you go into the storm! Are you all right?"

Ara replies, "Yes. We are. We spent the day dispersing the clouds. However, we likely only uncovered several hundred feet in that time."

Beside him, Belle steps out of the ocean in his human form. "Less than a mile," he confirms.

Liette jumps in surprise. "Oh! You did? But ... I didn't see you go – *rawr!* And ... *fwoom!* And ... "

Vocalise snorts.

Ara says, "I will continue to disperse the storm as I am doing – in my human form, Liette."

"It just seems like it'd be faster if – No, no, if that's what you're doing, it must be right." She peers out at the ocean to the east of Pica Pica. "I also thought I saw Captain Rath's ship leaving. Where are they going?"

"To help bring more provisions," Belle says.

"Oh, great! I was wondering when my streamers were coming."

Belle is quiet.

Marchand gently says, "I think they're delivering more food and other supplies for the people here to weather out the storm."

"I see! Those are great, too." She grins. "I've got this amazing idea for a STREAMER party. They're going to be everywhere! Like – *fwing!* And *shoom!*" She hops on each foot, shooting her arms up into air to the left and right. "What do you guys think?"

Vocalise says, "Sounds fun to me."

Maro smiles. "It's good that you seem to not be letting the storm trouble you, Liette."

"Oh, I'm terrified. Absolutely terrified. But – you guys are handling it! Yay!" She tilts her head to the side. "I mean ... I do wonder, though – not that I'm super strong like you or anything – if there was anything I could do? Like ... support?" She stands up tall. "I'm a great support."

Elvin says, "Actually, now that *PearlHeart* is engaged in another task, if we may ask for some rooms that we may stay in while we rest in between working on the storm?"

Liette claps her hands together. "Absolutely! Done. Follow me!" She starts singing to herself as she uses her traits to walk on air off the beach and above the partying crowds.

Ara watches her. "She has not changed in the slightest."

Oracle beams. "I think her bright attitude is infectious! It's no wonder her people are so happy all the time."

They follow Liette through the crowd. Very few people seem to notice that they are gods. Vocalise accepts a necklace of fabric flowers that he perches up on his nose, making Maro laugh. Oracle watches the bubbles rise in between the towers and Berceuse makes little gasps at the different booths and games. Marchand seems to be enjoying the festivities, too, but seems distracted as if thinking. Belle walks unbothered by the explosions of smoke above them or the confetti that endlessly rains down. Ara does as well, pulling his cloak close to him.

Liette leads them to the clock tower. The doors have bubble glass windows in bright rainbow colors. Inside, the clock face's shadow is laid on the square-tiled floor, with colored stones at each of the intersections. There are no stairs and those with Liette's Traits walk up 'steps' of their own. For those without, there is a pulley system operated by Liette's people with a team on each floor who haul up a wooden platform before handing the ropes off to the next team.

The gods travel all the way to the eighth floor where

grinning helpers let them off onto the balcony directly across from the clock face. There, Liette guides them past a large room to a hallway lined with doors on one side and windows on the other.

She spreads her arms. "Ta-da! Rooms for all of my brothers and sister! Well, just enough for you all anyway. I just now realized that we're all here together! How great is that?" She blushes. "No, really. I think it's really great. It makes me super happy."

They all smile and Marchand says, "It has been nice to be with one another again – although I wish the circumstances could have been different."

Elvin says, "Then, after this, we'll make an effort to! What do you all say?"

"Good with me," Vocalise says.

Maro says, "It's not always easy for me to leave Tecla, but I have enjoyed this time spent together."

Liette says, "Wonderful! It's a plan, then! The next time we're all available and there's NOT a world-threatening disaster going on – we're having a party! All together!"

Ara frowns. Belle does, too.

Marchand says, "We could also just get together and talk."

But Vocalise laughs. "Naw, I like the party idea. Sounds fun."

They all pick a room and go inside. Marchand collapses on his bed and snores. Elvin writes his thoughts in a journal at a desk before he rests. Oracle prepares her hair for bed. Vocalise juggles with his feet with his head at the foot of the bed. Maro reads in a book under the covers. Belle is already asleep on his stomach and the curtains are drawn. Berceuse is, too, but the curtains are open. Liette is humming merrily in the hallway, then realizes her siblings are probably sleeping and starts to hum more quietly.

Ara sits on his bed, looking at his hand. He practices heating the tips of his fingers a few times, then sighs. He lies back on the bed and falls asleep.

For the next few days, they travel to the storm over Daerce. Ara stands atop Elvin, swiping with his glowing red fingertips. The other gods work as well, protecting one another and dispersing the clouds up above.

Each evening, they return to the clock tower on Pica Pica.

The first two days when they return, they speak in the hallway with Liette, updating her on their progress, then return to their rooms to rest. However, by the end of the week, they begin to gather more and more in the larger room set in the center of the floor, with couches and chairs – a few have baskets of confetti tucked underneath them – and two small tables as well as a wood stove. Vocalise joins Liette first and they discuss parties together, then Marchand, and Oracle does the day after. Elvin does the next day and Belle follows.

While they talk, Ara sits in his room on his bed. He concentrates on both of his hands. This time, along with his fingertips, his palms glow red. He exhales abruptly and lets the glow fade. He hears the chatter of the others beyond his wall and hesitates. After a moment, he stands up and leaves his room.

As he enters the larger room, the others look up, surprised, but happy to see him. Liette says, "Ara!"

"Good evening." He sits down in one of the chairs.

Not long after he arrives, Maro walks in. He joins Vocalise on the bench by the window. "I thought I would save my next chapter for tomorrow."

Vocalise pats his back. "Good to see ya, buddy."

Sitting beside Berceuse, Marchand says, "We were thinking a game of cards – Marchand's Twist?"

Berceuse says, "Or Double Berceuse! Perhaps both? If all are willing."

Oracle says, "I would like to join."

The rest gather around, including Ara. Marchand and Berceuse simultaneously *Whoosh* decks of cards and they play together through the evening.

When they are going to bed, Liette says, "This was the best night ever! I'm just ... Thank you guys so much! See you tomorrow!" She skips down the hallway.

Vocalise says, "Yeah. This has been really nice. I enjoy being with you guys."

"That's surprisingly straight-forward of you, Vocalise," Marchand says, snorting a little.

"Blame your own. He's always super honest with his feelings."

Marchand smiles warmly. "I agree."

"It's no wonder One-Eye likes him so much."

At that, Berceuse clasps his hands together. "I fully agree!"

Marchand suddenly frowns. "Perhaps we shouldn't talk about them when they're not ... " He pauses. "One-Eye and Rath. Really? I should have guessed."

Berceuse says, "They are wonderful." He plays with his hair. "I do wonder how they are doing."

Ara says, "I would say admirably. From my interactions, Captain Rath seems to be a very diligent young man. His crew has proven much the same."

Oracle says, "Everyone on *PearlHeart* has been very helpful."

Elvin nods. "They truly have been instrumental in this past year."

Belle says, "Agreed."

"Most certainly," Berceuse says. "My dear ones are there as well. I hope Wagon-Pagu is enjoying their time, too. I would imagine being on a ship is rather new for them!"

Ara smiles. "It is. They said that it would be a 'brand new experience' for them. However, they seemed excited."

"I am so glad to hear that!"

They talk for a while longer before going to sleep. Ara rests well that night.

The following morning, to the east, *PearlHeart* arrives at the Southern Selachuu Military Base. The last crew members are carrying cargo up the gangplank from the ships that would not go inside Amara's barrier. Not long after, Rath and One-Eye walk down to the docks where a Selachuu captain is. He says, "Thanks much."

"Of course," Rath says. "We will return in two weeks for more cargo."

The captain nods, then frowns, looking at the other Pan ships unloading their cargo at the base instead of taking it to Pica Pica. He does not say anything, however, and just shakes his head, waves to Rath and One-Eye, and goes to direct them.

Just as Rath and One-Eye are walking up the gangplank to prepare the crew to cast off, a captain from one of the Pan ships walks up to them. "Hey – Captain Rath of *PearlHeart?*"

Rath turns. "Yes?" Then he gasps. "Lin!"

Lin, the man who had applied to be Rath's first mate on Pantrog the previous year, but had a broken foot, grins. "You've got it. Great to see both of you again," he says, including One-Eye. He waves his foot. "This is all good, too."

"I am very happy to see that."

"Me too. After it healed, I was able to get a position as first mate on another ship. Now, I'm a captain."

"Congratulations!"

"Thanks." Lin nods to Pica Pica, still encased in Amara's barrier. "You're going there?"

"Yes. We have been asked to."

"You don't have any concerns with it?"

"No."

Lin thinks. He turns to the Selachuu soldiers who are carrying cargo. "I feel bad about leaving them in the lurch" – he turns toward Pica Pica again – "and even more so for failing our delivery to the people on Pica Pica. My crew and I just don't know what to think about a barrier inside Ara's Storm." He pauses. "Would you tell me the conditions, if you know them? I'm thinking that would ease the fears of both me and my crew."

"Definitely."

One-Eye tells Rath, "I'll let the crew know we'll be casting off afterward."

"Thank you very much, One-Eye."

Rath begins speaking with Lin. He finishes, saying, " ... I would recommend easing the lines as you enter the barrier so that you may adjust them accordingly once your ship is fully inside. The wind speed is far lower within the barrier from our experience."

"Got it," Lin says, looking far more relaxed. He pats Rath's back. "Thank you. That helps a lot. We'll look into loading our cargo back up. Actually ... why don't we follow you? We would be able to see how you handle the change."

"That is a good idea."

"I'll tell them right now. We'll be ready to cast off in thirty minutes, if that works."

"Yes. We will wait for you."

Not long afterward, *PearlHeart* is pulling away from the docks and Lin's Pan ship – *TellTale* – seeing this, begins to as well. They sail with *PearlHeart* leading toward Amara's barrier.

By the end of the week, they have reached the edge. As *PearlHeart* enters, the crew eases the lines to gauge the new wind speed, then adjust accordingly.

Watching them, the crew on Captain Lin's ship do the same. Lin is by the wheel on the upper deck. "Good job, everyone!"

Once fully inside, his crew looks around at the white. They blink and turn to one other. "It's not that bad," one says.

The other shakes her head. "Yeah. Kinda just ... white."

The first gives a nervous chuckle. "Right?"

They reach Pica Pica that afternoon. While Lin's ship docks at the South Port, *PearlHeart* continues to the West Port. Lin waves from his ship, thanking them.

PearlHeart continues on and the further they go, the more Well-Pagu looks at the sky to the east curiously. Before, Ara's Storm had reached this far, but now the clouds have broken and blue skies peek through.

Wagon-Pagu flies over and sits down next to them on the console. "If I may say, Well-Pagu, it is Ara and his siblings who have done this." They tuck their hands in their lap, now wearing a much lighter dress than what they wore in Draconi. "It is wonderful."

"Good," Well-Pagu agrees. Then they say to Rath, who is standing near them. "Gone."

Rath had been looking east as well but turned to Well-Pagu when they spoke. "Yes. I was thinking the same."

One-Eye, at the wheel, asks, "The storm?"

"Indeed. Before, it reached this point. It seems to almost be gone over Daerce, too."

Well-Pagu says, "Ara." They pause. "Siblings."

"They are doing this?" Rath asks, surprised.

Well-Pagu nods.

"That is incredible."

Beside him, One-Eye looks surprised as well. He glances at Daerce and the barriers still over it, then forward, unsure how to feel.

Two weeks later, Ara and the other gods have finished working for the day.

Over Daerce, the green, yellow, and pale yellow barriers

remain. However, as the gods watch, they slowly fade, the yellow first, then the green, then the pale yellow last. All of them exhale in relief.

As they return to Pica Pica, Ara sits on top of Elvin's back, looking at his red palms. A bright red flame springs to life in one hand and he stares at it for a few seconds as it drags in the wind. Then he rubs his hands together, smothering it, and the glow fades.

Elvin speaks. "Thank you, Ara. Without you, we would not have been able to do this."

"That is true." He looks at his storm to the north. "However, there is still much to do. Thank you for your aid, Elvin."

"Of course!"

Below them, Vocalise is stopped on a rock, looking west.

Marchand starts to swim past him, then pauses. "What is it?"

Vocalise scratches his chin. "The Phoenae Sea. I kinda thought that what we were doing would've helped the storms there, too. Guess not."

Marchand looks. Lightning flashes, illuminating the downpour of rain in Phoenae's shadow. Thunder distantly rumbles. "You're right."

Ara, having heard them, says, "It would not. Storms are the nature of that place." He does not elaborate.

Vocalise says, "Huh. Got it," and leaps to the next rock.

As soon as they enter Amara's barrier, Berceuse gasps. "Oh! Everyone, look!"

Elvin sees immediately. "*PearlHeart!*"

The Delphaen, Pan, and Alliance flags flap from the mainmast from where *PearlHeart* is docked at the West Port. The gods hurry to it.

Rath and One-Eye have just finished directing the crew carrying the delivery when they hear Ara call, "Captain Rath!"

They turn and see all of the gods land or swim up, turning into their human forms to join them on the docks. Marchand hugs Rath tightly. "It is so good to see you."

"You as well, Marchand!" As they pull away, Rath smiles at the others and they return it. "Everyone, too."

Ara says, "Have your deliveries gone well?"

"Yes. Thank you for asking. We will be returning to the

Southern Selachuu Military Base for our second delivery."

"That is good of you to do."

Rath bows to the gods. "Thank you very much for everyone's help. The Pagu tell me that the storm is no longer in the east thanks to your work."

The Pagu – including Wagon-Pagu – had flown forward while he spoke. Flower-Pagu says to the gods, "You're doing amazing!"

Bucket-Pagu says, "Keep going!"

Well-Pagu says, "Together."

Wagon-Pagu beams proudly. "I fully concur!"

The gods stand up a little taller.

Marchand takes Rath's shoulder. "With your deliveries, I don't suppose you'll be staying the night here?"

"I am afraid not. We will be leaving soon."

"Then we'll just have to wait until we're both done with our work. I miss having meals with you and everyone aboard *PearlHeart*. I'm looking forward to when we can again."

"I-I as well," Rath says, flushing. "I have truly enjoyed it."

Marchand beams. "We'll be going to Liette's clock tower now to rest. Safe travels, Rath."

"You as well!"

While the gods join the crowd, Rath and the others board *PearlHeart*.

Inside the clock tower, the gods are gathered in the larger room.

Marchand says, "Now that Daerce is uncovered, there isn't much left over Pica Pica."

Vocalise asks Ara, "After that, Amara should be able to drop her barrier, right?"

"She should."

As they are going to their rooms for the night, Elvin pauses next to Ara's door. "Thank you again for your help."

"Thank you for yours," Ara replies.

Elvin glances down at his brother's hands. "May I ask how your traits are going?"

Ara seems surprised. "Did you see me practicing?"

With a gentle smile, Elvin says, "I have been carrying you for quite some time now. I haven't *seen* necessarily, but I have noticed the air growing much warmer above me."

"Not too warm?"

Elvin blinks. "Well, no. It is helping to disperse the storm."

"That is ... good, then." Ara continues, "They are going well. Thank you for asking."

"Of course. Rest well, Brother."

"You too, Elvin."

In his room, Ara sits on his bed and spreads both hands on his lap. They glow red, then twin flames spark to life. He lets them linger for a few seconds, then presses his palms together, cooling them and his hands.

The next day, they are to the north of Amara's barrier.

On top of Elvin, Ara stands up and, palm raised and glowing, creates a tiny flicker of a flame. He carries it with him as he waves his hand and they begin to work on the storm.

To the southeast, *PearlHeart* has just finished loading up their second load of cargo to be carried back to Pica Pica.

Rath is speaking with Farbourne, who was on duty at the time of their arrival at the Southern Selachuu Military Base. Farbourne says, "This will be the last load. Thanks for helping, Captain – also for what you said to Captain Lin." He grins. "Seeing you both go back and forth through Amara's barrier and what he's been telling the other captains that you told him has made it so a lot more of them are reloading their cargo and taking it there themselves."

"I see." Rath shifts. "You are welcome, however, I do not believe that it was what I said."

Farbourne shrugs. "Lin said it was. Your advice on entering the barrier has been helpful, too. We can't give that sort of advice to Pan ships or their crews with how different our Selachuu ships are."

Rath blinks, then nods. "I understand. I am happy to hear that."

Smiling, Farbourne says, "Safe travels back, Captain. Good to see you again."

"Thank you. You as well, Farbourne."

PearlHeart casts off, heading to Pica Pica for the last time.

While they travel, the gods continue to work on dispersing the storm to the north of the island. Elvin flies with Ara standing on top of him, two healthy flames on his raised palms.

Looking at the brighter skies around them, Elvin asks Ara, "Will that be enough?"

"I believe so." However, Ara frowns, knowing that Amara's barrier is still behind them. He takes a deep breath. "We will be sure. Please keep going."

Behind them, in her place on the ocean, Amara opens her eyes and sees the progress. After a moment, she closes them again, continuing her barrier.

The gods return every day for the next week. Now when Ara swings his arm, a steady stream of flames trails after his hand. The clouds disperse more quickly.

Vocalise and Maro swipe at them. Oracle flaps her wings. Berceuse, Marchand, and Belle keep barriers around them all while Elvin carries Ara. At the end of the week, Berceuse looks toward the ocean ahead of them, thoughtful.

When they return to Pica Pica, they gather in the larger room.

Hugging his knees, Berceuse says, "We are almost to where my Isles of Oct were. I cannot believe how much we have done."

Ara looks over. Vocalise has been trying to convince him into doing a wooden block puzzle on the floor. "Do you wish for your Isles to be uncovered as well?"

"Well ... " Berceuse looks away, brushing his hair back. "Truthfully, I can move them wherever I wish to – I had thought I might after all of this was over. But, I also do need to be able to reveal them where they were originally to do so."

"I see." Ara sighs. He finally takes the piece Vocalise has been holding out to him and immediately puts it in the correct place. "Then we will uncover them as well, if everyone is willing to do so."

The others seem surprised, but quickly nod. Marchand says, "Of course."

"Thank you, everyone," Berceuse says, blushing.

As they all go back to their own discussions, Vocalise holds out another puzzle piece to Ara.

Ara frowns at him. "I already laid down one."

Vocalise waves the piece. "That's not how a puzzle works, buddy."

Later, Ara sits on his bed in his room. He looks at the two

great flames he has created above his hands. He watches them grow, then hesitates. They start to fade, then extinguish on their own. When he tries to create another flame, it does not appear.

The next day, while they are out in the storm, he hesitates. His hands glow red, but there is no fire.

Elvin notices, and when they return to Pica Pica, he asks, "Are you all right?"

Vocalise says, "Didn't see much fire today."

Ara glares at him. There are bags under his eyes. "I would prefer not to today."

Belle looks at him, chewing on his toothpick. When they begin to gather in the room, he takes Ara's shoulder and says, "We should talk."

They sit out on one of the balconies off of the eighth floor. Belle says, "You're doing a lot of good. Liette has a different way of saying it, but she's right – you would do this faster if you used your traits to their fullest extent." Ara does not answer and Belle continues, "I can understand if you haven't used them in a while – I know you haven't. You're out of shape, but you've been getting better. Why are you holding back now?"

Ara looks past Belle, to the white barrier still around Pica Pica. Confetti flits in front of it like colored snow. "Because if I do ... Winter will end."

For a moment, surprise flickers across Belle's eyes, then he grows thoughtful.

But before he can say anything, Ara says, rubbing his face, "This is what I would prefer to do right now."

"It's causing problems here – you've seen your storm."

"I have. I will consider it." Ara pauses. "Do you still feel my object to the west?"

Belle raises an eyebrow at the subject change. He concentrates for a moment, then says, "Yeah. It hasn't moved."

Ara's expression loosens. "Then it is all right. I am glad."

The next day, they work slowly. Ara's palms are red, but no fire appears. When they meet again in the larger room, Vocalise asks Ara, "Hey. You wanna build this puzzle with me?" He holds out a bag and jiggles it, making the wooden pieces *clack* inside.

Looking tired, Ara sits down. "Very well. Hand me the first piece."

"Here ya' go."

Ara takes it and sets it down in the correct place. He puts out his hand again and Vocalise gives him the next piece. Vocalise watches as the towers slowly build.

"You're pretty good at this," Vocalise says.

"It is much like how I built my cathedral."

After Ara puts in several more, Vocalise says, "Didn't mean to be rude yesterday – sorry."

Ara glances at him. "No – you are correct. I have not been helping as much as needed."

"Why's that?"

Ara glares. "It is not what I would prefer at the moment."

Vocalise nods. "Got it."

When Vocalise merely accepts his answer, Ara hesitates. Finally, he says, finishing one tower, "I do not wish for Winter to end."

Vocalise lies down. "Yeah, but it's gotta, you know? Seasons go on."

Ara is quiet.

"I dunno," Vocalise says after a pause. "Sometimes we gotta do things we don't really want to do."

"Have you, Vocalise?"

"Yeah."

Ara stops. He finishes the second tower, then looks down at his younger brother.

Vocalise says, "I didn't really want to be a god, but it's what I needed to do." He swings his foot over his knee, waving it restlessly. "I don't like every day, but I like enough of them that I know it was the right decision." He grins up at Ara. "And I really love my people."

Ara nods. "As do I."

Vocalise's smile softens. He turns his head so he can see the puzzle. "You finished it. Good job."

"Have you ever completed one of these?"

"Nope."

"Didn't you invent them?"

"Ha, sure did."

Ara rubs his face.

Over the next few days, Ara uses more fire and it grows over the next.

They are now far from Pica Pica which looks like a small

white bubble on the horizon. Ara asks Berceuse, "Would this uncover all of your Isles?"

Berceuse swims around the area in his octopus form. He nods, saying brightly, "Yes! This should work perfectly!"

Ara smiles a little. "Good." He turns around, looking at the white barrier still around Pica Pica.

Vocalise scratches his head, sitting on a rock. "Amara's barrier isn't really needed anymore, is it?"

"No."

They make their way back. While the other gods return to the clock tower, Elvin lets Ara off near Amara, where a white path has already been created for him. She is now standing, facing him and as Elvin flies away, Ara walks up to her.

When he arrives, she looks past him toward the clear skies to the north, then focuses on her brother again. "You have done well." Her eyes narrow. "However, the need for it to have been done should not have been in the first place."

Ara winces. "I understand, Elder Sister."

She frowns at him for a moment. Her shoulders relax. "My duty here is thus complete and I shall depart for Unys." She studies him. "Your storm will not return to this area?"

"No. I promise you, Amara."

She nods slowly. Then she closes her eyes and breathes in.

Behind Ara, the white light begins to recede, rising up and above the towers of Pica Pica until they reach the center of the island where the clock tower is. There the light condenses, then disappears. Up above, the skies are now a brilliant blue, brightening the water around them, too.

Amara steps forward and, very carefully, touches Ara's shoulder. "Be well, Brother." Then she is off, galloping away in her unicorn form, headed south to Unys.

Ara watches her go, then walks along the path she left for him back to Pica Pica.

33

Ara sits with his siblings that night, thinking. At the table next to him, Marchand and Berceuse are playing cards.

"Double Berceuse!" Marchand says.

"Excellent job, my Brother!" Berceuse says.

On the couch, Liette is speaking with Vocalise. "So I ordered streamers in ALL the colors! Isn't that great?"

Vocalise leans back, arms crossed behind his head. "Sounds good to me."

Maro is explaining his book to Elvin while they sit on the bench near the window. "It is about a young Pagu looking to become a farmer. It's quite a charming tale."

"I see!" Elvin says, looking at the book with interest.

Seated at the table by the wood stove, Belle and Oracle are sipping tea. As Oracle lowers her cup, she says, "You've made an excellent brew, Brother!"

Belle smiles. "Thanks."

Ara suddenly speaks. "I believe we should move forward to Haliae."

The others pause in their activities and look at him.

Elvin pushes up his glasses. "A-Are you sure?"

Looking at him evenly, Ara says, "I think that it is only right."

Elvin can only swallow hard and nod.

Ara continues, "I will ask Captain Rath when he returns to Pica Pica if he would be willing to stay in the area while we do so."

Marchand smiles. "I'm sure Rath and his crew would be willing."

However, Oracle gasps. "Although, it is nearing the holiday. I hope they'll be all right with spending it here."

Maro sighs. "And us, too."

To Oracle, Marchand says, "I'm sure everyone aboard *PearlHeart* was aware of the possibility of spending the holiday elsewhere when they agreed to this journey. They truly want to help." He looks at Ara as he says this, who nods.

PearlHeart had been sailing toward Pica Pica when Amara released her barrier.

The next day, Rath watches Amara gallop past them. One-Eye joins him and looks up at the sky, now a bright blue all around them and Pica Pica. "They did it," he says.

Looking up as well, Rath says, "Indeed."

The Pagu, sitting on the rail, beam as the sun shines down on them.

PearlHeart arrives at the North Port later that week. The gods are returning when they do and Rath brightens when he sees them. As he walks down the gangplank to meet them, Ara is climbing down from Elvin's back. Seeing Rath, he says, "Good morning, Captain."

"Good morning, Ara." Addressing all of the gods, he says, "Thank you for the work that you have done. It is wonderful to see."

The gods smile. Ara says, "You are welcome."

Berceuse tells Rath brightly, "We have uncovered my Isles of Oct as well!"

"That is amazing!"

Ara looks at the crates being delivered by Rath's crew, then asks, "We would like to do the same for Haliae. Would you allow staying near Pica Pica while we do so?"

Rath eyebrows lift. "Of course." He turns to One-Eye and Well-Pagu, who are directing the delivery and the rest of his crew who are carrying it. "We all spoke and decided that if you needed this month that we would stay on Pica Pica for the holiday. Liette, too, extended an invitation to us to join in the festivities and for all of us to suggest our own." He blinks. "There were many sparkles on the envelope."

Ara smiles faintly. "That sounds very much like her."

"Would I be allowed to tell Sven, Pema, Hailcorn, and Fritz about Haliae? I think they would be very happy to hear it and would want to tell their people."

Ara hesitates, but says, "Yes, you may. However, I do not know when they will be able to return."

"I understand. I will communicate that to them. Thank you again, everyone. I truly appreciate the work that you are doing."

While the gods leave for Liette's clock tower, One-Eye meets with Rath. "Everything's off."

"Thank you very much," Rath says. "The gods tell me that they have uncovered the storm through the Isles of Oct and intend to do the same for Haliae. I think it is wonderful."

"It's ... " One-Eye huffs. "What they should be doing. That's good, though."

"I think so as well." Rath turns toward the clock tower in the center of the city. "I would like to tell Sven and everyone about it. Would you watch *PearlHeart* while I do so?"

"Yeah. How much longer do the gods need? I know for the holiday, but what about afterward?"

Rath frowns. "I cannot say. I will let you know as soon as I do."

One-Eye looks behind Rath at the colored smoke exploding in the air. "Thanks," he says.

Rath makes his way through the crowd toward the clock tower. When he reaches it, he goes up to the seventh floor and meets with Sven and Pema. They stand together on the balcony that the gods and Rath were on before.

"That would be amazing!" Sven says when Rath tells him about the gods' plan to uncover Haliae. He looks at Pema. "Goodness knows we would love to be able to go home. Thank you for letting us know, Rath."

"Of course."

"I'll make sure and let Father and Fritz know when they come back. They're helping to organize the supplies that have been coming in – part of it is likely what you just brought. It's good you were able to find work while the gods are doing this."

"I agree. I am glad that we were able to help."

Sven hums, leaning against the railing. "What about now? Haliae's quite a bit further north, so it may be a while until you leave. And you've done your last load."

"I cannot say."

Nudging him with an elbow, Sven says, "You could relax." On his shoulder, Pema's eyes sparkle. "I won't say that Pica Pica is exactly my ideal, but you might find it exciting."

"That is true." Rath watches rainbow bubbles float past the balcony.

Rath and Sven hug, then Rath lifts his finger for Pema to shake in their form of a goodbye. He goes back to *PearlHeart*, where he explains Ara's request to his crew. He finishes, saying, " ... we will remain on Pica Pica until the gods return from Haliae. Thank you for all of the work you do!"

"Thank you, Captain!"

The crew talks with one another, grateful for a break. Some go down the gangplank to join the festivities in Pica Pica, including Isaac, Perri, Franz, and Velt.

Rath is watching them when One-Eye walks up to him. "Are you going down there, too?"

"I might."

One-Eye hesitates, then says, "You should. I'll watch the ship while you're gone."

"I ... " Rath smiles. "Thank you, One-Eye." He pauses. "I think I will ask the Pagu if they would like to join."

He does so, and soon Well-Pagu, Bucket-Pagu, Flower-Pagu, and Wagon-Pagu – all wearing much lighter clothes due to the weather being warmer – are going down the gangplank with him. They wave to One-Eye, who waves back from the ship, then join the crowd.

Above them, people walk on air with Liette's Traits, talking and laughing. Confetti flits around and small colored explosions erupt while bubbles rise up into the bright sky. After a while, they go under an awning to get out of the sun and cool off.

Fanning themselves with their hat, Wagon-Pagu says, "There are truly so many people!"

"Indeed," Rath says.

Flower-Pagu giggles. "And they're so happy, too!"

Bucket-Pagu looks up. "Even more so with the blue skies."

Well-Pagu takes a drink from their little water bottle, then says, "Gods."

Rath says, "Yes. They are doing wonderful work. I am very grateful to them." Then he says, "It is nearly lunchtime. Would you four like to get something to eat?"

The Pagu all shoot their arms up and say, "Yes!"

They quickly find food – Pica Pica fare that is quite sweet – and eat on the edge of the fountain in front of the clock tower.

After Rath takes his first bite, Flower-Pagu asks, "What do you think, Captain?"

"It's so sweet! It's wonderful."

Wagon-Pagu takes a bite, then smiles. "It is really quite different from Draconi food, but I like it as well!" They look into the fountain. "I wonder how my dear friend, Fountain-Pagu is doing in Phoenae. Merp said that they are well, but it has truly been so long since I've seen them. Have you met them, Captain?"

Rath thinks. "No, I do not believe I have."

"I believe you will someday. They have been in Phoenae longer than I have been in Draconi."

"I see. May I ask what you will do after Ara finds his object? Will you return to Draconi?"

At that, Wagon-Pagu hesitates. "I ... have not decided yet. You are certain that Ara's object is to be found?"

"Yes. Belle says that he can sense it."

Wagon-Pagu laughs. "You are right!" They nibble on their food. "I think it is very wonderful that Ara trusts in his brother so. I would not have blamed him if he chose to go west first to seek out his object, but I am both delighted and surprised that he chose this path instead."

Rath looks north, where they can just see dark clouds on the horizon. "I hope that the gods are well on their journey to Haliae. I cannot say I know how you would disperse a storm like Ara's."

Flower-Pagu says, "I am sure that it is very hard for Ara."

Bucket-Pagu says, "But, he's still doing it!"

"Proud," Well-Pagu says.

Wagon-Pagu nods. "I am as well." They look up at Rath.

"Thank you, too, Captain, for welcoming me and Ara aboard *PearlHeart.* We have only been there for a very short time, but I have already felt so welcomed! It makes my heart very glad."

Rath looks touched. "I am very happy to hear that, Wagon-Pagu. I greatly enjoy having both of you aboard."

Wagon-Pagu beams up at him. They look back at their treat. "And, since I've left Draconi, I've had so many new and happy experiences! I wish to have more and I hope that Ara is feeling the same."

After they finish their food, Wagon-Pagu says, "I believe I saw a game that I wished to try! It seemed to be one with cones and small, colorful balls."

Rath says, "I saw the same. I thought it looked very fun."

They find it quickly and play for a good part of the evening. As the sun goes down, they find more food and this time, eat in a small park with soft grass. They listen to a group of musicians play on a stage with lights and Flower-Pagu dances with Bucket-Pagu while Rath, Well-Pagu, and Wagon-Pagu sit, enjoying the music.

Under a starry sky, they return to *PearlHeart.* One-Eye is on the deck, playing cards with Isaac and Oren in the light of the lanterns.

"Double Berceuse!" Isaac says.

One-Eye sees Rath and the Pagu return and One-Eye waves them over. "How was it?"

Rath sits with him and the others. "It was very loud. And very wonderful. I ate things that I never had before and played a new game with everyone. We also listened to very talented musicians and – " He blinks away the sleep from his eyes. "I apologize, we ... " Then he looks down at the box that he has been carrying and gasps. "That's right. I bought more of the treats that we ate earlier. I wished to share them with everyone here." He lifts the lid, revealing the multicolored sweets.

Isaac says, "Wow, thanks, Captain!" He reaches in and takes one.

"Yeah," Oren says, taking one as well.

One-Eye grabs one. "Thanks."

They all eat, sharing more about their evening on *PearlHeart* or Pica Pica before Rath covers another yawn with his hand.

"I believe I may go to sleep," Rath says. "I hope everyone

rests well when they do."

"Thanks, Captain," Isaac and Oren say.

"You, too," One-Eye says. After the others leave, he says to Rath, "Maybe ... Another day, we can go together. To there." He points at the city awkwardly.

His Lion bumps his head into One-Eye's calf.

Rath smiles warmly. "I would love that."

One-Eye returns the smile.

For the next several weeks, the gods disperse the storm in the North.

Ara, standing on top of Elvin with flames over his palms, looks out at what is left. Although they cannot see it, they are nearing Haliae. Ara lets his hands fall, cooling them. "We will stop here."

Vocalise asks, "Back to Pica Pica, then?"

Marchand says, "If I may – I've been thinking about that." Speaking to all of them, he says, "What would you think to possibly staying on Berceuse's Isles of Oct? We've reached a point that it would take far more time to travel back to Pica Pica and return here to work on the storm."

Near him, Belle says, "That's true."

Berceuse jumps, saying, "Oh! I would love that. To be on my Isles again ... What does everyone think? I am more than happy to reveal them."

Ara sits on Elvin's back and thinks. "It is a sound decision. I do not believe I have ever seen your Isles."

Maro says, "I am not sure any of us have."

Oracle says, "If I recall, Berceuse, you claimed them right before you hid them, correct?"

"Yes. Thinking back on it ... " Berceuse shakes himself. "Well, it is the decision I made." He beams at all of them. "Now, I am very happy to share it with you."

They travel south, Berceuse leading. After fifteen minutes, he stops and begins to concentrate, glowing bright purple. Slowly, the Isles of Oct are revealed – eight smaller islands surrounding one larger one. They are as green and lush and full of flowers as when Rath and everyone aboard *PearlHeart* saw them. "There we are!" Berceuse says.

Oracle looks delighted. "Oh! They're beautiful!"

"Thank you, Sister."

They move toward the largest isle. Maro looks at the flowers on the smaller isles while on top of Vocalise, who is jumping from rock to rock in the ocean. "I do not believe I've ever seen varieties like these."

Berceuse winks. "I've created them all! And the fruit!" He gasps. "Oh! We can have Together Fruit together! This will be wonderful."

Marchand swims next to him. "Rath has told me about it. He very much enjoyed it."

Vocalise jumps over them. "I'm looking forward to trying it."

When they arrive, they all turn into their human forms. Berceuse steps forward, the familiar warm sand beneath his feet. His smile fades.

Ara notices. "Is something wrong?"

"Well, these are my Isles, but my dear ones are no longer here. They left for Pagu Island a year ago." He smiles sadly. "I miss them terribly. They were what truly brought life to my home. It's rather quiet without them."

Vocalise raises his voice. "I mean, I could start – "

Marchand kindly says, "We'll be here for you. I can't say we're anything like them, but we are your family and I'm looking forward to this time to spend together."

Berceuse brightens. "As am I!"

Together, they explore the isle with Berceuse showing them the flowers and his small clearing. The hut Rath stayed in is still there as well as the fire pit and small pool that threads out to the ocean. They gather Together Fruit from the nearby trees, then *Whoosh* individualized cushions to sit on while they eat.

As the sky grows darker and the stars begin to come out, Ara lays his hand on the wood in the fire pit. He grips a piece and his hand glows red. The wood ignites, spreading to the others, warming Ara and the other gods. Ara watches the smoke drift up.

Beside him, Belle says, "You're getting better."

"I am trying to."

Berceuse leans back, his eyes sparkling. "The last time I was here, gathered like this, my Captain told us Elvin's constellation story. It was wonderful to hear him tell it."

Elvin says, "Truly?"

"Yes. It seems he knows ones from all but two of us, I believe Carlos said. I had asked if my Captain might tell me yours, Elvin. You were heavily on my mind at the time. It is also what began to convince me that I needed to leave my Isles and go see you – and see if I could help. It has only been a year since then, but so much has changed."

Ara says, "A year would not seem like much time – but, it is to you and your people, Elvin, correct?"

"I ... Well, yes, I must say that it is."

Ara looks into the fire. "Even being away from Draconi for several months has been difficult." He frowns. "We'd best sleep."

The rest agree and they all lie near one another, tucked around blankets that they *Whooshed*. Ara looks up at the stars, then closes his eyes and falls asleep.

The next day, they travel north to the edge of the storm.

However, when Ara stands up on Elvin's back, lifting up his hand, he hesitates. Very slowly, he lowers his hand. Then he says to Elvin, "I believe I will continue on my own. Thank you."

"What?"

But Ara leaps off. He glows and suddenly, a giant form shadows the ocean. Two very large wings appear and flap down, causing enormous waves to pulse outward as Ara – now in his dragon form – flies in place.

Vocalise jumps over to a rock to get a better look at him. "Huh. I thought you were bigger." He is about as big as Ara's claw.

Ara looks down, glaring at him. "I would prefer to remain this size."

Belle swims over. He is as big as Ara's eye. "It's good that you can maintain that form at all. Ready?"

"Yes." Ara looks ahead and inhales. When he breathes out, a steady stream of flames melt the snow and ice, carrying away the clouds with them. Blue skies shine down. Ara pauses, then flies forward, the other gods following him.

When they return to the Isles of Oct. Ara flies on his own, looking a little unsteady. He lands on the beach in his human form and rubs his arms. "I am exhausted," he says.

Belle steps out of the water in his human form and pats Ara's back. "It'll get better. Good work."

"Thank you, Belle."

The group sits on the beach together. The sun is low on the horizon, making the ocean orange. Vocalise says, "Seems like we got a lot farther than other days – thanks, Ara."

Ara nods.

Elvin says, "I truly appreciate it, Brother. This does not seem to be easy for you."

"It's not," Ara snaps.

They all look at him in surprise.

Ara rubs his temples. "My apologies. I am tired. I wish to eat and sleep."

Berceuse stands up. "I will gather food!"

Oracle says, "I'll help!"

They go off into the trees.

Ara pushes himself off the ground, and, with the others, goes to the clearing. They eat and afterward, Ara sleeps. Most of the other gods do as well.

However, Vocalise and Belle are still awake, sitting next to one another. The God of Pantrog looks at Ara. "He's all right, right?"

"Yeah," Belle replies. "He has to work through this." He looks at Vocalise. "Not tired?"

"Naw – I mean, with Mr. Dragon over there, I didn't have to do a whole lot – "

"Go to sleep, Vocalise."

"Yeah, Belle."

Throughout the next week, the gods grow closer to Haliae and Mella Island. Ara uses his dragon form, blowing fire directly at the clouds. By the end of the week, they can clearly see the outlines of both islands. Ara glances at Elvin, who is looking at the taller one – Haliae.

When they return to the Isles of Oct that night, Ara says, "I believe it will only take one more day."

Marchand says, "That's wonderful. How do you feel, Elvin?"

"W-Well, I ... " He smiles at the Together Fruit in his hands. "I don't feel that I can quite describe it. Sven and Pema, Hailcorn and Fritz – all of my people will be so happy."

Ara smiles gently.

When they return to the storm the next day, Ara faces Haliae and prepares his fire. But just before he exhales, he looks past it to Draconi, where the skies are still dark and the storm continues. He hesitates. However, then he looks at Elvin, who is flying steadily, his eyes locked on his home.

Ara breathes out.

A larger stream of fire erupts, soaring high above Haliae's peak and into the clouds above. All at once, they melt away, taking the ones over Mella Island and Pantha with them.

The sun begins to shine down on them and in the same moment, Elvin flies to Haliae. He lands softly on the snowy beach in his human form and looks around. Ara follows, turning into his human form as well, and joins him, quiet.

He sees Elvin take off his glasses and rub his eyes. When he turns around, his eyes are wet. "Thank you, Ara."

His brother frowns. "I am sorry you had to wait so long to return home."

Elvin shakes his head, stepping toward him. "But, I am here now." He looks toward the other gods, who are just arriving. "With my family, too." He turns back to Ara. "Would you allow that we stayed here tonight?"

"I will."

The other gods hear and join them.

Vocalise says, "Sooo, I want a full tour."

Elvin laughs, still crying a little. "I would be happy to oblige!" He adjusts his robes. "That's right – you've never been to Haliae, have you?"

"Nope. Should have, though. It's pretty great."

Elvin beams at his island. "It is magnificent."

They walk around, talking. Then, with Oracle and Elvin carrying the others, they go up to the city at the top of the mountain. Elvin steps down onto the snow-covered ground and walks toward the columned buildings. "It has been even longer since I've been here. We had to go inside the mountain when Sven and Pema determined the storm too dangerous, you see."

Ara nods. He looks out at the white marble and square architecture, hanging plants, and small, open-air courtyards. "My storm has destroyed it."

"No, no." Elvin walks forward to pick up a hanging plant. He cradles it in his arms, brushing off the snow. "We will rebuild and replant. These ones may even return," he says, holding up the planter.

Ara pauses. "Truly?"

"Yes. It always surprises me how much they can take – of course, Lady Azalea said that they would."

Ara is silent for a moment. "It's a seed."

Elvin's eyebrows shoot up.

The other gods gather around them.

"What I am looking for. It is a seed." Ara looks down at the poor plant in Elvin's arms miserably. "Perhaps the last one for my Frost Flowers."

Elvin lays the hanging plant down carefully, then they all sit together on the stone benches.

"But, Belle has found it, correct?" Elvin asks.

Ara looks to Belle, who says, "Yeah." He crosses his arms. "Thought it felt small."

Vocalise frowns. "I thought you had a lot of flowers – why do you think it's the only one?"

Ara's eyes flare. "Because – " He calms himself. "Centuries ago, North's Frost Flower Garden was large. She tended to it wonderfully. However" – he swallows – "after she disappeared, it was left to me. I ... knew that when Winter ended, they would die – North said that it was only natural that they did, like the snow each year. But, she said as long as there were seeds, that they would return the following Winter. I thought if Winter remained, there would be no need for them to die. Or to regrow.

"I restrained my traits so that Winter could last as long as it could and planted every seed that I could find. I thought that her garden would grow more, but ... there always seemed to be fewer seeds each year."

The gods listen, quiet.

Maro says gently, "You never allowed them to go dormant?"

"No. What if ... they never came back?"

"Ara, if I may ... did they not return when North was still present? When Draconi had Seasons?"

"That is true, however – " Ara quickly shakes his head. "But, if they never come back ... "

"You still have one seed," Belle tells him. "You can restart the garden."

"You say that you can feel the seed to the west, but is it even alive? How did it get there?"

Belle looks sympathetic. "I can't say."

Elvin turns toward the many potted plants around them. "If I may answer – I am sure that if Belle can feel it, it is alive. Plants and seeds are far stronger than you may realize."

"Even if it is not in its preferred climate?"

Belle says, "You'll just have to see for yourself."

Elvin says, "In the morning, we'll return to Pica Pica. We'll find Captain Rath and ask that he take us to the west, where your seed is."

"You will come with us?" Ara asks, startled. "What about Haliae?"

In response, Elvin smiles. "I intend to see this through to the end. I trust Hailcorn, Fritz, Sven, and Pema to make the necessary preparations for our people to move back here." He looks up at the sunny sky. "The snow will need time to melt, of course, too."

"Thank you, Elvin."

They spend the day in a makeshift campsite in the courtyard. As the sun goes down, they all help light the fire pit to stay warm and sleep around its large bright flame.

34

The next day, the gods travel away from Haliae, now under blue skies. They move past the Isles of Oct, then on to Pica Pica.

Two weeks later, they see *PearlHeart* at the North Port.

Inside the city, Rath and One-Eye are walking through the crowd. Rath is looking up at the confetti and bubbles while One-Eye watches his Spirit Lion leap through them.

They hear a bird call. William, with Phobos on his shoulder, runs up to them. "Captain! The gods have returned and requested to speak with you."

"I see. Thank you very much for letting us know, William, Phobos," Rath says.

They make their way back to the docks where the gods – including Liette – are in their human forms. Liette is hopping around, saying to her siblings, "You did it! I can't believe you actually did it!" She tackles Elvin. "I'm so happy for you!"

Elvin laughs. "As am I!"

Marchand sees Rath and the others and waves them over.

Looking around, Rath says, "Everyone seems to be very happy."

Elvin, his eyes gleaming, says, "My people and I can return

to Haliae, thanks to Ara and all of our efforts!"

They all look startled.

"That is incredible!" Rath says. "May I ask if Sven, Pema, and the others know?"

"Not yet. I'm just about to tell them."

Ara nods to Elvin. "Go. We will be here."

"Thank you, Brother." Elvin takes off in his eagle form, flying toward the clock tower.

Ara says to Rath, "On his return, I ask that we sail west, toward my object."

"I understand. I will notify my crew."

When Elvin returns, he looks tearful again, but happy as he joins his family and they all walk up *PearlHeart's* gangplank. They wait on the deck as the crew makes the final preparations for their departure.

Not long afterward, *PearlHeart* sails away from Pica Pica for the last time. Liette waves brightly to them from the docks.

They sail south past the Southern Selachuu Military Base and then southwest. Sir Ronan and Opal Starlight are no longer in the ocean there.

When *PearlHeart* nears Unys, they light the lanterns to see through the dense fog.

Two days after they enter it, Ara goes to Rath's door, asking to speak with him.

When they are seated at the table, Ara says, "I feel that it is only right that I tell you the object that I am looking for. It is a seed – one that I believe is the last of my Frost Flowers. It is very important that it is found."

Rath nods seriously. "I understand, Ara."

Ara pauses for a moment. "Yes. I suppose you do." He continues, "Maro tells me that from what I described, my flowers are not in good condition." He takes a breath. "It seems the answer is to allow them to go dormant and to do that, I must end my Winter in Draconi."

"That would make sense to me," Rath says. "Flowers – and all plants – need time to rest after their season has passed."

"I am ... considering this fact." Ara sighs. "However, it troubles me that I do not know the state of my last seed – especially in a climate so foreign. Are seeds truly so resilient?"

"Very." Rath smiles. "Two years ago, Flower-Pagu

discovered a Pantha Flower in my grandmother's garden whose seed flew all the way from Pantha. It had flowered, but it could not continue to grow in the environment it was in — it needed more sun. Flower-Pagu and I transplanted it together in Grandmother's South Garden. Now, it seems very happy, and the last time that I saw it, it had grown another flower."

"That is wonderful, Captain." Looking more relaxed, Ara says, "Thank you for speaking."

"Of course"

Later, Rath is eating with One-Eye in the captain's cabin. He has just told One-Eye what Ara's object is.

One-Eye chokes. "A seed?"

"Yes. Are you all right?"

"Fine. Just don't see how that's important enough for all of this. Why make the storm, then?"

"I cannot say. However, I would think that losing it deeply upset him."

One-Eye stares at him. He takes a bite, then says, "So, what happens if it's in the ocean?"

Rath looks up in surprise.

"Do we have to swim for it?" One-Eye gestures with his hand. "It would just — float away again."

Rath thinks. "That is true."

"Belle doesn't have an exact area, does he?"

"No, not that he has told me."

One-Eye nods and continues his meal. His Lion paws the floor next to him.

They sail through the open ocean to the south of the Phoenae Sea, then through the mist around Paradi.

When the rainbows come out and swirl around *PearlHeart*, Ara watches them with wide eyes, having never seen them before. Wagon-Pagu spins with the other Pagu in delight. Oracle stands by the upper deck, smiling at all of their reactions.

They arrive at Renet Island, where Captain Berkut performs customs for them. After they return to the deck, Berkut says, "You keep interesting company, Captain Rath."

Rath blinks. "I'm sorry?"

Berkut smiles a little. "The Gods. And ... an Elder God." His eyes look distant for a moment, then he says, "You are clear to leave. I pray that you are well for this Winter and ... that all are."

"I agree. And, thank you, Captain Berkut."

As Berkut leaves and Rath directs his crew to set sail once more, Elvin says to Belle, "He barely seemed surprised we were here!"

Belle says, "Of course not."

Vocalise stretches. "Belle's around his own all the time – what's there to be surprised about?"

They sail through the Delphaen Trade Route next. Ara stands with Rath near the prow. He looks out at all of the ships, underwater, above water like *PearlHeart,* and in the sky. "I've never seen so many."

Rath nods. "There are many during this time – Spring is the start of the sailing season."

"I see. You have been traveling for a very long time this year. I recall Elvin telling me you began your current journey last Spring. I pray that you will all rest after this?"

"Yes. We have decided to set out in the Summer this year instead so that all can return home before we do."

"I am glad to hear so."

Later that week, Ara stands with Oracle by the rail. Both are looking out at Cunica, now white with snow. "Does Cunica normally have such a heavy Winter?" Ara asks, frowning.

"Sometimes." Oracle hesitates. "That is, Rella's people believe that they have a far heavier one when there is harsher weather in the North. Near Draconi."

Ara sighs. "That would make sense."

"When we spoke last year, Rella believed that the Seasons would right themselves without our intervention."

"They would – North often said they always would – had I not imposed my own energy on them so that Draconi remained in Winter. I hadn't known that it would affect Haliae, Pantha, the Isles of Oct, Daerce, or Pica Pica so drastically. Or, that it would have effects this far south, either."

"But, now all of those places are better! Spring is coming to them."

"True, but Winter remains in Draconi."

Oracle nods.

They exit the Delphaen Trade Route two weeks later. Belle stands with Rath, One-Eye, Well-Pagu, and Ara. "It's closer," he says. "Five hundred miles west."

The others nod, but Rath looks thoughtful.

Ara says, "Is there an island there?"

"Yeah," Belle replies.

Rath says, "My grandmother's island."

Ara and the others turn toward him. Belle says, "That would follow."

They adjust their course and later that morning, Rath has tea with Carlos in the infirmary.

Carlos raises an eyebrow when Rath informs him of where Ara's seed is. "I suppose it does make sense." He takes a long sip and continues, "Lady Azalea's Island has a tendency to attract things that are needed at a certain time. I've come to expect it."

"I see," Rath says.

Later that week, the gods gather on the deck, watching Lady Azalea's Island – a small green island now visible on the horizon – grow closer. Rath, One-Eye, and Well-Pagu are on the upper deck, looking at it, too.

Finally, three weeks after exiting the Delphaen Trade Route, William calls, "Lady Azalea's Island ahead!" and Phobos gives a bright "Caw!"

PearlHeart arrives on the south side of the island. As soon as they tie off the mooring lines to the small dock, the gangplank is lowered and Rath, One-Eye, the Pagu, Carlos, Belle, and Ara go down to the beach.

As they join the forest path, Ara says to Wagon-Pagu, "Is there an expected form of introduction? To Lady Azalea?"

Wagon-Pagu shakes their head. "No, Ara. You just go as you are!" As they pass all of the Pagu homes – many look up at them in surprise – Wagon-Pagu is quiet. Then they say, "I have thought much of where I will go after this, Ara."

He hesitates with his next step, but listens.

Wagon-Pagu beams up at him. "I believe ... I will join my friends on Pagu Island. I am told that it is not far at all from this island. It will be wonderful to see my friends and family again."

Ara smiles, sad. "I see. Thank you, Wagon-Pagu."

"I am always here for you, Ara."

He nods.

They step out onto the front lawn of Lady Azalea's home, then up to the porch, where Rath knocks on the door and a surprised member of the staff opens it.

After Rath speaks to him, he guides them through the home to one of the anterooms. He holds the outside door open for them. "She is in her gardens," he says.

They walk along the side of Lady Azalea's home, past the windows and the hedge. They come to the hill, leading down into the main area of the garden. They follow Belle as he leads them further, past the gazebo and the small turtle pond, down another hill, then through the forest on a shaded path in between the trees.

They arrive at the South Garden.

There, Lady Azalea is tending to the plants, smiling softly.

Rath says, "Grandmother."

She straightens and turns. Rath meets her and they hold hands for a moment before Azalea looks at the others. As they approach, she smiles and says, "Well." She nods to them in turn. "Belle, Carlos, One-Eye, Well-Pagu, Bucket-Pagu, Flower-Pagu ... Ah, however, I do not believe I have met you two."

"I am Wagon-Pagu," they say, bowing. "It is a pleasure to meet you, Lady Azalea."

Beside them, Ara blurts, "You met my wife." He reddens, explaining, "North."

Azalea inhales at the name, then looks thoughtful. Understanding – if sad – blooms. "Ah, I remember now." She walks up to him. She is barely a third of his height. "It is very wonderful to meet you, Wagon-Pagu. And you, as well, Ara, Ruler of the Second World. I am Azalea of Sudines."

Ara nods. "One of Hep's. As you say, I am Ara, however, in this world, my role is as the Elder God of Draconi." He looks around. "Belle tells me that a seed of mine is here. It is from my Frost Flowers in Draconi."

Azalea's eyes widen. "Frost Flowers ... " She thinks. "I cannot say that I have ever seen any, however" – she smiles at Flower-Pagu – "I also did not know that there was a Pantha Flower here until Flower-Pagu showed it to my grandson so that we could transplant it here." She gestures to the flowers behind them, pointing their bright orange petals up at the sky. "I had always wished to see Frost Flowers. From what North told me, they are beautiful and unlike any plants in my gardens." She frowns. "But, also, from what I recall, they thrive best in cold climates."

Ara falters. "That is true."

"However, a seed ... " She laughs. "They can be quite resilient – stubborn, even. If Belle says that it is here, I'm sure it is and is only waiting for us to find it. Would you allow me to come with you?"

"Of course. These are your gardens." His expression softens. "They are beautiful."

Azalea smiles. "Thank you."

Belle concentrates. He nods toward the surrounding forest. "It's in there."

Together, they follow Belle. Rath and One-Eye walk alongside one another and Ara walks with Azalea, Carlos just behind them. The Pagu fly with everyone. They travel in between the trees, all quiet.

Then Belle slows to a stop in an area so thick with leaves, the sun cannot come through.

"Here," he says.

Ara frowns. "Where? I do not see it."

Belle kneels and points at the ground.

Azalea understands. "Ah." She kneels as well. "The poor dear must have gone dormant. It probably thinks Winter will never come for it."

Kneeling, too, Ara says, "Then, it's not – "

Azalea pats his hand. "No, no. Just dreaming. Imagining the day that it will become a beautiful flower, like all those that came before it."

Ara swallows, nodding.

Turing to Rath and One-Eye, she says, "My dears, would you retrieve one shovel for us to use and the Pagu shovels as well? I believe that this may take some delicate work at the end."

They both nod and Rath says, "Yes, Grandmother."

While they leave, Azalea says to Well-Pagu, Bucket-Pagu, and Flower-Pagu, "May I ask for your help in this?"

Flower-Pagu says, "Of course!"

Bucket-Pagu says, "We're always happy to!"

Well-Pagu says, "Dig."

When Rath and One-Eye return, Rath holds out the smaller shovels to the Pagu while One-Eye carries the larger one for him.

As One-Eye hands the other shovel to Rath, Azalea says to Flower-Pagu, "Would you help us know where we need to dig?"

"Definitely!" they say. They hand their shovel to Bucket-Pagu and carefully walk across the ground. Ara watches, still looking terribly nervous.

Flower-Pagu kneels in the same spot the others just were and concentrates. After a moment, they smile and pat the ground gently, saying, "Don't worry! We're going to help you get home!"

They get to work, patting the ground – little pink handprints appear – marking the area for Rath to dig in. As the group watches, their faces light up with the glow from the handprints in the heavily shaded forest. Once Flower-Pagu finishes, they brush off their pants and step away. They nod to Rath and he begins shoveling.

After he has taken out two clumps of soil, Azalea puts her hand on his arm. "There. That should be enough."

"Yes, Grandmother."

Azalea nods to the Pagu Trio of *PearlHeart*. "Would you like to do this part?"

"Yes, Lady Azalea!" Flower-Pagu and Bucket-Pagu say and "Yes!" Well-Pagu says. They fly down into the hole with their shovels. They work slowly, setting the soil behind them.

After they have been there for five minutes, Flower-Pagu gives a little gasp. "Oh!" Very tenderly, they kneel down and cup a little glass-like light blue seed in their hands. They raise it up to Ara. "Here it is."

Ara exhales swiftly. He goes down on his knees and holds out his hand. Flower-Pagu sets the seed in his palm and he can only stare at it for a long moment.

Flower-Pagu speaks softly. "Ara, you must promise to let this seed grow as it wishes to. It has had a lot of time to think on this."

"I do not understand."

Azalea says, "I believe what our little one means is that you must allow this seed to grow as its ancestors grew – going dormant for Spring, Summer, and Fall, and blooming in the Winter." She looks directly at him. "You must allow the Seasons to come and go, as they did before North's disappearance. This seed will not grow otherwise."

"But – " Ara pauses. "Yes, Lady Azalea. It will take time, however."

"Yes. But, it will be all worth it for this little one," she says, nodding to the seed. "Now, it will be a long journey home and when you arrive, it must rest. It must go dormant." She sighs heavily. "When the Seasons right themselves and Spring comes to Draconi, the other Frost Flowers will die, as they did before."

Ara's face tightens.

"However, in their place, this one will grow. I promise you that if you allow them to follow their cycle as they once did, they will grow and continue to for a very, very long time, coming back each Winter."

Ara gives a laugh, eyes wet. "I am accustomed to seeing them."

Azalea grows thoughtful. "There are other flowers – other plants, that grow in different seasons." She looks toward the sun, peeking through the edges of the forest. "Let us take a walk around my garden and I can tell you about them. However, you will need to go to Rella of Cunica for their seeds. Then, this little one can have a few friends on their long journey home."

Clutching the seed carefully in his hand, Ara says, "I do not know how to plant. My Frost Flowers – North and mine – are a testament to that."

"I think I know someone who can help with that. Rath, would you teach Ara? I have a few flowers that need to be planted now."

"I would love to," he says.

Grinning, Azalea says to Ara, "A long time ago, I taught him how to plant. Don't worry, he's an expert now!"

Flushing deeply, Rath says, "Ah, Grandmother – "

But Ara stands, saying, "Thank you, Captain."

"Of course."

Looking at the whole group, Azalea says, "Now, I do not think I am mistaken in that you all have had a very long journey. Rath, would you like to invite everyone to my island to rest? Ara and I will come find you when he is ready to learn how to plant."

"Yes, Grandmother." Rath brightens. "I think everyone would love that."

One-Eye smiles a little beside him.

Azalea laughs. "I would, too! It will be so nice to have everyone here together."

"Indeed," Rath says.

The Pagu hold one another's hands, beaming.

Then, Ara – gently holding the seed – walks beside Azalea, Rath, One-Eye, Carlos, and Belle, while the Pagu fly beside them, out of the shaded forest and into the light of Lady Azalea's gardens.

Acknowledgements

Journeys of PearlHeart began in 2016 when I was catsitting for a friend, became a comic that I would draw while going to college, a script version during the pandemic when I wanted to write something cheerful, and finally a real first draft in 2022 – then the revising began. During this time, many people supported me and I would like to thank them here.

Thank you to my family for believing in this story from the beginning, asking to stay updated on its progress, and listening to all of the different versions. There are some scenes we will never forget.

Thank you to my beta readers for your support and excitement for the characters.

Thank you as well to all of my friends who listened to me talk about my "ship story" and made publishing this possible – it's finally here!

And thank you for reading!

About the Author

Keilani McConnell has always enjoyed creating stories and sharing them with friends and family. She has a Bachelors of Music in Flute Performance and both teaches and performs in her local area. She also draws comics, animates, and makes jewelry. To relax, she likes to read, be outside, and play with her kitty, Midna. *Journeys of PearlHeart* is the first book in her *PearlHeart* series. She lives in Colorado. For more information, please see her website keilanimcconnellart.com

www.ingramcontent.com/pod-product-compliance
Lightning Source LLC
Chambersburg PA
CBHW030728310726
48969CB00005B/1134